ALSO BY RUSSELL BANKS

FICTION

The Reserve

The Darling

The Angel on the Roof

Cloudsplitter

Rule of the Bone

The Sweet Hereafter

Affliction

Success Stories

Continental Drift

The Relation of My Imprisonment

Trailerpark

The Book of Jamaica

The New World

Hamilton Stark

Family Life

Searching for Survivors

NONFICTION

Dreaming Up America

The Invisible Stranger (with Arturo Patten)

LOST
MEMORY
of SKIN

RUSSELL BANKS

THE CLERKENWELL PRESS

This paperback edition published in 2013

First published in Great Britain in 2012 by
PROFILE BOOKS LTD
3A Exmouth House
Pine Street
London EC1R 0JH
www.profilebooks.com

First published in the United States of America in 2011 by
ECCO, an imprint of HarperCollins Publishers

Copyright © Russell Banks, 2012, 2013

10 9 8 7 6 5 4 3 2 1

Printed and bound in Great Britain by
CPI Group (UK) Ltd, Croydon CR0 4YY

The moral right of the author has been asserted.

A CIP catalogue record for this book is available from the British Library.

ISBN 978 1 84668 577 4
eISBN 978 1 84765 785 5

MIX
Paper from
responsible sources
FSC FSC® C020471
www.fsc.org

To C.T.

And in memory, to F.T. B. (1914–2010)

Now I am ready to tell how bodies changed
into different bodies.

METAMORPHOSES

LOST
MEMORY
of SKIN

PART I

CHAPTER ONE

I T ISN'T LIKE THE KID IS LOCALLY FAMOUS
for doing a good or a bad thing and even if people knew his real
name it wouldn't change how they treat him unless they looked it
up online which is not something he wants to encourage. He himself
like most of the men living under the Causeway is legally prohibited
from going online but nonetheless one afternoon biking back from
work at the Mirador he strolls into the branch library down on Regis
Road like he has every legal right to be there.

The Kid isn't sure how to get this done. He's never been inside
a library before. The librarian is a fizzy lady—ginger-colored hair
glowing around her head like a bug light, pink lipstick, freckles—
wearing a floral print blouse and khaki slacks. She's a few inches
taller than the Kid, a small person above the waist but wide in the
hips like she'd be hard to tip over. The sign on the counter in front
of her says REFERENCE LIBRARIAN, GLORIA . . . something—the Kid
is too nervous to register her last name. She smiles without showing
her teeth and asks if she can help him.

Yeah. I mean, I guess so. I dunno, actually.

What are you looking for?

You're like the reference lady, right?

Right. Do you need to look up something in particular?

The air-conditioning is cranked and the place feels about ten degrees cooler now than it did when the Kid came through the door and he suddenly realizes he's shivering. But the Kid's not cold, he's scared. He's pretty sure he shouldn't be inside a public library even though he can't remember there being any rules specifically against entering one as long as he's not loitering and it's not a school library and there's no playground or school nearby. At least none that he's aware of. You can never be sure though. Playgrounds and schools are pretty much lurking everywhere. And children and teenagers probably come in here all the time this late in the day to pretend they're doing homework or just to hang out.

He looks around the large fluorescent-lit room, scans the long rows of floor-to-ceiling book-lined shelves—it's like a huge supermarket with nothing on the shelves but books. It smells like paper and glue, a little moldy and damp. Except for a geeky-looking black guy with glasses and a huge Adam's apple and big wind-catching ears sitting at a table with half-a-dozen thick books and no pictures opened in front of him like he's trying to look up his ancestors there's no other customers in the library.

A customer—that's what he is. He's not here to ask this lady for a job or looking to rent an apartment from her and he's not panhandling her and he's for sure not going to hit on her—she's way too old, probably forty or fifty at least and pretty low on the hotness scale. No, the Kid's a legitimate legal customer who's strolled into the library to get some information because libraries are where the information is.

So why is he shaking and his arms all covered with goose bumps like he's standing naked inside a meat locker? It's not just because he's never actually been inside a library before even when he was in high school and it was sort of required. He's shivering because he's afraid of the answer to the question that drove him here even though he already knows it.

Listen, can I ask you something? It's kinda personal, I guess.

Of course.

Well, see, I live out in the north end and the people in my neighborhood, my neighbors, they're all like telling me that there might be like a convicted sex offender living there. In the neighborhood. And they tell me that you can just go online to this site that tells you where he's living and all and they asked me if I'd check it out for them. For the neighborhood. Is it true?

Is what true?

You know, that you can just like go online and it'll tell you where the sex offender lives even if you don't know his name or anything.

Well, let's go see, she says like he asked her what's the capital of Vermont and leads the Kid across the room to a long table where six computers are lined up side by side and no one is using them. She sits down in front of one and does a quick Google search under convicted sex offenders and up pops the National Sex Offender Registry which links straight to www.familywatchdog.us. The Kid stands at a forward tilt behind her shifting his weight from one foot to the other. He thinks he should run now, get out of here fast before she clicks again but something he can't resist, something he knows is coming that is both scary and familiar keeps him staring over the librarian's shoulder at the screen the same way he used to get held to the screen when cruising pornography sites. The librarian clicks *find offenders* and then on the new menu hits *by location* and another menu jumps up and asks for the address.

You're from Calusa, right? What's your neighborhood's zip code?

It's . . . ah . . . 33135.

Any particular street you want to look up?

He gives her the name of the street where his mother lives and he used to live and she types it in and hits *search*. A pale green map of his street and the surrounding twenty or so blocks appears on the screen. Small red, green, and orange squares are scattered across the neighborhood like bits of confetti.

Any particular block?

The Kid reaches down to the screen and touches the map on the block where he lived his entire life until he enlisted in the army and where he lived again after he was discharged. A red piece of confetti covers his mother's bungalow and the backyard where he pitched his tent and built Iggy the iguana's outdoor cage.

The librarian clicks onto the tiny square and suddenly the Kid is looking at his mug shot—his forlorn bewildered face—and he feels all over again the shame and humiliation of the night he was booked. There's his full name, first, last, and middle, date of birth, height, weight, his race, color of his eyes and hair, and the details of his crime and conviction.

Slowly the librarian turns in her chair and looks up at the Kid's real face, then back at the computerized version.

That's . . . you. Isn't it?

I gotta go, he whispers. *I gotta leave.* He backs away from the woman who appears both stunned and saddened but not at all afraid which surprises him and for a few seconds he considers trying to explain how his face and his description and criminal record got there on the computer screen. But there's no way he can explain it to someone like her, a normal person, a lady reference librarian who helps people look up the whereabouts and crimes of people like him.

Wait. Don't leave.

I gotta go. I'm sorry. No kidding, I'm really sorry.

Don't be sorry.

No, I'm prob'ly not even supposed to be here, he says. *In the library, I mean.* He turns and walks stiff-legged away and then as he nears the door he breaks into a run and the Kid doesn't stop running until he's back up on his bike heading for the Causeway.

LIKE EVERYONE OVER A CERTAIN AGE THE KID has a name naturally but none of his neighbors under the Causeway knows it and he has no intention of giving it out unless the alternative is getting beat up or cut by one of the more occasionally violent wing-nuts living down there—although violence is not really their thing or why they're down there. Or unless he's required by law to give his full legal name which happens often enough to make the Kid stash his ID in his right sneaker where he can snatch and deliver it quickly if he needs to prove his age to buy booze or cigarettes or if a cop or an officer of the court or a social worker calls for it. Everyone else—the men who live alongside him under the Causeway and the waiters and waitresses and the other busboys he works with at the Mirador and even his boss Dario who because he hands out the paychecks actually does know his real name—everyone else calls him Kid and refers to him in his absence as the Kid.

I've been meaning to ask, what's he doing down here? Has the fellow a name?

"Meanin' to ask." *That's funny.* What're *you* doin down here? "Fellow."

Same as you, I assume.

Who the fuck you talkin 'bout anyhow?

The little white guy with the bike. Lives in the tent with the lizard.

Ask him yourself.

Most of the people he knew when he was a boy and in high school know the Kid by his real name and the guys he went through basic training with and his mother of course and some of her friends, they know it. But he hasn't spoken to any of them not even his mother in over a year and whenever he accidentally on the street spots somebody he once knew slightly from school or from hanging out at the mall in the old days or his job at the light store before he enlisted in the army which happens every now and then even though he never visits his old neighborhood anymore he stares straight ahead and keeps pedaling or if on foot cuts across the street or just turns on his heels and walks the other way.

No one he knew before wants to meet up with him anyhow so when they recognize him they do the same thing—turn around and walk the other way or check out the shoes in a Payless window or if there's no other way to avoid eye contact cover their face with a cap brim or sunglasses or even with their hands. In that sense things aren't much different now than they've always been. The way he sees it people have been avoiding him all his life except for the people he's become acquainted with in the past year. Not counting those who work for the state and have read his file as part of their job the men under the Causeway are in a sense the Kid's new and true friends and know nothing whatsoever about his private or public past and therefore do not noticeably avoid him and are okay with calling him Kid. It's superficial but it's what he's always preferred and maybe needs—strictly enforced surface relations with people—and with his buzz cut and thin pointed nose and nub of a chin and his big ears and being short and skinny as a jockey although pretty muscular if he says so himself it's what he looks like anyhow: a kid.

So what's your name, kid?

Dude, that is what it is. Thankyouverymuch. Good-bye.

What, like the Sundance Kid? Captain Kydd? The Cisco Kid? Billy the Kid?

Yeah, sure, all those guys. Who the fuck're you?

The Kid turns away and locks his bike to the concrete pillar next to his pup tent. The bike is an old dented Raleigh three-speed that he spotted unlocked in an alley between Rafer and Island Drive on his way to work one day and when he came back that evening it was still there. The bike was dark green and had a wire basket in front and a wide rack over the rear fender and no lock. He figured it was a rental abandoned by a drunk tourist who forgot where he left it or a throwaway or maybe a Chinese food delivery bike the delivery guy was too lazy to lock. He grabbed it and rode it back to the Causeway and later took it apart and spray painted it black just in case and bought a black carbon steel cable-lock for it.

Leashed to a cinder block by a somewhat longer link-chain is the Kid's iguana. Its name is Iggy which the Kid now thinks is sort of dumb but he was only ten when his mother presented him with the iguana and the singer Iggy Pop for some reason was the first thing that came into his head and eventually the iguana and its name became one the way he and his name Kid have become one and it was too late by then to change it. When it was a baby it was only eight or ten inches long and quick and bright green and cute. Almost decorative. Twelve years later it's the length and weight of a full-grown alligator—six feet long head to tail and twenty-seven pounds—and no longer cute. Definitely not decorative. Its thick muscular body is covered with dark gray scales. A raised jagged dorsal fin runs from its head along its back and down the long tail. It's a beast straight from the age of dinosaurs but to the Kid its appearance is as normal as his mother's. Dewlaps drape in soft fans from its boney jaw and there are thin fringes of flesh on its clawed toes that stiffen and rise as if saluting him when the Kid approaches. It wears its eardrums on the outside of its head behind and below the eyes. On top of its head is a primitive third eye—a gray waferlike lens that keeps a lookout for overhead predators which are large birds mainly. According to some experts the third eye tracks the sun and functions as a guidance system. Early on the Kid made a systematic online study of iguanas. He learned everything he could about the creature's body, its needs and desires, habits, fears, strengths and weaknesses. In school he never got a grade higher than a C- but if iguana had been a subject he would have received an A+. Iggy was the only creature other than himself that he had ever been obliged to care for and he decided to do it the way he wished someone had cared for him—as if the iguana were a human child and he were its parent.

He fed it a strictly vegetarian diet—bell peppers, okra, squash, and plenty of leafy greens and tropical fruits like papaya, mangoes, and melons—taking care to avoid vegetables known to be toxic to iguanas like potatoes and tomatoes and fruits with pits like plums and apricots. In the beginning he talked to it in his few words of junior high school Spanish because it was originally from Mexico but after a while when he got nowhere with Spanish he switched to English and still got nowhere. Eventually he stopped talking to the iguana altogether because he came to enjoy and trust the silence between them as if the two of them were buddies in an old-time silent movie. Mostly they spent a lot of time just staring at each other and making faces.

At first he kept it in his bedroom in a forty-gallon glass aquarium furnished with mossy rocks and coconut fiber and gravel. But iguanas grow fast and as it grew he had to buy bigger and bigger aquariums. Before long there were no pet store aquariums large enough. Also iguanas are arboreal and are happiest when they think they're in a tree. So after about two years when Iggy was a teenager the Kid pushed all the furniture in his room to one side and built a floor-to-ceiling chicken-wire cage that filled the other half of the room. He covered the floor of the cage with crushed bark and installed the trunk and leafless branches of a dead lemon tree he found at a construction site. He kept the temperature constant with a heat lamp and controlled the humidity with a small humidifier. It was Iggy's own private jungle.

Lawrence. Larry.

Larry what?

Somerset.

Larry Somerset. Lawrence Somerset. Rings a bell. You must've been famous once. Like in the news.

I had my fifteen minutes.

Yeah, tell me about it sometime. I got to feed my man here.

The Kid ducks into his tent and rummages through a plastic tub for the bag of wilted spinach and the overripe cantaloupe he foraged yesterday from the Dumpster behind the Whole Foods store on Bayfront Street. He wonders about this new guy. Except for the wrinkled pale gray suit and stained dress shirt he looks like another of the two dozen or so middle-aged and older homeless weirdos who've come to a final stop under the Causeway and like the others he acts as if everyone down here belongs to the same club and thinks the Kid in spite of his youth is a member too. He'll learn differently before long. The Kid is not a member of any club. At least not willingly. Other people can put him in this category or that and say he's one of those or these but in the Kid's mind he's a one-and-only one of a kind. A loner. That's what kind he is. And even among loners he's unique. Singular. Solo-fucking-mee-o.

The man named Larry Somerset is a little taller than the rest and soft in the face and belly like he's spent his life sitting in a padded chair signing official documents and giving orders to underlings. He wears a plain gold wedding ring. The Kid notices it at first glance because a wedding ring is unusual down here and the guy has a black brush of a goatee that looks dyed and long graying hair combed straight back to where it curls over the dirty collar of his shirt. The Kid is sure he's never met him before but something about the guy is familiar especially the name like he maybe read it in the *Calusa Times-Union*.

It's obvious even with his floppy wide-cuffed trousers that the guy's got a TrackerPAL GPS clamped to his right ankle. The Kid wonders if it's the same as his or if it's one of those cool new units he's heard about with the built-in cell phone that's connected to a monitoring center 24/7 and even pokes your caseworker's beeper if you forget to recharge your battery so the caseworker can phone in to make sure you haven't died. It's like being followed around by a CIA drone with a heat-seeking missile ready to fire. The new style TrackerPAL with the cell phone attachment intrigues the Kid simply because he's into the technology of surveillance but no way he wants an upgrade. The Kid's anklet is more like a simple antitheft tracking device for a stolen car that at least lets him piss in privacy.

The Kid sits down on his folding canvas camp-chair in front of his tent and lights his first cigarette since leaving work and right on schedule up under the Causeway the motor for the generator gasps and coughs and after a few seconds settles into a clattering diesel chug. Plato the Greek owns the generator and buys the fuel for it and runs it every evening from seven till nine and sometimes later depending on business. He has it wired to a twelve-outlet surge protector and the residents pay him a dollar each to recharge their cell phone if they have one and their anklet battery. Which they are required to do every forty-eight hours or more depending on the model or else in an office somewhere on the mainland a beeper will go off and in a few hours you'll see someone's caseworker or parole officer prowling through the camp looking for a guy he calls his client but who in actuality is his legal electronic prisoner and is probably only in his squat sleeping off a drunk or nodding off without having remembered to charge his now very dead battery. Sometimes though it's only a resident who has fallen into despair from living down here—a man with no job who's become a scavenger supporting himself by wandering the city with a shopping cart collecting and redeeming cans and bottles—and after months and even years of it opts for three hots and a cot because if you refuse to charge the battery that powers your electronic anklet you violate a key term of your parole and back you go to prison. Voluntary incarceration.

Outside the tent Larry Somerset takes a few cautious steps closer to the iguana and gives it a once-over. He says that he's not seen an iguana this large before and has to admire the Kid's use of it to guard his home and property. *Better than a pit bull,* he says. *Certainly uglier than a pit bull.*

Iggy's chain-link leash is long enough to let him lie in the front entry of the tent but still able to scramble around to the back if someone tries sneaking in that way. The iguana looks lethargic and slow but they're often seen streaking across golf course fairways and putting greens at astonishing speed—low to the ground on short legs but fast as a greyhound. The eyes of the iguana are round and large as marbles and watchful and like its scales dry and cold. It stares motionless at Larry—eyelids sliding slowly up and down like thin scrims. Every few seconds its forked tongue slips from between its jaws and flicks the air as if tasting it for flavor, passes quickly in front of its nostrils to read the odor of the air and withdraws. When the iguana swallows, its dewlaps loosely flap.

Larry keeps a respectful distance from the iguana. Everyone does. Except for the Kid. He loves the lizard. He could say Iggy is the only person he loves. But he wouldn't. It was a birthday present from his mother. The summer before he turned eleven she left him home alone and took off a week from the beauty parlor where she was and still is a hairdresser and traveled with a group of seven other women to Mexico to participate in a summer solstice sun ceremony in the Yucatán. It was an annual spiritual rebirthing ritual designed and led by her yoga teacher and held in the main plaza of the Mayan ruins at Chichén Itzá. During the overnight layover in Mérida on the way home she purchased a baby iguana from a street vendor and smuggled it into the States in her suitcase. It was illegal but three other women in the group—all mothers—did the same for their kids and none of them got caught by customs because except for the yoga teacher they were women in their forties traveling home as a group to the same city and looked like American sex tourists which in a sense they were because all of them had gotten laid by Mexicans while in Mérida.

His mother's name is Adele and she was not married to the Kid's biological father who was a roofer who drove his pickup down from the North for work after one of the bigger hurricanes and was a sort of boyfriend for a few months but when she got pregnant with the Kid the roofer moved back to Somerville, Massachusetts, where he was from originally. She told the Kid his father's name and not much else because there wasn't much else to tell or so she said. Except that he was a short good-looking Irishman and had a funny accent and drank too much. After the roofer left and the Kid was born she had boyfriends pretty constantly who lived in her house with her and the Kid for up to six months on a few occasions but none of them stuck around long enough to claim the Kid as his own or take responsibility for educating or protecting him. Adele needs men to want her but she doesn't want men to need her. In fact she doesn't want anyone to need her—not even the Kid although she does not know that and would deny it if asked. She believes that she loves her son and has done everything for him that a single parent could and has sacrificed much of her youth for him and therefore cannot be blamed for the way he's turned out.

It might have been different she believes and has often said if she'd had a husband to help raise her son and be a role model for him but most men at least the men she was attracted to as soon as they found out she shared her concrete block shotgun bungalow in the north end of the city with a young son weren't interested in much more than sex for a while and someone to cook breakfast for them the next morning. There may have been men out there hoping to marry a good-looking red-haired woman with a terrific body in her thirties and then forties who owned her own house and had a steady job and was raising a boy on her own but she hadn't met any. At least not any who turned her on sexually or even had a good sense of humor which she likes to say is as good a substitute for sex as anything else. She says she can live without one or the other—humor or sex—but not both. But then after her son turned eighteen and joined the army and moved out she looked in the mirror one day and she was fifty years old and was coloring the gray out of her red hair and unable to keep the weight off her hips and waist and almost any man who paid attention to her would do. Forget sense of humor. Forget good sex.

What about him, the lizard? Does he have a name?

Yeah, sure. Iggy. He's not a lizard by the way. He's an iguana. Iggy's short for iguana. It's a stupid name, I know, but we're both used to it.

How long have you owned him?

Eleven-twelve years maybe. Since I was a kid. But I don't exactly own him. I mean it's not like he's my slave or something.

He's your friend.

Yeah. You could say that. You know, if you're the guy named Lawrence Somerset I'm thinking of you're kind of a freak. Even down here.

Don't believe everything you read.

I don't. But be careful of Iggy. He doesn't like freaks.

On the flat a short ways behind the Kid's tent a shirtless yellow-skinned man named Paco lies on his back on a homemade weight bench pumping iron. Paco is a surly Dominican with muscles in his arms like tattooed bowling balls and a stomach like corrugated iron. He drops the barbell onto the rack with a loud clank. He sits up straight and calls over to the Kid, *Just blow him off, man! The dude's a fuckin' baby-banger.*

That true, Larry? You a baby-banger?

God, no!

If you are then you must not be the dude I'm thinking of. He was into little girls.

Everyone down here is the same, I thought. Everyone's here for the same reasons, right?

Fuck no. Baby-bangers, man, those guys are the worst. The lowest of the low.

What, some of us are worse than others? C'mon. I don't buy it.

Buy it, man. Guys here for rape or what they call sexual contact with teenaged girls, they're on top. Like ol' Paco there. He claims to be a rapist. Maybe he is, maybe he isn't. Then come guys convicted of sexual contact with young boys. And below them are guys who did time for sexual contact with young girls. And way way below them are the baby-bangers. There's other categories too. Like fags and straights. Straights are ranked higher than fags.

Well, I'm certainly straight. And I'm no baby-banger. Jesus! That's disgusting.

You're disgusted, eh? I told you there was a kind of ranking.

What about you, Kid? Where are you in the offender hierarchy?

The Kid turns his back and ducks into his tent. *Figure it out for yourself, man. I gotta feed my pit bull.*

CHAPTER TWO

IGGY HAS BEEN THE KID'S MAIN FRIEND FOR all these years and sometimes his only friend but their relationship did not get off to a good start. The Kid's mom arrived home from her trip to Mexico in a cab and lugged her suitcase up the crumbling cement walk to the porch and when she couldn't find her key she banged impatiently on the screened door. The Kid was alone in his bedroom at the back of the house, a small dark room that was once a toolshed made of plywood located under a mango tree at the far end of the backyard until Kyle who was one of his mother's boyfriends and wanted a little more privacy shoved the shed on two-by-four skids up to the back of the house where he bolted the shed to the exterior wall with metal straps and cut a door into the cinder block wall where a window off the kitchen had been. Until then it had been a single-bedroom house and the one bedroom had belonged to his mom and whoever was sleeping with her and the Kid slept on the couch in the living room which wasn't too bad since he got to watch a lot of what he wanted on TV. At first when thanks to Kyle he got his own room he missed having all-night access to the TV and being able to keep track of the men who passed back and forth through the living room on their way to the kitchen from his mother's bedroom but when his mother finally bought him a laptop computer which was required that year for every middle school student in the state he was glad to spend all his time in the new little dark room in back and lost track both of what was on TV and who was sleeping with his mother. Although now and then he took a peek at both. More than now and then actually. Especially the TV. When she was out at night he watched porn on pay-per-view until finally the monthly bills from the cable company got so high she checked the specific charges and ordered the parental control option. *No more watching porn on my dime, mister!*

She banged on his bedroom window which was opposite his computer screen and could have given her a view of what he was watching there so he clicked away to a different website and then looked over at his mother. Her face was red and sweating from the summer heat.

For God's sake open the damn door and let me in! Didn't you hear me knock?

He got up and slid open the window and smiled in the way he knew calmed people when they were excited or angry.

I had the air conditioner on high, Mom. I couldn't hear you. Welcome home, Mom.

I can't find my keys. Come and open the door and help me with my suitcase. I've got a present for you. The house better not be a mess.

It's not, Mom. Don't worry.

And it wasn't. He was a neat boy, more orderly and in fact a better housekeeper than his mother and whenever she left him alone at home and came back the house was cleaner than when she left. He actually enjoyed the chance to live in the house alone for a few days and nights and put everything right—squaring the pillows on the couch and mopping the tile floors and scrubbing the kitchen counters and restacking the dishes according to size and use and lining up the cups and glasses in military rows. When he could busy himself cleaning and rationally organizing the house he was less lonely and almost didn't notice his mother's absence and sometimes even forgot to remember when she was returning.

He opened the door and grabbed onto her suitcase and dragged it into the living room and she followed. She kissed him on the cheek and chucked him under the chin with her thumb and forefinger as was her habit. Her smell was a vinegary mix of sweat and cologne and her thick red hair was damp and tangled and her mascara was smeared from the heat. She wore a pale blue nylon tracksuit for comfort and bright yellow high-top sneakers as a fashion statement. She looked tired and not especially happy to be home from Mexico.

I thought you wasn't coming back till tomorrow or the next day.

I brought you a present you're gonna just love. Wait'll you see it.

She lifted the suitcase onto the sofa and flipped the latches, opened it, and took out a shoe box–size carton with a thin blue ribbon around it. She handed him the carton and hugged him.

It's for your birthday! Happy birthday, little buddy.

My birthday's not till September.

So? It's a problem I'm a little early?

Two months early.

Better than two months late, ingrate. Go ahead, open it!

He slowly untied the ribbon and lifted the top off the box and there in a pile of straw lay the pepper green baby iguana, eyes closed, its body shaped like a carving knife unmoving as if sleeping or maybe dead, he couldn't be sure which. Or maybe neither sleeping nor dead but instead carved out of jade. It was a beautiful thing. It looked like an ancient piece of Mayan jewelry on a fine gold chain that a brocaded priest dressed in robes for a religious ceremony hangs from his neck.

The Kid reached into the cardboard box and picked up the iguana and suddenly it came to life and twisted its body around as if it were a snake and bit the Kid on the meat of his hand between his thumb and forefinger, clamping onto it like pliers and refusing to let go even when the Kid as if he'd been scalded shook his hand in the air trying to get rid of it. He yowled in pain and kept flipping his hand to shake off the lizard but it clung by its dry-boned mouth to

the soft lump of skin and muscle, not chewing or biting hard enough
to break through the flesh but clipped precisely to it by rows of small
inward-slanting serrated teeth so that it could not be removed without tearing the flesh.

Get it off me! Ma, get it off!

She yanked on the iguana but it wouldn't let go. She was afraid
that if she pulled any harder she would rip away a chunk of her son's
hand which was already swelling around the creature's beak. The Kid
was bawling now. She decided to call 911. Fifteen minutes later the
ambulance arrived and the EMT aides and the driver took one look
at the iguana and the Kid's hand and half-laughed and drove him
and his mother to the emergency room way over at Cameron-Kelly
Hospital on Northwest Fiftieth.

They waited for thirty or so minutes before a doctor could see
them. By then the Kid had stopped crying. His hand had ballooned
out like a baseball glove and had gone numb and he had gotten used
to the sight of the iguana clamped onto him and because the bite
didn't hurt now it seemed almost affectionate, a kind of hard ongoing kiss, and he wasn't afraid of the creature anymore. In the waiting
room the eight or ten other people waiting for a doctor stared at the
iguana, repelled by it, and felt sorry for the Kid even though most of
them were in much worse shape than he with busted feet and cuts
and concussions and mysterious pain from places deep inside their
bodies, but all their attackers had long since fled or been arrested and
here he was still under attack.

His mother sat beside him and stroked his head with her left hand
and flipped through a *People* magazine with the other. Finally a nurse
called his name and led him and his mother down a long tiled hall.
The nurse carefully averted her eyes from the Kid and the iguana
which creeped her out and walked fast in front of him and his mom
so they had to trot to keep up.

In the treatment room the Kid sat on a paper-covered bench
while the doctor examined his hand and the iguana attached to it.

The doctor was a slender light brown Asian-looking man with a shiny bald head and a thick black mustache.

Well, my friend, this is a problem, yes, but a problem easily solved. If you don't object to a little blood. Okay?

What? No! Don't cut off my hand! Please, mister, don't!

I would not think of doing such a terrible thing as that. No, I am going to cut off the little animal's head. A very simple solution to your problem.

Don't worry, honey, it'll be over in a minute. God, I wish I'd thought of that before calling the ambulance. I could've done it at home myself with a kitchen knife. This is going to cost me a pretty penny. I don't have insurance.

No-o-o! Please don't kill it!

When the head has no body, when its spinal cord has been severed that is, the muscles that contract to control the mouth relax. You are very fortunate that the iguana is only a little baby. They grow to be very big, you know. Where I come from they are known to kill and eat dogs and even people sometimes. Especially babies. They like to eat babies. They are dragons. They are known to inject their prey with a poison that causes fatal internal bleeding. This one is only a baby itself and is not of the poisonous type anyhow. Which is very fortunate for you, eh?

Can't you just like put him to sleep or something? Like with a needle?

You want your little friend to live and grow big and eat dogs and babies, eh?

Yes.

Does it have a name?

The Kid suddenly thought that if the iguana had a name the doctor might not be so eager to cut off its head. He said the iguana's name was Iggy.

Hmmm. Iggy. Cute.

Yeah. I guess.

The doctor reflected a moment and walked to a cabinet and removed a glass vial from a drawer of vials. He doused a large square patch of gauze with chloroform and wrapped it around the face of the iguana and after a few seconds the body of the iguana went limp and its color changed from green to gray. Its mouth opened and released the Kid's hand. The iguana plopped onto the tiled floor. Ignoring it the doctor examined the Kid's hand, saw that there were no breaks in the skin other than a curved line of pinpricks on the top of his hand and another on the bottom between the thumb and forefinger. After applying antiseptic to the Kid's hand the doctor dropped Iggy into a plastic HAZMAT bag and sent the foolish boy and his even more foolish mother and their sleeping baby dragon on their way.

CHAPTER THREE

WHILE HE WAITS FOR THE BLUE BUTANE flame of his camp stove to heat his supper the Kid stands beside his tent in the damp semidarkness beneath the Claybourne Causeway and contemplates the smooth blue waters of the wide Calusa Bay and the southern outflow of the thousand-mile-long Atlantic Intracoastal Waterway. Bumper-to-bumper cars, trucks, buses, and intermittent motorcycles rumble overhead crossing between the mainland and the barrier islands on the eastern side of the Bay. It's the end of a long late-summer day. Everyone's headed home. Everyone's home is in one place or the other, the mainland or the islands. There. Or over there. Definitely not here. Not here on the broad flat concrete peninsula that anchors the rusting steel piers that hold up the Causeway.

He pretends that he is alone down here. He turns away from the polyethylene lean-tos and tents and the salvaged plywood huts nearby and the men who live in them standing around like bored ghosts and he gazes out at the Bay, thinking not of where he is but of where he would like to be. This is how he has learned to endure being where he is without bawling like a little lost boy. Or worse: trying to escape from this place.

He peers out at the Bay. He tracks charter fishing boats and a few large white yachts and dozens of small private fishing and pleasure boats returning from open waters after a long day's pleasure at sea and in some cases work. He would like to be aboard one of those boats. A pleasure boat or a charter fishing boat or a shrimper. Any one of them would do. That one. Or that one. Or that fifty-foot cabin cruiser shaped like an arrow. The flotilla passes through Kydd's Cut from the open sea into Calusa Bay and plows steadily northward keeping downtown Calusa portside and the Great Barrier Isles off to starboard. Individual boats peel off and make their way to the thousands of marinas, dockyards, and piers scattered along the mainland and the islets and canals that filigree both the mainland side of the Bay and the Barriers, where the fleet finally disintegrates.

The official name for the twenty-mile linked chain of narrow flat mostly man-made islands between the Bay and the open sea is the Calusa Great Barrier Isles. Real estate developers, speculators, politicians, and hoteliers a hundred years ago invented the Calusa Great Barrier Isles by dredging muck and crushed limestone from the bottom of the shallow Bay and filling in the mosquito- and crocodile-infested mangrove swamps from Bougainvillea Shores twenty miles to the north all the way south to Kydd's Cut, the deep-water channel that opens the international port of Calusa to the Atlantic Ocean. The Realtors, speculators, politicians, and hoteliers hauled ten thousand tons of white sand from beaches in another state hundreds of miles north of here and made with it a wide fine-grained sun-reflecting beach running along the ocean side of the islands from one end of the Barriers to the other. They connected the island chain to the mainland with bridges at each end and a four-lane causeway in the middle—the Archie B. Claybourne Causeway, named after the president of the corporation that financed the development—and laid down a grid of streets, carved out Venetian-style canals, planted palms, and built marinas, beachfront hotels, golf courses, and high-rise apartment buildings with ocean views.

The value of real estate rose by 10 and 15 percent a year for a hundred years. And as the price per square foot of land rose the height of the hotels and apartment buildings rose and now the Barriers are lined for twenty miles with terraced pastel-glass towers filled with northern retirees and tourists, South American entrepreneurs and drug lords, European fashion models and the men who photograph them, aging out-of-work Latin American dictators and generalissimos. Most of the people who serve them, sell to them, park their cars, and clean their condos and hotel rooms live on the mainland north of downtown Calusa in barrios, slums, ghettos, and subsidized housing projects and ride the buses across the Causeway and bridges to work and back. Most of their supervisors and managers live west of downtown in middle-class suburbs and gated communities and drive east in their cars daily through ten, twenty, and even thirty miles of clotted traffic to the Barriers and in the evening drive back again through the same jams.

The Kid listens to the rumble and roar overhead of day's-end traffic crossing the Claybourne Causeway and trying to hear his thoughts he turns and looks south across the lower Bay at the clustered skyscrapers of downtown Calusa—fifty-story towers of smoked glass and gleaming sheets of aluminum and steel high-rise hotels here too, but these are Marriotts and Hyatts and Holiday Inns built for business travelers instead of tourists. There are domed convention centers and international banking and insurance company office buildings and whole colonies of condominiums stacked on top of one another like gigantic poker chips. A condo downtown would be fine, he thinks. He doesn't need to live on the Barriers. Even a small studio on a low floor without a view would do. He'd furnish it simply for one person alone with a single bed and a table and two chairs and a lamp or two and a dresser. Maybe a few small pictures. Some dishes and pots and pans. Sheets and blankets and towels. Keep it simple. Keep it neat and clean. He doesn't really require a view but it would be nice to have one. To stroll to the fridge and take out a frosty Corona and crack it open and flop in his La-Z-Boy recliner and check out the city below.

At this time of day he'd watch the glass and metal towers cast their long shadows over the cluttered port where cranes and gigantic elevators load and off-load rows of room-size steel shipping containers from wheezing freighters headed to or from China, India, and Brazil. He'd consider the three creamy cruise ships lined up like floating amusement parks beside the docks and warehouses sleepily waiting to be restocked with food and liquor and refilled with fresh island-hopping limbo-dancing tourists from the North. If the Kid were a deckhand he'd have his own bunk in one of those ships. He'd have access to a galley where the cook prepares meals and the crew eats them. A recreation room for watching TV and movies on DVD. He'd be able to travel to Asia or South America or to the islands of the Caribbean.

Out where the sprawling city dwindles and finally ends, beyond where the malls and bungalows and gated communities of the suburbs turn into trailer parks and the trailer parks eventually merge with palmetto scrub and cane fields and mangrove marsh, out beyond the Great Panzacola Swamp a flattened red sun glimmers near the low unbroken horizon. Streaked with tangerine strips of cloud the western sky turns turquoise and then orange all over and finally scarlet. The Kid can see that evening sky from here beneath the Causeway but only if he walks out to the end of the concrete peninsula and stands at the water's lapping edge and looks up. A pair of 747s departs simultaneously from the international airport west of downtown. Parallel white contrails scratch the darkening sky. Then directly overhead one plane slowly veers northeast in a long arc toward England while the other bisects the dark sky above the blackened green Gulf Stream on a line that follows the Tropic of Cancer straight east all the way to North Africa and beyond.

Here below the Causeway he gazes along the smaller Great Barrier Isles and the canals between them and the bayside backsides of the palatial homes of singers, professional athletes, and movie stars and the men and women who import and export drugs and manage and launder other people's ill-gotten and sometimes inherited money in hedge funds and offshore accounts in the Caymans, Turks and Caicos, and Bahamas. Along the canals the mostly Moorish-style estates hide floodlit manicured gardens, terraces, and Olympic-size pools behind ten-foot walls alarmed and topped with razor wire. Looking east beyond them he can see the tall seaside hotels, their pastel walls splashed with warm light. Neon signs chum the names of the hotels against the purple eastern sky and blot out the stars: CONQUISTADOR. CASA CALUSA. MONTAGUE. MIRADOR.

The cars, buses, and trucks on the Causeway and bridges and the north-south Interstate and the traffic-jammed turnpikes to the suburbs have switched their headlights on. In the high-rises and sky-scrapers downtown fluorescent night-lights ignite floor after floor as the cleaners and janitors and watchmen begin their night's work and from the rooftops and penthouses slender beacons reach like long pale arms into the darkness. An offshore breeze puts a sudden chill in the air. Night has fallen in the city of Calusa and along the Great Barrier Isles and down here under the wide loud Causeway that connects the two.

CHAPTER FOUR

T HE KID CLICKS HIS HEADLAMP ON. HE
shuts off his stove and holds the hot tin can with a gloved
hand and spoons chili con carne onto a paper plate and
starts eating his supper, washing it down with a warm can of Corona
beer. The iguana settles in beside him and watches while he eats as
if waiting for leftovers but there are none. Iggy's an herbivore anyhow. Pure vegan. The Kid crushes the chili can underfoot and drops
it into his recycling bag and lights and burns the paper plate on the
ground. He opens a second Corona and places the empty into the
bag where he stores returnables.

Waste not want not. Carry out what you carry in. The Kid is
a good camper. His habits go back to when he was fourteen and
behind his mother's house pitched the same Boy Scout pup tent that
he lives in now. He placed it in the shade of the mango tree where
the toolshed that became his bedroom had been located before his
mother's then-boyfriend Kyle attached it to the house. That first
summer he rarely spent more than a single night at a time out there
but he discovered that he loved the privacy and solitude of it. When
later that summer his mother got her own computer and a wireless
router he had Internet access in the tent. He strung a long extension cord from the house to the tent for charging his laptop and cell
phone. In the fall when he started attending North Village High

where he didn't know anybody and no one wanted to hang with him and wouldn't let him join any of the sets which were mostly black kids anyway he made the tent his semipermanent residence.

Next to his tent he built a new outdoor cage for Iggy six feet high and four feet wide and deep with a perch, a bathtub, a bed of mulch, and a heat lamp. Nights when he needed company or when the temperature dropped into the fifties and occasionally into the forties as winter came on he brought Iggy into the tent with him and visited the house only when his mother wasn't home for food supplies and to use the toilet and every few days to shower and do his laundry. Most of the time when he wasn't at school or taking care of Iggy or the two of them were just sitting there staring at each other he watched pornography online and charged it to his mother's Visa.

At first his mother didn't seem to know. He told himself he didn't care. He did care but didn't want to be the one who drew her attention to the facts. But she barely noticed that he'd moved out or that he was running up bigger and bigger monthly charges on her Visa— although she did notice and complained when he took food from the cupboard and fridge that she'd bought for herself and whomever she was sleeping with and making breakfast for. She said, *For Christ's sake, why don't you get a part-time after-school job and buy your own damn groceries? And no more drinking my beer! Or smoking my cigarettes! It's enough already that I'm putting a roof over your head and buying your clothes. Besides, that food, beer, and cigarettes aren't always only mine, you know.*

A few weeks into October walking home alone one afternoon after class he saw a hand-painted sign, PART-TIME HELPER WANTED, in the window of a wholesale lighting store on Northwest Primavera Street on the edge of Haiti Town. The owner's name was Tony Perez, a gaunt pale-skinned Cuban in his early fifties with a shaved head and Fu Manchu mustache and a small gold hoop in each earlobe. He needed someone a few hours a day to sweep the place and dust the thousands of lamps hanging from the ceiling and pack the sold lamps for shipping. He said he was the first cousin and had the same name of the famous Cincinnati Reds first baseman Tony Perez who the Kid had never heard of which Tony said was too bad, he was a great first baseman.

Tony didn't mind that the Kid was small and underage. He was energetic at least and seemed intelligent enough and told Tony that he had no problema being paid in cash off the books. Tony admitted that he hadn't wanted to hire Haitians from the neighborhood because most of them couldn't speak English well enough and no way he was going to learn their lingo. Not at his age.

The Kid figured Tony was racist and wouldn't have hired anyone who wasn't white like him anyhow or someone almost white but that didn't bother him and instead made him feel lucky that both his biological parents were white people. He had never met his real father or seen a picture of him but he was pretty sure if his father wasn't a white guy his mother would have told him as she was in no way a racist and now and then actually seemed to be attracted to men who weren't white since at least three of the boyfriends that he knew about were black dudes and two others were very dark Cuban or Dominican guys, one or the other, he wasn't sure and they never said. She told him black men were sexier than white men and were better hung which he wasn't sure of even after being in the army and seeing lots of black guys naked. She said it didn't matter but he had a feeling it did. Because he's never actually made love to a woman the value of having a large penis is one of the many things about sex and women that he still wonders about. He does know from watching porn that big looks better.

He kept the job at the light store all through high school and worked there full-time after he graduated right up until he enlisted in the army. Tony never promoted him or gave him a raise but the Kid was okay with that because he was able to cover all his expenses with what he made. He lived at his mother's rent free so he only needed enough money to pay for cigarettes and his and Iggy's food and his increasingly regular visits to Internet porn sites. He put most of his earnings into a savings account at the Wells Fargo neighbor-hood bank branch and was given a debit card that he could use to pay for his porn, his phone cards, and other incidental expenses. Once a week he gave Tony enough cash plus a ten-dollar surcharge to buy him a case of beer. He had no friends—only acquaintances—and no girlfriends and essentially no family either. He wasn't sure if this should bother him but since he had no idea how to go about obtaining friends or girlfriends or family he made the best of the situation and not only never complained—who would listen, who would have cared?—he told himself that actually he preferred things this way because he at least had Iggy and didn't have to answer to anyone except Tony Perez and even Tony he could say fuck you to and walk away if he felt like it. Back then there were all kinds of jobs—thousands of them—available to a kid like him that were just as good as his job at the light store.

Larry Somerset the new guy lugs a large dark green duffel bag over to the Kid's tent and sets it on the ground and smiling in a contrived casual way hunkers down beside him on the side opposite Iggy like an overfriendly uncle. He's positioned himself a little too close to the Kid for comfort and his breath smells like old moldy cheese. The Kid looks beyond him and over his shoulder thinking maybe he ought to pull somebody else into this conversation since this guy Larry is a little creepy somehow. Maybe he is a baby-banger. The Kid isn't afraid of Larry. He just feels trapped by the bright insincere light of the guy's smile. Very few people down here ever smile like that. Very few people down here smile at all. The Kid can't remember the last time he smiled.

In the shadows he sees Otis the Rabbit leaning against a girder watching them. Otis is maybe the oldest resident although probably not eighty-five as he claims, more like seventy-five but being eighty-five gets him a certain amount of admiration and status as does his claim that he was a professional featherweight boxer who fought in Madison Square Garden on the undercard twice back in the 1950s.

He's a short dark-brown man tight and trim with a white grizzle of a beard and a bald head that he covers with a black beret. He has the professional fighter's squashed nose and ridge of scar tissue above the eyes and he stammers a little which might be a result of too many blows to the head.

Otis the Rabbit Washington was his fighting name because of his quickness he likes to say but once he confessed to the Kid with a certain small pride that he got the name because he was an expert rabbit-puncher and could knock a man out with it and get away with it even though it was illegal. He says the reason he's here is because he was caught pissing in a parking lot next to an apartment house in broad daylight and a white woman looked out a first-floor window a few feet away and saw him and claimed he was showing her his dick. He likes to say that a black woman would never have done that. But he was homeless to start with, he says, sleeping in the parks and behind Dumpsters and getting constantly rousted by cops and square-badge security personnel so for him becoming a sexual offender and landing under the Causeway with official permission was in a way a move up. He's a juicer who supports his habit by canning recyclables and with as much of his Social Security check as his sister will give him after she takes her cut for acting as a mail drop.

Otis the Rabbit likes the Kid and the Kid likes him and unlike most of the other residents they do favors for each other. Now and then when they have nothing better to do Otis shows the Kid a few moves and has promised to show him his patented secret version of the rabbit punch someday. He says he taught a legal version to the welterweight champ Kid Gavilan that Gavilan made famous as the bolo punch. You deliver it with your left hand after a hopping side step to the left but need to set it up with a wide-swinging right which opens you up in front and makes it a risky punch. Otis thinks the Kid has possibilities as a bantamweight except that at twenty-two he's almost too old to start now and is probably not allowed to train or fight in public anyhow especially wearing an electronic ankle bracelet.

The Kid stands up and ignoring Larry Somerset stretches his arms, rolls his neck, and touches his toes once. Larry stands too, still making that toothy smile. The Kid flips his cigarette butt in a bright arc into the Bay. He's trying to quit smoking by cutting out one cigarette a day every week and is down to thirteen a day now. Next week he'll be down to twelve a day. In twelve weeks one a day. Then zero. The Kid is nothing if not self-disciplined. Actually he's more patient than self-disciplined.

Say, Kid, I'm wondering if you could give me a little advice, me being a newcomer here. So to speak.

What kind of advice?

Well . . . I need a place to sleep. You know, shelter from the storm, as the song says.

Can't help you, man. Everybody here's on his own. So to speak.

I can pay you, if that's the problem. Really, I need help. I just need a place for tonight. Until I can set up my own place. You know, get my own tent set up. I had to sleep outside on the ground in Centennial Park last night. No fun. I'll go downtown tomorrow. Pick up a tent and whatever I need for cooking and so on at a Target or something. I only just got here and wasn't aware that it was so . . . open. I didn't expect to be met with such hostility. I mean, they told me at the park that there were cots and so forth. Like it was a kind of unofficial shelter for people. People like us.

Yeah, well, you were told wrong.

Evidently.

I don't think I'm like you anyhow. Nobody's like anybody else down here.

What would you charge for letting me sleep in your tent? Just this one night. I have cash. I have my own sleeping bag in my duffel there.

Dude, forget about it. I don't need your money. I only got room for me and Iggy anyhow.

Shadowy figures have slowly gathered around Plato the Greek's generator silently waiting their turn to charge their anklets and cell phones. There are small driftwood fires burning here and there in barrels and fire pits lined with cinder blocks and the occasional blue-flamed butane camp stove like the Kid's. The smells of burning charcoal and woodsmoke and food cooking—burgers and beans and franks and coffee—mingle with the salt-smell off the Bay.

It is hard to know if there are twenty men living under the Causeway or fifty or even a hundred. What little conversation that takes place among them is low and mumbled and is scattered into the night by the steady thumping of the traffic overhead and the offshore breeze. Every now and then the beam of a flashlight snaps on as someone makes his way down to the water and stands there and pees into the Bay or just stares out at the lights of the city. Farther down a man fishes for his supper with a bamboo pole. Other figures stand in pairs in the shadows smoking and swapping pulls from a bottle. Where the off-ramp descends to the mainland the concrete isle underneath is closed off on both sides and beneath the sloped ceiling is a wide dark cavern. Deep inside the cavern a Coleman lamp flares up illuminating a half-dozen low shanties made of salvaged lumber. The shanties belong to the old-timers, men who have been in residence here the longest like Otis the Rabbit who is finishing his fifth year under the Causeway. The shanties look almost permanent and in the white glow of the lamp the four men·playing dominoes are seated on overturned buckets around a spindly table made from a cast-off scrap of Masonite.

C'mon, Kid, just this one night, till I get my own set-up. It's probably a little dangerous for me to be sleeping out in the open, right? I mean, some of these guys are a little weird, I think, and some of them are on drugs. And what about rats? I've seen a couple of rats already. This is not what I expected or I'd have come a little better prepared.

How long you been down here?

Oh, just a couple hours. My wife dropped me off at the Park yesterday and I walked over from there.

Your wife.

Yes.

Larry. Larry Somerset. Are you the Lawrence Somerset I'm thinking of? The asshole state senator who got bagged last spring at the airport hotel with a coupla little girls?

You don't have to put it quite that way. There weren't any little girls. It was a set-up. A sting.

Yeah, sure. That's what everybody says. I read about you in the papers. Came to the door of a hotel room naked with all kinds of sex toys. Not very smart for a state senator.

It wasn't quite like that. It was a sting. Entrapment.

It always is. But I don't have to ask what brings you here. Do I?

I might say the same for you.

You might. But don't.

The Kid needs advice from an elder. He throws a wave in the direction of the Rabbit.

The Rabbit saunters over to the Kid's tent. Seventy-five or eighty-five, it doesn't matter, he walks like a man half his age with more grace than sprightliness although he watches where he puts his feet as if his eyesight is bad. Which it is. He just can't afford eyeglasses, he says. Or false teeth. The Kid thinks he wants people to believe he's older than he really is so he'll get more respect from the younger men down here. He'd rather be seen as a very old toothless and nearly blind ex-boxer than just another pathetic homeless old drunk.

He keeps silent while the Kid explains the newcomer's situation. The Rabbit doesn't particularly cotton to the man who seems to have an attitude as if he thinks he doesn't belong down here and they do. And he doesn't trust the cat's interest in the Kid. But maybe there'll be something in it for the Kid since the guy obviously has money in his pocket and if so then there will likely be something in it for the Rabbit too. The Kid can be a generous little bugger sometimes.

So what d'you think? Should I give Mr. Somerset here Iggy's bed for the night?

You running a fuckin' flophouse for Level Threes?

No way.

How do you know I'm a Level Three?

You wouldn't be down here if you wasn't, amigo. Charge him what he'd hafta pay a hotel on the Barriers, Kid. Coupla hundred bucks a night.

Whaddaya say, Mr. Somerset? Two hundred bucks for the night in the comfort and safety of my bayside condo? Good views of the water. Breakfast not included however. Payable in advance. Cash only. We don't take credit cards.

What about the lizard?

What about him?

Does he sleep in the tent too?

You can have Iggy's bed. He's fine sleeping outside if it don't rain. It's still summer. If it rains though I'll hafta bring him in. Iguanas don't like rain.

The man gives it a moment's thought, then agrees and turns away from the Rabbit and the Kid. He removes two one-hundred-dollar bills from his money belt. The Kid and the Rabbit watch and talk on as if the man can't hear them. The Kid tells the Rabbit he'll take care of him in the morning. He thinks maybe twenty bucks ought to be enough of a thanks. More than twenty is a retainer for future services, less is a cheapjack insult. When you're in the Kid's position sharing is carefully calculated. His golden rule is do no more for others than you expect you'll need them to do for you. Even with friends. Although the Kid doesn't really believe he has any friends. People he likes, yes. The Rabbit for instance. But no friends.

Just gimme a holler the guy gives you any trouble.

I don't think he's into guys. Paco thinks he's a baby-banger, I'm betting he's into little girls. Tweeners.

You sure he ain't into iguanas?

CHAPTER FIVE

I T'S AN HOUR BEFORE DAWN. THE TIDE HAS turned and the sulfur stink of the mudflat beyond the Causeway and the nearby mangrove marshes laces the cool night air. In the east where the sea meets the sky a gray velvet blanket of clouds leaches darkness from the night and dims the stars overhead one by one. It's still too early for the traffic to commence its daily rumble over the Causeway. There are the steady slaps of low waves against the edge of the concrete peninsula below the Causeway and the sporadic cries of solitary seagulls cruising low over the Bay. There are the occasional coughs of sleepers in their huts and the low drawn-out groan of a man curled in a thin blanket sheltered from the salty dew by a plastic tarp. There are the snores of the deepest sleepers like the Kid's new and decidedly temporary tent-mate whose raucous adenoidal snoring has kept the Kid awake most of the night.

The encampment is otherwise silent and still and lies in darkness invisible to the world. The fires have all burned to cold ash. Fully clothed the Kid lies awake in his sleeping bag and for a few seconds he imagines the dream of the man snoring in the sleeping bag next to his and shudders and stops himself cold. Children have come onto his radar and entered his no-go zone. Little pink-skinned girls barely older than toddlers. How do you even *talk* to kids that young? he wonders. He's never been able to figure out what to say to children anyhow. Or at least children under the age of twelve or thirteen. They always make him self-conscious and insecure. Especially girls.

Little girls. Just thinking about them—never mind talking to them—makes him self-conscious and insecure. And oddly scared. With little boys he can at least pretend they're as old as he is himself no matter how young they are in reality and he can talk to them the same as he would a grown man. Boys like it when you talk to them as if they were grown men—at least he always did when he was a kid—because they pretend that's what they are anyhow, grown-up men, and they do it for their entire lives. Even old men playing golf or pinochle or watching TV in their retirement homes or sitting half-asleep in a Jacuzzi tub are only pretending to be adult men. But little girls are more complicated and mysterious than little boys. At least to the Kid they are. They don't want you to talk to them like they're grown-up women. Maybe it's because grown-up women aren't like men. Maybe women really are adults and not little kids in disguise.

But what about the women who when they were little girls got hurt somehow? Hurt so bad they got stuck there scared of having to grow up and as a result they never grow up and like men have to fake being an adult. The Kid is pretty sure from what she's told him about her childhood and what she left out his mother is that type of woman. A fake woman. Same as he's a fake man. It may be the only thing he has in common with his mother. He never had to deal with being beaten black and blue by his father the way she did. And he was never sexually abused or raped by anyone male or female the way his mother has hinted happened to her when she was a little girl. And he was never abandoned by his mother to the state foster-care system like her mother did to her and shuttled from one temporary family to another.

The way he sees it his mother was always there for him. That's her phrase, that she was always there for him, and it means two things to him: that he was a burden to her and that he never took full advantage of that fact. He never accepted her love and loyalty. The phrase makes him feel ashamed twice over. She's a better person overall than he. She has a good excuse for refusing to grow up and he doesn't. Her being a fake woman makes sense; his being a fake man doesn't.

He thinks all this has something to do with his no-go zone reaction to Larry Somerset. He wonders why he let the Rabbit talk him into taking the man's money and letting him sleep in his tent. It isn't like he needs the money especially. He has a job and almost no expenses. And it's not like he's fond of playing the Good Samaritan. He knows who the guy Larry Somerset is or rather was and what he got busted for and while the Kid's in no position to judge Larry Somerset or anyone else living beneath the Causeway he still has a fearful attitude toward the guy and it's not just because Larry Somerset is a cheese ball and was once a big-time state senator with all the power and prestige and money of that office and might still have some of it left over.

The Kid has glimpsed kiddie porn by accident lots of times back in the day cruising the Internet looking for company late at night but he always quickly clicked off—scared but not sure why. Nothing he's seen on the Internet has scared him like that and he's seen a lot. And it isn't fear of being caught and punished for doing something illegal or weird or breaking a taboo like incest or sex with animals. That's a whole different kind of fear than what scares him about Larry Somerset.

It's what he felt in the not-too-distant past spending his nights maxing out his mother's credit card and then his own debit card on porn sites and role-playing and swapping endless sex-talks with strangers in chat rooms when he'd sometimes click his way unintentionally into a website or a chat room where the hinted-at subject was sex with children. Which is immoral. Maybe worse—if there is something worse. Well, baby-banging is worse.

It wasn't that he was afraid of getting caught unless by his mother and she didn't bother for years to check on where he went in real life—never mind where he went on his computer. He might not have been raised by wolves exactly but he was a feral child. He was pretty sure that back when he was still living at his mother's house none of his digital travel was illegal or expressly prohibited as long as he did it on his own time which since he got sent back from Fort Drum became almost all the time.

Fear of being caught and punished for doing something most people disapprove of and some people prohibit or is illegal is only what goes with playing a high-stakes game of chance. If you win you feel lucky and if you lose you feel unlucky and you just take your punishment like a man. Either way you don't feel ashamed or guilty. It's almost never colored by shame or guilt like it would if it was immoral.

The Kid hears a car overhead or maybe it's a truck because it's moving too slowly to be a commuter's car and while he waits for it to thump off the bridge onto the highway to the Barriers he hears a second vehicle also moving slowly but on the opposite side coming from the Barriers toward the mainland and then he hears both vehicles crunch to a stop somewhere up there on the Causeway. For a long moment, silence. Until several more cars or vans—he can't be sure which except he knows they're not trucks or buses—arrive from both directions and stop overhead. More silence. The Kid sits up and listens. Nothing. The man lying next to him turns fitfully in his sleep, rolls onto his left side facing away from the Kid and yanks the top of his sleeping bag over his head against the chill and goes back to dreaming whatever a guy like that dreams. The Kid doesn't want to know.

Iggy's chain clanks and the Kid knows that the iguana is awake and alert. The chain is locked onto a cinder block and Iggy can drag the block a fair distance but not easily and is lazy enough not to bother unless someone accidentally drops trash that he thinks is food just out of his reach. It's one of the reasons the Kid keeps his campsite clean and gets pissed off at anyone who tosses his garbage and wrappers from McDonald's or an empty pizza box anywhere close to his tent.

The Kid's heart rate has picked up. He's spooked but doesn't know why. He's almost never spooked down here. The other residents might be weird and even squalid because of the difficult living conditions and some of them are drunks like the Rabbit or high on drugs and a few of them are potential if not actual thieves but so far none of them has been violent. At least not against him. It's violence from outsiders that you worry about. Besides, all of the residents except for the Rabbit are afraid of Iggy the best guard dog a man can have and even the Rabbit is cautious around Iggy. Not that the iguana would ever actually attack a human other than to defend himself and probably not even then but nobody except the Kid knows that for sure. The only person in danger of being attacked by a male iguana is another male iguana. And that's in breeding season when there's a female iguana in the neighborhood.

He reaches forward and partially unzips the front tent flap and looks out. The predawn light in the east hasn't reached the camp yet and it's like being in a cave out there. He grabs his headlamp and switches on its narrow beam. The light is dim. Nearly out. Batteries need replacing. Always happens when you need it. The Kid drops the pale beam of light onto Iggy, who has run his chain out to the end. The iguana's sawtooth crest is rigid and on high alert. He follows Iggy's stare and casts his headlamp's useless fading yellow light in the direction of the off-ramp but it falls short. A narrow bare-dirt path starts at its base and switchbacks up the steep incline from the encampment to the guardrail and highway. It's the only entrance and exit. Unless you arrive or leave by boat or jump into the Bay and swim from the mainland against the tidal current—where to keep from drowning you'd have to be an Olympic-level swimmer— there's no other way in or out.

Maybe Iggy hears one of the residents sneaking home after curfew and because of his electronic anklet already caught without knowing it and scheduled for trouble or maybe jail time. Why bother to sneak in when you know they've already nailed you? Why not just stroll home openly?

Old habits, the Kid guesses.

He snaps off the useless light and glances back toward the path one last time and against a gray swatch of the eastern sky spots the moving silhouette of a man. The man carries what looks like a baseball bat or possibly a rifle. A weapon anyhow. He's wearing some kind of helmet with a visor. Behind him comes a second man who also wears a helmet and carries a club or a gun. They're big guys and they're walking carefully in the darkness as if they aren't familiar with the pathway down and don't have any flashlights or don't want to reveal their presence by using them. The Kid remembers training in the dark at Fort Drum wearing helmets fitted out with night vision and how useless they were for walking on rough unfamiliar ground and wonders if these two are using night vision.

Behind the first two come a whole bunch more big guys wearing helmets and carrying weapons. It's some kind of raid or a military-style takedown by a platoon of cops or soldiers or a SWAT team. But why the hell would they be making a raid down here? Nobody down here deals drugs in any quantity larger than the occasional nickel bag or a few tabs of Ecstasy. No illegal aliens. No terrorists plotting the overthrow of the state. There's nobody here but people like the Kid and the Rabbit and Larry Somerset and Paco and the Greek. Practically everyone in Calusa has known for years what kind of people live here and why and has never given a damn as long as they stay put. The newspapers write about it like it's a leper colony. Even the TV news has covered it a few times. The only authorities who ever visit the camp are plainclothes cops and parole officers or caseworkers looking for their clients gone missing or the occasional bored state trooper dropping by to waste time looking for drugs or following up on a possible lead to some real criminal he's investigating elsewhere. And they don't come at night. They come during daylight hours as if even though the doctors say the disease the residents carry isn't contagious people think it is—cops included. They're afraid they'll catch it if they come at night. The Kid watches the strangers in helmets gather together in a clot at the bottom of the steep incline. There are twenty to twenty-five of them. Maybe more. And here come five or six more guys but without helmets or uniforms—civilians in regular sports clothes.

As if at a signal he somehow missed the entire SWAT team or cops or soldiers or whatever charge full speed into the encampment. Their boots slap heavily against the concrete and their clubs are raised—the Kid sees now they're uniformed cops carrying batons not guns—ready to bust somebody's bones while the half-dozen civilians stand back and watch from the sidelines like they're embedded reporters. When the raiders reach the tents and shanties they break into teams of two and three and go to work kicking over the flimsy huts and yanking down the tarps and as the residents stumble befuddled and terrified out from under the wreckage of their collapsed shelters the cops bellow at them—*Get the fuck outa here! Move move move! Get your shit, get the fuck out outa here!*—and call them names—*Motherfucking pervs! Faggots! Kid-fuckers!* The frightened residents cover their heads with their arms and try vainly to dodge the riot sticks but it's no good and the cops club their shoulders and backs and skulls and whack them across the face. Blood spurts from noses and mouths and ears. People howl in pain.

The Kid sees a pair of cops lurching toward his tent. He grabs his backpack and unzips the rear flap of the tent from inside and ducks out and escapes into the darkness just beyond when he flashes on Iggy and turns back. The cops have already grabbed onto the front end of his tent and are yanking it down when one of them sees Iggy on his chain stalking steadily toward him fearless and on the attack with his mouth open and his long forked tongue flicking the air.

Holy shit! What the fuck's that? the first cop says.

The second cop pauses in the destruction of the Kid's tent. He takes a look at the iguana and his eyes widen. *It's a goddam lizard! Shoot it! Shoot the fucking thing!*

We got orders to keep our guns holstered.

Unless physically threatened, man!

While the cops argue the Kid's roommate wearing only his baggy boxer shorts and T-shirt and black socks like an old-time European porn actor escapes from under the collapsed tent through the open flap at the back the same way the Kid got out. He scrambles on his hands and knees into the relative safety of darkness and comes up on the Kid.

Good God, what's happening? What are they doing?

The first cop has his revolver out and aims it down at Iggy who keeps on coming toward the second cop.

I call that threatening. That's physically threatening, man! Shoot the goddam thing! Shoot it!

Too much fucking paperwork. It's on a chain anyhow.

The Kid hears the sickening crack of a club against bone and he glances in that direction and sees the Rabbit go down, then slowly get back up and stagger off, dragging his right leg as if the thigh bone is fractured. Most of the rest flee into the darkness running and stumbling past the embedded reporters or whatever they are gathered at the bottom of the incline. Those who can do it scramble up the pathway to the Causeway and hop over the guardrail and run down the highway. The few residents who refuse to run or like the Rabbit are unable to run are herded together and shoved into a group off to the side close to the civilians where they're guarded by a pair of cops with flashlights and guns while the Kid and Larry Somerset watch unseen from the edge of darkness.

I said shoot it! For Christ's sake, he's gonna bite me!

The Kid suddenly stands, *Don't shoot!* he cries. *He's friendly! He won't hurt you!*

The cop swings his helmeted head around and peers through

night-vision glasses at the Kid and Larry Somerset. He looks like a giant bug standing on its hind legs. He brings his gun up and aims it at the Kid.

You got ten seconds to get the fuck outa here. You and the other guy. Otherwise you're busted back to prison.

For what? We haven't done nothing!

Obstructing a police officer. Now get the fuck outa here you disgusting little creep before I change my mind and bust both of you and your fucking lizard for resisting arrest.

The Kid turns and runs. He's got no alternative. Larry tries to follow him but he doesn't know the camp in the dark the way the Kid does and after a few steps he stumbles and falls. The Kid hears his face smack against the concrete—*Kid, help me! I'm hurt! I'm bleeding!*—but keeps on running anyhow. The hell with him. It's every man for himself. As he races past the civilians at the bottom of the pathway he sees that they actually are reporters—they're holding skinny notebooks and are writing furiously in them and a couple of them are talking into digital recorders. They have strange little smirks on their faces like they're customers at a sex show who don't want you to know it's turning them on.

The Kid keeps running. He sees bright red and yellow and white lights flashing up on the Causeway and hears sirens wailing as ambulances and paddy wagons and more cruisers arrive. TV crews too. He keeps running. He makes it up the path to the guardrail, jumps over the rail onto the Causeway, then races panting down the ramp onto the highway that leads to the Barriers. He's still running. His heart is pounding. His lungs feel like they're on fire. Turning back he sees a pair of patrol boats cutting full speed across the Bay toward the encampment. Coming to pick up the guys who couldn't make it up to the ambulances and paddy wagons parked on the Causeway—probably including the Rabbit, oh Jesus, the poor fucking Rabbit who looked like his leg got broken and Larry Somerset who looked too scared and bloody to get up and run after he fell. The hell with them. Nothing he could do for them anyhow. He slows to a jog. Then he walks.

The Kid wishes he had taken his bike but there was no way that cop would have let him. He's lucky he thought to grab his backpack. He's lucky he slept with his clothes on because he was creeped out by Larry Somerset even though he's not gay. He's worried about Iggy but figures once he and Larry took off there was no reason for the cop to shoot Iggy anymore. If they do anything they'll turn him over to the SPCA or Animal Rescue and he'll end up in Reptile Village. As soon as the Kid has a new home set up he'll check in with the SPCA and Animal Rescue people and try to retrieve him. If he's not with the SPCA or Animal Rescue he'll be at Reptile Village, which is probably where he ought to be anyhow. Living with other reptiles instead of with humans.

The Kid is rationalizing, he knows. He is going to miss Iggy. But the iguana was getting harder and harder to feed and care for properly especially down under the Causeway and he knows that Iggy will be better off living a more natural life with his own kind than chained to a cinder block down where there isn't much sunlight and there are no other snakes or lizards for company. Just rats and homeless sex offenders. And no trees to climb.

The sun has broken the horizon and the rumpled silver gray clouds overhead are pushed halfway back by the emerging blue sky. The Bay on either side glistens in the clean new light. Palm trees clatter in the offshore breeze. Traffic has started to build as commuters from the mainland head for work on the islands and the residents of the islands start the daily drive from their homes to their jobs on the mainland. The Kid still has a couple hours to kill before he has to show up for work at the Mirador. The eastbound cars flash past him and to get safely out of their way he steps over the guardrail onto the grass and walks there.

Things could be worse, he thinks. He escaped. And no one's chasing him. He could be locked in a paddy wagon like Larry Somerset probably is: on his way to court and hauled back to jail for breaking parole by resisting arrest or refusing to disperse or whatever phony charge they come up with. He could be injured or worse like the Rabbit and a couple others he saw getting clubbed by the cops. But he's not, he's a free man. More or less. And it's morning in Calusa.

CHAPTER SIX

I T TAKES THE KID OVER AN HOUR TO WALK from the Causeway over to the Barriers and south onto Clifton Road and then the half-mile residential curl alongside the Bayshore Golf Club. From the sidewalk at Clifton and West Twenty-third he watches with a willed curiosity the retirees out for their first eighteen holes. His legs are still wobbly weak and his lungs burn from the long run to safety and ten years of smoking cigarettes, a habit he caught back when he was twelve and hoped that dangling a ciggie from his lips might make him seem older because people kept mistaking him for nine or ten due to his being short and skinny and big-eared. He was eager to be noticed back then but not for that.

Now he's eager not to be noticed for anything.

He tries distracting himself with the sight of elderly pink people in pastel shorts and shirts whacking with sticks at little white balls, the kind of people he's never known personally or even spoken to except to say, *May I clear, sir?* at the restaurant, people whose thoughts he cannot imagine, whose past, present, and future lives are incomprehensible to him. As if they were members of a different species. He wants to understand what it must feel like to be them. To wake in the morning and shower and shave and read the *Wall Street Journal* or whatever at breakfast—freshly squeezed orange juice and bacon and eggs cooked just the way you like them by a Jamaican lady who is employed by you—and then you take your bag of golf clubs from the trunk of your S-Class Benz and walk from your walled-in rancho de luxe across Clifton Road to the Bayshore Golf Club where you meet two or three fellow retirees from New York or Philadelphia and stroll out to the first tee chatting knowledgeably about yesterday's Dow Jones average and the gross national product.

Whatever they are.

Who are *those fucking people?* the Kid wonders and beneath his wondering hopes that the question will keep him from thinking about what he just went through back at the encampment beneath the Causeway. He can keep the shock of the police and press raid pretty well out of his mind almost as if it never happened but it's harder for him to ignore the fact that now he's scared of being picked up by the cops and charged with resisting arrest or unlawful flight or any of the other dozen charges they could easily stick on him if they wanted to because no one will believe that he's innocent of anything. Even of just being alive. He's guilty of that too. Being alive. Besides that he's lost his squat, his safe haven, his home. And he's worried about Otis the Rabbit and Iggy and feels sorry and a little ashamed that he abandoned Larry Somerset in spite of finding the guy creepy. Guilty and ashamed. Like he did something immoral by running for his life.

CHAPTER SEVEN

H E'S SITTING ALONE AT A CAFÉ TABLE outside a small bookstore on the fifteen-block-long section of Rampart Road that's given over to pedestrians—a chic sprawl of sidewalk cafés, restaurants, bars, brasseries, and upscale shops for people who want to be seen by each other alongside souvenir stores for short-term sunburnt tourists and sunglass and sneaker stores for young people who like to think of themselves as raging against the machine. A fine mingling spot for people-watching if you're into that but the Kid is here because it's still early in the day and there aren't many customers and no one wants his table so he's free to idle away a few hours over a cup of coffee and not get nudged off it by the waiter. It's a bookstore café with a newsstand and a sprinkling of people are sitting nearby reading newspapers just as he is although he's not reading his newspaper exactly. He's cashed one of Larry Somerset's hundred-dollar bills at the bank on the corner of Clifton and Rampart and has bought a city map at the newsstand and a cup of coffee and an apricot muffin at the café. He's opened the paper to the real estate section and is working his way down the listings for studio apartment rentals.

Parc Bay Plaza Apartments
2341 North Bayshore Drive

$750–$1378. Live up to ONE MONTH FREE in selected apartments when move-in by the end of September. Prices listed reflect the one month free. Enjoy breathtaking views of Calusa Bay and downtown Calusa. Our lovely studio and 1- and 2-bedroom apartments for rent are beautifully appointed with spacious living areas. Many of our homes have large patios and balconies. Our controlled access community includes a swimming pool and a 24-hour fitness center. Catch a flick in our big screen surround sound movie room or play pool, table tennis and air hockey in our game room. Call today to schedule a personal tour: 866-510-1424.

A tall very thin guy in his forties with long lemon yellow hair carrying a purple velvet clutch purse and wearing nothing but a gold lamé Speedo, flip-flops, and an all-body leathery tan swings past and catches the Kid's eye. He's anorectic thin with a lace mesh of wrinkles for a face and is weighed down with gold rings dangling from his ears, nostrils, nipples, and navel. He flashes a toothy smile and waves at the Kid, flips his hair and cruises in a half-circle up to the Kid's table and stops.

Hello, Kid. A little early to be working the street, isn't it?

The Kid gives him a cold stare and looks down at his map. It's a very detailed map of the entire city with the Calusa Isles segment scaled at five hundred yards to the inch.

Oh, I forgot, you're holding down a regular job now. Like a real quote family man unquote.

Fuck off, Molly.

Molly spins in a feigned huff and walks away. The Kid retrieves his cell phone from his backpack and punches in a number.

Parc Bay Realty. How may I help you?

He says he's calling about a furnished studio with kitchenette and bath. Always he asks first for the price and then the square footage. It's the drill—the same old Q's, the same old A's. Regarding price he's looking strictly at the low end. Location is irrelevant as long as it's within biking distance of his job but he knows it's reassuring to the rental agent so he politely inquires into the related questions of neighborhood safety and building security. While the woman at the other end goes on about how it's perfectly safe even after dark and the building has excellent twenty-four-hour security he dots the street address on the map with his ballpoint and draws a circle with a diameter of two inches—one thousand yards, three thousand feet—around it.

There are a half-dozen kindergartens, day care centers, public and private schools, and three or four public playgrounds inside the circle. There are kids' ballet studios, martial arts studios, art classes, music classes, and SAT preparation classes located inside the circle. Inside the circle everywhere you look the children are already gathering.

He makes an appointment anyhow to come by and check out the room as soon as he gets off work at the Mirador and she says fine. He takes a box of Marlboro Gold from his backpack, knocks a cigarette loose, and lights it. He asks about pets and she says no dogs or cats.

He says, *Oh,* followed by a longish pause. *How about a pet iguana?*

She knows what an iguana is. She asks how big is it.

Not big, he lies. *It sleeps all day and can live in a box under the bed. It doesn't make any noise and won't damage anything.*

She says she'll have to see it first and then decide.

He's okay with that. He says he was thinking of giving him away anyhow. *To a friend,* he lies again.

Then she asks his name. As usual he wants to tell her Kid. But no way he can get away with it. End of interview. He knows what she'll do with the information as soon as he gets off the phone. He says his real name anyhow. He has to.

They say good-bye and he clicks off. He imagines her going straight to the Internet to run his name. He's been through all this before—how many times? Fifty? A hundred? It's a total waste of time, energy, and hope and he knows he won't bother to show up at the appointed time and place. Even so he'll make a call to a second agent. And a third. And probably a fourth. Before finally once again he'll give up the search for a home.

It's an hour before the Kid has to be a busboy again and pedestrian traffic has thickened somewhat with tourists, brunchers, and dog walkers strolling past the café and grabbing seats nearby in increasing numbers until all the tables are taken and the Kid has noticed a clutch of people gathered by the headwaiter's stand staring pointedly in his direction. He folds up his map and is about to leave the café and does not see the two bottle-blond girls in bikinis Rollerblading his way until they circle his table eyeing him like a pair of hawks riding a rising thermal high above a distracted mouse. As their shadows cross him he looks up and instinctively ducks. He wishes he had a hole to dive into. One bikini is pink polka-dotted, the other is tiger striped. Both girls wear carefully tousled honey-colored manes, black fingernail polish, lovingly applied makeup, and the usual navel rings. Polka-dot snaps one of his ears with her thumb and forefinger and keeps circling. Rolling along behind her Tiger-stripe does the same to his other ear.

Ow-w! Cut that shit out, man!

They flash their gleaming teeth and make a second loop. They are both genetic wonders, their smooth tight bodies evenly toasted a golden brown, flesh firm as an unripe Bosc pear, symmetrical faces with pertly sculpted noses and chins. They're not quite twins, probably not even sisters—Polka's cheekbones are a little higher than Tiger's and she's maybe two inches taller—but have been manufactured from the same prototype by a bored God for no better reason than to satisfy His private eyes.

But for the Kid as the girls skate arabesques around his table everything mingles and blurs. Gold bracelets and earrings glint in the late-morning sun. Flocks of screeching green parrots watch like an aroused audience from the palms and tamarind trees that crowd the center of the mall.

The Kid wants the girls to go away, please go away, and he wants them to stay and stay, please stay. He glances at each girl's plum-shaped breasts as she passes, her taut belly, the sweet little pouch between her legs and he looks quickly off and up to her mischievously smiling face and as she swirls past and disappears in back of him he switches to the other girl's face and down to breasts, belly, and pouch and then off her body at once *bang* and when she disappears behind him his gaze swings back to the face of the first girl again. He mustn't linger on her body anywhere *he mustn't* and tries fixing on her face but can't keep himself located there for more than a second. His head nods up and down like a stringed puppet's saying yes yes yes and flops side to side from one girl to the other saying no no no until finally they stop circling over him and Polka dives for the chair next to his and plants her elbows on the table and cups her head in her hands and gazes through half-lidded jade green contacts into his blinking eyes. All her moves very exact, very studied, very likely practiced in front of a mirror. Tiger comes to a stop too but stands next to him and watches as if holding a tray waiting her turn at a cafeteria counter. He feels his throat start to close and his blood thickens all through his body and he swallows hard but then suddenly realizes that seen up close like this the girls are not what they seem, they're not grown women, eighteen- or twenty-year-old women. They're girls. Teenage girls. A glistening pearl of sweat slips from Polka's throat across her chest and slides between her breasts. Thirteen- or at best fourteen-year-old girls.

You guys . . . you guys oughta get the fuck outa here.

Aw, c'mon, little dude, we're only trying to turn you on.

Yeah? Well, I ain't turned on so forget about it, man. I got places to go, things to do.

You look so sad and cute sitting here all by yourself we figured you wanted company. We're like cheerleaders. You know, like for cheering people up. Doncha wanna get cheered up?

The Kid sits back in his chair, folds his arms over his chest, and crosses one leg over the other trying to look gruff and casual at the same time. A grown man. Ex-military.

Tiger reaches down, pats his ankle through his jeans, and tugs his cuff back a few inches. *What's that thing?*

Whaddaya mean? Nothin'.

No, what is it? It's cool-looking.

Polka leans across the table for a look-see and the Kid quickly yanks his cuff back to his sneaker but can't help peering down Polka's bikini top. He can see between her breasts all the way to her dangling navel ring. Her glistening tanned skin is wet with sweat down there. And guaranteed warm to the touch.

Polka says, *Show me. What is it?*

Tiger says, *Is it some kind of camera? Or a secret recorder? Are you a spy, little dude? You must be a secret spy working for the government, like in the CIA.*

It's nothin'.

I bet you're spying on people. I can tell. Okay? You're like sitting here pretending to read the paper and stuff only you're really like a private detective checking on somebody's wife meeting her boyfriend for sex.

Polka says, *Cool!* and yanks his cuff halfway up his calf. The Kid uncrosses his legs and plants both feet on the pavement under the table and shakes his cuff down.

No! It's only . . . it's like a kind of monitor. I got a heart condition and it monitors my heartbeat.

Awesome! Let's see it work then. Let's check your heartbeat. See if we can get it racing. See if we can give you a heart attack. That'd be really cool. Get you excited enough to have a heart attack. What's your name?

Kid.

Awesome! I'm Stephanie and she's Latisha. You want to play with us, Kid?

What do you mean, play with you?

Whatever you like. You got any money?

No.

Okay. You got a ATM card? I see you got a map there. We can show you some fun places if you want. You got a car? Where's your hotel?

I'm not a tourist. I live here.

Where's your place? We can go to your place if you want.

Why aren't you two in school where you should be?

We graduated!

Yeah, sure. Babes on blades.

Slowly the Kid pushes back his chair and stands. He looks down and sees with relief that his pants are loose enough that his woodie doesn't show. He takes a last lingering look at the two and almost choking says *I'm outa here.* Stuffs his map, newspaper, cigarettes, and cell phone into his backpack. Turns and walks away.

The girls watch him go, shrug and giggle and skate off in the opposite direction. Halfway down the block the Kid glances back as they roll past Victoria's Secret. He sees them lifted quickly off the pavement by warm updrafts and over the heads of the pedestrians into the air. They soar above the trees and the flocks of squawking green parrots into the blue sky where they make slow interlocked circles and renew their search for unwary prey below. On the corner of Mantle and Rampart Road the man called Molly who carries a clutch bag and wears only a gold lamé Speedo and flip-flops gazes up at them mildly amused by their audacity and deftly rolls a joint without having to look at his hands. He looks down the block at the Kid and flashes him a wink and a pinkie-wave.

CHAPTER EIGHT

THE KID LIKES HIS JOB AT THE MIRADOR. He's a noon-to-ten-at-night busboy in a beachfront hotel restaurant the size of a major airport terminal which is pleasant enough—no previous experience required, no hierarchy among the busboys, no Babes on Blades—but beyond all that the job appeals to his innate affection for order and cleanliness. He gets to clear away dirty dishes, silverware, glassware, and crumpled napkins and strip the tablecloths off the tables. He gets to cart everything back to the kitchen and separate out the plates, cups, and saucers from the silverware and glassware and rack them in separate dishwashers and drop the used tablecloths into one basket and the stained napkins into another. Then he gets to go back to the dining room and shake out a fresh clean tablecloth and lay down four or six or eight shiny new place settings for the next batch of diners. He likes all this. He enjoys squaring the circle of the plate with the knives, spoons, and forks and folding the napkins into little cloth pyramids and placing them just so in the exact center of the plate. He takes pleasure in delivering the basket of bread and plate of little shell-shaped butter pats and filling the glasses with ice water and then disappearing until the meal is finished. And he likes wearing the starched white jacket with the mandarin collar. It makes him feel like he's a scientist.

Most of all he likes the anonymity of a busboy. No one checks him out. No one asks his name. No one remembers him. It's almost like being invisible. He'd make better money if he were a waiter but then he'd have to interact with the diners, describe the daily specials to them, reassure them about portion size, degree of spiciness, ask and answer dumb questions about hotness, coldness, well done, medium or rare, whether or not it really is kosher, endure the diners' complaints and make small talk and smile all the while. He'd have to say, *My name is Kid and I'll be your server today*. He'd have to come regularly to the table and ask, *How is everything?* He'd have to bring them their food and say, *Bon appétit* or *Enjoy*. Some of the waiters, usually the gay guys, just say, *Enjoy*. That is definitely not the Kid's style. But neither is *Bon appétit*.

Actually the Kid doesn't have a style. He can't be pegged as one kind of person or another except by age, race, and gender. He's a white guy in his early twenties. Otherwise he's almost invisible. Which is the way he likes it. When he was a teenager in high school or working at the light store and later in the army at Fort Drum in upstate New York it bothered him that no one could seem to see him or remember having met him before or simply forgot he was present even when he was trying to draw attention to himself. It puzzled and irritated him and made him even more insecure than when he was alone and every now and then he tried to effect a personal style—he tried gangsta for a few months, then preppie. He tried techno-geek, goth, surfer dude, urban cowboy. Once at Fort Drum he tried sex machine and told the guys in his outfit that he'd auditioned for a porn flick but they needed nine and a half inches and he only had nine. The part about auditioning for a porn flick was a total lie but the part about nine inches was close enough. He had the biggest dick in the outfit but when his fellow soldiers dragged him into the showers and stripped him they just laughed at it and acted like it was wasted on him. Which it was.

Nowadays though he's happy to be invisible. Sometimes when he's clearing a table even though the waiters and waitresses wear black tuxedo-style jackets and the busboys are in white a diner mistakes him for a waiter and asks him to bring another menu or more bread or the check but he just pretends he doesn't speak English and turns his back.

Table seven is a large round VIP table over by a floor-to-ceiling window with a view of the beach and crashing waves and the turquoise ocean beyond. It's usually bused by the pretty little Mexican girl who wants to be promoted to waitress so she does a lot of smiling and leaves the top two buttons of her jacket unbuttoned. But she called in sick today so as soon as the Kid comes into the kitchen ready for work Dario the manager assigns it to him.

Hurry the fuck up and clear seven, they've already ordered dessert.

Dario is Italian from Philly in his late thirties, dainty as a dancer with little hands and tiny wedge-shaped feet but hard-bodied, a man who works out regularly and dresses the same way every day like a prosperous gangster or an actor playing one in a black silk T-shirt, black Armani suit, sockless black Bally loafers, and a large faux-diamond pinkie ring. He has straight black hair in a ponytail and keeps a fresh carnation in his lapel and likes to be seen sniffing it. He reminds the Kid of Al Pacino in *Scarface* only without the scar.

Dude, it's only noon. What is it, a late breakfast? Brunch? We haven't started serving brunch, have we?

Don't fuck with me, Kid. I let 'em in early. They got a golf game or something and needed to eat now.

Must be big cheeses.

Never mind that. Just get out there and clear the fucking table.

There are four large beefy men at table seven, a thick-necked black guy with his back to the Kid facing the window and three white guys with barrel-bellies, all of them in pastel-colored golf clothes. Mob friends of Dario down from Philly, the Kid decides although he's pretty sure Dario isn't a real mobster, only a guy who likes to be regarded as one. He goes all smarmy and overhospitable whenever the real thing shows up at the restaurant. One of the white guys at the table looks Spanish and has a bad dye job on his black pencil-thin mustache and comb-over. The big black guy wears a baseball cap and even from behind looks familiar to the Kid. Usually he avoids looking at the diners' faces when he clears the table but this time as he goes for the black guy's plate and silverware he glances up and recognizes him.

His legs go all watery and his breathing turns shallow and fast. O. J. Simpson is in the house! How weird is that? the Kid says to himself. More than weird, it's a little scary because to his knowledge at least the Kid has never been this close to a real cold-blooded killer before. He somehow hadn't realized O. J. Simpson was a real person and not just a famous killer who existed only on TV since nothing you know only from TV is real. Not even the news. Not even the president. He wonders what O. J. would do if the Kid accidentally knocked over his half-filled glass of red wine and it splashed into his large lap or dropped his plate of half-eaten ketchup-covered fries onto the floor and got ketchup all over O. J.'s spotless pale green slacks and white shoes.

He sets the tray onto the folding stand beside the table and very carefully removes first O. J.'s knife, then the dishes and the rest of the silverware and the empty glasses. When he nervously reaches for O. J.'s wineglass the man places his brown football-size hand over it and shakes his head no and the Kid quickly backs off.

Sorry sorry. Very sorry.

I'll have another glass of the Rhône.

Yessir. I'll tell your waiter.

The man the Kid thinks is Spanish says, *Bring me half a pear.*

O. J. laughs and says, *Fucking half a pear! Why do you want only half a fucking pear? Get a whole one, for chrissakes, and eat half if you only want half a fucking pear.*

I only want half a pear. I wanted a whole fucking pear I'd order a whole fucking pear.

O. J. says to the Kid, *Bring my fastidious friend here half a fucking pear.*

Yessir.

Dario is standing at the headwaiter's desk by the door going over lunch reservations. As the Kid passes with his tray of dishes and silver and glassware from table seven he stops for a second and says, *O. J. wants another glass of wine. Rhône. Want me to bring him his wine?*

I'll take care of it. Fucking guy never buys a decent fucking bottle himself unless somebody else's paying. Like he expects to get comped his whole fucking life.

And there's an asshole over there who wants half a fucking pear.

At that moment the asshole—the Spanish-looking guy with the bad hair—passes behind the Kid on his way to the men's room. The Kid realizes he's been overheard.

Oh yeah and this gentleman wants the other half!

The gentleman nods, smiles, and moves on to the men's room.

Dario places a hand on the Kid's shoulder. *That "gentleman" is the Nicaraguan consul.*

No shit? The guy with O. J.?

No shit.

I thought in Nicaragua everyone was a soccer player or a hooker.

Dario gives the Kid a cold look. Then he turns his attention back to the lunch reservations. In a low voice he says, *You some kinda wiseguy? My wife's from Nicaragua. You know that. Everybody works here knows that.*

Jeez, Dario, I didn't even know you were married. What team'd she play for?

Dario takes a step back and squints at the Kid. Is he serious? Is he putting me on? Is he insulting my wife? Or me? The Kid confuses Dario. He's confused him since the day he walked in and asked for a job that almost always went to a Honduran or a dry-footed Cuban off the boat or a wet-footed Haitian with phony papers. A normal-looking little white American guy in his twenties with a high school diploma, a type that almost never wants to bus dishes except temporarily as a way to become a waiter. He took the Kid's application anyhow and ran the usual background check. It turned out the Kid was a listed sex offender on parole and was wearing an electronic ankle bracelet. Dario got the picture. But the Kid didn't seem mentally retarded and he spoke decent English and a little Spanish so he went ahead and hired him anyhow. He figured because of his record and the risk of being sent back to jail he wasn't likely to cause trouble or steal anything.

He called the Kid in and told him he knew about his past. The Kid said it was all a stupid mistake, he was innocent of everything, he was set up. It looked like he was going to break into tears right there in Dario's office and Dario felt sorry for him which he rarely felt for anyone especially someone he was interviewing for a job. In the past he'd hired ex-cons, recovering alcoholics, and addicts just out of rehab, men and women he knew were illegals with doctored documents and they usually made good dishwashers, pot scrubbers, and busboys at least for a few months or a season until they fell off the wagon or reverted to their old petty criminal habits or got busted by the INS or Homeland Security and deported or locked up. He figured the shadow hanging over the Kid would keep him in line. Which it has.

But that was ten months ago and the Kid is starting to get on Dario's nerves. Not for anything he does as much as for what comes out of his mouth. The Kid is a good worker but he's also a wiseguy. A smart-ass. You never know what he's going to say or not say. He makes Dario nervous as if the Kid doesn't give a damn about his job and is periodically tempting Dario to fire him. This is one of those times, Dario decides. Enough already.

Kid, put your tray in the kitchen and take off your jacket and go home.

What?

You heard me. You're through. Come by the end of the week for what you're owed.

Why are you firing me?

You got a fucking big mouth. You don't show respect.

Dario sniffs his carnation, turns away from the Kid, and walks toward the bar. *I gotta get the wife-killer his fucking cheap glass of bar wine. Don't be here when I get back.*

Okay. I won't.

The Kid slowly hefts the loaded tray to his shoulder and heads for the kitchen. To himself since no one's listening anymore he says, *I don't know where I will be though. I got nowhere left to go.*

CHAPTER NINE

NOWHERE, EXCEPT BACK TO THE CAMP
beneath the Causeway. So he goes there. By the time he
steps over the guardrail and cuts down the sharp slope to
the concrete island below it's late afternoon and the camp is shrouded
in semidarkness. A few of the rousted residents have returned and are
struggling to prop their shanties back up and hanging plastic sheeting over jerry-built frames of PVC tubing and cast-off lumber but
otherwise the place is mostly deserted. They too have nowhere else
to go. They ignore the Kid and he ignores them. Nothing new—
that's how they usually act. Like they're covered with shame and are
ashamed of each other as well. Him included.

The camp looks like a small tornado blasted through—clothing
and papers and blankets lie scattered in no discernible pattern, shacks
and shanties have been turned into piles of rubble, tents have been
pulled down and tossed into rumpled heaps of canvas and torn pieces
of plastic. The Greek's generator lies on its side half in the water and
half out. A strong shove would dump it permanently into the Bay.
The few returning survivors of the raid move slowly and silently in
the gloom as if merely trying to make the best temporary use of the
wreckage they can but with no evident ambition to restore what
they built before the raid when it was practically a village down here,
a settlement of men, grim and minimal and squalid but an extension

of the city nonetheless as if the city had deliberately colonized this dark corner of itself with its outcasts.

A couple of residents are fishing for their supper from the edge of the island. Someone in the cavern beneath the far on-ramp has set a grill on bricks and built a driftwood fire and is boiling water in a pan probably for spaghetti or a one-pot meal from a box. These are the only signs of domestic intent.

From a short distance the Kid spots his bike still chained to the pier where he left it and his tent collapsed in a pile next to it. No sign of Iggy—which he's desperate enough to take as a good sign. This is not the same as optimism. The Kid is definitely not an optimist. Even so he thinks maybe Iggy somehow escaped and is hiding in the shadows or under a pile of wreckage waiting for the Kid to come back for him. It's possible but not very likely that the cops called the SPCA or some kindly animal rescue organization and they unhooked his chain from the cinder block and hauled him off to Reptile Village where he's already found himself a cave to sleep in and a tree to climb and a friendly female iguana to warm his cold reptilian blood.

The Kid knows what he's going to find but just can't face it yet.

No sign of Larry Somerset either and none of Otis the Rabbit Washington which doesn't surprise him. The Rabbit is probably in the hospital and bound for jail as soon as he's discharged while Larry Somerset has his pin-striped lawyer arguing that in no way did his client violate the terms of his parole and Senator Somerset should therefore be released on his own recognizance immediately which will very likely happen although the Kid doubts he'll come back to the encampment after this. He's got options the rest of the men don't have. He could live in a rented trailer out on the Keys or beyond the suburbs someplace close to the Great Panzacola Swamp where no children live. The Kid figures Somerset's lawyers if they can't get him off parole will cut him a deal with the city. He'll probably end up living down on one of the Keys and teaching a class on good governance and homelessness at the Keys branch of Calusa Community College. It might have to be via the Internet though—there's lots of college students under the age of eighteen who have to be kept 2,500 feet from sexual offenders.

For months the Kid knew the raid was in the political opportunism pipeline but he didn't really expect it to happen. Newspaper and TV editorials have been calling incessantly for a "solution" to the "problem" posed by the underground colony of homeless men living beneath the Causeway. State and local tourist boards and hotel and restaurant associations have been lobbying city government to ship the settlers out of the city to someplace where tourists never go—someplace that's isolated and feels far away, like a homegrown version of Tasmania or Devil's Island. Church groups and religious leaders and talk radio commentators and their call-in listeners for months have been demanding permanent punishment of sex offenders and even potential sex offenders by means of chemical castration or better yet life sentences without parole or even better execution to be followed if possible by eternal damnation.

The county commission and mayoral elections are only six weeks off and candidates from all political persuasions have been working to outdo each other in the effort to protect American children and defend the American family from the dark desires and intentions of perverts. First they scream for laws that prohibit anyone convicted as a sexual offender from living within 2,500 feet which is almost half a mile from a school or day care center or playground or wherever children are known to gather together or from living in a home where anyone under the age of eighteen happens to reside. Which means pretty much the entire city and its suburbs are off-limits. Except under the Causeway and one or two other locations in Calusa County like the airport and the Great Panzacola Swamp. Then they turn around and call for an immediate solution to the problem of the growing number of convicted sex offenders living under the Causeway.

The Kid's no psychologist and he hasn't much insight into what makes a sex offender offend but he has more sympathy for the men he's been living with lately than with the people who put them there even though he knows that most of the men living here himself included have done very bad things. The papers have taken to calling them the Bridge People which he thinks makes sense in another way because they are a bridge between what passes for normal human beings and animals. They're like chimpanzees or Neanderthals who eventually would have evolved into normal human beings if it weren't for their DNA having got scrambled somehow making them forget how they're supposed to act when it comes to sex so that what seems natural to them seems unnatural to everyone else even though everyone else has the same DNA except it isn't scrambled the same way theirs is. The Kid wonders if all across America there is some kind of strange invisible radioactive leakage like from high-tension wires or cell phones or road and mall parking lot asphalt that is turning thousands of American men young and old of all races into sex offenders so that instead of being attracted to grown women their own age they're attracted to young girls and little children. He worries that it's an environmentally caused degenerative disease. He's heard about Twinkies having chemicals that can change a normal person into a murderer. Maybe junk food like Big Macs and Whoppers can damage the immune system of certain susceptible men and convert them into sexual offenders. He wonders if his still being attracted to girls like the Babes on Blades earlier today on Rampart Road is a sign that he will someday be attracted to female children. He wonders if when he's middle-aged he'll end up like Larry Somerset and rent a motel room and over the phone arrange for a clucker mother to bring her two little daughters to the room where he'll plan to greet them with porn videos and sex toys and the crackhead mother will turn out to be an undercover cop.

Finally he sees Iggy. Poor Iggy! He walked past him twice and didn't notice him because the iguana had turned the same shade of gray as the concrete and in the shadows was almost invisible. He's dead. Shot in the top of his head where his third eye was located. Shot at close range it looks like. The hole is large—the size of one of Dario's carnations without much blood showing due to his being a reptile and cold-blooded. The eyes on the sides of his head are open but dry and glassy like marbles. With his dewlaps deflated and his dorsal crest and spikes folded back he seems shrunken and old. His feet are hidden beneath him as if he was holding on to his belly when he was shot or maybe he was shot first in the belly and was holding his guts in when the cop finished him off with a shot to the head.

He is still attached to the chain and the chain is hooked to the cinder block but he dragged it about twenty feet away from the tent and the Kid wonders if he did that after he was shot and his final effort in life was either to get away from the cops or to attack them.

Knowing Iggy he was on the attack. Iggy was always braver than the Kid. Iggy would never run from a fight. Not that he'd had many opportunities—in all the years he lived with the Kid Iggy never met another male iguana. And the Kid always protected him from dogs except when he was in basic training at Fort Drum when he made his mother swear not to let him out of his cage except when she cleaned the cage and then to make sure the door to his bedroom was closed tight and the windows down so he couldn't escape into the dangerous outside world. Down here under the Causeway no one bothered Iggy. He was sort of a mascot anyhow as if he somehow represented not just the Kid but all the men living under the Causeway to the world at large. To the residents under the Causeway Iggy was more than a pet and less. To the Kid however he was more than a human being and less. He was his best friend. He never should have abandoned him during the raid. He never should have trusted the cops to ignore him especially when that one cop drew his gun and the other cop yelled for him to shoot Iggy.

Tears are running down his cheeks and he feels like a big baby. He's ashamed of himself not for crying but for having been such a coward and though he feels rightly punished by having his best friend taken away forever Iggy did not deserve to die. Iggy never once did anything to be ashamed of. All he did all his life was be his natural self. Unlike the Kid. Who doesn't even know what his natural self is.

There's no way he can bury Iggy down here so the Kid drags Larry Somerset's sleeping bag out from under the collapsed tent and unzips it and rolls Iggy's body and the chain and cinder block into the sleeping bag and zips it back up. Then he lifts the bundle in his arms and cradling it walks down the sloping concrete island to the water. With Iggy's body which weighs twenty-seven pounds plus the cinder block and chain the sleeping bag is too heavy for him to toss so he drops it straight into the Bay and then takes a nearby two-by-four and pushes it out into the deeper water where it slowly sinks to the bottom.

The Kid loved Iggy—maybe the only creature he has ever loved except his mother and he's not really sure he loves her because sometimes it's hard to distinguish between lifelong dependency and love especially for someone you can't be sure loves you back. But he knows that from the day Iggy clamped onto his hand with his little beak and the doctor wanted to cut off his head to make him let go the Kid has loved Iggy. And now that Iggy is dead and his body is at the bottom of the Bay the Kid wants to be dead and at the bottom of the Bay too.

Slowly he turns away from Iggy's watery grave site and walks back to his ravaged campsite. Larry Somerset's duffel is still there alongside his own supplies and sleeping bag and clothing and his cook-kit and stove. There's even a can of Corona beer and a bag of Cheetos left over from last night's supper. The tent poles and lines are intact and the tent itself wasn't torn. He's able to reset it quickly and in an hour he has restored his camp to its original neat four-square condition. While he drinks the beer and eats the Cheetos he pokes through Larry Somerset's bag: corduroy trousers, a Brooks Brothers

V-neck sweater and two folded dress shirts, some underwear and socks, a shaving kit and miscellaneous toiletries, a pair of flip-flops and a bath towel. Also a Bible which doesn't surprise him since guys like Larry Somerset are usually Bible thumpers and a thin leather briefcase stuffed with legal-looking papers that the Kid intends to read in the morning light as it's nearly dark and he remembers that his headlamp batteries are weak.

On the north side of the Causeway a couple of the survivors of the raid have put the shower pail back up on its stand and have repaired the latrine which is basically a large plastic bucket half-hidden behind a floral shower curtain stretched over a tripod of bamboo poles. One of the men—a guy named P.C. who is around fifty and says in his previous life he was a high school track coach—passes by his camp and the Kid asks him what happened to Rabbit.

P.C. is a fleshy white man with a steel gray buzz cut. He wears baggy bermuda shorts and white basketball sneakers, a faded green Calusa Tarpons T-shirt and a Boston Red Sox baseball cap and is lugging a second plastic bucket to the latrine for when the first bucket is full. He looks like a suburban dad off to wash his station wagon in the driveway. You'd never think he was a sex offender but what's a sex offender look like anyhow? The Kid doesn't know what P.C. stands for but he's pretty sure it isn't "politically correct." More likely it's "partly correct" because he's one of those guys who speaks with total authority about things he knows almost nothing about. Also there is something sly about him that the Kid can't quite name. Something compulsively deceitful—like he would say it's raining, it's definitely raining, when you can see for yourself that the sun is shining. He doesn't trust the guy. Not the way he trusts the Rabbit. Or even Paco and most of the other residents.

Rabbit? Oh yeah, he got his leg busted up pretty bad. They took him and some others in the ambulances. Paco just took off on his motorcycle and no one followed him on account of being so busy busting everybody else.

Anybody killed?

A heart attack or two and one guy who tried swimming to the mainland but got caught in the rip and drowned.

P.C., that's gotta be bullshit. It woulda been in the paper and I read the paper today. I woulda seen it.

They're keeping it quiet on account of politics. A lot of us just ran like hell. Once people heard the cop's gun from when he shot your lizard everybody who hadn't already gotten the hell out of here like you and me froze and behaved themselves and got hauled off in the paddy wagons. Hey, too bad about your lizard, Kid.

You think they'll be back? I mean the cops and all?

Not tonight. This whole thing was staged for the press. The media. An election year photo op. A few days though an' there'll be reporters back to write their follow-ups and if they find us still here and write about it the cops'll be all over this place again.

I thought you said they were keeping it quiet on account of the politics.

Trust me. Better pack your stuff and find a new place to live, Kid. At least till after the election.

Why do I think you're trying to keep people from coming back, P.C.? You got your eye on one of those empty shacks?

Come morning I'm outa here myself.

Where can we go?

There's no "we," Kid. My advice is go alone. The same way you came here in the first place. Being homeless ain't a team sport. And keep moving is my advice. And never sleep in the same place twice. Hey, good luck out there, my little friend.

Yeah, thanks.

You might try Benbow's over on Anaconda Key for a few nights. It doesn't look like it but it's a business so he won't let you camp there permanently. You know Benbow's?

You're just making it up, P.C., like everything else. Benbow's is probably some kind of beach resort where they'll run me off as soon as they see me start to pitch my tent. Or they'll bust me. You're trying to get me busted, aren't

*you? You want my spot here beneath the Causeway with the great view of
the Bay and beautiful downtown Calusa.*

*Naw, Benbow's an old squatters' shrimper camp. Trust me. They sell beer
and smoked fish and shrimp. But guys down on their luck hang out sometimes for a week or two and nobody bugs 'em for it unless they want to make
it permanent. Benbow and a bunch of old Vietnam vets run the place. Crazy
guys but harmless. Him included. Other side of the South Bay Causeway.
On Anaconda Key out by the sewage treatment plant. Can't miss it. They
make movies there sometimes.*

What kinda movies?

*I heard skin flicks, porn. Cheap shit that goes straight to the Internet.
Trust me.*

Yeah, right. The Kid says he'll think about it. Tomorrow. Tonight
he's too fucked up by the death of Iggy to think about anything that
might be considered his future or his past. Tonight all he wants to
think about is the immediate present.

P.C. says, *Suit yourself, Kid. But you're going to need a power source to
charge your anklet battery. The Greek's generator is permanently out of business. This place is totally over, Kid.*

CHAPTER TEN

THE KID FLICKS HIS BIC AND LIGHTS A candle and crawls into his sleeping bag. Above him shadows flutter like restless crows across the pale green skin of the nylon tent. He forgot to buy batteries for his headlamp. Dumb. Lying back, elbow bent, head on his upper arm, he lights up a cigarette. His thirteenth smoke of the day. He'll be down to twelve next week. But who's counting, right? At least he's not thinking about Iggy or about being fired from his job or about having to find a new place to live. The Kid is good at keeping in cages the things that trouble his mind.

He opens Larry Somerset's Holy Bible. It's the only book in the tent. The Kid's never been much of a reader and he has hoped for a long time, ever since he first heard of it, that he suffers from attention deficit disorder because in school and in the army most people regarded him as borderline retarded. He's pretty sure that he's not but he's had a hard time coming up with a better explanation for what's gone wrong with his life so maybe he is borderline retarded.

He's not actually read the Bible before. All or even in part. His mother never made him go to Sunday school or church but he's known about the Bible all his life of course and he respects it—just as he knows about and respects the U.S. Constitution and the Declaration of Independence which he's also never read and Shakespeare and a few other famous writings that weren't required reading in school and some that were but which he never got around to reading. Supposedly those are the chief books and documents where people set down in print the basic rules that you have to obey in order to live a good productive legal life. A moral life. Everyone in authority when you got down to basics concerning right versus wrong quotes from them or at least refers to them but the Kid always figured that since every rule and regulation in the world was based on them you didn't have to read the originals.

But lately he's started to wonder if the authorities have been misrepresenting the originals here and there or at least interpreting them in a way that is more to their own advantage than to the good use of people like the Kid who are both ignorant and pretty much powerless and therefore usually have to depend on the authorities to tell them what's right and what's wrong.

For instance he wonders where in the Holy Bible or the U.S. Constitution or the Declaration of Independence or Shakespeare it says you aren't supposed to try and have sex with anyone under the age of eighteen. He's pretty sure that somewhere in the Bible it says God doesn't want you to have sex with animals or with your mother or your sister or daughter. Shakespeare was probably against all that too. Who wouldn't be? But what about sex with hard-bodied flirtatious fourteen-year-old girls with navel rings and tattoos and you're not related to them? What does the Bible have to say about going online and trying to have sex with them? Shakespeare might even be *for* it.

Some things have been viewed as obviously wrong for thousands of years which is the main reason they're illegal. At first they're regarded as immoral pure and simple—God's law whether you believe in Him or not—and then when people keep doing those immoral things anyhow which is the same as breaking God's law the majority of human beings gets together and votes to make them illegal as well. Man's law. That's okay, the Kid can live with laws like that. It's democracy in action and everybody including the Kid is in favor of democracy.

Then there are man-laws that are more like rules you agree to obey only they aren't backed up by the Bible or any of those other ancient writings and if you break them you're punished which is to be expected but it's not because you've done something morally wrong. You've not broken God's law, you've just broken a rule. Like when you join the U.S. Army which has a rule against distributing porn and you go ahead and do it anyhow because you want all your buddies to have a DVD starring your favorite porn actress and you want them to like and respect you but you aren't aware of the rule against distributing porn so you get kicked out of the army. That's like breaking a contract because you didn't read the fine print. Or you didn't realize that the lease said no pets. Too bad for you is all. It's not necessarily wrong. Just stupid. Nobody pretends it's immoral or against the Holy Bible or Shakespeare the way they do if you try to have sex with someone who says she's fourteen years old and tells you to come on over.

The Kid needs to check out God's law. So he opens Larry Somerset's Holy Bible to the book of Genesis and starts reading. It's the King James Version and he can tell right away that even though it's supposed to be in English it's in more like a foreign language than any English he's ever read before. Still with a little work and concentration he can figure out most of what's being said there. It reminds him of the dialogue in certain video games and movies about Vikings that are set in medieval times.

Right from the start God seems to be the president or the king of the universe and in charge of everything in it including the sea that surrounds it and the skies above. The various firmaments. Seven days go by in which He sets everything up so He can rule without any opposition and if He wants can even kick back and rest every seventh day. By then He's got people living there, a man anyhow that He made from blowing into a pile of dust. God's first real citizen. God's homey. His name is Adam.

The Kid sort of knows where this story is going but he keeps on reading anyhow. For the details. He likes the details. He can visualize the story and what you can visualize you can imagine. He's imagining Calusa thousands of years before the white people arrived. Calusa and the Bay and the Barrier Isles and Keys and the Great Panzacola Swamp back when there weren't any people living here, not even the Panzacola Indians. Only Adam and Eve. And no skyscrapers or hotels or malls or interstate highways and the whole of this part of the continent was covered with jungle and mangroves and the waters were filled with manatees and porpoises and crocodiles and endless schools of fish and whenever vast flocks of birds crossed overhead the skies darkened as if the sun were blocked by passing clouds.

He can't quite picture God except as a huge ball of light with an old man's deep voice like in the pickup truck ads on TV coming out of the ball of light dictating the way everything in Eden is supposed to work. God's got one big rule—no eating from the tree of knowledge of good and evil. This is the first real basic right-versus-wrong rule that he's seen in the Bible so far.

No eating the fruit from the tree of knowledge of good and evil, okay?

He likes that distinction: there's good and there's evil. Evil is worse than bad. And it's a lot worse than merely dumb or unlucky or illegal. That's what makes God's rules superior to all other rules: if you break one you're not just dumb or even bad, you're fucking *evil*! You have knowingly disobeyed God. To be evil is to be bad in an extreme way—sentenced to life without parole and locked up in hell for eternity after you die. If you believe in hell, that is. Which the Kid does although he does not believe in heaven. When you've had a life like the Kid's so far it's a lot easier to believe in hell than in heaven. Same as with God whom the Kid believes in when things go right but not when things go wrong. Which doesn't make him an atheist exactly or an agnostic. Just inconsistent.

Finally the talking snake comes into the story and it gets seriously interesting to the Kid especially because the Snake which in the

Bible is called a serpent reminds him of Iggy somehow. He wonders if Iggy who is definitely a reptile could properly be called a serpent as well. *Don't go there, Kid.* He doesn't want to think about Iggy wrapped in a sleeping bag at the bottom of the Bay. But he doesn't want to fall asleep either because he's afraid the cops might come back in spite of what P.C. told him. And he's afraid of his dreams. *Don't go there either.* So he keeps reading.

The Snake complicates the story which makes it suspenseful for the first time. The Kid tries to warn Adam and Eve: *Don't fall for it! The Snake's only trying to make trouble between us humans and God!* But he's too late. The woman—probably because women are more trusting than men or at least they were back then in the beginning— believes the Snake. And of course once she's taken a taste and likes it she talks Adam into eating the fruit of the tree of knowledge of good and evil too. And suddenly they go from feeling innocent and like babies not even aware that they don't have any clothes on to feeling guilty and also ashamed which is worse than just feeling guilty and when God shows up again to check on how His garden's doing they hide in the bushes. When God calls Adam out at first Adam says *I didn't do it.* Then he claims that actually the woman made him do it. And the woman turns around and says the Snake made her do it.

The Kid knows how they feel. He's felt that way since he was about eight or nine. Maybe even younger. First you deny that you did it and then when it's obvious you're lying you blame somebody else. It's what people do when they're ashamed. It's always about sex too. First it was from watching his mother making it with some guy and then it was from jerking off all the time since he was ten and then skin magazines and Internet porn and when he got older it was porn DVDs and shows at sex clubs and sex chat room conversations on the Internet with teenage girls until finally he got caught in the act so to speak and busted by the cops and it's all on YouTube for the whole world to watch and judge.

The Kid wonders if it's possible that this whole tree of knowledge of good and evil thing was set up by God as a kind of prehistoric sex-sting with the Snake as the decoy. Maybe from the beginning the Snake was secretly working for God who was mainly interested in testing Adam and Eve because in spite of being all-seeing and all-knowing He couldn't be there in the Garden of Eden 24/7 to watch over them and protect their innocence. If God was going to trust them to behave themselves and follow His rules when He was elsewhere in the universe they would have to be capable of protecting their innocence from temptation on their own. They would have to be like angels. God probably wasn't sure they could do that. Maybe God didn't know what sort of creature He'd actually created when He blew into that handful of dust and came up with Adam and then later took out one of Adam's ribs and made Eve.

Without knowing it the Kid is drifting toward sleep and his theological and philosophical speculations are starting to shape and misshape his reading. According to the Kid the punishment that God lays on the Snake for beguiling the woman into eating the fruit from the tree of knowledge of good and evil is to wrap the Snake in a sex offender's sleeping bag and sink it to the bottom of the Bay, there to lie forgotten and despised by all mankind and mourned by none except for Adam who in a cowardly moment exposed himself to the fear of men with guns and abandoned the serpent to suffer their wrath. God punishes the woman by making her bear a son who will be dependent upon her for many years and will restrict her in her enjoyment of the company of men until she reaches the age when she no longer attracts them and then the son will disappoint the woman and publicly humiliate and shame her all the remaining days of her life. And because Adam listened to the woman and ate of the fruit of the tree of knowledge of good and evil he is condemned to homelessness living in a tent somewhere east of Eden until he turns back into the dust from whence he came. Then there is something about Adam becoming a farmer and fathering two sons with Eve and naming them Cain and Abel but by now the Kid's candle has burned down nearly to a stub and he is asleep and dreaming freely.

All of a sudden the flap is pulled back and a bright white light floods the inside of the tent. The Kid wakes and sits up and rubs his eyes with his fists like a child. He hitches himself away from the light toward the rear of the tent. His first thought is to say *What the fuck?* but it might be God so he doesn't say anything. The white light splashes against the sides and roof of the tent and bathes the Kid all over. It probably *is* God. And He's finally found him although He must've known all along where on the planet the Kid was hiding because He's all-seeing and all-knowing. He must've decided that because the Kid has been reading the Bible now is the right moment to confront him with the cold irrefutable fact that the Kid is evil and He's come down from heaven to the Causeway to tell him in person and reveal the nature of his punishment.

A low voice speaks from the source of the light which is located at the open tent flap—a man's voice dark and old and thickly layered like the bass register on a church organ. It has a noticeable southern accent cleanly spoken but a little drawled and homey like some of those TV evangelists.

I realize, my friend, that it's late. But I would enjoy talking with you.

Now?

I will take only a few moments of your time, as it's late for me as much as for you. To tell the truth, I did not expect to find anyone still here.

The source of the bright tent-filling light drops and the Kid sees that it's a high-intensity emergency lamp held by an enormous white man with a gray beard and a tangled mass of gray hair. His long shaggy beard and messy nest of hair look like He got buffeted by hurricane-force winds when He flew down from the sky or wherever He came from. He has red puffy lips and a face as broad as a shovel. His body is as wide as the tent and He's very tall. He's the largest man the Kid has ever seen. Assuming he *is* a man and not God—the Kid's still not sure. He's never seen a portrait of God before. No one has. Besides God can probably take any form He chooses depending on the circumstance and who He's talking to. Right now He's a gigantic bearded fat man in his early sixties dressed like a lawyer or a banker in a chocolate brown suit and white dress shirt and brown-and-yellow-striped tie and a vest buttoned tightly over his enormous belly.

What . . . what do you want to talk to me about?

Maybe this isn't a good time. I didn't think there'd be anyone still here. I just stopped on my way home to see the site of last night's raid.

On your way home.

Yes.

From?

From the university.

What do you want from me?

A chat.

This ain't a chat room.

Would you agree to talk in the morning? I don't have a recorder with me tonight anyhow. It's a bit of a surprise to find someone still here.

Who the fuck are you anyhow?

It doesn't matter. I'm a professor at Calusa State. Chair of the sociology department.

Why are you here?

I moderated a panel discussion this evening at the university and was driving myself home. Listening to the local news on the car radio I heard what happened here last night. So I parked up there on the Causeway and made my way down to see where people like you have been living.

People like me.

It's sort of my area. My academic specialization. Homelessness. Its causes.

Okay. Whatever.

Would you meet with me tomorrow morning? I'd like to interview you.

I won't be here in the morning. I'm moving.

Where are you moving to?

Why should I tell you, Professor?

I can meet you there. We can do the interview wherever you like.

The Kid thinks it over. The Professor is clearly not God and he's not likely a cop or someone working for the state either so the Kid has nothing to lose in talking to him in the form of an interview. He can always lie or refuse to answer questions that might incriminate him: *Did you or did you not eat of the fruit from the tree of knowledge of good and evil? On advice of counsel I refuse to answer on the grounds that it may incriminate me.*

It sounds like the Professor will do most of the talking anyhow. He's a professor, after all. It's possible the guy can help the Kid find a job at the university on the grounds crew or something and a more or less permanent place to live. You never know. The Kid has never met a real professor before but they're supposed to be smart and people respect them and they don't work for the cops or the state. Besides they're like priests and shrinks, right? Everything you tell them is strictly confidential.

You know where Benbow's is?

Benbow's? Is it a restaurant? A homeless shelter?

I can't go to a homeless shelter. Not where there's likely to be kids. It's supposedly an old shrimpers' camp on Anaconda Key. Out beyond the sewage treatment plant. That's where I'm going tomorrow. Look for me in a day or two at Benbow's, okay?

I know how to get to Anaconda Key. And I've smelled the sewage treatment plant numerous times when the wind blows out of the south. Now tell me your name, young man.

Kid. Just ask for the Kid.

I have classes all day tomorrow. And meetings at night. I'll have to get together with you late the following day, if that's all right.

Not this late.

The Professor rumbles a laugh and says, *No, son, not this late.* He lowers his lamp and closes the tent flap and walks away. The Kid listens to his slick shoes crunching against the concrete. It must have been hard for a guy that fat to make his way down the path from the Causeway. And a lot harder getting back up. A guy his size could have a heart attack just getting out of his chair.

The Kid lights his stub of a candle and opens Larry Somerset's Holy Bible again and picks up reading where he left off. But after the story of Cain and Abel he comes to a whole lot of *begat*s which except for the fact that everybody back then was living for hundreds of years at a time is really boring to the Kid.

He closes the Bible and blows out his candle and lies back in the darkness with his eyes wide open and as he has done nearly every night of his life even when he was a little boy he plans his day tomorrow step by step. Break camp. Pack tent sleeping bag clothes cooking utensils containers toilet kit and other gear into backpack and duffel. Include some of Larry Somerset's stuff. Tie duffel to bike rack, wear backpack, and ride or if it's too much stuff walk bike to South Bay Causeway four miles south and cross to Anaconda Key. Find Benbow's. Find Benbow himself if P.C. didn't lie and he's a real person and talk him into letting him pitch his tent temporarily and maybe ask for a job there as a busboy if it's a restaurant and try to cadge a meal or two. Meanwhile make a quick late-night Dumpster dive and replenish home food supply. And hope things change for the better soon. He's pretty sure they can't get worse.

PART II

CHAPTER ONE

THE PROFESSOR DIGS CLASSICAL JAZZ AND
swing, music made in the 1930s, the decade before he was
born in Clinton, Alabama, and in the 1940s, the decade of
his early childhood. He was an only child, his mother the town librarian and his father an accountant for U. S. Steel. They were northern-
ers, originally from Pittsburgh, Pennsylvania. Both his parents were
college educated, Episcopalians, suspected locally of being support-
ers of Franklin Roosevelt, and despite his father's white-collar job at
U. S. Steel, pro-union.

The Professor's father's name was Jason. He kept the books that
monitored the costs of inmates hired and often purchased outright
from the state and county prisons and local jails. They were, with few
exceptions, black men, de facto slaves housed in the company labor
camps, serving out their sentences in the dark airless mine shafts
deep beneath the red hills. His mother, a high-spirited, easily bored
post-debutante from an old Pittsburgh banking family, was named
Cynthia.

Classical jazz and swing was music made mostly by black people—
Duke Ellington, Louis Armstrong, Benny Carter, and Lester Young—
and raffish whites like Jack Teagarden and Benny Goodman. It was
the dance music of the Professor's parents' northern youth. When he
was a child, he watched them after supper spike a stack of records on

the old Victrola, set the needle, and as the music began, they would stroll hand in hand from the living room to the wide screened porch that faced the tree-lined street. Invariably the boy put down his book and followed his parents and climbed onto the porch glider. With the soles of his sneakers barely touching the floor, the boy got the glider swinging back and forth in time to the music. His mother and father were already dancing. It was as if they were putting their northern sophistication on defiant display. He watched his handsome young parents happily dance on the open porch where their disapproving white Southern Baptist neighbors could see them, and he fell in love as much with their public defiance as with their private music.

But it's music he himself never danced to, except when he was alone and no one, especially the neighbors, could see. Even after he went north at the age of fifteen to attend Kenyon College in Ohio and later in graduate school at Yale, he refused to be seen dancing to the music that he and his parents loved. He tapped his hands and feet to it and bobbed his head, keeping time. But he would not put himself on the dance floor for the simple reason that when he was a youngster he was both morbidly obese and taller by a head than any of his contemporaries. He was a child imprisoned in the body of a very fat adult, a boy who was strong and otherwise healthy but believed that when it came to taking part in physical activities of any kind—sports and outdoor games, hunting and fishing, even physical labor around the house, like mowing the lawn or planting flowers with his mother, but especially when it came to dancing—if he did not keep entirely to himself and out of public sight, he would look ridiculous.

Despite being in most ways a sociable boy who appeared actually to seek out and enjoy the company of other children, he could not be said to play well with others, especially with children his own age or near it. Early on this conflict became problematic for him. Year after year he skipped grades, making him to an increasing degree the youngest in his class, although perennially the largest. He had a gift for languages and a near photographic memory and retained vast stores of data. Precociously intelligent and verbally gifted, he developed a compulsion to explain everything, at first just to other children, but then to adults as well. He explained geography, local, regional, national, and international history, politics, statistics and mathematics, physics and chemistry, sociology, anthropology, and, before it became a subject, game theory. Whether they wanted him to or not he explained things. He did it in a friendly way that was neither condescending nor showing off, and children and adults alike, all of whom were astounded by his mental acuity and linguistic clarity, were for the most part grateful for and sometimes amused by his eagerness to reveal the world to them. From kindergarten on, adults and children called him Professor, and mostly they meant it as a compliment.

He had a mass of curly dark brown hair, smooth pale skin, rosebud lips, and round brown eyes with long lashes, and although his face, due to his obesity, was flattened somewhat, he was nonetheless a conventionally pretty child. But he was not like other children, and he knew it. From the time he learned to walk (delayed because of his weight until he was nearly two and a half years old), he positioned himself on the sideline of every group activity with arms crossed over his bulging chest and assumed the facial expression of a cool, skeptical observer: bemused smile, cold eyes, head tilted back slightly, not in disdain so much as ironic detachment.

It was a self-protective disguise, an affect and posture designed to make his outsized body as irrelevant and close to invisible as possible. But it didn't work. Adults couldn't help noting and commenting on his body, and their comments, even when they took the approximate outer form of praise (*That's a real big steamroller of a boy, ain't he?* and, *Bet you gonna be half the Tide's offensive line all by yourself when you get down to Tuscaloosa!* and, *That boy sure mus' like his biscuits an' gravy!*), ridiculed him. Consequently, he knew all too well what he would look like to parents, teachers, coaches, and especially to the other children if he waddled over to join them on the playground in their games of kickball, Red Rover, and capture the flag; or if in middle school he lumbered onto the sports field prepared to play baseball or football; or when finally in high school, if he shuffled shyly up to the pretty blond girl named Ashley Tarbox at the school dance and asked her to come onto the dance floor with him and jitterbug to Artie Shaw's "I Get a Kick Out of You." He knew that he would look ridiculous. So he never did any of those things.

CHAPTER TWO

I T ' S   T H E   S O N G   T H A T ' S   P L A Y I N G   N O W   O N   T H E
CD player of his van as he crosses the narrow bridge from
Calusa onto Anaconda Key—Artie Shaw's version of "I Get a
Kick Out of You." His fingertips tap in time against the steering
wheel. *I get no kick from champagne. Mere alcohol doesn't thrill me at all.*
He passes the sewage treatment plant on his left and inside the air-
conditioned van, even with the windows closed, catches a whiff of
the wind-blown vegetal stink. On his right through a snaggy wall
of mangroves he glimpses a narrow channel and the peeling hull of
an abandoned, half-sunk shrimp boat. At a fork in the road he spots
a tilted, hand-painted sign: BENBOW'S. He turns right and follows
the winding, crushed-shell and coral lane into the low live oak and
palmetto woods. He shuts down the CD player so he can better concentrate his attention, and as he bumps along the lane he searches in
among the trees for the Kid's tent.

He's excited about this meeting. Two nights ago when he made
his way down to the encampment beneath the Claybourne Causeway he had not expected to find any of the homeless sex offenders who'd been living in abject squalor there. For months he had
intended to visit the camp and regretted having postponed it so
long, and after hearing on the car radio that the camp had been
raided by the police, he expected all the residents, twenty-four hours

later, to have been scattered by now or carted back to jail. Although most of his colleagues at the university—indeed, most of the good citizens of Calusa—denied knowing of the camp, there had been numerous newspaper stories and online commentaries and Internet blogs decrying its existence and urging its dissolution and the removal of the colony. There was no agreement, of course, on where the sex offenders should be removed *to*. They were pariahs of the most extreme sort, American untouchables, a caste of men ranked far below the merely alcoholic, addicted, or deranged homeless. They were men beyond redemption, care, or cure, both despicable and impossible to remove and thus by most people simply wished out of existence.

The Professor was not one of these people. Homelessness, its causes and possible solutions, interested him professionally. The legal apparatus designed to deal with sexual offenses also interested him. And so did the psychology of denial, although that was more a personal interest than professional. He'd leave any professional examination of collective and individual denial to the psychology department. When he stopped on his way home from the university and parked his van at the side of the road and made his way in the dark down under the Causeway, he expected only to see the place where these men had been living, not the men themselves. He wanted to observe what sort of habitation they had made for themselves before the city sanitation workers had a chance to come in and clean it up.

Thus he was elated to discover the Kid asleep inside his tent. The fellow wasn't much more than a boy. The Professor guessed him to be twenty or twenty-one at most. He acted suspicious and was a little hostile, perhaps. Testy. But why not, after what he'd been through, especially after the raid?

Soon, with no sight of the Kid's tent—*Of course he'd want to hide himself, the poor kid must be terrified*—the lane ends at what the Professor assumes is Benbow's. He parks the van in a clearing where there are several other vehicles: a rusting Toyota pickup, a yellow

Calusa city cab, and a gleaming, meticulously restored 1965 Harley-Davidson chromed front to back and top to bottom with an American flag drooping from a rod attached to the rear fender. Last of the FLH panheads, the Professor notes. First of the electric starters.

Beyond the clearing, scattered in the shade of live oaks and palm trees, in no evident pattern and to no recognizable purpose, are a half-dozen unpainted shanties and low, shedlike buildings with corrugated iron roofs. It's a random-seeming collection of old handmade buildings, most of them windowless and half-open to the elements. Beyond the buildings a rusted, dented, twenty-foot Airstream housetrailer with flattened tires has been set on cinder blocks. A handpainted wooden plaque with the name BENBOW is bolted to the aluminum outer wall above the entrance.

From his van the Professor can see on the far side of the trailer the dark green waters of the Bay fading to azure in the distance and in flashes through the tangled mangroves the wide channel that surrounds the small key where four or five partially sunk hulks, fishing boats and shrimpers, have been left by the shore to rot, too far gone to claim or repair. Looking north across the Bay he can see the Calusa skyline and the arch of the Claybourne Causeway. The purpose of Benbow's is unclear to him, but the place looks like a staging area for refugees waiting for the arrival of the man with the boat who will smuggle them from their native land across the sea to America.

Phrases and names have been scrawled and spray painted here and there on the faded plywood and warped board walls of the nearby buildings, more like messages left for a search party than graffiti: BOOM-BOOM BENBOW RULES! and TRINIDAD BOB WAS HERE! THIS IS THE PLACE! EVERYTHING IS PERMITTED! One of the sheds is set up like an open-air bar with a plank counter, an old-fashioned zinc-lined cooler visible behind the counter, and a fourteen-inch TV set with a rabbit ears antenna and VCR perched on a shelf above it. A small wire cage with a large gray parrot snoozing inside hangs next to the

TV. Nearby an oil drum overflows with empty beer cans and bottles spilling onto the bare ground.

Keeping their backs to him, as if they haven't heard his van ease over the crushed coral to a stop barely twenty feet away, two men, one with a shaved head, the other with long, lank, silver-gray hair, lean against the plank, drinking beer from cans. They are scrawny men the same approximate age as the Professor with arms, shoulders, and necks smattered with ancient tattoos too faded and wrinkled to decipher. They are both shirtless, wearing cutoffs, and barefoot, their slack-skinned bodies tanned the color of old bricks. The bald man has bright blue eyes and smokes a large, yellowed meerschaum pipe; the other wears a stringy billy-goat beard and a large gold hoop in his left ear and jangled sets of gold bracelets on his wrists. The TV screen is blank, but both men watch it intently as if it's the seventh game of the World Series. The Professor decides that the man with the pipe is Boom-Boom Benbow; the one with the gold is Trinidad Bob. A pair of permanently stalled Vietnam vets.

A yellow mixed-breed dog skulks toward the Professor's van, too sick and undernourished to bark or even growl or glare, but unlike the pair at the bar is unable to resist the instinct to challenge an intruder. She's an old bitch with sagging teats who's been allowed to breed too many times. The Professor eases himself from his van to the ground, and a wave of sweat instantly sweeps down his broad face into his beard. The sweet smell of woodsmoke and the damp salt smell off the briny Bay and open sea beyond mingle in the sulfurous breeze that wafts across the Key from the sewage treatment plant. The mix of smells is almost pleasant to him. He's wearing faded blue farmer's overalls, fisherman's sandals, and a yellow seersucker short-sleeved shirt—clothing that makes him look even larger than he is. Sweat circles spread from his armpits across his upper chest where tufts of white hair peek out from the open collar of his shirt. He has a pale blue baseball cap on his head, and his abundant long hair pokes through the plastic, unhooked hatband at the back.

He stares down the yellow dog and dismisses it with a flip of his hand, and the dog, glad for the dominance, flops in the shade of the van and closes her eyes. Slowly the Professor approaches the men at the bar and takes a position next to the one with the shaved head, the man he believes is Benbow, and watches the blank TV screen with them. Neither man acknowledges his presence. The other, Trinidad Bob, finishes his beer and tosses the can in the general direction of the barrel of empties. He reaches over the bar and fishes a fresh can from the cooler and cracks it open.

Got one of those for sale?

Trinidad Bob answers by hauling another can of beer, Miller, from the cooler and slides it down the plank to the Professor.

How much?

Two bucks.

The Professor lays three singles onto the plank in front of him and waits. After thirty seconds Benbow grabs the bills and stuffs them into his pocket. He relights his meerschaum pipe.

Tobacco smells good. Not many people smoke a pipe anymore.

Trinidad Bob laughs, halfway between a chortle and a giggle. *Not many people smoke anything anymore! 'Cept mary-juana!* He knocks a cigarette from a pack of Parliaments and lights it. *Mary-wanna. Mary Jane. Merry Christmas. You here for fish? Got some fresh smoked marlin today.* He points to a large rusty oil barrel that's been converted into a primitive smoker with a low-burning fire beneath it, the source of the sweet-smelling woodsmoke the Professor noticed earlier. *Been makin' it since mornin'. Came in yesterday afternoon. Seven bucks a pound.*

Actually, I'm looking for someone. A friend of mine.

Benbow turns and looks the Professor over once, top to bottom, then goes back to the blank TV screen. *What's his name?*

Kid. Just Kid. Young fellow, said he'd meet me here around now.

Never heard of him. You ever heard of him, Bob?

Trinidad Bob hesitates a few seconds, then says, *Nope. Never heard of him. 'Course, we had a crowd here last night, mostly youngsters over from*

Calusa an' the Barriers. He might've been one of them people. Lots of pretty girls in bikinis an' mini skirts dancin' an' drinkin' and partying like crazy! I was sort of distracted by all that so could've missed your friend named Kid. They all wanted to talk to Trinidad Bob. That's me. Them little chickies like talkin' to Trinidad Bob.

Because you're so fuckin' handsome. Without looking at him, Benbow says to the Professor: *I take you for a cop.*

I'm a teacher. A professor at Calusa State.

I still take you for a cop.

I take you for a vet. 'Nam. Noncommissioned officer, E-5, Air cav, probably. Or else BRO. Two tours, early 1970s. Bronze Star and a Purple Heart. I take Trinidad Bob there as a vet too. A blueleg E-2 who never got to E-3. One tour, late 1960s, maybe early 1970s like you. BRO, but not in your outfit. Took some shrapnel in the head. Like they say, FUBAR. Fucked up in the head.

Trinidad Bob says, *Hey, that's pretty good, Professor! How'd you know all that?*

'Cause he's some kinda fuckin' cop is how. Turn on the TV, Bob. The news is over. It's time for Jeopardy!

Bob says, *Me, I always wanna watch* Wheel of Fortune, *but Boom, he prefers* Jeopardy! *So he says, anyhow. He likes questioning answers, he says. But* Wheel of Fortune *has Vanna White, man. Fuckin' Vanna White! You ever check her out? Can't get enough of that bitch, man!* Bob quick-steps around the plank bar and switches on the TV, fiddles with the controls until the picture comes up on *Jeopardy!*

Don't think I've ever seen the show, the Professor says.

You'd know if you did. They was gonna shoot an episode of that show here at Benbow's one time, on account of so many TV shows an' modelin' shit and movies that gets shot here. Only at the last minute they decide to do it over on the Barriers at a fancy fuckin' hotel instead. Too bad. I really was hopin' to meet Vanna White in person an' maybe get me a lick of that, y' know what I'm sayin'? Chicks dig me, man.

The Professor glances left at the sound of a door opening and sees a thin woman in her late forties or early fifties step from the Airstream trailer, followed by a slightly older man in jeans and motorcycle boots and a muscle shirt. He has short, stiff, shoe-polish-black hair and a pure white handlebar mustache. He's a man who lifts weights regularly—broad meaty shoulders, thick neck muscles, and slabbed biceps decorated with tattoos of overlapping dragons and unicorns. He falls into a bow-legged swagger as he nears the men. A competitive power-lifter who just got laid or a blow job, the Professor decides. Senior heavyweight division. Not a bodybuilder. Bodybuilders favor the deliberately cut look over bulk and brute strength and avoid tattoos. She must be the smoked marlin.

The man takes a position at the bar beside Trinidad Bob. The woman walks behind the bar, pulls two beers from the cooler and passes one to her companion. Her face is freckled and blotched from too much sun. She has a web of fine lines around her green eyes and a vertical cluster of smoker's lines above her upper lip. Her thick coppery hair is cropped short, chopped rather than layered, and streaked with gray, as if the copper-red dye needs to be replenished. She's her own hairdresser, the Professor observes. She's full-breasted for such a thin woman and wears a loose, black chenille skirt with a dangling, ripped hem and a faded red T-shirt with *I GOT CRABS AT HALEY'S CRAB SHACK* printed across the front.

She smiles and says to the Professor, *How're you doin' today, big man?*

Trinidad Bob says, *Boom-Boom thinks he's a cop!*

That's interestin'. Are you?

I'm a professor at CSU. Calusa State. I'm looking for a young friend who was supposed to meet me here.

One of your students?

Sort of. A small young man in his early twenties with a buzz cut and big ears. I think he hoped to camp out here on the Key for a few days.

Sure, the Kid. He's here. He's still here, ain't he, Boom?

Shut the fuck up, Yvonne.

You don't look like a cop. Or a professor, either. I mean the way you're dressed an' all. What's with the overalls?

I said shut the fuck up, Yvonne.

The weight lifter takes a final gulp from his beer and cleans his mustache with his paw like a schnauzer. *I'm outa here. Check you later, Boom.* He steps away from the bar, drops the can into the barrel, and walks quickly to his motorcycle. In seconds he is gone.

Yvonne smirks after him. *No good-bye even? Jeez.*

Cops make Paco antsy.

He said his name was Tom.

Yeah. Whatever.

Trinidad Bob looks over at the Professor. *If you ain't a cop how'd you know so much about me an' Boom-Boom so fast? You a vet? You in 'Nam?*

Would it make a difference if I were?

Without looking away from *Jeopardy!* Benbow says, *What branch?*

101st Airborne.

Yeah, you an' everybody else. The 101st's like Woodstock. Everybody and his brother over fifty got high and got laid at Woodstock. What year were you in 'Nam?

In-country from December fourth, 1968, to September twentieth, 1969.

Based where?

Long Binh. And mostly up in the A Shau Valley. What is this, a quiz show? Benbow's version of Jeopardy!*?*

Yeah. Except in Jeopardy! *you get told the answer first and the contestant has to come up with the right question.*

Fair enough. Here's an answer. "Pup tent."

Trinidad Bob slaps his hand on the plank to ring the buzzer. *I got it! "Where's the Kid?"*

Right. Next answer, "On the beach on the far side of the trailer."

"Where'd the Kid pitch his pup tent?" Man, this is too fucking easy!

Shut the fuck up, Bob.

Here's the final answer. Get it right, I buy a round of beers. "Yes."

"Yes"? What the fuck kind of answer is that?

Think of a question that's answered with "yes."

Trinidad Bob scratches his head in puzzlement. Yvonne peers around Bob and Benbow at the Professor and says, *Ah, how about, "Okay if I visit the Kid in his pup tent on the beach on the far side of the trailer?"*

The Professor smiles and pulls a twenty–dollar bill from his wallet and lays it on the counter. *Correct. She beat you, Bob. But here's a couple of rounds' worth. A bonus prize.*

Yvonne reaches into the cooler and pulls out two cans of Miller and sets them on the counter in front of her. Trinidad Bob does the same. Benbow pockets the twenty. He says, *You may not be a cop. But you ain't no Vietnam vet.*

The Professor moves away from the bar and starts walking toward the Airstream. *Well, I sure wasn't getting I-and-I at Woodstock the third week in August of 1969. So I must've been getting stoned and laid in Vietnam.*

Benbow calls after him, *Here's an answer, fat man! "BOHICA"!*

The Professor stops, turns, looks over at the quiz master, and coolly smiles. He tilts his head back a notch and crosses his arms over the bib of his overalls: *What's "Bend over, here it comes again"? Don't worry, Benbow, nobody's gonna get fucked this time.* He turns and shambles on.

Trinidad Bob says, *Did he get it right, Boom?*

Shut the fuck up an' drink your beer.

Yvonne says, *He ain't no cop. But he ain't no Vietnam vet, neither.*

How do you know that?

He's too fuckin' fat.

What is he then?

I dunno. A fuckin' professor. Like he said.

Yeah, like you're a cabdriver, Yvonne.

Trinidad Bob laughs and slaps his palm on an imaginary buzzer. *I got it! "How does Yvonne make a living?"*

Benbow says to Yvonne, *Gimme,* and extends his hand palm up.

Yvonne pulls two twenties from her pocket and passes them over to him.

Trinidad Bob laughs. *How does Benbow make a living?*

Just shut the fuck up, Bob.

The big gray parrot in the cage squawks and says, *Shut the fuck up, Bob!*

A PAIR OF WHITE-BREASTED TERNS DANCES along the shoreline. Farther out a cackling gang of gulls spots a cruise ship passing slowly from the Bay through Kydd's Cut into the Atlantic, wheels, and speeds off to hunt and gather in the ship's garbage-strewn wake. The Kid has pitched his tent and dropped his duffel and cooler beside the crumbling concrete breakwater where Benbow's property meets the sea, a spot of bare ground with a clear view of the city and the Bay and in the distance the Causeway and the Barriers. The Kid's bicycle leans against the spindly crutchlike limbs of a nearby screw pine that's large enough to cast a platter of all-day shade over the nylon tent. It's an intelligent almost picturesque campsite.

A little exposed to the wind however. The Kid squats in front of his butane stove and with one hand cups his lighter flame against the blustery offshore breeze and struggles to get the stove lit. The wind keeps blowing his flame out, forcing him to start over: turn off the gas, pump up the pressure again, turn on the gas, shield the Bic, and flick it. The Kid curses—*Shit, shit, shit!*—and lets himself fall backward into a sitting position on the ground and stares angrily at the cold windblown stove.

He ate half a watermelon for breakfast and a chunk of raclette cheese and most of a box of Kashi seven-grain stone-ground crackers for lunch but he specifically wants hard-boiled extra-large organic eggs for supper, at least two from the box of eleven perfect brown eggs plus one slightly cracked egg that he grabbed last night along with the watermelon, cheese, and crackers out behind Bingo's Wholesome Foods. He's got a craving for healthy food and knew he needed a nutritional break from his usual diet of Cheetos and canned stew. He rode his bike over to the mainland after dark arriving early at the Dumpster an hour before the store closed catching a primo spot where the hungry and the homeless Dumpster-divers line up by the chain-link fence behind the store all waiting as patiently and politely as the paying customers inside with their overflowing carts at the cash register. When the store closes and the workers shut off the lights and go home the scavengers one by one scale the fence each in his turn.

With rare exceptions they honor the three rules of Dumpster diving: first-come first-dibs; never take more than you need; leave it cleaner than when you arrived. Since you can only take what the Dumpster gives, you can't control your menu much. But everyone on the streets knows that upscale shoppers and the people who prepare their food are fussy about their diet and in a nice convergence of economics and marketing the high-end organic and natural foods stores like Trader Joe's, Whole Foods, and Bingo's throw out more and better food—especially fresh produce, meats, fish, bread, and dairy products—than the big chain supermarkets like Publix and Price Chopper. If there's a single cracked egg in a dozen the entire box goes into the Dumpster. If one avocado is bad the entire bag gets tossed. A spot of mold on a cheese wheel disqualifies the wheel, one head of lettuce with rusted tips ruins the crate, and a few bruised apples in a basket spoil the basket. The day before their sell-by date whole boxes and trays of baked goods, milk, hamburger, chickens, even steaks and chops get thrown out. It's a feast of imperfect but perfectly edible organic and all-natural pesticide- and preservative-free groceries.

Back when the Kid was gainfully employed he had enough cash in hand to pay for his food and though no one ever told him he knew there was a fourth rule in the Dumpster-divers' code: If you can afford to pay at the register inside, do it. Leave the castoffs for those who have no choice but to forage for food or starve. Now that he's been fired and has no prospects for future employment he's decided that even though he's still got a few bucks left in his pocket it's okay to hit the high-end Dumpsters and fill his pantry. With no more than what he can carry back in his bicycle basket however— the watermelon, cheese, crackers, and eggs. Enough for two days, possibly three. If he can get his fucking stove lit so he can cook some of these eggs.

The Professor approaches the Kid slowly from behind, unseen. He's wary and anxious and not sure why. He has no reason to be afraid of the Kid and is confident that the fellow will eventually consent to be interviewed on the subject of his present circumstance. How a citizen of Calusa becomes homeless is common knowledge. At least among Calusans who, like the Professor, view homelessness as a social blight, who regard it sociologically as a community's debilitating, possibly fatal disease and who, when naming its causes, point to alcoholism, drug addiction, mental illness. Commonplace observations. It's not as easy, however, to identify how a citizen of Calusa becomes a convicted sex offender. It's the combination of the two that intrigues the Professor—men who are both homeless and convicted sex offenders—and their growing numbers here in Calusa and across the country. It shouldn't be hard to get the Kid talking about his homelessness. But it may be difficult to get him to tell the truth about what he did to end up a convicted sex offender. He's bound to be evasive about that. They all are.

Once again the Professor feels like an anthropologist who has ventured deep into the jungle and has stumbled upon a survivor of a tribe long thought to be lost or exterminated. He mustn't frighten or anger the lad. He needs to be sensitive to the Kid's cultural norms, even though he's mostly ignorant of them. He can't project onto the young man his own middle-class, academic cultural norms and assumptions. His first task will be to obtain the fellow's trust, to overcome his understandable suspicion that he's being objectified in the Professor's eyes, that he's viewed as a curiosity or as part of a social science research project, rather than as a human being.

Once he's obtained the Kid's trust, he'll try for friendship. He can't pay him for his trust and friendship, of course; that would corrupt the truthfulness of the subject's narrative. But when the Professor learns what the fellow needs—other than a safe, more or less permanent home and social respectability, both of which the Kid will probably never be allowed to possess again, if he even had them in the first place—he can offer him certain types of small help. Occasional transportation, the odd household item that the Professor and his wife would otherwise put into a yard sale, and possibly, if he needs a job, help finding one.

This could turn into a long-term project and could eventually produce important data and proposals for dealing with both sexual offenders and the problem of homelessness here and elsewhere. For the Professor, the stakes, like the opportunities, are high. He has tenure but wouldn't mind acquiring a Distinguished University Professorship. Or an offer from a Washington think tank.

Can I give you a hand with that?

The Kid turns and peers up at the huge man blocking the late-afternoon sun. *Yeah. Stop the fucking wind. You're big enough.*

The Professor chuckles. He's used to chuckling; it's his default form of laughter. He believes that overt, open-mouthed laughter makes him look too much like a jolly fat man; thus he tends not to laugh at all and rarely even smiles. If he must show pleasure or amusement or delight, he'd rather be seen as a chuckler, another stereotype, perhaps, but a slightly more serious one than that of the jolly fat man. He eases himself down to the ground and takes a position next to the Kid that effectively blocks the wind. The Kid tries again to light his stove and this time succeeds. The two sit there and watch the flame flare yellow and settle quickly back into a steadily purring blue blur.

Thanks.

You're welcome.

For several minutes they are silent until the Kid stands and visits his tent and returns with the carton of eggs, a gallon jug of water, and a blackened saucepan. He pours three inches of water into the pan and sets it on the stove and sits back down on the ground beside the Professor.

Fresh eggs, man. Organic.

Pretty thin pickings, I'd say. For a growing boy.

Yeah? You into hitting on me or something? You some kinda faggot?

The Professor chuckles. *Not in a million years, Kid.*

What's with them old-timey overalls, then? They look pretty faggoty to me, if you wanna know the truth. Especially on a guy built like you.

I just spent the day pretending I'm a carpenter building a house. It's a volunteer project, Habitat for Humanity.

What's that?

We build houses for poor people. Remember Jimmy Carter?

Yeah. Sort of. He was like the president way back.

Correct. The thirty-ninth president of the United States, and afterward he did volunteer work for Habitat for Humanity. Among other good things.

I s'pose he wore old-timey overalls too? And hippie sandals?

Not while he was president.

That's good.

So how do you like it here at Benbow's? Better than under the Causeway?

The water in the saucepan has come to a boil. With a spoon the Kid carefully places two eggs into the pan. He seems to consider the Professor's question for a moment. Finally he points to his electronic ankle bracelet and says, *I can't stay here, except for a coupla days at most.*

You can't? Why not? Benbow's is surely more than twenty-five hundred feet from a school or playground.

Yeah. But I don't think Benbow's is what it seems.

What is it, then? If it's not what it seems.

I dunno. It's sort of like a movie set maybe. That dude Trinidad Bob says among other things they shoot lots of commercials here but my parole officer says they're only pretending like it's some kind of funky island beach club with old guys hanging out making like they're fucked-up Vietnam vets or something. They're like wearing Vietnam vet costumes, she says. For TV and fashion magazines an' shit. Mostly models in bathing suits and underwear and other filmy items. A lot of the models are under eighteen. At least that's what my parole officer told me. I hadda let her know where I was living after I left the Causeway, and she checked in with Benbow, who ended up telling her they had a shoot scheduled this week for Gap Kids or something and there's gonna be lots of little kids running around posing for the cameras in bathing suits and underwear. Besides, Benbow's sort of paranoid about having me camped out here in the first place. Me and people like Paco, we attract attention from cops an' shit. There's probably a certain amount of illicit substances being circulated, if you know what I mean. Due to the fashion industry being here so much. And who knows what the fuck they really photograph and film out here? Other than Gap and magazine fashion ads.

Who's Paco?

A biker dude from under the Causeway. Friend of mine. He came out here when I did.

We just met. I think he suspects I'm an undercover cop.

Paco's like a part-time mechanic at a biker garage up in North Calusa. He's got a job at least. Unlike me. But Benbow's not cool with him being a permanent resident. He told me he's gonna move back under the Causeway tomorrow. I guess I will too.

But why?

No place else to go, man. Same as with Paco. Same as with everybody who was living there. They're all gonna come drifting back to the Causeway eventually. Too bad. I kinda like the view here. The sewer factory stinks when the wind's offshore, but that's only about half the time. Plus I was hoping maybe I could get Benbow to hire me to help smoke the fish when it comes in and sell it to people or tend bar or something. Or just keep the place cleaned or painting it. I'm good at that. But he doesn't want it cleaned or painted. They need it looking fucked-up and funky. For the cameras. I guess it turns people on. The desert island fantasy.

I rather doubt he'd hire you to help sell the smoked fish. But maybe he could use you to tend bar.

All he needs for that is the other dude, Trinidad Bob. Trinidad Bob's part of the act. Like he's a prop. Even the old dog out there is a prop. And the parrot. You see the parrot in the cage by the bar?

I did.

The whole fucking island's like a movie set. Probably the whole city of Calusa is. Maybe we're all only props, like Trinidad Bob and that old broken-down dog and the parrot. You kinda look like a prop, y' know. Like one of those TV wrestlers from WWF. You could be Professor Humungous Haystack.

Very funny. But won't the police just come back to the Causeway and throw you out again?

Yeah. Prob'ly.

Where will you go then?

I'm starting to think three hots and a cot.

What do you mean?

Jail, man. Get myself busted for shoplifting a six-pack from a 7-Eleven.

You can't mean that!

No money, no job, no legal squat. You got any better ideas, Humungous?

The Kid reminds the Professor of Huckleberry Finn somehow. Here he is now, long after he lit out for the Territory, grown older and as deep into the Territory as you can go, camped out alone where the continent and all the rivers meet the sea and there's no farther place he can run to. The Professor wants to know what happened to that ignorant, abused, honest American boy between the end of the book and now. After he ran from Aunt Sally and her "sivilizin'," how did he come years later to having "no money, no job, no legal squat"? In twenty-first-century America.

How old are you, Kid?

Twenty-two. Why?

Just wondering. How long have you been living like this?

Like what?

Well, under the Causeway. And now here. Homeless. And on permanent parole, so to speak.

Little over a year. Since I did my time. And I'm not on permanent parole. Just ten years. Nine to go.

How much actual time did you do?

Three months up in Hastings. Minimum security. I got three months off for good behavior, though. Or it would've been six months.

You want to tell me what you were convicted of?

No, not especially. Anyhow, you can look it up.

Not if I don't know your real name.

No shit.

So do you want to tell me your real name?

What is this, a fucking quiz show?

The Professor chuckles. Quiz shows seem to be on everyone's mind today. The coincidence amuses him and the irony comforts him: quizzes, tests, exams of all kinds are his specialty and have been since he was a schoolboy answering every question correctly on every test from kindergarten through graduate school; going off the charts on IQ tests, pulling perfect scores on his SATs and GREs; and even after graduate school rising through the ranks and becoming the highest nationally rated Mensa member before he was thirty years old. More recently he has moved beyond Mensa to the even more exclusive Prometheus Society, which requires applicants to take the Langdon Adult Intelligence Test, a test specifically designed to winnow qualified membership down to the one-per-million level, compared to Mensa's paltry one-per-thirty-thousand. The Professor likes tests. It would be more accurate to say that he likes questions, questions with answers that nearly no one other than the Professor can answer. One person in a million.

It shouldn't be difficult to answer the question of the Kid's real name. No need to sit around waiting for the Kid to volunteer it. All he has to do is Google his way onto the National Sex Offender Registry, click *find offenders,* then *search by location*, and type in *Calusa*. A map will pop up pocked with little colored boxes, each box representing the location of a convicted sex offender, color-coded red, yellow, blue, and green to indicate the nature of the offense. Red is for offenses against children; yellow is for rape; blue is for sexual battery; and green is for "other offenses," which is everything from "second-degree sodomy" and "second-degree sexual abuse" to "lewd and lascivious behavior." That's probably the Kid's color, given the relatively short length of his sentence.

Blank boxes indicate the location of a school or playground. For a city the size of Calusa there would be thousands of blank squares and hundreds of green squares on the map, and it would take a while, unless he were lucky, for the Professor to click randomly onto the Kid's box, and suddenly there on the screen he'd see a mug shot of the Kid, with his real name beneath it, a descriptive history of his convictions, his age at the time of the offense and the age of his victim, last known address, employer's address, his race, height, weight, eye color, date of birth, and markings. Everything the Professor needs to know in order to start finding out what he wants to know.

It would be more pleasing to him, however, if he could pop the Kid's real name into the conversation unaided. Relying on the National Sex Offender Registry feels a little like cheating, not that different from his students' reliance on Wikipedia and other search engines to research their papers. It's not exactly plagiarism, especially if they acknowledge the source, which they seldom do, but it is lazy and topic specific, so the students rarely learn anything beyond the narrow subject they've typed into the subject line. And what they do learn about the subject is no more reliable or authoritative or detailed than what the little colored squares reveal about the Kid's offense. Yes, his mug shot may come up from under a green box, and maybe he will turn out to have been convicted on a certain date of "second-degree sexual abuse" against an unnamed victim who was eleven years old at the time, let's say. But was the victim a girl or a boy? Was he or she a family member, a friend, an acquaintance, or a stranger? What exactly did he do to that little girl or boy? Was it a first offense? Was he alone? And why did he do it?

From his past study of the sexual offender laws of his home state of Alabama, he remembers that a person commits "sexual abuse in the second degree" (1) if he subjects another person to sexual contact who is incapable of consent by reason of some factor other than being less than sixteen years old; or (2) if he, being nineteen years old or older, subjects another person to sexual contact who is less than sixteen years old, but more than twelve years old. The Professor also remembers that in Alabama sexual abuse in the second degree is a Class A misdemeanor, unless that person commits a second or subsequent offense of sexual abuse in the second degree within one year of another sexual offense, in which case the offense is a Class C felony. Calusa's not in the state of Alabama, but the Professor believes the definition is boilerplate for most southern states. He can check it easily enough. The Professor calls to mind the Internet address of the statute: Code of Alabama/1975/13A-6-67. Acts 1977, No. 607, p. 812, §2321; Act 2000-728, p. 1566, §1.

"Kid" is an alias, I take it.

You could say that.

Is it a first name or a last?

Both.

Sort of like Kydd's Cut, then.

What d' you mean?

The deep-water channel out there running between the Barriers and Anaconda Key. Kydd's Cut. It leads from the Bay out to the ocean.

News to me.

Supposedly, the famous pirate Captain Kydd used it when he was prowling the Spanish Main and Calusa was his base of operations. All the other channels between the ocean and the low mangrove islands that were filled in and are now called the Barriers were too shallow for a ship to enter. The only way in or out of the Bay was through that one channel, which Kydd could easily defend with the cannon emplacements that he located here on Anaconda Key and over there by the high-rises on what's now called Bougainvillea Shores.

No shit. The Kid has finished his eggs. He lights a cigarette and extends the pack to the Professor. *Smoke?*

No, thanks.

Quit?

Never smoked cigarettes.

Yeah, well, I'm in the process of quitting myself. Tell me more about this Captain Kydd dude, the pirate. How'd he spell it? Like, was it K-I-D, or what?

Variously, as K-Y-D-D and K-I-D-D. A few documents have it as K-I-D-D-E. He was Scottish, born around 1645, a commoner who ran away to sea at a young age. He was executed in London by the British crown in 1701. Actually, he was executed twice. The rope broke the first time, and they had to do it over. Then, as a warning to would-be pirates, they locked his body in an iron cage and hung it from a pole over the Thames River to rot. It hung there for twenty years until it finally disintegrated and the remaining parts fell into the river.

That's hard, man. The fucking Brits. They're fucking hard.

He left among his papers a piece of a coded map of the island where he buried his treasure, but no one's been able to figure out where the island is located. Some think it was off Long Island, others say it's Oak Island in Nova Scotia. There's even a possibility he buried his loot on an island off the coast of Vietnam, where he sailed late in his career. On his map the body of water that surrounds the island is called the China Sea, which most people take to be code for Long Island Sound or the Bay of Fundy. But some of us believe it may refer to the actual China Sea, Nan Hai. Which would suggest the island of Cu Loo

Hon or possibly Hon Tre, off the coast of Vietnam. I got a little bit involved with that myself back in the early 1980s.

No shit? Have you seen the actual map? Does it have like, "X marks the spot"?

I've seen the map. There is indeed an X. But no scale, so you can't tell if it's a big island or a small one. The truth is, Captain Kydd's treasure could be buried in any one of hundreds of islands from the Bay of Fundy to the waters west of Madagascar. It could even be buried right here on Anaconda Key.

Now you're shitting me, Professor.

No, I'm not. Kydd's map fits nicely over the topography of Calusa Bay and Anaconda Key as they existed in the middle of the seventeenth century, when no one was living here, other than the Calusa Indians and the last of the Panzacolas. From time to time Captain Kydd and his men came ashore for fresh water and to trade for food with the Indians, heal their battle wounds, and repair their ship. Every now and then an old coin or shoe buckle or bullet shows up at a construction site, confirming the presence of Europeans here long before there was anything like a permanent settlement in this part of the state, which didn't happen till the mid-nineteenth century, as you know.

I didn't know. I thought Calusa was always American. I mean, except for when the Indians were here. Before Columbus an' shit. I thought the Europeans only started coming here recently. You know, like tourists and models and movie stars and wannabes. For drugs and sex an' shit and to make commercials and movies and TV shows. Those are the only Europeans I know about. Except for us Americans and black people, the ones who are also Americans, I mean, I thought everyone else in Calusa was from places like Cuba and Nicaragua and the Caribbean islands like Haiti and Jamaica.

No, before the Americans there were Europeans here. And Captain Kydd, who was from Scotland, was one of them.

Cool. So what was Captain Kydd's first name?

William. They called him Billy.

Billy? No shit? Billy Kydd? The original? Like Billy the Kid?

Well, no. He came later.

Oh. Yeah, sure. I knew that. The Kid looks out to sea with a dreamy, fearful half-smile on his face, like an adopted boy who's just been handed the name and address of his birth father. After a long silence in a voice barely above a whisper he says: *I hate the idea of going back to living under the Causeway, y'know. I like it here. It really is almost like a deserted island. Except for Benbow and them.*

You want me to speak to Benbow on your behalf?

There's still my parole officer. She calls herself my caseworker, but she's really just a glorified cop.

Maybe since you're so out of the way here, so far from schools and playgrounds and so on, she'll cut you a little slack.

I guess it can't hurt. Sure, go ahead and talk to Benbow. If I could stay out here on the Key, maybe I could sniff out ol' Captain Kydd's buried treasure. What d' you think?

The Professor rolls onto his side and placing both hands against the ground, shoves his huge body into a standing position. *I have a copy of Captain Kydd's map somewhere in my files. I'll get it to you. But first I'll have a chat with Mr. Benbow.*

That would be awesome, Haystack. You want a boiled egg? I got like nine more.

No, thanks. Not while I'm working. I'll eat at home. Very generous of you, though.

CHAPTER FOUR

I T'S DUSK, AND A HALF-MOON HAS RISEN IN the southwest and hangs like a silver locket over the Bay. An offshore wind riffles the palms and palmettos, flips the leaves of the live oaks onto their gray backsides, and blows the stink of the sewage treatment plant away from Anaconda Key, across the Bay in the direction of downtown Calusa. Shambling across the compound toward the bar, now lit with strings of blinking red and green Christmas tree lights, comes the Professor. At the bar the television has been turned off, and speakers hanging in the nearby trees and under the eaves of the half-dozen ramshackle buildings broadcast a skein of Jimmy Buffett tunes about getting high in Key West.

The unblinking gray parrot, a key part of the scene, studies the set from its cage. The poor old yellow dog lies in the sand by the bar, licking water from a bowl, completing the scene. Trinidad Bob is mixing a blender of margaritas for a man and two slender young women in miniskirts and silk T-shirts. The man is in his middle fifties and looks like Jimmy Buffett himself—shoulder-length curling white hair, evenly distributed tan, Hawaiian shirt, Bermuda shorts, flip-flops. One of the women jiggles her gold bracelets in time to the music; the other examines her purple fingernails. The man talks to them, but the music muffles his words. The Professor makes out *busted condom* and *equity*. Both women laugh. Trinidad

Bob fills three glasses from the blender and serves the man and his companions.

Out of long habit the Professor avoids taking a barstool and instead stands at the far end of the counter. He nods at Trinidad Bob and zips a thin smile at the others, which they return in kind. The lights of an arriving BMW flash over the bar, and from the car come two more men, younger than the Jimmy Buffett look-alike, more athletic and predatory, casting their gaze around the compound as if in search of potential prey. There are four or five cars in the parking area now, in addition to the Professor's van, the pickup truck, which probably belongs to Trinidad Bob, and the taxi, where Yvonne sits smoking in the passenger seat. She has the door wide open, a newspaper in her lap, her dress pulled up to advertise her long legs to anyone who happens to pass by. The two newcomers check her out, shrug, make a slow circle of the compound, and eventually approach the bar.

The Professor tells Trinidad Bob he'd like a beer, a Corona.

Bob places a frosted bottle in front of him and asks, *What can I get ya?*

The Professor says, *I see we're drinking from bottles now, instead of cans.*

What changes at Benbow's when it gets dark?

The Professor says, *The prices, too, I suppose.*

What else changes at Benbow's when it gets dark?

The Professor looks over the four men and two women at the bar and says, *Auditions.*

What's happenin'?

The Professor pulls a five-dollar bill from his wallet and pushes it across the counter. He asks Bob if Benbow's around. He'd like to have a private chat with him.

Trinidad Bob grabs the five and stuffs it into the cash register drawer. *No, you hafta give me an answer first, then I'm s'posed to come up with the right question.*

Oh, right. Try this one. "In the trailer."

Where's Boom-Boom Benbow?

You're tonight's winner. Congratulations. The Professor slides him another five and carries his beer across the sand to the trailer and knocks at the shut door. A few seconds later, the door opens to Boom–Boom Benbow, holding a long-stemmed balloon wineglass half-filled with red wine. He's heavily cologned, head freshly shaved, and wearing a crisp white guayabera shirt and tan slacks, tasseled black loafers. He looks like a small-time film producer with plans for a dinner meeting with potential financiers at a Dominican restaurant on the mainland. Or a man who runs a midlevel escort service. He takes a sip of wine and waits for the Professor to speak.

I'm interested in having the Kid stay out here in his tent for a while.

How interested?

Enough to pay his rent for him.

I expect you plan on coming out to visit him every now and then.

Correct.

This ain't exactly a whorehouse, you know. You can't keep your boy here.

I know. How much a week?

This is a place of business. The kid's a convicted sex offender. I don't want cops and social workers crawling all over the place. I already hadda talk to his caseworker or whatever the fuck she is.

I'll take care of the caseworker. The Kid will only be here for a while anyhow, until I find him proper housing and a job. Maybe you could put him to work a few hours a day a few days a week.

I don't need helpers. Unless you feel like paying his fucking salary too.

Depends. How much will you charge for his rent?

Let's say two hundred a week. Up front.

And his salary?

Ten bucks an hour for cannin' the empties and raking the place and whatever other janitorial duties I think up. Let's say two hours a day times six days a week. That's a hundred and twenty bucks a week. Three-twenty a week for the package.

Make it an even three hundred.

I still think you're a cop. Except it's usually me paying the cops, not vice versa.

I'll be back in the morning with the first three hundred. You needn't mention my involvement to the Kid. Let him think you're merely a warm-hearted benefactor taking pity on him.

Your call.

Thanks.

Stick around and party awhile, Professor. The night's young.

Can't. Got to get home to the wife and kids.

Yeah. Sure.

CHAPTER FIVE

THE PROFESSOR'S SEVEN-YEAR-OLD FRA-
ternal twins are named Rani and Biswas. His wife is named
Gloria, but from the day they met he has called her Glory.
She's his pride and glory, he tells her. She's small and conventionally
pretty and knows it's an indirect, self-deprecating reference, tinged
with irony, to his obesity, though she would never say it to him or
even to herself. She takes it as a compliment. When he is exasperated
by something she has done or said, attempting to soften irony with
affection, he lapses into his marshmallowy Alabama accent and calls
her Glory-Glory-Hallelujah! As in: *Glory-Glory-Hallelujah! Please
stop asking me so many questions about the distant past. Damn! Why do
y'all insist on hearing from me a narrative y'all can never personally evaluate
or corroborate?*

I'm not insisting. I'm just—

*I've said it before, I'll say it again. What folks cain't observe, folks cain't
measure at all. And what we observe, we disturb by observing and thus cain't
measure accurately. The only reliable information about our lives that's available to us comes to us indirectly via algorithms based upon data generated by
our bodies' auto-response systems. The rest, Glory-Glory-Hallelujah, the rest
ain't nothin' but fantasy and fear, darlin', nothin' but self-serving delusion
and illusion.*

Oh, please!

Life is a dream, m' dear. It ain't that y'all don't need to know my distant past. It's that y'all cain't know it. No one can. Not even me. It's why they call it the past, m' dear. It's more like the future than it is the present. And y'all never think to ask me about the future, do you now?

It's not your "distant past" I'm asking about, for God's sake. And I don't need another lecture about your philosophy of life. All I want to know is where you've been so late.

She expected him home in time to drive the twins to their flute lesson at 5 P.M., so she could prepare dinner for them and they could eat together as a family, and here it is nearly eight and he has missed dinner altogether, and the kids and she once again have found themselves eating alone in front of the TV.

Gloria is a librarian employed at a branch of the Calusa County library system out on the Barriers and is the reason why the Professor has ended up serving on the library board of directors: her descriptions at home of her working conditions and the overall incompetence of her colleagues and superiors convinced him that the entire library system was woefully mismanaged by the cadre of elderly civic do-gooders who sat on the board. There's not a professional book person, educator, or scientist among them, he noted. The Professor, although a social scientist, rather than a so-called natural or theoretical scientist, was all three. He put his name on the ballot, sent out e-mails to the membership listing his qualifications, and was promptly elected by an overwhelming majority.

Of the four candidates running for the position, one of whom was the eighty-seven-year-old incumbent, the Professor's résumé was easily the most impressive. Included among his many qualifications were his *summa cum laude* (Phi Beta Kappa) bachelor's degree from Kenyon College and his master's degree in American studies and doctorate in sociology from Yale, his membership in Mensa and the Prometheus Society, his many professional publications and the several anthologies of monographic studies of homelessness that he has edited, his rank of senior tenured professor at Calusa State University, his position as deacon for the First Congregational Church of Calusa, and his volunteer work for Habitat for Humanity.

Which is pretty much everything his wife Gloria knows about him too—at least all she knows about his near and distant past. That plus the few additional bits and pieces of what he calls data that he's conveyed to her in a seemingly casual way during their courtship and the nearly nine years they've been married: that he is an only child, and his father worked as an accountant for U. S. Steel in Alabama; that both parents were killed in an automobile crash when he was in his early twenties off doing fieldwork in Lima, Peru, and he has no other living family members that he's close to; that he traveled widely for many years doing independent research for private foundations in Asia, Central and South America, and the Caribbean, before settling down to academic life in his middle forties here in Calusa; that he was never previously married nor, as far as he knew, has he fathered any children other than Rani and Biswas (a datum offered in a jocular fashion that implies a possibly hedonistic period in his youth).

The reason I'm late, then. The usual reason. Research. I've befriended a young homeless man who's one of those sex offenders I told you about who are living under the Claybourne Causeway. I was arranging to interview the fellow. He's naturally suspicious and needs to be courted a little first. He's camped out on Anaconda Key for now. I went there after finishing my Saturday stint for Habitat.

You might have called me.

Would you have done anything differently if I had?

No. But I wouldn't have worried.

Did you worry?

No.

Well, there you are, then.

He heads for the restaurant-size refrigerator that they purchased the first week of their marriage, when they realized they'd be sharing food storage, pulls open the door and scans the gleaming contents. Dozens of topped-off plastic, paper, and cardboard containers of ready-to-eat food—potato salad, macaroni and cheese, beef stew, lamb stew, curried chicken, fried chicken, pork dumplings, chicken pot pies, half a ham, chunks of cheese, egg salad, tuna salad, sliced meats, marinated tuna steaks, mashed squash, creamed spinach, meat loaf, Cuban, Chinese, and Indian takeout, Dominican meat patties and Mexican fajitas, and much, much more—all prepared over the last few days by Gloria or, as instructed and listed by the Professor, purchased at the Watson New York Deli or delivered to the house by the nearby ethnic restaurants, everything ready to be eaten cold or else easily heated in the microwave. In addition, stored for his eventual delectation, there's plenty of backup in the freezer—loaves of bread, cakes, ice cream, custard pies, pizzas and chicken fingers, french fries, onion rings, waffles, and more. He also has a standing order with his wife to keep at the ready a gallon jug of sweetened iced tea and two unopened liters of Diet Coke and a gallon of milk.

The Professor likes to eat standing up at the kitchen counter, alone, unseen, without his intake being observed, quantified, and judged, and he arranges to do so at least four times a week and would do it every night, if Gloria did not complain that he should spend more time with his children, since the kids' bedtime is eight-thirty and they can only be together as a family when they all sit down to dinner. So three and sometimes four times a week, he manages to arrive home from the university by 6 P.M. where he presides over the evening meal—eating restaurant-size portions only, nothing excessive—and afterward conducts a brief interrogation of his children as to the particulars of their schoolwork and extracurricular activities and a television program or two that he personally selects and oversees.

Later, long after the twins have been sent to bed and Gloria, a fan of crime and forensic dramas, has retired to their bedroom to watch television alone, he slips into the kitchen again and again, long into the night, and frequently even after he has gone to bed himself the

Professor rises, wraps his body in his bathrobe and strolls through the darkened house, as if he is merely restless, unable to sleep, ending his walk at the kitchen, there to swing open the wide refrigerator door and in the cold light spread onto a platter slabs of meat loaf, piles of potato salad and various vegetables, meat patties, ice cream bars, and so on, an entire multicourse meal, which he proceeds for the next half hour or more to serve himself, chewing and swallowing and cutting off another slice and chewing and swallowing that and spooning another clump and chewing and swallowing that, until the ache in his cells has faded, and he can wash his plate and utensils and pack up the tubs, boxes, and plastic containers, switch off the kitchen light, and return to his study and resume reading or, as dawn approaches, slip back under the covers of his queen-size bed that stands next to his wife's narrow twin bed and for another hour or two, while his stomach and intestines, injecting the undigested food with enzymes and chemicals, contract and expand and extrude, and his involuntary organs, his kidneys, liver, pancreas, and colon, like miners deep in the dark of the earth, do their mindless slow work, and he falls back to sleep. He sleeps soundly until the work in the dark recesses of his bowels is complete, and then the ache in his cells gradually returns and wakes him again, and it's time to return to the kitchen again, before Gloria and the kids wake.

His outer body, its enormous size and shape and its social and physical liabilities, is a significant, unavoidable part of the Professor's public life, seen and in his absence commented on by all. For this reason, he avoids mirrors and cameras and reflecting glass windows and doors. His inner body and its needs, however, are his secret life, which by and large he keeps locked away, even from himself. No one comments on his inner life; no one even observes it: not his colleagues nor students nor any of his friends and acquaintances; not his wife anymore nor his children, for whom their papa's inner life is a threatening, demanding, impossible-to-please-or-penetrate mystery. No one. Since childhood, the only treatment for the Professor's sickness that he has been able to imagine is more of the sickness itself. Like a drug addict, he has compartmentalized his life, not simply in order to remain an addict, but so that he can continue to treat his addiction with more of what he's addicted to without contaminating any other part of his life, public or private, outer or inner.

He has not proven to be a particularly adept participant in any of the forms of therapy or the various self-help and twelve-step programs designed to treat his addiction. All his life he has believed that he is the most intelligent person in the room, and—if you measure intelligence by IQ and memory—he has been for the most part correct. He talks, but rarely listens. And then he leaves the room. At the urging of Gloria, he agreed after the second year of their marriage to attend weekly group sessions with a psychotherapist who specialized in treating eating disorders like bulimia and anorexia and on occasion simple overeating. Judgmental terms like *glutton, self-indulgent,* and *vain* were forbidden. Everyone in the group pointed accusing fingers at parents, especially mothers. Even so, it went nowhere. At least for him. After a half-dozen meetings with the group, which was made up of four adolescent girls, who, he believed, were obsessed with media celebrity, like most American adolescents, and two perpetually dieting, slightly overweight middle-aged women, women who he felt were indeed gluttonous, self-indulgent, and vain, he announced to the group and the therapist, *There is no apparent conflict between my "body image" and my perfectionism. And my parents had nothing to do with shaping either. In fact, I find the former, "body image," an essentially meaningless construct, and the latter, "perfectionism," a virtue worthy of cultivation, an aspect of my character and personality that I actually admire and take credit for having instilled in myself and for which I therefore blame no one. But there's no polarity between the two, my "body image" and my perfectionism. Only a distinction without a difference. I therefore bid you a fond and respectful good-bye.*

After that—again to satisfy Gloria, who was still trying to ignore the dietary needs of her husband's inner body, his appetite, the way early in their courtship she had learned to ignore the visible size and shape of his outer body—the Professor agreed to attend meetings of Overeaters Anonymous, a twelve-step program based on Alcoholics Anonymous. But he never got to the first step. He didn't even get beyond the threshold. Meetings were held in a basement room at the Watson Unitarian Church, and the room turned out to be filled with fat people. He left immediately after the group recited the pledge to change what they could change and accept and give over to a higher power what they could not change. *Those people offend my eye and dull my mind, especially in such numbers,* he explained to Gloria. *It's like being in a room full of remorseful self-mutilating amputees. I am not an aesthete, but there is an aesthetic aspect of the human body which, seen whole, pleases my eye and relaxes, even as it sharpens, my mind.*

You can get over that. Can't you get over that?

Why should I?

Dear, it's a prejudice. A prejudice against fat people.

Au contraire. It's a delight in the observable beauty of the human body. How can I be prejudiced against fat people when I am one myself? No, it's about my aesthetic life, my appreciation of the visible beauty of the human body and the sensual pleasure I take from it. Male or female, it doesn't matter. Y'all wouldn't have me give that up, now, would y'all? Just watching y'all undress, for instance, thrills me more and with greater complexity today than it ever did in the past.

No, dear, I wouldn't want you to give that up. As long as it's me you're looking at, and not some other woman taking off her clothes.

Glory-Glory-Hallelujah. There ain't no other woman I'd rather see naked than y'all.

You smooth talker, you.

The Professor is not merely flattering her. He does indeed like looking at her when she is naked. Several times a month, wearing only his size XXXL terry cloth bathrobe, he sits across from her in their bedroom in his forest green leather Barcalounger, and she takes off her clothes, slowly, article by article, and then poses on her narrow bed, as if modeling for an artist, while he masturbates. That's the nature and extent of their sexual activities. They did not have sex as such—normal intercourse—more than a few times before the twins were born and have attempted it only once since then. A failed attempt. But they did not marry for sex in the first place, nor was it ever an essential part of their relationship. Sexual intercourse, at least in the beginning, was merely a requirement, an obligation on both their parts determined mostly by convention and proximity and her wish to have a child, rather than by attraction or desire.

Gloria is shy, withdrawn, sexually naive and, because of it, insecure. She is the sort of conventionally pretty woman who disappears into the background of group photographs or fails to be properly introduced at social gatherings or office parties. She is a quietly competent person whose calm self-containment masks a resentful feeling of superiority, contradictory characteristics that make other women feel judged by her. Men detect that contradiction from halfway across the room, and alarmed by it back off to an even greater distance. All her adult life, therefore, until the Professor came along, Gloria was a very lonely woman.

The Professor was the first man who treated her as if he were sexually attracted to her. He was not. He was merely looking for a particular kind of wife. She was thirty-one years old at the time, and he had recently purchased a home in the suburb of Watson. He strolled into the branch of the Calusa library closest to his university office one morning before class ostensibly to examine its public programs and holdings, especially the reference section and Internet access and number of computer terminals, as a way of evaluating the educational level and interests of the community. *Public libraries are the sole community centers left in America,* he explained to her. *The degree to which a branch of the local library is connected to the larger culture is a reflection of the degree to which the community itself is connected to the larger culture.*

Gloria was attracted to the way the man spoke: complete sentences and organized, coherent paragraphs that were essentially pronouncements, beyond opinions or observations. The clarity and authority of his words and grammar made her stomach tighten and loosened the muscles in her legs. But not only his words and grammar drew her to him: it was also the way he spoke, his crisply articulated pronunciation smoothed and diluted by the remnants of a rural Alabama accent that every now and then in a slightly self-mocking way he brought into full use. She also liked the authority of his enormous body, the way it took up so much space in a room, her office, when he first presented himself. When the Professor stands in front of you, no one else in the room is visible: either your eye is drawn to his unusual girth and height, which he does little to disguise, or else he literally blocks everyone else out—even in a very large room, as Gloria discovered when she led him from her office to the reference section of the main hall. The scattered patrons and other library staff members turned toward them and stared at the bearded man walking beside her and saw no one else, especially not Gloria, the short, slender, bespectacled librarian. It was almost as if she had been absorbed by him, as if she had become huge too, four times her usual size, with all the authority and high visibility of a lone adult in a schoolyard surrounded by children.

Until this moment, she had not realized that all her life she had been waiting to feel exactly this. Large and central. As if spotlighted on a stage. It was an emotion without a name, not exactly orgasmic—as she showed the Professor their encyclopedias and dictionaries, English, Spanish, French, Haitian Creole, Mandarin, Russian, German, Italian, and Swahili, and their extensive collection of supplementary reference materials, technical and scientific dictionaries, atlases, medical dictionaries, thesauruses, dictionaries of slang, biography, history, and myth—but close.

You should be careful, hanging out with sex offenders. Especially homeless sex offenders. Don't you find them . . . creepy? Scary? Some of them are rapists, I heard. Child molesters.

Nothing they have done or will do offends or frightens me. I view them scientifically. Like lab specimens. They're less violent, at least toward other men, than the general population. Quite often they themselves have been the victims of violence, and almost all of them have been sexually abused as children. This young man I mentioned particularly interests me. He calls himself the Kid. He wouldn't tell me his real name, but I'm sure it's William Kid, spelled either K-Y-D-D-E or K-I-D-D-E. He's fairly bright and articulate, and he's nicely, realistically defiant, unlike most sex offenders, who are usually unintelligent and secretive, either from shame, which is understandable, or because they're hoping for an opportunity to commit their crime again in the future. They're unforthcoming, to say the least. And if they do speak of their offenses at all, they justify and rationalize them. They attack the interrogator and blame the victim. This fellow seems unusually honest. I think from him I'll get the straight story, the truth.

The truth? The truth about what? His crime?

No. The reasons for his crime.

There have to be all kinds of reasons why a person does . . . what they do. What they've done.

I don't think so, Glory-Glory-Hallelujah. It's why they often go back and recommit the crime again and again. It's why sex offenders are viewed as incurable.

Maybe they're just programmed to do what they do. You know, hardwired.

These men are human beings, not chimpanzees or gorillas. They belong to the same species as we do. And we're not hardwired to commit these acts. If, as it appears, the proportion of the male population who commit these acts has increased exponentially in recent years, and it's not simply because of the criminalization of the behavior and a consequent increase in the reportage of these crimes, then there's something in the wider culture itself that has changed in recent years, and these men are like the canary in the mine shaft, the first among us to respond to that change, as if their social and ethical immune systems, the controls over their behavior, have been somehow damaged or compromised. And if we don't identify the specific changes in our culture that are attacking our social and ethical immune systems, which we usually refer to as taboos, then before long we'll all succumb. We'll all become sex offenders, Gloria. Perhaps in a sense we already are.

Oh, please.

We cast them out, we treat them like pariahs, when in fact we should be studying them up close, sheltering them and protecting them from harm, as if indeed they were fellow human beings who have inexplicably reverted to being chimpanzees or gorillas, and whose genetic identity with us and their shared ancestry with us can teach us what we ourselves are capable of becoming if we don't reverse or alter the social elements that caused them to abandon a particularly useful set of sexual taboos in the first place.

This is a little boring, you know. And far-fetched. These people are sick. That's all. Sick. Are you coming to bed soon?

First I have to check the sex offender registry for Calusa and find out how to spell the Kid's real name.

You like him, don't you?

Personally? I don't really feel anything personal for him one way or the other. I suppose I admire him somewhat.

Admire him? He's a convicted sex offender!

He's plucky. And his defiance doesn't take the form of denial, like most of them.

"Plucky."

Go to bed, Gloria. Please.

CHAPTER SIX

THE PROFESSOR STANDS BESIDE HIS VAN IN the parking area at the edge of Benbow's and watches the Kid drag a large plastic bag across the sand between the buildings and in among the low bushes and trees and mangroves, stopping here and there to collect dropped and discarded empty beer cans and bottles. There's no one else in sight. The Kid stops for a moment by the bar and appears to be talking with the caged parrot—a short two-way conversation. He listens and talks. The parrot listens and talks. The Kid laughs, as if the parrot's told a parrot joke, waves good-bye to the bird, and moves on.

When the bag is filled to bulging, the Kid drags it to the tailgate of the red, rusted-out pickup truck parked next to the Professor's van, where he separates bottles from cans and tosses them into a pair of metal barrels placed in the bed of the truck. Though it's still early in the day, the sun is already pounding down and the air is thick as syrup. The Kid moves slowly. He knows how to work in the heat. He's wearing a T-shirt and cutoffs and sockless sneakers and a baseball cap. The Professor wears his usual dark three-piece vested suit, and though he stands in the shade of his van, sheets of sweat run down his entire body, soaking his underwear and socks. He wipes his face and neck with his handkerchief and folds and tucks it neatly back into the breast pocket of his suit coat.

The Kid, who until now has not acknowledged the Professor's presence, tosses a glance in his direction and looks away.

I see that you are now gainfully employed. Good.

Benbow told me the deal. Not clear who I'm working for, though. Him or you.

You're employed by Benbow. You answer to him. I'm merely the guarantor of your salary. He's your boss.

Whatever.

I brought you a few items.

Yeah? What?

Household items. For your campsite.

The Professor slides back the side door of his van and pulls out a cardboard box and sets it on the ground. The Kid walks up to the box. He purses his lips, crinkles his brow, and peers skeptically into it, as if wondering what this weird fat dude wants in return. It's got to be some kind of trick. What's the exchange rate here?

Early this morning before leaving for his office, the Professor raked through the kitchen cupboards, linen and cleaning closets, filling the box. Gloria asked him what he was doing, and he told her he was bringing a few things to the Kid. *Necessaries,* he called them. She said nothing in response, just stood with her back to the stove and watched in silence, wondering: What's the exchange rate here? What does her husband really want from this person?

The Kid reaches down and pokes through the contents: a cast iron skillet, a large pot, a spatula, a small wooden salad bowl and serving spoons, a set of old mismatched bath towels, laundry detergent, several bars of hand soap, a gallon-size thermos jug.

The Kid grunts. *I can't use this shit. I can't use any of this shit, man. I travel light.*

What could you use, then?

A Mercedes S-Class coupe. A condo twenty-five hundred feet in the air in a building where no children are allowed. That'd be enough, I guess. For a start.

No, seriously, Kid. You might be settled here for a while now.

I don't think so, man. Benbow didn't give me no guaranteed lease or anything. He could boot my ass outa here anytime he wants.

No, he can't. I arranged for you to stay.

There's still the problem with my parole officer, man. My caseworker, she calls herself. But she's a parole officer and she can pretty much ruin my life if she wants to. The part that isn't already ruined. Anyhow, she don't want me settling here. She didn't say it, but she wants me to go back to the Causeway. Did you bring the map? The treasure map?

It's in a file in my office at the university. I'll bring it next time. I'll speak with her. Your parole officer.

The Professor pulls out his cell phone and hands it to the Kid. He instructs the Kid to call the woman and tell her that someone wants to discuss the Kid's housing situation with her. *I'll take it from there.*

The Kid shrugs and punches in the caseworker's direct number, which after these many months of reporting in to her every week he has memorized. Her name, he tells the Professor, is Dahlia Freed. She's a black lady, he adds. *Cold. And hard. Goes by the friggin' manual.*

When Dahlia Freed picks up, the Kid in a flat, uninflected voice tells her that he has someone here who wants to speak with her about his housing situation. *The guy's some kind of professor. He'll explain,* he says and passes the phone to the Professor.

Benbow has stepped from his trailer and stands on the steps watching the Kid. Benbow pointedly looks at his watch, and the Kid immediately goes back to work picking up bottles and cans, leaving the Professor alone by his van to speak with Dahlia Freed.

He introduces himself to the woman and informs her that he is a professor of sociology at Calusa State University.

She is not impressed. She sounds bored and skeptical. *Okay, so what's the purpose of your call?* She has a Brooklyn or Queens accent. Queens, he decides. She was probably a New York City cop before coming to Calusa. Half the Calusa police force are ex-cops from northern cities. Snowbirds with badges and guns.

The Professor explains that he's doing field research for a paper on convicted sex offenders and the causes of their high rate of homelessness and low rate of recidivism. He wants to interview young Mr. Kydd, who has agreed to talk with him about his present situation and his personal history. He invites Ms. Freed to verify his academic credentials and the seriousness of his project by checking the faculty listings on the university's website or by looking him up on google .com, where he has many listings. She can visit his personal website as well. *You will find that I am a legitimate researcher and social scientist and have published numerous monographs and studies on the subject of homelessness. I'm now trying to expand my research into the lives of convicted sex offenders who happen also to be homeless. A subject I'm sure you're more than familiar with.*

So why call me? You want to interview him, go ahead and do it. You don't need my permission.

He explains that it would be helpful to him if Mr. Kydd could remain in residence here at Benbow's while he's being interviewed, since he's already encamped here and has even arranged to be employed by Mr. Benbow. *Otherwise it may be very difficult for me to track him down again and interview him in an ongoing way for the length of time required by my project. I need to meet with him many times over several months in order to test the veracity of what he tells me.*

Yeah, yeah.

This is very important work I'm doing, Ms. Freed. Someday it may turn out to be helpful to you in your line of work as well. In fact, I might want to interview you yourself. I'm sure your perspective would be helpful. I would give you proper credit in print, of course. Which might be useful to you down the line. With your department head, when you seek promotion.

She barks a laugh. *Maybe. Maybe not. But I don't like him living at that place. Benbow's. It's got a reputation. Supposedly they do all kinds of fashion shoots there. Fashionistas. It's like a whaddaya call it, a location. But even if that's all they do there, it's still clothes coming off and on, cameras rolling, lights, et cetera. It's only a step or two removed from the porn industry.*

Which is something I heard they've done over there in the past anyhow, make porn films, and are probably doing it still. So-called adult films. It's not illegal, although you ask me it oughta be illegal. Besides, Benbow's is a known hangout for upscale junkies. Which means there's dealers present—we're talking coke mainly and smack. Lots of soft money moving around. And where there's upscale drugs being bought and sold, Professor, there's pretty little sex workers standing on the sidelines looking for work, male and female. And some of them are underage. He's gonna get caught up in that, one way or the other. At one end of the trade or the other.

The Professor decides to deal with her as if she were the worried parent of a teenage son, not a parole officer. He tells her that he understands her concerns, and he sympathizes. He's willing to help her by checking in on the Kid daily and reporting to her afterward, either directly by phone or, if she prefers to have a written record of his visits, by e-mail. The Kid, of course, would continue to check in with her on his own once a week as required. His camp is not really at Benbow's anyhow, he points out. He's pitched his tent in an isolated spot outside the area where people gather, on a piece of property owned by Benbow, close to the Bay. His job is as a maintenance man, a part-time day job, so he's not around the place at night. And as for the filming, there seems to be no evidence of it at present, and he, the Professor, would be sure to keep the Kid away from the scene if a crew and actors showed up and started to make an adult film. He certainly wouldn't want the Kid mixed up in any of that!

He's thinking, however, that maybe it would be interesting to interview some of the actors—a separate research project—and find out how they came to this line of work, how the males manage to keep their erections for so long, and do the females have actual orgasms or do they fake it? Do the actors take sexual pleasure from their work? Do the directors and the crew get turned on while filming? Or is it all, for everyone concerned, purely and simply *work?* Skilled labor. The manufacture of a product. Do they take pride in their product? Do they in a Marxist sense identify with it?

He's in no sense an expert, but he's seen plenty of porn films in his time—who hasn't? Anyone who's spent a night in a hotel or motel room has seen a porn film. Anyone with a computer and an Internet connection has watched clips from porn films. He's seen enough of them both ways, films and Internet clips, to find pornography too boring to watch anymore, even when he has an itch to masturbate and is alone. But he's never seen one being made, has never seen a porn film *live,* as it were. Never been in the audience for a live sex show. At least not in America, and suddenly for the first time in years the Professor is remembering live sex shows in Thailand and Malaysia. He recalls being a member of an audience, being pressured by the audience, all men, mostly Europeans and Americans, to become aroused by the coupling taking place on the stage. The members of the audience nudged one another with their elbows, laughed and cheered, whistled and stomped, then settled into rapt silence, their hands buried in their trousers. No matter how odd or bizarre—male performers with grotesquely large penises, racial mixes, dwarves, huge multicolored dildos, chains, whips and rubber suits, twins, once even a set of triplets—it didn't work for him. His fly stayed zipped, his cock remained stubbornly flaccid, buried beneath rolls of belly fat. Somehow the pressure he felt from the other men in the audience interfered with his ability to respond sexually to the show. He grew quickly bored, then detached, and finally analytical. He ended up considering the cruelly exploitive politics of the event. Another instance of late capitalist imperialism.

It would be a lot more interesting, possibly a lot more arousing, he thinks, to watch a porn film being *made,* to be on the actual set, close enough to the actors to see their sweating faces and the women's breasts and nipples and their vaginas and anuses and the men's huge thrusting penises, and to know that everything, the sucking, licking, squirming, jamming, and ramming, is being done, not for the sexual stimulation of the director and crew or for the other performers, but for the camera. For an audience that's not present and is not situated *in* the present, either, but is instead located somewhere out there in the future, unknown and alone in a darkened motel room or at home in front of a computer screen, invisible to the performers and to the people observing and filming them live in real time. For pay. For money fed to the computer or the TV pay-per-view cable company by credit card number.

The parole officer, Dahlia Freed, says, *Okay, I'll give it a shot. Only temporary, though. I gotta check out the situation in person first.*

When? I'd like to be here and introduce myself.

I don't give advance notice when I make my visits. And you've already introduced yourself, thanks.

Well, perhaps I'll come by your office.

Call ahead.

I will.

CHAPTER SEVEN

K: *So you're back. And lugging another gift box, I see. Whaddaya got for me this time, Haystack? No more household goods, I hope.*

P: *I think you'll find these items somewhat more useful. Sorry I misread your needs this morning. Here we have a Swiss Army knife. Many blades, nine by my count. Very handy, given your circumstances. And this terrific little radio. Doesn't need batteries. You just crank the handle and it charges the radio for eight hours' playing time.*

K: *Cool.*

P: *And a portable telescope. To help while away the time while you're sitting here by your tent.*

K: *I ain't a peeper, y' know.*

P: *Yes, I know. But you could watch the cruise ships come and go and the birds and keep track of cars and check out the visitors arriving at Benbow's from right here by your tent. You could watch the stars at night.*

K: *What're you, like the white explorer bringing high-tech presents to the low-tech Indians?*

P: *(laughs) Something like that.*

K: *What's the Indian supposed to do in return? Carry all your shit on his back into the jungle?*

P: *Just talk into the little black box for an hour or so every few days.*

K: *It don't look like no recorder. Is it running? I thought you was just gonna use a tape recorder.*

P: *It's a digital camera. A minicamera. Very useful for making both a visual and aural record of interviews. In my field visual cues are as telling as linguistic cues. I'll just set it on its little tripod here in the sand . . . and we can forget about it. It's miked, of course. It has a very good microphone. We can speak normally and just forget it's there.*

K: *You can forget about it maybe. Not me though. It's a fucking camera. I don't mind recorders but cameras make me nervous, man. Surveillance cameras, hidden cameras, cameras you don't know are watching. And cameras you forget are there. Especially them. Is it running?*

P: *It's running. Okay, where do you want to start?*

K: *No, where do you want to start? You ask the first question. Then I'll like decide if I want to answer it. I'm only doing this because I guess I owe you. Like for talking with Dahlia this morning and cutting the deal with Benbow and all. And bringing me the knife and radio and shit. But that don't mean I hafta tell you shit I don't feel like telling you. Right? You're not interrogating me, you're interviewing me. There's a difference, man. You're not a cop, you're a professor. Correct?*

P: *Correct. This is an interview, not an interrogation. So let's begin by talking about your family. Everything starts there, doesn't it? Tell me about them. Your mother, your father, and so on. Your siblings.*

K: *My family. That's a joke. Siblings, that's like brothers and sisters, correct?*

P: *Correct.*

K: *Okay. No siblings.*

P: *An only child then. Everyone has a mother and a father, however. At least in the beginning they do. Tell me about your parents.*

K: *Sure. I have a mother. No father though. I mean my mother raised me, not my father. Like there was someone who "fathered" me, but nobody who was my father. My moms, she's the one who gave birth to me and you could say she took care of me, at least till I was a teenager and was more or less on my own. She's alive and I guess well and lives right here in Calusa. She's out in the north end in a house she owns where I used to live and where she has a job as a beautician that she's had since Day One. My moms is okay. At least I assume she's okay. I haven't seen her in a while.*

P: *How long is that?*

K: *Not since I got convicted and sent up. About two years now, I guess.*

P: *Does she know you were living under the Causeway?*

K: *No. Unless she figured it out on her own when it got into the newspapers and such. Though the papers never used my name or singled me out. She's not much for newspapers anyhow. I know she didn't learn it from me. Not that she'd give a shit. Which I can understand.*

P: *I'll come back to that. What about your father?*

K: *Yeah, right, what about him? My so-called father took off as soon as he knocked up my mother. They should have a different word than "father" for someone who just happened to fuck your mother and she got pregnant from it. To me he's not even got a name. They were never married or anything. That's why my last name's the same as my mother's. He was from up north and went back there supposedly where he probably already had a wife and kids. He was like a roofer or something. Even my mother doesn't know much about him. One of those northern guys with a pickup and a set of tools who shows up for work after the hurricanes. They fuck all the women and girls for a few months, spend a lot of government and insurance money on booze and drugs and then disappear back north till the next hurricane. My mother's a sucker for those guys. Especially the black dudes. She likes only black dudes with northern accents though. The same with Latinos. Like Puerto Ricans from New York. That's what she says anyhow. Maybe she thinks inside they're really northern white guys, only outside they're these sexy dark types, if you know what I mean. It's sort of racist but she doesn't have a clue. She thinks it's liberal and all. My mother's okay but kind of a dim bulb.*

P: *Was your father black?*

K: *You shittin' me?*

P: *Latino?*

K: *Look at me, for chrissake.*

P: *How old is she? Your mother.*

K: *I dunno. Maybe in her late forties.*

P: *How old are you? The registry says you're twenty-two.*

K: *Registry?*

P: *The National Sex Offender Registry. I looked you up online this morning.*

K: *Oh yeah. So you know everything worth knowing about me already. Why bother interviewing me then?*

P: *To learn what the registry leaves out. And to let you tell your story yourself. Like about your mother. Tell me more about her. And about your childhood. Would you say you had a happy childhood?*

K: *C'mon, man, what's a happy childhood? Anybody says he had a happy childhood is bullshitting. But mine was okay I guess. At least nobody beat on me and I didn't starve and I always had a roof over my head, thanks to my mother, which are things she always likes to remind me of. Until I enlisted in the army anyhow. Although afterward when I got out she let me have my old room back. So I can't complain about my childhood. Or my mother. Not really.*

P: *You were in the army?*

K: *Yeah. For a while. I signed up when I was twenty right after I lost my job at this light store which closed on account of the guy that owned it got killed in a robbery. It happened on my day off, so for a while there the cops thought I was involved and almost busted me for it, but I had an alibi. My mother. Another thing she did for me and won't let me forget. She said I was home with her all day. Which was basically true, since I really was home all day, only not with her, because she was at the beach working on her tan with her boyfriend of the moment. That's okay. I was home alone with my friend Iggy but he's an iguana and couldn't testify. Or he was an iguana. He's dead now.*

P: *I'm sorry. You were in the army? For how long? Did you get sent to Iraq or Afghanistan?*

K: *I really wanted to. Yeah, Afghanistan, man. I was jonesing for Afghanistan. But no. I only got as far as basic training at Fort Drum in New York State which is way the fuck up by the Canadian border in the middle of winter, man. Freeze your ass off up there. Not exactly good preparation for desert warfare. Except you get really buff in basic, plus you learn how to use your weapon and shit.*

P: *You didn't complete basic training?*

K: *You could say I got discharged early. Not a dishonorable though. I got what they call a general discharge. So I never made it to Afghanistan. Pissed me off. I think I would've done good there, kicked some serious Arab ass. I could like kill people with my bare hands, man. They teach you that in basic.*

P: *Why were you discharged early?*

K: (long pause) *Porn. Distributing pornography, they said.*

P: *Pornography! What type of pornography? You mean children?*

K: *No, no! Just the usual kind. Videos. Triple and quadruple X. Your basic hard-core. I wasn't really distributing them anyhow. I was only giving them away free to my buddies. Some DVDs I bought and paid for myself. It's a long stupid story. You don't wanna hear it.*

P: *I do want to hear it. Tell me.*

K: *Well, like I said, I was stationed up at Fort Drum which is only about an hour's drive from the Canadian border, and over there in Ottawa on the French side of the river there's a lot of strip clubs and such, and I overheard some of the guys in my outfit saying that this actress who's my favorite porn star was appearing in a place called Lucky Pierre's. Her name's Willow. Just Willow. Which is cool. No last name. I mean she has a last name but she doesn't use it in her profession. And she's really special. At least to me. Not like your regular suck-'n'-fuck porn actresses with tats on their butts and clit rings and nipple rings and shaved pussies and who all they do is moan and groan and squeal and can't act for shit. Willow's different.*

P: *How do you mean, "different"?*

K: *I dunno. Most guys don't really get off on her. Her Internet videos only get one or two, sometimes two and a half stars instead of five and not many hits compared to Cassidey Rae say or Brianna Banks or Hannah Hilton who look like they've had these huge breast implants installed and get thousands of hits. Maybe not Cassidey Rae. Her tits are pretty normal-looking. But Willow's tits are kind of small. Like plums. With these dark almost purple nipples. Willow's more natural, if you know what I mean. Also her teeth aren't perfect white, and she has curly brown hair instead of straight blond like she's maybe Italian or Jewish. She's got this fantastic warm smile. Actually, I bet she's French Canadian, which is why she was performing at Lucky Pierre's. It's on the French side of the river in Ottawa where they've put all the strip clubs and hookers for the Canadian politicians that keep their offices and homes over on the English side. She was probably in town visiting her family and took the gig to pay off some of their overdue bills. She looks like she comes from a poor family. Her website says she was born in Colorado and went to college in Southern California and studied architecture, but they always lie on those websites. They'd never say things like she's French Canadian from Ottawa, Canada, and dropped out of high school and got into stripping and porn to help support her family. But that's what she looks like, and that's one reason why she's my favorite porn star. Or was. I don't have any favorites anymore.*

P: *Why not?*

K: *Dude, get a clue! On account of I can't watch porn anymore! I'd get busted. Back then though, like all the guys in my outfit, I watched porn all the time on my computer, and I really wanted to meet Willow, so I hitched up to Ottawa on a two-day pass. I had to hitch because none of the guys who had cars wanted to take me where they went on passes and hung out, and none of them gave a shit about Willow, and to tell the truth I wasn't tight enough with anyone to ask any favors, let alone borrow their car. Besides, I didn't have a driver's license. I pretty much kept to myself most of the time because from the first day of basic guys gave me a lot of shit. Not just the sergeants and officers. Every outfit has somebody who gets shit on by everyone else, and I guess I ended up being that somebody. You know what I'm saying?*

P: *Why, do you think?*

K: *I dunno. It's my personality maybe. Most people's personalities have like a specialty. They tell jokes good or they know a lot about cars or computers and video games or heavy metal music or they excel at some sport or at least if they don't play sports they know everything about the NFL say or the NBA. Or they're religious and can talk about Jesus and the Bible and shit. There were some guys like that in my outfit. Jesus freaks. Or they can talk about all the women they fucked. My personality just doesn't have any specialty. All I know about is iguanas, and who gives a shit about iguanas? Plus I'm shorter than most guys and kind of skinny for my age, so I look younger than I'm supposed to be, which means that guys my age and even younger tend to treat me like their stupid little brother. Or they just ignore me. It was like that in school. It's always been like that for me. You get used to it, and I didn't mind it after a few years. It was weirder in the army, though, because it was the first time I had to shower naked with other people, and I had the biggest dick in the outfit, and you'd think that would have got me some props—*

P: *Wait a minute! You had the biggest penis in your outfit?*

K: *Yeah. Not the thickest. A guy from Akron had the thickest. I had the longest. But they just treated it like it was a joke. Like it was wasted on me, which was sort of right. I think it's because I didn't know how to brag about it. You know. And show it off. That sort of thing. I mean, I didn't have a lot of sexual experience, to say the least, and was kind of shy about my dick and actually didn't realize it was unusually long until I was in the army, because I didn't play sports in school and the only other dicks I had seen up to then belonged to male porn stars, and their dicks, except for the really freaky gonzo-size ones, were the same size as mine more or less. Or when I was a kid and sometimes accidentally saw the dicks of the guys who stayed at our house with my mom, which from a little kid's perspective seemed really huge, even though they didn't even have a hard-on at the time and were just walking naked from her bedroom to the bathroom or the kitchen or sitting on the couch in their skivvies watching TV and their cock and balls would fall out.*

P: *So what happened with Willow up in Ottawa?*

K: *Oh, man, it was awesome! It was a pretty cool club, better than anything I'd seen in Calusa. And for sure not what you'd expect to see in Canada. They had a couple of small stages for the pole dancers and a Plexiglas booth where they put on shower shows—*

P: *Shower shows?*

K: *Yeah, like a naked woman takes a shower in this see-through shower stall, and you get to watch. It's kind of cool if you've never seen it before, but once you have it gets sort of boring, unless she flips her button and jerks herself off or has a dildo to play with. That can be interesting. Anyhow after a couple of numbers by the local talent, which wasn't much, Willow comes on. She's dressed in a tight nurse's outfit with furry white boots and pretty soon she's down to a thong and the boots and then just the boots. It's supposed to be a little story about a doctor's office visit and she's the nurse and she's wearing a stethoscope that she puts the head of it into her pussy and then sucks it and so on. But mostly she pole dances. The DJ's playing these old Bee Gees songs, but Willow's a real good dancer so the audience is into it, especially me, because her and me are having serious eye contact, like she knows I know she's special and probably because I'm not like the rest of the guys in the audience, who are all these red-faced Canadians, most of them drunk and older than me and yelling and grabbing their junk and so on, while I'm just sitting there quiet all by myself watching her pole dance like she's dancing for me and nobody else. Like we're alone together. Y' know?*

P: *Yes. I know the feeling. It's a good feeling.*

K: *Yeah. Anyhow, at the end she does a split and a couple of final butt flashes from the pole and starts scooping up all the cash the guys in the audience have been tossing up there. I snake my way up to the stage and hand her an American twenty, which stands out because the rest of the money is mostly Canadian twos and fives, and she takes the bill, looks at it a second, then looks at me and purses her lips in a pretend kiss. "American?" she asks and I say, "Yeah, U.S. Army," and she says, "Awesome." Then she prances off-stage. But a minute later she's back, wearing just the thong and the furry booties and sitting at a table at the end of the stage with this huge stack of DVDs of her newest movie, Willow's Day Off, that she's selling and autographing. There's only a couple of wrinkled, red-faced, old guys who're buying the DVD, and I feel kind of sorry for her and pissed off at these Canadian guys, who don't know what they've got. They don't know how lucky they are. So when there's nobody else in line I go up to the table and tell her I want to buy twenty copies of* Willow's Day Off. *She goes, "Wow, dude! What do you want with twenty of them?" And I go, "They're for the guys in my outfit back at Fort Drum. You're our favorite porn star. They sent me up here to buy them each a copy of the DVD," I tell her. Which isn't exactly true, but it makes her feel real good, I can tell. She asks if I'm going to Afghanistan, and I say, "Yeah we'll be shipping out in a few weeks." Which was true. I promise her we'll take her DVDs with us and share them with the other guys over there, which practically gets her crying. No shit, real tears in her eyes. You never see porn stars cry, man. Never. They're like trained not to cry. "You're real sweet," she tells me. And she goes, "You guys're risking your lives over there to protect our freedoms from the terrorists. I'm gonna give you a free lap dance," she says, and when the music comes back on, that's what she does. Gives me a free lap dance. Right there in front of everybody. I could smell her perfume, man.*

P: *That's incredible.*

K: *That's what I thought. It was like the best night of my whole life. But then after that everything went downhill.*

P: *How do you mean?* (to the dog) *G'wan, scat! Go home!*

K: *No, she's okay. Let her hang out with us awhile. Those guys, Benbow and whatzisname, Trinidad Bill, they treat her like shit over there. They treat the parrot like shit too. Both those guys are a buncha turds, if you ask me. They like to throw pennies at the parrot and make him yell swears at them so people'll laugh.* (to the dog) *C'mere, girl. Wanna treat, Annie? Want a Cheez-It?* (to the Professor) *She likes Cheez-Its, which is good because I like them too, and it's the only treat I got for her. Her name's Annie they told me. For Raggedy Ann and because she's got red hair. Reddish yellow hair. Only I like thinking it's for Little Orphan Annie instead, on account of there was this porn movie named* Raggedy Ann and Andy *that I never liked. It was all about sex dolls that suck and fuck. There's probably a porn movie named* Little Orphan Annie *too, but if so, I've never seen it. Iggy used to like Cheez-Its.*

P: *Iggy?*

K: *My iguana. The cops blew him away the other night when they raided the camp at the Causeway. I hadda bury him at sea. But don't get me started on Iggy. Jesus!*

P: *Okay. Tell me how everything went downhill after that night in Ottawa with Willow.*

K: *You know what a GO-1A is?*

P: *Hmm-m. General Order Number 1A?*

K: *Right. You must've been in the service, Professor. They passed it in the first Iraq War and updated it after 9/11. It bans you from drinking alcohol in Muslim countries plus doing other shit the Arabs dislike that Americans sort of take for granted, like gambling and drugs and borrowing money with interest, which means no credit cards except on the base. And no promoting Christianity. And no pornography. No porn at all. Nada. Not even skin magazines. Not when you're stationed in an Arab country. The rest of the time the army don't bother you about porn, so everyone is into it. I mean, what else are you gonna do with your free time? Everybody's into porn, even the officers. Especially over there in Iraq and Afghanistan I heard. In spite of the rules. It's practically un-American not to be into porn. Especially if you're a guy although I heard the female soldiers are into porn pretty heavy too. Downloading from the Internet onto your computers and iPhones and swapping with your friends and family members and sending out pictures of your dick and your wife's or girlfriend's tits and bush to your friends and exchanging sex organ pictures with your wife or girlfriend back home to let her know you're thinking of her and of course triple and quadruple X hard-core DVDs and jack-off magazines and other shit like that. Except for distribution. That's out. You can collect and swap skin magazines with your buddies. You can watch porn videos and share them with your homies and exchange sex-oriented family photos with your wife or girlfriend or if you're a female soldier with your boyfriend or husband. But if you're U.S. military personnel you can't like distribute porn, even here in the free world. Which is a pretty fine distinction, if you ask me. Between consuming and distributing. You can be one but not the other. Anyhow, I get back to the base from Ottawa with my stash of twenty copies of* Willow's Day Off, *and before I have a chance to give them away to the guys, they do a surprise search of the barracks, and they find the DVDs. It's called a "Health and Welfare Inspection," but all it is is a drugs and non–U.S. Army issue weapons search. So they grab all my DVDs, even the ones in my personal collection, and impound my computer and toss me in the brig until a week later, when they haul me before the base commander where they had this hearing, and they shit-can me. They gave me a general discharge and my pay and returned my computer, but they kept all the DVDs and my signing bonus money and handed me a one-way bus ticket to Calusa. None of which made my mother happy, except that she was sick of taking care of Iggy by then and could turn his care and feeding back over to me. A good thing for Iggy as it turned out, because in another week or two my mother would've probably given him away or dropped him off at a golf course. He was practically dead of starvation anyhow when I got home.*

P: *Iggy. The iguana.*

K: *Yeah.*

P: *So there you are, back in Calusa, living in your mother's house, without a job, no friends except Iggy. No girlfriend, I assume.*

K: *Yeah. I never had an actual girlfriend anyhow.*

P: *So what'd you do?*

K: *Pretty much stayed in my old bedroom. Watched television. Watched a lot of porn on my computer. I tried to get a job, but when they found out I was discharged from the army before completing basic, they said forget it. Plus my only work experience was in shipping for a light store, and the guy who owned it was murdered and the new guy still thought I was involved, but I wasn't. I had a little money left over from my army pay and a debit card. So I started making friends and talking with people on the Internet. Not real people, just people I met in chat rooms and such. I mean, they were real enough. They were real girls who liked to talk about stuff. Some of it sex stuff, but mostly just passing the time. Only not people I knew like in person.*

P: *We've talked for an hour already. That went fast, didn't it? Let's quit for now and come back to this in a day or so. I still have a lot of questions. Incidentally, Kid, I really appreciate your doing this.*

K: *No problem. What about the treasure map? Did you bring it?*

P: *Oh, I'm sorry! I forgot it again! I'll bring it next time, I promise.*

K: *Yeah. Try and remember, okay? It's sort of our deal is how I understand it. Maybe you can bring a compass and one of those GPS things that can locate coordinates like latitude and longitude. You probably know how to use that kind of gear, being a professor and all. Were you in the military? They teach you how to use those things in the military, but I never got to that particular lesson, so I don't know how to use a map to find a spot that's marked with an X.*

P: *Was I in the military? No. When I was your age it was the 1960s, and I was deeply involved with the movement to oppose the war in Vietnam. The only honorable path for me when I was drafted into the army was to refuse to serve, which I did. I spent a little time in the brig myself. I was in effect a draft dodger. And I've never regretted it.*

K: *No shit. How'd you dodge the draft? I heard that was hard unless you said you were a fag. Was it by being so fat?*

P: *Neither. It's a long story, Kid. I'll tell it to you sometime.*

K: *Yeah, I'd like to hear it sometime. That and the treasure map. I'd like to see that map sometime.*

P: *You will. I'll bring it tomorrow. I promise.*

CHAPTER EIGHT

A THICK MIST HAS SPREAD ACROSS BENBOW'S settlement. It hovers low over the sandy grounds between the shacks and the bar and trailers, spreading into the mangroves toward the narrow inlet on one side and over the berm out to the point, where the Kid has pitched his tent, and on to the back side of the settlement, where the pickup truck and several vans, SUVs, and panel trucks are parked. As it grows in density and height it blocks the morning sun and blue sky above. The vehicles slowly disappear from view. The half-dozen men and women standing near them fade and are gone. The buildings and trailers and barrels filled with trash and empty bottles and beer cans are embraced and then swallowed by the silver-gray mist.

It's hard to tell where the mist is coming from or if the entire island has been devoured by it or possibly the whole city of Calusa and its suburbs all the way west to the Great Panzacola Swamp and beyond to the Gulf of Mexico. Or if it originates out there in the Gulf and has been blown east across the vast swamp to the city and the Bay and Anaconda Island, driven by the morning breeze off the Gulf, the breeze stirred to life by the colossal swirl of a tropical storm named George three hundred miles at sea.

The mist here at Benbow's is now so thick the Kid can't see a person, building, or vehicle farther than ten feet away from where he stands. It muffles sounds—the lap of low waves off the Bay, the seagulls and waterbirds, the softly rocking, derelict shrimp boats tied to the posts of the crumbling, half-rotted dock by the inlet.

He knows he is not alone here; there must be dozens of other people close by. He heard their cars and trucks crackle across the crushed coral earlier, heard the doors of their vehicles open and slam shut. He heard them talking to one another, giving orders, arguing and discussing work of some kind. But he can't hear them anymore, as if, when the mist swept in and settled and thickened, one by one everyone left Benbow's settlement and the island. He can't see or hear the parrot, because he can't see the bar where its cage is kept; he doesn't know north, south, east, or west, for the sun has long since disappeared; he can barely tell right from left.

It's been a long time since the Kid has seen the dog, Annie. Or has it been a long time? When he wandered from his camp into the settlement the mist had already gathered at his feet and was starting to grow thicker and to rise from the ground and spread across the place, but now he can't tell if that was moments ago or half a day earlier. He's sure there are people nearby; there must be. He can't be the only person left on the island. He can sense their ghostlike presence close by and standing farther off in twos and threes, but he can neither see nor hear them, except for an occasional shadowy shift in the gray mist, as if a low wind has blown across a wide curtain. He hears a murmur of human voices, as if someone were speaking quietly into a phone behind a closed door in a language he can't identify.

He's almost forgotten why he came out here in the first place. Then he remembers that he left his tent to find Benbow so he could learn what his job will be today. But it's not a memory; it's a glimpse of one, and it's gone. He remembers for a second that the Professor is coming to bring the copy of the map today and make a second interview with him. But then he forgets.

For anyone other than the Professor and the Kid there are a hundred different reasons to drive out from Calusa, cross the narrow bridge onto Anaconda Island, and find oneself standing at the center of a cloud that has erased all sights and sounds of the known world and its inhabitants. You might have come in a delivery truck to restock the bar with beer and beverages or a panel truck loaded with ten cases of liquor. Maybe you came with drugs to sell, pot or Ecstasy or meth or coke; maybe you came to buy. You might have come out here to sample and purchase a half pound of Benbow's famous smoked marlin. Maybe you're a cop or an inspector from a government agency come to investigate a crime committed elsewhere in the city but with a possible connection to activities at Benbow's; or you're here to investigate a violation of county health board regulations. You may have left the city and come to the island for a fashion shoot or to make a pornographic film or act in one. Whatever brought you here this morning, you've lost touch with your intentions and desires for being here, as if you've taken a drug and can no longer remember the need or desire that induced you to swallow, smoke, or inject it in the first place. For there is something soothing about the enveloping mist: it's placed you halfway between sleep and wakefulness, halfway into a dream and halfway out. The line of demarcation between inside and outside, between subject and object, has been erased, and a zone that is neither and both has replaced it. You feel like you're watching a movie or making a movie or acting in one. Or all three at once.

And then, stepping free of the mist on your right not far away, a child. Or is it a child? A very small person, female, white, and wearing a gauzy white scrap of cloth draped across one shoulder and over her belly and wrapped once around her pelvis. Bare shoulders, legs, arms, wearing sandals with thin golden straps. Her hair is long, blond, combed forward and covering her face. She drifts a few slow steps toward you, her arms floating at her sides, then rising to above her head, as if she is plucking a forbidden fruit from a tree. She turns and returns to the mist and disappears inside it.

Another child floats toward you, this one a boy, also white and blond, also looped in a piece of gauzy white cloth, like a dancer in the role of an angel in a silent ballet. But a child; clearly a human child. A beautiful little boy. His eyes, like the eyes of the girl who preceded him, are expressionless, and his face is as still and unsmiling as a mannikin's. A third beautiful angelic child, a boy with light brown skin and black locks covering his face, parts the mist. The piece of cloth that half covers, half reveals, his body is thin and loose like the others', but is black, and the boy slowly approaches the first boy, touches his fingertips on both hands with his own, as if passing an electric current through them from one boy to the other, and the two boys turn on an axis, as if welded together at the tips of their fingers, a slow, erotic dance around an invisible Maypole, a dance that, despite its eroticism, is strangely chaste, impersonal, without desire or even shared awareness of the other. The blond girl now joins them, and a fourth child comes into view, a dark-haired white girl, and the four children hold hands in a circle, raise their hands over their heads and come close, face-to-face, expressionless, somber, cold, dead-eyed, turning clockwise.

Behind them, nearly invisible but clearly there, are the dark shapes of four or five adults watching the dance of the children, the nearly naked, dancing children. The beautiful children. One can make out the boxy, black silhouettes of machinery back there, and scaffolding with bright squares of phosphorous light attached. Adult male voices now and then break through the silence, men giving quiet directions to other men and to women, who answer with insecure interrogatories, *Here? Okay now? Slightly to my right or yours?* They all speak English, both those giving orders and those following them, but without any knowledge of the subject, they might be speaking in a foreign language. The adults are either standing in the middle of the heavy mist or on the other side of it, for perhaps the mist is not as widespread as the Kid thought, perhaps it originates and has settled only here on the island, only here at Benbow's. Perhaps it's not natural, is made by one of the machines back there beyond the enchanted children.

Their dance spirals forward out of the cloud and recedes into it, comes forward again, then halfway back. Are they enchanted, though? Entranced is more like it. Lost in a trance, mildly hypnotized or sedated. Their movements are choreographed and directed by someone you can't see but can hear now in a voice amplified electronically, a man telling the children to turn and face him and *come slowly toward the camera holding hands, that's good, that's very pretty, keep coming, don't stop, come right to the camera, you two part to the right of the camera, you two to the left.*

And cut!

CHAPTER NINE

FOR CLOSE TO AN HOUR THE PROFESSOR HAS sat in his van, watching the shoot. He thought at first that the cameras and crew and the scantily clad children and their handlers were filming a commercial for television and tried to figure out what product the commercial was designed to promote. Not clothing, surely. Except for the pieces of cloth draped across them, the children were naked, or appeared to be naked. No electronic toys or games or sports equipment or team paraphernalia were visible, no bicycles, boogie boards, or plastic aboveground swimming pools, no sneakers or shoes, except for the gold-strapped sandals, no shampoos or soaps or toothpaste evident. No musical instruments, Frisbees, Hula Hoops, trampolines, or jungle gyms; nothing for children to play with or on or in, nothing to eat or drink or wear.

There would be music added later, of course, and a voice-over to make the images cohere around the pitch, the sales pitch. But what are they selling? the Professor wonders. What product, what manufactured item, made probably in Mexico or China or Indonesia or Ecuador, could possibly be advertised using images of nearly naked children doing a faintly erotic slow-motion dance in a mist generated by a machine with shacks and shanties and rusting house trailers in the background, palms and mangroves and what appears to be the open ocean beyond, glimpsed for a second whenever the mist shifts and parts and then closes over the children again? It's an island, yes, but not a deserted island. They must be filming a story about children for children. It's an abandoned island, he decides, abandoned by castaway adults who have been rescued or have built themselves a raft of flotsam and moved on to another island, leaving behind these ghosts of their lost children, lost memories of childhood.

The Professor suddenly realizes his mistake. He thought the images of children were being directed at children. No, the viewers are meant to be adults. Adult men, not women. Men with money. Young men too, and even adolescent boys. The dance would be meaningless to children and women, even as a mood or atmosphere. The figures of two boys and two girls caught between movement and stillness like figures on a Grecian urn would have no sexual charge and no ability to arouse in anyone a possessive desire of even a material nature—except in an adolescent or adult American male. Maybe not just strictly American males. Maybe all males above the age of puberty would feel erotic heat from the sight, once the digital work was done and some thumping music added. You wouldn't even need a narrative voice-over to get the job of selling done. The images of nearly naked children floating through clouds in an abandoned shantytown on an island thousands of miles from civilization—that could be enough to sell the targeted male viewer anything. A luxury automobile, cologne, a ticket on an airplane, a bottle of vodka, a hip hotel room with an oversize flat-screen plasma TV at the foot of the king-size bed and a full-length mirror on the opposite wall.

The Professor eases himself from the van and peers into the fog, looking for the Kid. It's like a London fog, only without cold, damp, uptight London. It's a semitropical island set instead, it's the end-of-the-road, beyond, before or after the rise and fall of civilization, where nothing matters and everything is permitted.

They are selling an atmosphere, a mood, a feeling of low-key, nonthreatening sexual arousal that can be associated with a product, any product. The advertisers will add the product later digitally.

Its mere name will be enough, or a flash of the thing itself, if the product is indeed a thing and not a singer or a song laid in behind the imagery. But can't a singer or a song be construed as a thing? A product. It's the imagery that does the selling, the Professor reasons, and the imagery is sexual, an old story, except that in this case, it's sex of a particular kind: barely conscious fantasies of pedophilia.

He wonders if it was always so, if it's characteristic of the species for adult males to lust after the very young of the species. No other mammal shares this trait, if indeed it is a trait and is not, as he suspects, socially determined. He is a sociologist, after all, not an anthropologist or biologist. For him, social forces are the primary determinants of human behavior.

Even among the other higher primates, our cousins the chimpanzees, gorillas, orangutans, and bonobos, the adult males show no sexual interest in young females until after they pass menarche and are capable of breeding. But for the higher primate that we call *Homo sapiens,* the most socially determined creature of all, was it always so? Have Catholic priests always preyed on their young charges to such a scandalous degree that no parish in the world seems to be without a priest mutually masturbating his pretty young altar boys? Have cities in the past ever found themselves struggling to monitor and house whole colonies of pedophiles, creating an entire body of law and a nationwide tracking system designed to protect the young from sexual predators? The Professor doesn't think so.

To learn which crimes flourished in a specific period social scientists look to the period's legal code. For the Professor, the need to reason backward from prohibition to behavior is a fundamental principle. He teaches it early and often. Specific laws against piracy, slavery, infanticide, sedition, and ground and air pollution and smoking reveal the antisocial activities likely to attract a reckless, greedy, frightened, mentally disturbed, or merely weak man or woman of a specific era. Until the modern, postindustrial era there have been very few laws against pedophilia, the Professor reasons, because there was not thought to be a need for one. Adult males of the species were not thought to be sexually attracted to premenarche children. If on occasion they were, it was sufficiently regulated by the family's interests in protecting their young from predation. It generally only happened within the family anyhow—the weird uncle or cousin was not allowed to babysit the kids. Thus, until recent years, very few laws were passed against it. It was not thought necessary. The family, or at most the tribal elders, can handle it. Keep it in the village.

What the hell is this?

Startled, the Professor turns to face a short, round, black woman, her shining face fisted with angry disgust. Her thick arms are crossed over her pillowy chest. She is wearing tight jeans, running shoes, and a black T-shirt. No jewelry. No earrings. Close-cut hair. The Kid's caseworker, the Professor assumes. A tough, uncompromising, lesbian cop with a Queens accent.

I take it they're shooting a commercial of some sort, he says. The Professor blankets the woman with his large shadow.

You the guy I spoke to yesterday? The professor?

Yes.

You parta this?

No.

So where's the Kid?

I haven't seen him today yet. His camp is over by the Bay. I'll show it to you if you like.

He parta this too?

No. Neither of us has a thing to do with it.

You got ID?

The Professor hands her his card and his university ID, and with her lips pursed, as if memorizing the information, she studies them both carefully for a full minute: name, title, office address, home address, e-mail, telephone. She keeps the card and passes back his ID and tells him to take her to the Kid's camp.

This shit gives me the creeps, she mutters. *I don't know how these people find each other.*

What people?

The parents of those half-naked kids over there. They gotta have parents. And the creeps making their fucking kiddie porn.

It's probably just a commercial. An ad for TV.

Yeah, right. And I'm Jack Sprat.

WITH THE COP AT HIS SHOULDER, THE PROFESsor unzips and folds back the Kid's tent flap and peers in. The Cop has a name, and the Professor knows it, but to him she's the Cop—not the Caseworker or the Kid's Parole Officer. The Cop. She has a steel grid in front of her mind, and for anything in the outer world to reach her it first has to squeeze through the bars of that grid. Information has to be broken into small cubes; information and data packaged in two-dimensional squares are preferable to three-dimensional cubes however: they pass through the grid more quickly and once they reach the Cop's mind take up less space there.

The Kid has cocooned himself in his sleeping bag. The dog, Annie, lies curled at his feet. Neither the Kid nor Annie acknowledges the arrival of the Professor and the Cop. They're not sleeping; they're hiding, both of them, the Kid from the children being filmed at Benbow's, Annie from the people who don't want her accidental presence to screw up their movie.

The Cop tells the sleeping bag that the Kid inside it will have to pack up his stuff and move from here immediately. He'll have to be gone by noon. Or the Cop will bust him back to prison. No arguments. No discussion. End of story.

From inside the bag the Kid's muffled voice asks where should he go?

The Professor asks the same thing, *Yes, where should the lad go?*

Gimme a fuckin' break. The lad's a felon, a convicted sex offender. You got kids? You want him in your neighborhood?

He's paid his debt to society.

It's not about paying your debt to society. It's not about punishment. These fuckin' guys are incurable.

I'm not so sure. It depends on the nature and the cause of the offense. On what he did and why he did it. That's why I'm interviewing him.

You think he's innocent?

Legally innocent? No, of course not.

You think he's cured?

I don't know yet what he did and why.

The Kid has sat up and is gently scratching the forehead of the dog, who appears now to be deeply asleep. Without looking at the Cop or the Professor, the Kid says: *Why are you talking about me like I'm not even here?*

They look at him, the Cop with impatience, the Professor with compassion, in both cases mixed with mild curiosity. The Cop wonders if the Kid will decide to cut through his anklet and leave Calusa, go off surveillance and disappear into some other state far from here like an illegal immigrant, a Mexican or Haitian without a green card working in a motel somewhere out west. The Professor wonders what exactly the Kid did that made him a convicted sex offender. Whom he touched, if indeed he touched anyone, and exactly where.

You got till noon to get yourself and your shit off this island.

Can I take Annie with me? The dog?

Am I in charge of your pets now? Jesus!

The Professor says to the Kid: *I'll help you move.*

To where?

I don't know. We'll think of something.

Can I bring the parrot? These guys are really cruel to animals, y'know. Benbow and them. I'll have to steal it. They use the parrot for like a kind of prop.

Yes, bring the parrot.

What about the map? Did you bring the map?

If you're thinking of going off the reservation, Kid, fuggetabout it.

It's a treasure map, the Kid explains.

The Cop looks at the Professor, and he nods slightly, leave it alone, please, and she returns his nod, all right, just get him the hell outa here.

I brought the map. It's in the van. I'll show it to you later.

Cool. Very cool.

The Kid crawls over the sleeping dog and out of the tent. He stands in the sun and stretches.

The fog machine is silent now, the mist has dispersed, and the children and the people filming them appear to have left Benbow's, perhaps for another location—a suburban split-level home with a pool or a dingy motel room in the far North End or a white-walled downtown studio loft with large pillows on the floor, or maybe they've got enough footage now to head straight to the editing room.

EVERYTHING THE KID OWNS, INCLUDING his bicycle, the dog Annie, and Einstein, the gray parrot, has been stashed in the Professor's van. The Cop watched as they loaded the vehicle, though she took a little walk when the Kid stole the parrot and its cage from the bar and afterward said, *I didn't see that.* The Professor distracted Benbow in his trailer by explaining why the Kid had to leave the island. Trinidad Bob for reasons unknown had gone off with the film crew. The Professor paid Benbow the Kid's rent for a week and half a week's salary, and Benbow said fine, the Kid was a lousy worker anyway, and he attracted cops like the dog attracted fleas, so he was glad to be rid of both of them. Not that there was anything illegal going on here. He just doesn't like cops. Or fleas.

When the Professor returned from Benbow's trailer to his van the parrot cage and parrot were in the rear on the floor covered by the Kid's sleeping bag. He explained to the Professor that when you cover them like that, parrots think it's night and go to sleep. *They're real smart except for that. As smart as iguanas. And they talk. I'm gonna teach him to have like real conversations. When can I see the map?*

The Professor says later, when he gets the Kid settled. The Kid wants to know if he really thinks that the spot marked *X* is on Anaconda Island. He hopes not, now that he's been kicked off it. There are hundreds of these little offshore islands scattered around the Bay and up and down the coast close enough to Calusa for pirates to hide out while they bury their treasure. He brags that he's lived in Calusa all his life and knows these islands like the palm of his hand.

The Professor doubts that. But says nothing to discourage the Kid.

The Professor is now in charge of the Kid. It's unofficial and the Kid is free to walk away if he wants, but with the addition of the dog and the parrot to his household, the Kid needs the Professor now more than he did yesterday, and the Professor will do what he can to make certain the Kid needs him even more tomorrow. He has a plan for the Kid, still vaguely formed, but a plan nonetheless. Unlike the Kid, the Professor makes a sharp distinction between plans and fantasies. And when he makes a plan he almost always implements it. The Kid doesn't make plans. He never has.

The Professor intends to cure the Kid of his pedophilia. Not with psychotherapy or drugs or more radical means like feeding him female hormones or chemical castration. He intends to cure the Kid by changing his social circumstances. By giving him power in the world. Autonomy. Putting his fate and thus his character in his own hands. He believes that one's sexual identity is shaped by one's self-perceived social identity, that pedophilia, rightly understood, is about not sex, but power. More precisely, it's about one's personal perception of one's power.

Where are we going?

They've crossed the bridge off Anaconda Island and have passed through downtown Calusa heading north along the Bay. Across the Bay the long line of beach hotels faces the open sea like lookouts.

Back to the Causeway.

Definitely not cool. Lemme out right here. Me and Annie and Einstein. And my stuff.

Don't worry. I have a plan.

Yeah, right. I think you're just another fuckin' weirdo perv, you wanna know the truth. All you guys got "plans."

This has got nothing to do with that. This has to do with getting you a home. And a job. Giving you control over your shelter and your economy.

Make fuckin' sense, Haystack.

The Professor explains to his young charge that he has spoken with a friend who is a county commissioner and another friend who is an advocate for the homeless in Calusa and a third friend who is a state legislator. All have agreed that if the settlement of convicted sex offenders beneath the Causeway can be organized in such a way as to meet Calusa city and county health and safety ordinances and no criminal activities are taking place there, then convicted sex offenders up to a number yet to be determined will be allowed to reside there without interference or harassment by city, county, or state officials. Except for the international airport and the eastern edge of the Great Panzacola Swamp, the Causeway that crosses the Bay between the mainland and the man-made offshore string of barrier islands is the only place in Calusa County that is not also within twenty-five hundred feet of a school or playground or park where children gather and where illegal activities like those taking place on other islands, such as Benbow's on Anaconda Island, do not occur. Or rather, need not occur. The pretext for the recent police raid at the Causeway, which was indeed driven by local politics and the upcoming municipal elections, was that health and safety ordinances were being violated there and criminal activities like drug use and prostitution were rampant.

If one eliminates the pretext, the Professor explains, there will be no more raids by the police, regardless of the politics. In fact, the problem, basically a housing problem, will have been solved by the residents themselves, and the politicians will be scrambling to take credit for it.

"Eliminate the pretext," the Kid says. *How the fuck do you do that? It's a fuckin' open sewer down there. Half those guys who end up there are junkies, the other half are total losers, drunks and nutcases or just fucked-up in the head like. . . .*

Like who?

Well, like me, I guess.

I don't believe you're fucked-up in the head, Kid.

You don't, eh? What do you know about me? Other than what you got off the Internet. And what I told you yesterday. None of that might be true, y'know. Except what's on the Internet about me being a convicted sex offender. That's true. As far as it goes. But it don't go very far, does it? Believe me, I'm fucked-up in the head. Just like the rest of those guys down there.

The Professor pulls over and parks the van on the shoulder at the farther end of the Causeway. He gets out and follows the Kid, who's carrying the parrot in its cage, and Annie down the steep, zigzagging pathway to the concrete island below.

Be careful, Haystack. One slip and you're in the Bay, and I don't think anybody here can get you out.

The Professor chuckles. "Haystack." He likes the Kid's sense of humor. He thinks it's the key to his personality structure, the way in. It's the only apparent opening the Kid has kept to the outside world, evidence that he still has an opening to the outside world. With enough support and encouragement, the Kid will be able eventually to widen that opening on his own and gain sufficient control of the world so that, for the first time in his life, he'll feel powerful. Powerful enough not to need to demonstrate to himself that he has control of children. And animals. Iguanas, dogs, and parrots.

The Professor sits down on a tractor tire next to the parrot cage and, as instructed by the Kid, holds on to Annie's collar while the Kid returns to the van for the rest of his belongings. The Professor's theories about pedophilia are rapidly evolving. When a society commodifies its children by making them into a consumer group, dehumanizing them by converting them into a crucial, locked-in segment of the economy, and then proceeds to eroticize its products in order to sell them, the children gradually come to be perceived by the rest of the community and by the children themselves as sexual objects. And on the ladder of power, where power is construed sexually instead of economically, the children end up at the bottom rung.

The Kid may indeed be fucked-up in the head, but it's because he's a weak, relatively powerless member of a society that is fucked-up in the head. It's led the Kid to believe that, except for him, there's no one in the community who has less control over his or her fate than a child. A female child, the Professor surmises. He's confident that the Kid is not sexually attracted to males. Although it wouldn't alter his theory or change his equations a jot if the Kid had a pre-dilection for male children. Because it's not about sex, and it's not about gender; they carry no weight in the equation. It's about power. Control. Dominion. Dominance? Well, yes. When you feel you have nothing and no one you can dominate, you turn to children. And when children have been transformed into sexual objects and you have no other way of controlling them, you dominate them sexually. Thus the obsessive interest in pornography, the literal addiction to it: for the pornographic narrative is always a tale of dominance. Of men over women; of adults over children. If the Professor has lost himself in theory, a thing inconceivable to him, the Kid is lost in fantasy, a thing the Professor is now quite sure of.

When the Kid has lugged all his worldly possessions back down under the Causeway to his old campsite and has dutifully repitched his tent where it was before, he looks around him at the sad wreck-age and desolation of the place and sighs and sits heavily down on the cast-off tractor tire next to the Professor. Most of the shacks and tents and polyethylene tarps have been restored to their earlier disheveled state. A few cook fires are burning in the distance. The place smells badly of human urine and feces. A scrawny gray cat spots Annie and changes its path to avoid her, but Annie seems not to notice. The parrot Einstein squawks twice and fluffs his feathers to get rid of some of the dampness of the place. It's early afternoon but has already grown dark down here. A tinny radio speaker in the distance plays a country tune. Someone has a portable TV going and is watching Martha Stewart's show, an irony not lost on the Professor, but not noticed by the Kid. To him it's just part of the background noise, mixed with the quiet rhythmic slap of waves against the concrete pilings that hold up the Causeway, the rumble of vehicles passing overhead, the screeches of scavenging gulls, and the occasional dull honk of a boat horn from the Bay. There are a dozen or more gray figures moving about in the gloom, but they keep to themselves and are silent—the Kid recognizes several of the men out there by shape and posture and walk, but none of them comes to greet him. It's as if he and the Professor and Annie and Einstein are invisible.

The Professor asks the Kid if he can make the parrot talk. He's not heard the bird speak—not at Benbow's and not in the van or here, either.

Not much. I think he only talks with that guy, Trinidad Bob. Actually, I never heard him talk with Trinidad Bob, either. He's a loser parrot, I guess. A loser dog and a loser parrot. I don't know why I took them with me. I guess I was just missing Iggy so much, y'know?

The Professor points out that Annie seems to be genuinely attached to him, and if he feeds and shelters her, she'll prove to be a useful watchdog who will protect him and guard his campsite when he's away from it.

The Kid says, *No, man, she's too fuckin' old and feeble.*

The Professor doubts she's as old as she looks. She's just malnourished and sick with mange and suffering from having been physically abused. She needs to be examined and treated by a veterinarian. Both these creatures need to be seen by a veterinarian, and once restored to health, they'll make fine and faithful companions.

The Professor makes his first offer. He'll carry both the dog and the parrot to a veterinarian in his van and pay for their treatment, even including having poor old Annie, who's probably not that old, spayed and de-fleaed and X-rayed, if necessary. She may have broken bones or damaged internal organs. Einstein too needs to be properly fed and kindly treated. In short order they will be like family to him. He will be like the head of the family.

The Kid likes that idea. He smiles. *Hey, what about the map? The treasure map!*

Ah, yes. The map. It's in my briefcase in the van.

The Kid says not to worry, he'll get it. He jumps to his feet and scrambles up to the Causeway. A few moments later he's back, looking puzzled and downcast, with no briefcase.

It's gone. The fuckin' briefcase. Where was it?

On the backseat.

Well, it ain't there now, man. Some asshole stole it. We shoulda locked the van, Professor. The Kid is close to tears. *It's my fault. I shoulda locked it.*

The Professor stands and places a hand on the Kid's bony shoulder. *No, it's my fault. I wasn't thinking. But don't fret, son. There was nothing irreplaceable in it. Everything's backed up on my computer.*

Nothing irreplaceable? The map, Professor! What about the map? Was it the original? You don't have that backed up on your computer, do you?

The Professor says no, it was a copy he drew of the original map ten years ago in Washington, D.C., at the Library of Congress. But the Kid can relax, the Professor says he has a photographic memory and can redraw the map exactly, even though he hasn't examined it closely in a decade.

The Kid doesn't believe him. But the Professor is telling the truth. At least the part about his photographic memory and his ability to redraw a map he copied by hand years ago. The map, however, the original, as it were, was not in a dusty archive of eighteenth-century documents and charts at the Library of Congress in Washington, D.C. And it was not ten years ago that he copied it onto a sheet of notepaper for a report he was writing. The map he copied was the frontispiece in a 1911 edition of the novel *Treasure Island,* by Robert Louis Stevenson, illustrated by N. C. Wyeth. The Professor was twelve years old at the time, already a sophomore in high school, writing a book report that attempted to prove that the novel, far from being merely a children's adventure story, was in fact an encoded philosophical treatise on the ethical and religious implications of Charles Darwin's *On the Origin of Species*.

The Professor tells the Kid none of this, of course. He wants the Kid to believe in the map's authenticity. It's the means by which he has ingratiated himself with the Kid, and he needs it, now that the Kid's imagination has seized on it, to buy him cover and time enough to earn the Kid's complete trust. Without that trust, he'll not learn from the Kid what he needs to know in order to cure him of his pedophilia. And he needs to cure the Kid in order to prove his theory that pedophilia is the result of social forces, a sexual malfunction shaped by a malfunctioning society. It's not a mystery; it's not even a psychological disorder. Because if it is a mental illness, then the entire society is to one degree or another sick with it. Which makes it normal.

I'll redraw the map tonight and bring it to you tomorrow. But first we have work to do here on this island.

Whaddaya mean?

Eliminating the pretexts. Remember? You've got to get this place cleaned up and made safe.

Who, me? No fucking way.

The Professor proposes to pay the Kid a small salary for organizing the residents into clean-up crews and establishing a public safety force. They will begin, he explains, by calling a meeting of all the men currently residing under the Causeway. The Professor will address the group and will inform them that he has hired the Kid to be the official director of the community until such time that the members of the community decide by secret ballot to replace him. A set of rules and regulations for all residents will be drawn up by a special committee appointed and chaired by the Kid. Anyone who violates those rules or refuses to abide by them will not be permitted to reside under the Causeway.

The Kid thinks this is the stupidest idea he's ever heard and says so.

The Professor explains that all human beings need and want to be organized into social units that guarantee their comfort and safety. You start with what they have in common and build upon it. The men down here share a great deal: geography; gender; forced alienation from the larger community that they came from. And their basic needs are pretty much the same: shelter; sanitation; protection of property and self; freedom from harassment and persecution by outsiders. With a little organization and enlightened leadership, all these needs can be met. A problem can be turned into a solution. A negative can be made a positive. The citizens of Calusa will thank them—the Kid and his men who have been forced to live beneath the Claybourne Causeway. And if they are successful, if they are able to construct a coherent, efficiently functioning society of convicted sex offenders down here, then it may become a model for cities all across America to emulate. Communities of convicted sex offenders able to provide themselves with basic services while residing more than 2,500 feet from any-place where children gather will start appearing beneath overpasses, causeways, bridges, and in abandoned buildings in hundreds of cities large and small. They could become linked into a nationwide network. As the number of convicted sex offenders grows—and the Profes-sor knows that it will increase exponentially, keeping pace with the increase in law enforcement and fear of pedophilia among the gen-eral population—the political and economic power of convicted sex offenders will grow.

Sounds good to me, Professor. But what about the map? The pirate's treasure map.

I'll bring it tomorrow. First, let's call a meeting of the current residents.

And don't forget the veterinarian. I gotta take care of Little Orphan Annie here and Einstein.

Tomorrow, Kid. Tomorrow. After you've formed your safety committee and can leave the island for a few hours and know that your property is protected.

Yeah. Sure. Tomorrow.

PART III

CHAPTER ONE

THE PROFESSOR WANTS TO CALL A MEET-
ing of the residents which the Kid thinks is a useless idea.
Useless and therefore dumb. Despite being a fantasist or
perhaps because of it the Kid is a pragmatist. The eight or ten guys
he can make out in the gloom under the Causeway are all loners
pretty much. Like him. Not the meeting types. They're not exactly
his friends or friends of each other and not colleagues for sure and
this isn't a condo or a fraternal order and if any of them has anything that resembles a social life it's only with people who live elsewhere—what the residents call "off-island": family members left
behind when they became convicted sex offenders and wives and
girlfriends for those that have them, friends from before their arrest
and conviction all of whom have enough problems of their own,
legal, sexual, and otherwise, not to give a damn about other people's
problems, legal, sexual, and otherwise. Yes, there are people whom
the residents work with and for when they have jobs like the Kid
had at the Mirador before Dario fired him for being a wiseass punk
and of course the social workers and psychologists and counselors
and even in some cases the parole officers when those relationships
evolve as they sometimes do into something more personal than
merely professional and obligatory.

Otherwise the men who live beneath the Causeway mostly keep

to themselves. They give themselves or each other names that are not the names they're known by on the National Sex Offender Registry. There's the Rabbit and Plato the Greek and Paco the biker-bodybuilder and P.C. the coach and Ginger and Froot Loop and probably by now Lawrence Somerset is no longer Lawrence Somerset, the Kid thinks and wonders what the creep is calling himself now that he's had a few days to ditch his old name. Those old names are like what black people call their slave names, the names by which they're known to the cops and caseworkers and on the registry, the names they're called by the people who knew them when they weren't convicted sex offenders and by the people they work with and for, those that have jobs. There's something tainted about their old names, their real names, something shameful about them or at best embarrassing and controlling so that a new name like Kid or Paco or Ginger or even a weird name like Froot Loop can be liberating in a small way. For a minute or at least for as long as you're under the Causeway you're almost off the registry of sex offenders. You're almost somebody else and not anonymous either but a real person. Or almost real. As real as a character in a book anyhow.

The Kid tries convincing the Professor that it's a dumb idea to try to get his neighbors to meet together but the Professor doesn't listen which the Kid has decided is typical of him and maybe typical of all professors although this is the only real professor he's ever actually met in person. Assuming he is a real professor because you can't be sure that anybody is what he says he is. Or she. He's remembering the night he got busted and the watery feeling he got all over his body when he realized that nothing was what he thought it was and no one was who he and she claimed to be. He wonders if the guy that day at the Mirador he thought was O. J. Simpson really was the famous ex–football player and movie star who supposedly sliced up his wife and the guy she was with who the Kid heard was gay anyhow. If O. J. had known that, he probably wouldn't have thought the guy was fucking his wife and he wouldn't have killed them and he'd still be a rich and famous and beloved ex–football player and movie star instead of a guy playing golf in Calusa with an out-of-work small-time Central American diplomat. He'd be hanging in L.A. with Arnold and Sly. Maybe he wasn't O. J. Maybe he was just a big black dude who happens to look enough like O. J. that he can fool these star-fuckers into buying him a fancy lunch at the Mirador and get Dario to comp him the best Rhône wine in his cellar. The world is full of people who aren't who or what they say they are. The people who believe them aren't who or what they say they are either. That's the main thing the Kid has learned since the night he got busted and became a sex offender. Nobody's who he says he is.

One by one the returnees to the Causeway are introduced to the Professor by the Kid. The first is the Rabbit because the Kid can actually call him a friend unlike the others whom he thinks of as neighbors is all. Acquaintances. People who if he saw them off-island he'd only acknowledge with a nod and otherwise avoid. Also he's worried about the Rabbit because he's old and the last he saw of him a cop was whaling on one of his legs with a club the size of a baseball bat.

The Rabbit is wearing a thick blue cast and boot on his right leg, the leg without the anklet the Kid notices, which is lucky. He hobbles along with a metal crutch toward the water with a bamboo fishing pole in his free hand.

Yo, Rabbit, wassup?

The old man turns and checks out the Kid and his huge companion in a three-piece suit and tie and he frowns with puzzlement and slight irritation. *Who the fuck's this?* he says meaning the Professor who smiles through his beard at the Rabbit and extends his right hand and introduces himself by name and title.

The Kid says, *The Professor's okay, he's doing some kinda research for the university. Go ahead, Professor, you do the talking.*

The Professor more or less repeats what he told the Kid earlier about eliminating the pretexts for the police raids political and otherwise by organizing the residents beneath the Causeway into a law-abiding community that meets the Calusa city and county sanitary and safety regulations. He explains the need for a meeting of the current residents and the composition of a binding charter that will include a set of rules that all who choose to reside here must sign and obey. Also the formation of at least two committees, one to provide physical safety and protection of property and the other to be responsible for sanitation. They will need an executive committee of at least three persons that will make and administer policy with an executive director or chair of the executive committee who will act as spokesperson for the residents.

The Rabbit stares at the Professor for a long moment. Finally he says, *I gotta catch a fuckin' fish for my supper.* And starts to hobble away.

I told you it was a dumb idea.

The Professor calls after the Rabbit that everyone will meet in one hour at the Kid's tent but the Rabbit ignores him and makes his slow limping way down to the edge of the Bay where he takes over a folding metal lawn chair abandoned there and tosses a few bread crumbs into the water to attract his supper and baits his line with a balled chunk of white bread.

The Professor asks the Kid if he thinks the Rabbit will show up for the meeting. The Kid thinks so but only if he manages to catch a fish by then. He'll probably come out of curiosity if nothing else. He points out that the Rabbit has a good sense of humor and will come for a laugh. The others—forget it.

Undeterred the Professor heads for the next closest person who turns out to be Paco, and the Kid reluctantly follows. The Professor tells the Kid that he recognizes the man from Benbow's and the Kid shrugs whatever. Paco's pumping iron. He's always pumping iron when he's not riding his motorcycle or getting laid although the Kid's not sure he gets laid as much as he claims or if he's just making it up so you won't think he's one of those buff beach-buddy types with a tiny dick in a G-string who only wants to be looked at and not touched. He's lying on his back on his weight bench which is a board held up by two cinder blocks doing presses with his homemade weights that he built from a boxcar axle and steel wheels he stole from the rail yard. His tattoo'd arm and shoulder muscles are like illustrated drawstring bags of coconuts. His abs are like writhing pythons. To the Kid he's a cartoon character. Harmless and not very bright. The only complicated thing about him is the fact that he's a sex offender. The Kid isn't sure of the nature of his offense—the Rabbit figures he's into giving blow jobs to teenage boys. That's complicated, the Kid thinks: a guy built like a superhero from a video game likes hookers but still wants to suck teenage dick so he uses his huge muscles to attract the only kind of people who think a body like his is cool and sexy. With his ankle bracelet exposed as if he thinks it's a come-on to teenage boys. Maybe it is. Maybe in combination with the muscles it turns them on. The Kid can hardly bear to look at Paco's body. And it's always out there to look at, shirtless and wearing cutoffs. When he introduces the Professor to him the Kid looks off at the Bay.

Paco clanks his barbell to the ground and sits up, checks out the Professor and when the Professor extends his paw to shake Paco takes it in his and gives it a crunch. The Professor crunches back and Paco winces in pain.

You don't want to hurt my hand, bro! Paco speaks with a slightly tinted Spanish accent and though he looks like a café-au-lait Cuban or maybe Dominican the Kid suspects the accent is faked and Paco is really an all-American white guy with a tan. The chalk white brush of a mustache looks dyed and the Kid for the first time notices that he's wearing eyeliner. Also his hair, glistening black, long and tied back with a rubber band, is way too black. Definitely a bad dye job. Maybe the only person he's interested in turning on is himself, like his own looks instead of other people's are what give him a hard-on and that's why he looks the way he does.

Paco says to the Kid, *What you doing down here, man? I thought you was squattin' over at Benbow's.*

My parole officer made me split from there.

I can dig it, man. Them guys is too wiggy when you get down to it, y'know? But here, man, is living like animals, no?

Yeah, like animals.

So, who's this dude, amigo? What's up with him? I seen him at Benbow's. Them guys thought he was a cop. He a cop?

He's some kinda professor or something. The Kid doesn't want to talk about the Professor. He's the only civilian the Kid knows right now but he's getting a little sick of the man. He takes up too much space, uses too many words, has too many theories and ideas. The Kid doesn't want the Professor's ideas and plans and words and his size to become his, the Kid's. He likes living without any plans, not talking much, keeping to himself and making his life as small as possible.

The Kid tells the Professor he should explain what he has in mind for the men who live under the Causeway and he steps back a ways and looks off in the distance again: the Bay, seagulls, boats, the skyline, cruise ships, stacks of gray clouds coming in from the east promising rain.

Paco says sure he'll come to a meeting if it helps get this place cleaned up and keeps the cops off their backs and the Kid and the Professor move on to the others. The Kid is surprised that Paco didn't blow off the Professor's plan and is even more surprised when Plato and P.C. and the others agree to meet together. Even Froot Loop who claims to be a surrealist whatever that is and Ginger, a redheaded black guy in his thirties whose main activity is pushing a pick through his Afro and checking out his freckles in a handheld mirror in search of skin cancer he says because his Irish father and his brother died of melanoma.

And then there's Lawrence Somerset who the Kid thought would not have to come back to the Causeway because of his political connections. But once you're a convicted sex offender all your connections to society are broken no matter how much money you've got in the bank or how many houses you own or how big your boat is or how much power political or otherwise you used to have back when you were committing sex offenses in his case on little girls and buying kiddie porn and probably distributing it to other villains. That's the word the Kid uses when he thinks of Lawrence Somerset—villain. It has the right old-fashioned association with a black top hat and a black suit and a long tweaked mustache and big white teeth with fangs that appear when he smiles like a vampire.

He is a vampire, the Kid thinks. That's what he'd name him if it was up to him—Vampire. Or Dracula. A guy who sucks the blood out of little girls, turning them into vampires too who can't stand the light of day and have to live forever prowling the streets of Calusa at night and sneaking into the beds of other little girls and boys and sucking their blood while they sleep making more vampires forever and ever while the parents sit downstairs in the living room watching ha-ha TV shows.

The Professor introduces himself to Lawrence Somerset. The Kid won't do it even though at one time barely forty-eight hours ago he was willing to share his tent with him. Something happened at Benbow's that darkened his view of Lawrence Somerset. He's not sure what but it wasn't the weird film those guys were shooting of the kids dancing half-naked in the mist which was probably only for a TV ad or a music video even though it looked like a trailer for a kiddie porn film. Actually the Kid thought the filming was interesting to watch because from the start he'd been behind the scenes and saw the crew set up the fog machine and lights and cameras and knew all along that it was real so he never saw it transformed into fantasy on a screen. He never saw the illusion they were creating. Just the tools they were using. Even the kids were tools. They were actors, not half-naked children. They had mothers or people who acted like mothers and agents who brought them to Benbow's in the family van and probably dropped them off at school after the shoot.

Maybe it was the story about the pirate and the treasure map and X marking the spot that the Professor told him about. When he first heard it the Kid felt his chest expand as if with helium and it made him feel lifted up. Literally uplifted as if he might float up and off the island and drift over the Bay high enough to see all the way west to the Great Panzacola Swamp. The Panzacola Swamp with its thousands of mangrove islands and mazelike waterways would have been a smart place to bury treasure. Maybe, the Kid thinks, the island on the Professor's map is way inland someplace in the middle of the swamp. Maybe Captain Kydd and his men anchored their ship here in the Bay and rowed one of their lifeboats up the Calusa River for miles to where it originates in the endless shallow waters of the swamp where there are thousands of low hummocks and mangrove-covered islands and buried their treasure on one of the larger islands and using their compass and measuring rods drew a map of the island and wrote the exact longitude and latitude in code on it right where X marks the spot. A code the Kid with the Professor's help could break.

Call me Shyster, Larry Somerset says to the Professor.

Really?Shyster. How'd you come by a name like that?

The fellow over there fishing, Rabbit, he started it. I didn't care for it at first, but now I rather like it. The irony of it.

I take it you're a practicing attorney.

In a past life. An earlier incarnation, let us say.

What was your name then?

It doesn't matter. Shyster will do well enough, thank you.

Shyster looks a little beat up and bedraggled. He's still wearing his suit coat and dirty white shirt but one sleeve of the jacket is half torn off at the shoulder and he has a raw contusion on his right temple the size of a poppy blossom. His narrow flat cheeks are covered with black and white stubble. He looks like he spent the last few nights sleeping in a Dumpster.

Kid, you abandoned me! I don't mean to whine, but we were tent-mates. Everyone for himself, Shyster.

The Professor interrupts to say that's just the sort of mentality he's trying to eliminate here and proceeds to unfold his plan to Shyster. The ex-legislator quickly agrees. He'll gladly cooperate and will volunteer his expertise as sergeant at arms for the meeting and will provide pro bono legal advice for such matters as the composition of the charter and other questions regarding the law should any happen to arise.

I assume you've been disbarred, Shyster.

True. But I haven't been subjected to brain surgery. I still know what I knew and am willing to share it with my cohabitors here. In our common interests, of course.

Thank you very much. Shyster, yours is precisely the attitude I'm hoping to foster here. We'll see you at the meeting. We'll be following Robert's Rules of Order.

The Kid can tell the Professor likes Shyster which disappoints him in the Professor and when they part from Shyster and make their way back to the Kid's tent he reveals the lawyer's real name to the Professor who immediately recognizes it. He remembers the case. Three years ago it made big news all across the state. The Honorable Senator Lawrence Somerset arranged on the Internet to meet at a hotel close by the airport with a woman who claimed to be the mother of two little girls, nine and seven years old. She was to bring her daughters to his room and in exchange for five thousand dollars in cash leave them with him for the night. They were to be freshly bathed and wearing party dresses. When the senator at the prearranged time answered the knock on his hotel room door he was wearing only his underpants. There were some reports that he was stark naked. But there were no little girls awaiting him. The woman claiming to be their mother was a police officer and with her was a pair of state troopers. They arrested and handcuffed the senator, threw a blanket over his paunchy body, and marched him off to jail. They held a press conference the following day at the Calusa County Courthouse where it was revealed that the near-naked state legislator, who had sat on the state parole board, had brought to the hotel room his laptop computer on which were found dozens of downloaded child pornography films. He also had in his possession what were described as "miscellaneous sex toys" and a jar of Vaseline and "a tube of lubricant commonly used by male homosexuals to facilitate anal sex." Although the senator's wife in a written statement declared her ongoing support for him and after describing his long struggle with alcoholism her belief in his essential innocence, his two grown sons shut down their real estate business, moved out of state, and changed their names. The senator was sentenced to ten years in prison but after serving two was released because of good behavior which had included weekly attendance at Alcoholics Anonymous meetings and group therapy for sex offenders.

The Professor knew his story up to the time of his release from prison from the newspapers. Now he knows the rest of it.

The guy's wife brought him here, the Kid adds. *Dropped him off after he got out of jail and split. That's what everybody does. Wives, mothers, girlfriends, it don't matter,* he explains. *They fuckin' stand by their man so long as he's in jail but when he gets out they drop him off someplace where the sun never shines and don't return his phone calls or answer his letters anymore. You can't blame 'em though.*

Why not?

People in prison. They're not quite real people. Except to each other. It's only when you get out that you're real again. Only now you're a registered sex offender. It's like you're a leper and they let you out of the leper colony.

Is that what happened to you? Your mother dropped you off here and now ignores your letters and phone calls?

I don't give her the chance. Look, it's complicated, okay? Forget about it. The Kid doesn't want to think about his mother; it gives him a headache. It makes him start missing Iggy again.

I gotta feed my dog and my bird. He ducks into his tent and grabs a can of Spam for Annie and two plain doughnuts for Einstein. Tomorrow he'll go to Paws 'n' Claws and buy them proper dog and parrot food. He's got to learn about parrot care. He's never had to feed a bird before. He figures he's got enough cash in his pocket and in his ATM account left from the money the Shyster laid on him his first night under the Causeway to last the three of them a week or possibly ten days although he thinks he's soon going to be able to touch the Professor for what he'll call a loan but it'll actually be payment for these interviews he wants.

The Kid has decided to embellish his story a little here and there, make it more interesting to the Professor so he'll think he's converting the Kid from being a sex offender into a regular law-abiding citizen with a normal sex life. Whatever that is. The Kid believes that in some sense he already has a normal sex life, as normal as anyone he's ever known well enough to get a good idea of what they do. Except of course that he's never done anything with or to anyone himself and is still technically a virgin. That's not normal. He also admits that it probably was not normal to watch as much pornography as he did from the age of almost eleven until he was busted. Seven to eight hours a day and sometimes more from the time he got home from his afterschool job at the light store well into the night until he finally fell asleep in the gray dawn light. When his mother came in to wake him for school his computer screen would be showing three naked guys fucking a Chinese girl. His mother takes the mouse in her hand and says, *You're too young for this. You better be paying for it yourself this time, buster.* Then she sits down at the computer and with her eyes dimming watches the gangbang drag out in front of her as if it was a Ninja video game. *Hurry up and get dressed, you're gonna be late for school.*

Plus he knows—or rather he believes as he has no evidence to the contrary—that it was not normal for him to be jerking off five to ten times a day especially as he grew into his late teens and should have been getting blow jobs from girls like the other guys at school. But masturbating had become as automatic and normal a bodily function as swallowing or clearing his throat of phlegm.

On the other hand it's not normal that he hasn't masturbated once since the night he was arrested. He tried a couple of times to jerk off but he couldn't make his dick get hard no matter what porn video he played in his mind, even the kinky scenes that used to make him come without his even having to touch himself. Nothing worked. So he gave up trying. He was only doing it because he thought he should be jerking off once a day given his youth or at least a couple times a week. Once he gave up trying to get hard, once he accepted that he really wasn't sexually normal, he felt better. Calmer. As if by giving up trying to scratch an itch that he couldn't reach the itch went away.

As the seven other current residents of the camp beneath the Causeway one by one approach the Kid's tent more or less at the appointed time to be greeted by the Professor in a to-the-Kid strangely hearty way, the Kid squats next to his dog and his parrot and feeds them. He cuts the cube of Spam into small chunks for Annie and breaks the doughnuts into walnut-size pieces that he hands piece by piece to Einstein. The parrot takes each piece of doughnut gently from the Kid's fingers with one clawed foot like a prehistoric hand and studies it for a second as if examining it for dirt or contamination and passes it onto his beak and swallows and blinks. He opens his mouth and shows his yellow tongue and seems about to speak. The Kid opens his mouth too. Silence. The Kid hands the parrot another piece of doughnut. The parrot takes it in his claws and stares at the Kid. The Kid hears Einstein say in a creaky but clear voice: *Thank you. I like you. You're a good kid. You may be fucked-up sexually, but you're normal.*

The Kid looks over at Annie who has finished off the Spam and is now smiling gratefully at the Kid. He says to the dog, *Did you hear that, Annie?*

Annie nods and wags her tail slowly.

The Professor turns and says, *Hear what?*

The Parrot. Einstein.

I'm afraid I missed it. Sounded like a squawk to me.

Yeah. I guess that's all it was. A squawk.

CHAPTER TWO

I T'S A MOTLEY BAND OF BROTHERS THAT HAS gathered around the Professor. The Kid is surprised that they answered his call except maybe for the Rabbit who has a mocking way of looking at life and enjoys finding ways to express it. It's something he shares with the Kid. Or rather it's something the Kid learned from the Rabbit and now applies to almost everything and everyone that comes to him. When he first arrived at the Causeway settlement—after living for a month on the streets of Calusa and in the public parks and the occasional abandoned building and being hassled and chased off by cops and private security guards and maintenance people—the Kid didn't have an attitude other than the one that had got him safely through three months in the minimum security prison in Hastings.

A "correctional facility" it was called—he was being corrected, he believed, and made every effort to help them succeed. He was passive and obedient and cooperative. Everyone including the guards liked him and thought he was a little simple. Maybe borderline retarded. It was how he had behaved all his life in school and at his job at the light store and in the army. Until the night he took the initiative to hitchhike up to Ottawa to see Willow his favorite porn star and brought back all those DVDs to give to his buddies at Fort Drum. Big mistake. After that one initiative, that one departure from his usual compliant docility, he'd gone quickly back to his old tried-and-true personality like a turtle into its shell. For him for years his computer and its access to the Internet and pornography and sex-talk chat rooms had provided the shell and kept him from loneliness and dismay and the explosive desperation that often follows hard upon. His computer kept him from turning violent and he was self-medicating with an addiction to pornography to the point where he was no longer using it to get high or hard but merely not to be bored or harmful to others.

Maddie who ran the weekly group therapy sessions at Hastings explained all this to him. She told him that it was as if he had been addicted to heroin during those years and the only real cure was for him to look inside himself and learn what or who was the true cause of his rage. She was a small thin brittle-looking woman in her early thirties with a cloud of curly green-tinted hair. She painted her fingernails black like a 1990s punk queen and said she had a pierced nose and tongue and other piercings on her body that she had to take off and check in a locker every time she came to the prison which she probably thought impressed the inmates in group. But the men serving time at Hastings were mostly upscale white guys convicted of fraud and embezzlement and Type 2 and 3 sex offenders like the Kid none of whom was particularly impressed. Especially not the Kid who saw her as just one more of the kind of girls and women who thought he was weird and pathetic and treated him accordingly.

They got no argument from the Kid. He *was* weird and pathetic. Had always been that way. Even his mother thought he was weird and pathetic. Many times when she didn't think the Kid was listening he heard her say it to her women friends or to the guy she happened to be sleeping with and sometimes she even said it to the Kid himself right to his face. Although she always said it with a warm affectionate smile as if she actually preferred weird and pathetic to normal and praiseworthy. So that on one level it made the Kid feel good when she said it: *You're such a loner, such a loser, your only friend is that goddam iguana you're obsessed with, you're scared of girls, you don't play sports like the other boys but at least I don't have to worry about you getting into a gang or doing drugs, you never seem to have any friends at all, you're not interested in cars like other boys your age, you're not turned on by video games, your clothes are like an old retired janitor's clothes, you spend all your hard-earned money maxing out first my credit card and now your own debit card on Internet porn sites that you have to be eighteen or older to watch anyhow, mister. Don't forget that.* She tousles his hair and smiles and her eyes fill. *You're so short for your age and so skinny. It's my fault you're the way you are, honey. I tried. Lord knows, I tried, and I might have found a father for you if I believed that any father is better than no father at all. But I didn't believe that when you were little, and I sure as hell don't believe it now.*

The Kid would like to take a hard-ass attitude toward the Professor and his plan to organize the men living under the Causeway into some kind of gated community for homeless sex offenders. But he's having trouble generating the necessary cynicism. He's starting to trust the man's intentions—a little, only a little so far. There doesn't seem to be anything in it for the Professor except maybe bragging rights if it actually works out and nothing lost if it doesn't except some wasted time spent down here with people who to a guy like the Professor must seem like aliens from another planet. People who to a professor of sociology (or at least that's what he claims) ought to be worth studying and writing up in a book: a small tribe of men forced to live together in a cave in the middle of the city.

He runs a good tight meeting, the Professor. The Kid admires the ease with which the big man masters the names of the residents—Rabbit, Shyster, Paco, Plato the Greek, Ginger, Froot Loop, and P.C.—and applies them liberally so they feel special and singled out whenever he asks for their opinions which he does often: their opinions on how a security committee should operate, its rules and responsibilities and who should serve on it; their thoughts on the proper number of members of an executive committee (three) and its powers and restraints; the length of term of membership for the three-man sanitation committee (three months—no one is willing to serve longer than that). They agree that the security committee only needs two members. Paco is an obvious choice and is eager to serve but no one else wants the job so it's left to the executive committee to appoint the second member as soon as they have agreed on the three for that committee and the three on the sanitation committee.

The Kid notices that the Professor is smoothly maneuvering the group into doing exactly what he wants without their realizing it. He defines and narrows their choices his way because they don't really have any alternatives in mind. Having never imagined taking control of their environment down here under the Causeway, the residents regard the Professor's options as the only available options. He proposes and they dispose. Or so they think.

How many members of the Executive Committee, Paco? Two or three? Of course we ought to have an odd number, in case of a tie, right, Shyster? And do we want the three to be equal or should we have a rotating chairman so we can have a single spokesman to represent all of us to the police and other authorities? Shall we nominate candidates for the Executive Committee then? One by one, please state your nominees, starting with you, Rabbit, going in reverse alphabetical order.

Predictably Rabbit shrugs and nominates the Kid, and Shyster interrupts the process to note that he should have made the first nomination because in reverse alphabetical order *Shyster* comes before *Rabbit*.

The Professor acknowledges his mistake and invites Shyster to nominate a candidate and Shyster adds the Greek to the list. Rabbit sticks with his candidate the Kid. Plato and Paco argue over who goes next and the Professor refers the question to Shyster who invokes reverse alphabetical order again and finds for Paco as they're more inclined to call Plato "the Greek" instead of just Plato except when addressing him face-to-face. Paco declines to serve, says he's happy taking care of security and doesn't need or want no more responsibilities in life. He smiles and nominates the Shyster for membership in the Executive Committee. No sense giving the Greek more power and authority than he already possesses as the owner-operator of their power source, the diesel-fueled generator that the Greek has managed to drag out of the Bay and after a day of drying once again has it charging their cell phones and anklets. Then it's the Greek's turn to nominate a candidate and he says, *The Rabbit would be good, since he's been living down here longer than anyone else,* and all seven men nod approvingly. The Professor calls for additional candidates but no one volunteers which makes it unanimous that the Executive Committee will be made up of the Kid, Shyster, and Rabbit. The Committee for Safety and Security is made up of Paco and Ginger with Paco officiating as chief of Safety and Security. Ginger is his deputy. They will each be issued a baseball bat to be purchased by the Professor at Rick's Sporting Goods. The Sanitation Committee is Froot Loop and the Greek and P.C., which displeases Froot Loop and the Greek who take small comfort in the brevity of their term of office but pleases P.C. who had previously and unofficially functioned as a one-man sanitation committee taking it upon himself to provide trash barrels stolen from the park at Twenty-third and Herrington at the western end of the Causeway and regularly emptying the latrine bucket into the Bay, a practice the Professor says will no longer be tolerated.

So what're we supposed to do with our shit? P.C. wants to know. Yeah, the Kid thinks. Answer that one, Haystack.

The Professor explains that he will arrange for a private contractor to install a portable toilet for their use and until he locates a private donor to pay for the regular removal of their wastes he himself will pay for the service. *We have to show the public and their elected officials that we're at least as capable of meeting local sanitation ordinances on our site as a construction company.* The Kid notices his use of *we* and *our* and wonders where this is all leading. Or is it just another way for the Professor to get them to do what he wants them to do? For his own mysterious purposes.

The Kid is starting to feel vaguely like a laboratory rat.

CHAPTER THREE

A S CHAIRMAN OF THE EXECUTIVE COM- mittee the Kid is essentially in charge of the settlement and that first night back his first executive action is to allow five sex offenders to return to the Causeway and reestablish their homes there. The next morning three more returnees arrive and are told by Paco, who is taking his policing responsibilities seriously, that they must petition the Kid for the right to settle under the Causeway. It's become routine now. The homeless sex offender either gets the word on the street or simply drifts back to the Causeway because he's got no other place in Calusa to sleep and is told by Paco on arrival that there is a whole new set of rules of governance operating now, a whole new structure. The applicant is quickly interviewed by the Kid whose main interest is to verify that the man is a genu- ine convicted sex offender whereupon he is assigned a spot under the Causeway where he is allowed to set up a tent or lean-to or stretch a tarp over a frame. He is instructed on the new sanitation and security rules—all trash and garbage that's not recyclable has to be carried out by the individual resident and daily deposited off- island in a Dumpster; no urinating or defecating except in the rented Porta Potti that the Professor has arranged to be placed up alongside the Causeway on the shoulder of the highway several hundred feet beyond the bridge; no drugs bought, sold, or consumed anyplace within a thousand feet of the settlement; no drug paraphernalia or needles; no possession of stolen goods allowed; no acts of violence or pilferage permitted. Pets are allowed as long as the resident leashes or otherwise restrains them and cleans up after them. But no aggressive dogs. No cockfighting. No keeping live animals for food or religious sacrifices, not even chickens.

As long as we obey Calusa city and county rules and regulations and don't commit no crimes down here the cops'll leave us alone. The Kid has bought the Professor's party line. To which in his wisdom he adds one further prohibition: *No sex offending down here. No weenie-wagging. No knob-jobbing.* He makes it clear in a way the Professor never could or would that in spite of the presence among them of predatory wolves and ex-prison punks, come-freaks and chubby-chasers, Charlies and chomos—all kind of sexual weirdos who've been arrested, tried, and convicted for their acts—none of them, no matter how much or what kind of therapy and rehab they've done, none of them is not a sexual weirdo. They are all sexually offensive. Some in fact may have been made even more obsessed with committing illegal and strange sexual acts by their conviction and time in prison than they were before being arrested. But not here beneath the Causeway. What they do with their dicks and hands and mouths and assholes anywhere else is their business. What they do here is his business, the Kid's.

The Kid likes his new authority. He might in some oddly undefined way be working for the Professor but he's never before held any power over anyone else. Except for Iggy. And now Einstein and Annie. A parrot who won't talk and a watchdog too sick to bark. Now however he has the power to admit or exclude at his discretion any of the growing number of applicants for a spot under the Causeway.

By midafternoon of the second day of his return from Anaconda Key there is a total of nineteen residents, twelve more than the seven who are now running the place. And more will come. The word is spreading that it's safe beneath the Causeway now and relatively clean. Police cruisers pass overhead without even slowing so word must have reached them too. Just as the Professor predicted the cops are practically relieved to know where all the convicted sex offenders are located at least at night and except for those who have jobs to go to most days as well. They're fishing in the Bay, scavenging food from the Dumpsters and trash bins behind restaurants and supermarkets, repairing and cleaning their tents and huts, and have even started picking up the trash tossed from cars passing over the Causeway between the mainland and the Great Barrier Isles, bagging beer cans, food wrappers, plastic bottles, as if they've adopted that section of the highway like any other civic organization. This place is theirs.

CHAPTER FOUR

THE MORNING OF THE THIRD DAY OF THE Kid's return to the Causeway the Professor shows up early and checks the place out and is pleased by what he sees. He's red-faced and sweating from the effort of descending from his van on the roadway above. The Kid remembers reading in Shyster's Bible the story of Genesis. The Professor is like God stopping by to visit the Garden of Eden and approving the way his human beings are running the place.

Nice work, Kid. The number of residents is multiplying. But that means it's going to be harder to keep order, the Professor notes and suggests adding two or more members to the security committee.

The Kid says he'll take that under consideration. He doesn't want the Professor to think he's God and in charge down here even though in a sense he is. *I'll talk it over with Paco.* He informs the Professor that he's thinking of forming a construction and maintenance committee. They need to build a shower stall and some of the shanties have to be rebuilt. *Most of these guys can't buckle their belts or tie their fuckin' shoes right let alone pitch a tent or build a hut outa old boards and plastic.*

The Professor nods as if approving and tells the Kid to follow him and leads the Kid away from the others out of earshot. He sits his enormous body down on a grassy slope near the path down from the roadway and pats the ground next to him. *Take a seat. I have something to show you.*

The Kid doesn't quite sit where he's told; he squats three feet away ready to stand up in case the Professor reaches out and lays one of his meaty paws on his thigh. He still doesn't quite get the Professor's interest and deepening involvement with the men living under the Causeway. Unless he's a sex offender himself only not convicted. Although for the Kid it's very hard to imagine a guy that fat having any kind of sex life at all, even in his head. He knows about chubby-chasers, guys who are into sex with fatties, but they usually aren't fatties themselves. And the Professor's not just fat, he's two or three times fat. He's enormous all over and wears clothes that make him look even fatter than he is as if he's trying to warn people off his mountain of flesh. His three-piece suit and buttoned-up shirt and wide necktie strangling his neck with a Windsor knot the size of a fist and his hard leather brogans are like body armor. Plus his beard and long hair enlarge his head and make him look like he's wearing a hair helmet.

Whaddaya got?

What you've been waiting for, my friend.

The Professor pulls a folded sheet of paper from his inside jacket pocket, carefully unfolds it and passes it to the Kid.

The map! Very cool. Very very cool.

It's only a copy of the original. A copy of a copy, actually. The original is in Washington, D.C., at the Library of Congress, where I expect no one except for me has seen it in two hundred years.

The Kid gives it a once-over, then a closer look, then gazes a little wistfully out across the Bay to the Calusa skyline and beyond to Anaconda Key and west to the Barriers and the stacked hotels facing the ocean there. He's trying to place the map of the island onto the world that surrounds him. The map is hand drawn and to the Kid looks old-fashioned enough to have been made by Captain Kydd himself even though it's on a standard sheet of typing paper but like the Professor said it's a copy of a copy. The original is probably an old sheet of parchment and much larger and faded by time.

The island is shaped sort of like a diving whale with its mouth wide open as if about to swallow a much smaller island. The smaller island has the words SKELETON ISLAND written next to it. The mouth of the whale looks like a bay, unnamed like the whale-shaped island which has a second segment attached to its backside as if a shark were riding piggyback on the whale or maybe it's the whale's baby and the mother whale is diving for a chunk of food for her baby. There are other words written on the map: CAPE OF YE WOODS, SPYEGLASS HILL, NORTH INLET, SWAMP, WHITE ROCK, and so on, and in the water surrounding the island are numbers indicating the depths, the Kid figures, none of them over 14 and most of them low numbers, 3, 4, and 5 and so on.

Pretty shallow waters, the Kid observes to himself. Maybe Calusa Bay didn't used to be as deep as it is now since they dredged it out to make the Barrier Isles and the Cut between the Barriers and Anaconda Key for deep-water freighters and cruise ships to come and go. Maybe back then two hundred or more years ago this place didn't look like it does now. He's sure the sky was the same huge blue dome spreading from horizon to horizon from the Atlantic Ocean and the Caribbean in the east and south and in a vast sweep overhead to the endless Great Panzacola Swamp on to the far side of the swamp to the Thousand Islands and west of the islands the Gulf of Mexico. The sky never changes. He knows that the land between the horizons was flat as a table from shore to shore barely two or three feet above sea level with low sandy ridges and mounds heaped up in places here and there by the hurricanes that for centuries roared out of the Gulf and the Caribbean every summer and fall just as they do today. There were no buildings anywhere then—no skyscrapers, no hotels, no miles and miles of condo developments, gated communities, suburban ranches, and bungalows. No geometrically laid-out fields of sugarcane, vegetables, strawberries, citrus orchards.

No mile after mile of drainage and irrigation dikes and canals carrying off the waters of the Great Panzacola Swamp and the overflow from the huge lakes in the central portion of the state. No highways, cloverleafs, bridges, overpasses and underpasses, no causeways. No Claybourne Causeway for sure. No Great Barrier Isles. No Mirador Hotel & Restaurant, Rampart Road with its boutiques, cafés, restaurants, tourists, and hustlers. No airport or Boeing 747s cutting across the sky. No cars, trucks, buses rumbling back and forth day and night between the mainland and the Barriers. No Barriers even, because they're man-made. No people! Mainly that. No people and everything they've done to the land and the water and all the animals that live on the land and the creatures that swim in the waters and the birds that fly above.

The Kid is imagining his city the way the pirates under Captain Kydd saw it when they first sailed into what's now called Calusa Bay. He doesn't know their story or the history of this place but with the map in his hand he can imagine it. They'd approach the mainland from the east-southeast sailing up from the Caribbean atop that deep green current called the Gulf Stream. They'd be on the run after pulling off a set of daring raids in the waters off the coast of Hispaniola, their ship loaded down with bars and coins of stolen gold. The Kid would've climbed to the crow's nest atop the mainmast, sent up by the Captain to keep a sharp lookout: *Keep your starboard eyeball on the glass for ships sailing north behind us, lad. And use your portside eye for the dear old harbor on the east coast of the mainland.* That dear old harbor would be Calusa Bay though it's not yet named and isn't on any maps yet, not even the Captain's.

Between the string of low-lying coastal islands and the mainland a meandering river that drains the mainland dissolves in a marshy delta and empties into a broad bay so that when you enter the bay your first sight of the mainland is of a long green line dividing the sea from the cloudless sky. It's midday with a light breeze out of the east and where the bow slides through the low waves the water glitters like silver coins. After decades of pillage and flight Captain Kydd knows these waters better than any other man. He takes the wheel himself, orders the mainsails down, and brings his ship straight in toward shore as if he plans to run it aground on the offshore mangrove islets. It's high tide and from above in the crow's nest you can see the narrow cut between two of the islets, a channel deep enough at high tide and just wide enough to let the ship slip past the islets into the broad blue-green bay.

The waters on the seaward side of the mangrove isles are thick with schools of silver fish surging and turning in huge sweeping motions, wide rivers of fish just beneath the surface so closely crowded that you can drop a bucket into the sea and bring it back filled with flopping gasping fish. You can drag a weighted basket across the sandy bottom and a minute later pull it back to the ship and dump dozens of large spiny lobsters onto the deck. As the ship approaches, flocks of birds—anhingas, pelicans, cormorants, egrets, and herons—rise from the mangroves into the sky where they thicken into layers of birds and spread out until they block the sun and cover the sea and ship below in darkness as if evening has come on. Herds of sea cows, enormous lumbering manatees, part for the ship, making room for it to pass from the sea into the bay, then gather behind it into a massed crowd of animals, hundreds of them, gently watchful, trusting, and almost politely deferring to the ship.

All sails are furled now and the crew has been sent to man the lifeboats and tow the ship slowly across the bay toward the mainland. As the Kid rows, he looks back over his shoulder at the lush flowering trees, the jacaranda and lignum vitae and the flame-colored poincianas and the forests of thatch palms and palmettos and groves of slash pine spreading inland from the sandy shore. There are sea grapes and along the islets where the streams empty into the bay white, red, and black mangroves float on their stilts.

Captain Kydd stands in the bow of the lead lifeboat. The first mate sits in the stern manning the rudder while the Captain indicates with his one good arm where to aim the boat. There are eight men rowing, their backs bent to their destination, and though the Kid doesn't want to be seen slacking off every now and then he turns in his seat and steals a look at where he's headed. They're moving north in the bay a few hundred yards off the mainland, slowly towing the ship toward what appears to be a large low-lying island at the far end of the bay. He spots a protective shelf of land with hills high enough to look out over the tops of the mangrove islets one way to see if danger is approaching by sea and over the tops of the pines and palms and lush flowering trees the other way to see if danger is approaching by land.

From the top of the highest hill which the Captain has named Spyeglass Hill you can survey the entire island. It's shaped like a whale with a shark riding its back. The mouth of the whale is wide open and about to swallow the smaller island. The ship has been anchored in the shallow waters on the leeward side of the smaller island. When the tide turns and the waters empty from the cove turning it into a mudflat the ship's hull will be exposed to the sun and air. One crew will go to work scraping it free of barnacles and sea worms. A second crew will cut trees and construct a small fort atop Spyeglass Hill and a palisade in case they are attacked either by the murderous Indians or by a contingent of European or American sailors. A third crew carefully selected by the Captain for their loyalty to him will carry from the ship his treasure—trunks and wooden cases filled with gold bars and coins, jewels and precious stones, a ton or more in all—sweating in the afternoon sun, lugging the booty from the ship across the mudflat into the jungle to a spot near the center of the island that only the Captain knows how to find, where there is a cave that he has used for years as a hiding place for his stolen cargo. The cave is like an enormous vault known only to a handful of men who have been sworn to secrecy in exchange for a promise to share out the treasure when the time comes for the Captain to give up piracy on the high seas and return to land and a life of respectable law-abiding luxury. The Captain holds five shares of the treasure and the five men he's chosen to divide it with hold one share each.

Who are the five? The Kid believes he is one. *X* marks the spot and the Kid puts his finger on it and says to the Professor, *Here's where they buried their treasure.*

Correct. But where is the island?

Right here, man. Right where we're standing.

The Professor chuckles. He's amused that the Kid seems to have taken seriously the map that the Professor drew from his memory of the map drawn by Robert Louis Stevenson to illustrate his novel *Treasure Island*. Amused and a little disappointed. He meant it as a joke and a tease. But is it funny if the Kid doesn't get the joke and doesn't realize he's being teased?

No, seriously, dude. I bet we're standing on Captain Kydd's original island. What's left of it.

How do you know?

I just know.

You could be right. But from the map it could be anywhere. I've seen a dozen islands that correspond to its approximate shape and contours. From Nova Scotia to the Caribbean to the South Seas. Captain Kydd anchored at hundreds of islands and harbors like this. The Professor squints and studies the map as if searching for something he may have missed in all the times he's studied it. He says to the Kid, *Of course, he probably passed by this bay, Calusa Bay or whatever it was called then, more often than any other. And no doubt there was an island already here when they dredged the Bay for the soil to build the Great Barriers and put up the Causeway to connect the Barriers to the mainland. So it's certainly possible, my friend. Yes, Captain Kydd's treasure may well lie beneath us.*

More than possible, man. It's fucking here. I can feel it.

How do you plan to locate it?

I don't know. Maybe I could use one of those forked sticks people find underground water with. I have the vibe on this, Professor.

Dowse for it? Why not? But assuming you locate the spot where it's buried, how do you propose getting it out from under this concrete island and the Causeway overhead? Dynamite?

I dunno. Maybe something a little less explosive. I gotta focus on it awhile first. Once I nail down the exact spot where it's buried I'll concentrate on how to get it out. One step at a time, Professor.

Have you considered the possibility that the map is a fake?

You mean the one you copied the copy from? The original?

Yes. The original.

That's like asking have I considered the possibility that you were lying to me.

Exactly.

Why would you lie to me about something like that?

Why, indeed?

I mean, I can see it if you were trying to keep the treasure all for yourself so you drew me a phony map that sent me to the wrong place to dig for it. But if you wanted the treasure all to yourself, why tell me about it in the first place?

Exactly.

Unless there wasn't any treasure in the first place or even an original map to copy from. And you only wanted to make fun of me. And make yourself feel superior.

The Professor says, *I wouldn't do that to you, Kid.* But his smile tells the Kid that's what he's done. The Kid stands and turns and walks back to his camp and his dog and parrot.

CHAPTER FIVE

P ROBABLY THE KID SHOULDN'T BE ALLOWED to own a dog or a parrot. They are helpless dependent creatures, neither of them very healthy, and both unable to function normally especially Einstein whose wings were broken at Benbow's and tied back so that when they healed and the strings were cut he'd be unable to fly more than a few feet at a time. He'd never be able to escape to the trees above Rampart and breed with the parrots there and spend his days cadging dropped bread and leftovers at the sidewalk cafés, squawking with the flocks of other escapees and their offspring and gawking at the humans down below. And Annie's like an old lady on a walker, frail and slow and cross. They are rescues is how the Kid sees them but in spite of his limited abilities to take proper care of them he still believes they're better off under the Causeway with him than they were at Benbow's.

He wonders if the Professor can give him a lift over to the Barriers to Paws 'n' Claws the pet food store on Rampart or maybe he'll hold on to his dwindling cash reserves and hit Bingo's Wholesome on the mainland for a Dumpster dive. There'll be three-day-old organic chickens and marrow bones for Annie and plenty of nuts, crackers, and berries a day too stale for the yuppy vegetarians but perfect for Einstein. The Kid used to dive at Bingo's twice a week at least because of the abundance of the leafy greens that Iggy so loved. But since Iggy went down the Kid's only been diving at Bingo's once.

He figures if he can restore Annie's health she'll be a serviceable watchdog who can at least stay awake while he sleeps and bark if someone tries to sneak into his tent or cut his bike chain. A little food, kindness, and respect can do wonders for an animal of any kind. It worked with Iggy. It kept him close by and attentive and loyal and fiercely protective which was what got him killed of course but will keep him always in the Kid's only memory of being loved. In a sense Iggy is responsible for what little capacity the Kid possesses for loving others.

You might think the Kid's mother loved him—she certainly thinks so—because she bore him after all and had no help from anyone else in raising him. She wasn't cruel to him or violent and for many years she provided him with food, shelter, and clothing and she offered him companionship from time to time when there was no one else around, no boyfriend or some guy about to become her boyfriend or another guy on the way out. She wasn't on meth or crack, just weed and the occasional blow. Mostly he remembers her going out the door in the mornings for work at the salon, his box of Coco Pops on the kitchen table, slightly sour milk in the fridge, school lunch money next to his plate. Then he remembers her coming home after afterwork drinks at the Bide-a-Wile with her girlfriends from the salon, putting a microwaved box meal in front of him while they both watch music videos on MTV, and then she puts on her makeup and tight jeans and sleeveless tee with the good cleavage and heads back to the Bide-a-Wile or someplace else where she's agreed to meet up with her girlfriends to begin the night's prowl.

That was when she had no boyfriend or as she put it, *No beau.* Once she found herself a beau he usually moved in with her or at least moved into her bedroom and kitchen and took half the couch in front of the TV. The Kid would hole up in his bedroom with Iggy and his computer so he wasn't seeing her any more when the beau was around than when she was out looking for one. It was a pretty boring lonely life for the Kid whether his mom was with a beau or without, whether she was at home nights and Sundays or on the prowl. Until he was almost eleven, that is, and clicked his way for the first time onto porn sites. After that if he got bored and lonely it was only the porn that was boring and making him lonely but by then it was working on him like a drug that created a need that only it could satisfy and brought with it a need for more of the same.

Officially then until he was eleven or twelve and could take care of himself more or less the Kid's mother was neglectful because she left him home alone unattended so much of the time. Unofficially she might still have loved him. People do that sometimes—love somebody they appear not to notice is alive. But she was the kind of person for whom love was only a word and a tone of voice and a ready-made set of facial expressions and body movements. As long as she employed the word and made the right faces and provided the appropriate hugs, kisses, and whatever else was required of her body to support her use of the word she believed that she loved her son just as she believed she was in love with many of the men she brought home and had sex with. They believed it too, her son and some of the men who shared her bed. For a while anyhow. The men that is. For a day or two. Sometimes weeks. Her son however believed for years and years that his mother loved him. Even now he believes that she loved him all his life right up till he became a convicted sex offender and then she stopped. Which the Kid thinks was understandable.

The night he was busted in West Calusa Gardens after they finished interrogating and booking him he called her from the police station to explain why he wouldn't be coming home unless she could put up a twenty-thousand-dollar bail bond. She demanded to know what he did. She didn't ask him what he was charged with.

Nothing, really.

If you didn't do anything, why did they arrest you, then?

On account of the way it looked. I did something really stupid.

Then you did something. And they arrested you for it, and now you want me to bail you out with money I don't have.

Well, they said you could put your house up if you own it.

Who's "they"?

The guy who set bail. The judge, I guess he is.

You're not innocent. You're guilty of a crime, and you want me to risk my house just to get you out of jail. What kind of crime did you commit? Was it drugs? It better not be drugs, mister. 'Cause if it is, you can forget about me bailing you out. You can forget about me bailing you out anyhow, since you're not innocent. Was it drugs? Did you rob somebody?

No, it was a sex crime.

Oh, Jesus!

That's when she hung up. It was the last time he spoke with his mother. At his trial he looked for her in the audience which was made up mostly of the families and friends of other people being tried that day and their lawyers but she wasn't there which he understood because by then there had been at least two lengthy articles in the *Times-Union* about child pornography and a five-part series on the nightly TV news about protecting children from sexual predators prowling the Internet. He didn't blame her for staying home.

At first once he was convicted, sentenced, and in jail, he didn't miss her very much. But then after he got out of jail and started living under the Causeway and knew that she was living and working only a short bus ride away he began to miss her. Before he left home for the army and everything went bad for him there and when he came back to Calusa and resumed living in his old bedroom again she cracked jokes like she used to and teased him sometimes as if he were still a little boy and asked him what he thought about her clothes and makeup and hair when she was about to go out. She wasn't mad at him for getting kicked out of the army—not after he explained the circumstances. She actually thought it was kind of funny and the army was being stupid for making it illegal for our young men and women in uniform to buy and sell and watch pornography when we were engaged in a worldwide war against Islamic terrorists.

Plus she was somebody to report to. Everybody needs somebody to report to at the end of the day or in the morning when you wake. But here under the Causeway the Kid has no one to report to. Not even the Rabbit who never asks what the Kid did today or last night. No one down here asks questions except on the first day or two like the Shyster did when he first arrived. It was like a code: Don't ask and don't tell. So with no one to report to after a while the Kid missed his mother.

Now however the Professor has come into his life and because he doesn't live under the Causeway he feels free to ignore the Don't Ask Don't Tell code and the Professor asks all kinds of questions of the Kid. In spite of the games he sometimes plays the Professor has gradually gained the Kid's trust—the bit about the map actually helped because it provoked a temporary feeling of intimacy. At least on the Kid's part. Plus the stuff he brought the Kid and carrying him and Einstein and Annie and all his worldly possessions in his van from Benbow's back here to the Causeway. And now he's helping the Kid organize the settlement and make it clean and safe—or at least cleaner and safer than it was—and has eased the Kid into a position of authority and responsibility down here which the Kid to his surprise enjoys. The fat man's even willing to help the Kid get food and medicine for Annie and Einstein.

But payback time is on the horizon, the Kid knows. On the drive over to the pet shop on Rampart he asks the Professor what's all this going to cost him?

You mean for dog food and birdseed and maybe a salve for Annie's sores? Probably not much. Under twenty dollars for the next four weeks. Do you need money?

Not for that. Not now. I can cover expenses for the next few weeks. Till I find another job busing tables or whatever. No, I mean, what's it gonna cost me for this, the rides, setting things up back there under the Causeway and shit like that? And the stuff you gave me? What's in it for you? From me?

The Professor smiles and drives on.

CHAPTER SIX

K: *I get to see all this footage and shit and listen to it and give my permission or maybe not give it depending on how I feel about it, right? I ain't signed any kind of permission slip or anything yet, y'know.*

P: *Don't worry, I'll make you a copy and you can review it before signing a release. It's not for public distribution anyhow.*

K: *What's it for then?*

P: *Research.*

K: *Whose?*

P: *Mine.*

K: *What're you researching? Convicted sex offenders? Homeless people?*

P: *Both. When they're the same.*

K: *Yeah, well, usually they are the same. Is that thing running?*

P: *It's running.*

K: *You planning on interviewing the other guys living down here after you finish with me? 'Cause most of them won't do it, you know.*

P: *They're . . . what? Shy?*

K: *Fuck no. Ashamed. Scared maybe. Mostly ashamed though. Even though most of 'em don't think they did anything wrong.*

P: *What about you? Do you think you did anything wrong?*

K: *(long pause) Illegal for sure. And stupid. Really stupid. I hadda do group therapy in prison, y'know. We hadda talk about all this right-versus-wrong shit. It never did get cleared up except when guys were lying about it and saying oh yeah it was really wrong what I did and I'll never do it again for sure, I'm not a come-freak anymore, no more kid fruit for me, no more peeping, no more quail hunting for me, nossir, I've learned my lesson, no more weenie-wagging for this old guy. But it was all bullshit. Especially for the chomos.*

P: *Chomos?*

K: *You know, child molesters. Guys who're into little kids.*

P: *I take it you're not a chomo.*

K: *I'm not "into" anything, man. Okay, maybe I used to be like into porn and banging the bishop a little too hard for what's considered normal, but it was always your normal porn showing the usual run of normal sexual activities between two and sometimes three or more consenting adults. The kind of stuff you can see on pay-per-view TV or your computer screen any night anywhere in America even where Jesus rules. As for banging the bishop all the time, I pretty much had a woodie every minute of the day due to my youth so what else was I gonna do except stroke it? Like I said, I never had a regular girlfriend I could fuck or who would blow me. Listen, is this all being recorded and like on film? 'Cause you're gonna hafta edit a lot of this shit out on account of the language.*

P: *Don't worry, no one but me will ever see or listen to it. Just use the occasion to tell your side of the story. That's all I'm looking for, your side of the story.*

K: *That's not so easy to do, tell my side of the story.*

P: *Why not?*

K: *It's hard to know where it begins and where it ends. Or if it ends. With other people's versions of your story it's easy. The cops' version, the lawyers', the judges', even your mother's version. They can pick and choose where your story begins and what it leads to because they weren't really there when it began. They weren't inside you when you were eleven or twelve and started whacking off under the blanket with a flashlight and a beat sheet. You ever wonder why they call them skin mags and skin flicks, by the way?*

P: *Can't say I—*

K: (interrupts) *Me neither. I mean they're not really skin, they're just pictures of skin. The only skin they get you touching is your own.*

P: *I don't understand.*

K: *Never mind.*

P: *So where do you think your story, your side of the story, begins?*

K: *Good question. I kinda think my story's pretty much the same as most guys my age up to when I got shit-canned outa the army. Most guys means guys like me who're pretty much normal sexually speaking but don't have a regular sex life with another person. No girlfriend and no wife and no prospects on the horizon, so to speak. And no money for ho's. I never went to a ho. Lap dances. I had a lap dance once. I tell you about that? Yeah, I did. All most guys like me got for sex is their computer and their chubby. Most guys are like that, and face it, most guys my age could end up doing what I did easy.*

P: *Most guys your age aren't convicted sex offenders.*

K: *Don't remind me.*

P: *Were you guilty as charged?*

K: *I pleaded guilty. My lawyer said it would go easier on me if I did. He was only a public defender, but I guess he was right. Six months is a long time for what I did, though. Six months and ten years' parole and the rest of my life. 'Course I only got to wear this electronic foot collar for ten. But even when I get to take it off I'll still be on the fucking registry for the rest of my life. I'll still be homeless and living under the Causeway or someplace like it that's more than twenty-five hundred feet from wherever there are kids gathered or else I'll be living in some wilderness where there's only animals for neighbors, like I'm an animal myself, one of those pet store pythons that people get tired of feeding mice to so they drive out to the Panzacola Swamp and leave them by the side of the road and drive off while the python slithers down from the road into a culvert or under a causeway or an overpass and makes his home there for a while. Until the park rangers decide they can't have giant pythons from like Asia and South America living in the Great Panzacola Swamp so they raid the place with dogs and baseball bats*

*and guns and bust the pythons and shoot them. For the public's safety.
That's my fate, I'm pretty sure.*

P: *Don't be so sure.*

K: *I said "pretty" sure.*

P: *What did you end up pleading guilty to? All it says on the registry is you
were convicted of a Class Two felony.*

K: *I don't feel like going there. I gotta spend some time with my animals. I
gotta get Einstein talking. I gotta encourage Annie here to act like a regular fucking watchdog. All she wants to do is sleep. Maybe I'll get Rabbit
or somebody to try and sneak up on me while I'm pretending to sleep
in my tent, and if she barks give her a treat to reward her. Sort of get her
started.*

P: *Why don't you feel like going there?*

K: *Where?*

P: *Telling me what you pleaded to.*

K: *I'm not telling you, I'm telling that fucking little black box. I don't like
little black boxes. Besides, it sounds worse than what I actually did. What
I'm actually guilty of.*

P: *Are you ashamed of what you did? What you're actually guilty of?*

K: *No. Not really. Except it was stupid, like I said. But I'm not ashamed.
Actually, yeah, maybe I am.*

P: *If you're unsure, maybe you should tell me what you did. It may help you
make up your mind about how to feel.*

K: *You can't make up your mind about how you'll feel, man. How you feel
is how you feel. Besides, you'll just think I'm like the rest of these guys
down here, making up excuses and shit. Lying and blaming the victim,
like they say, or I'm like the Shyster and some of the other weirdos who
don't have a moral compass, like they say, and think there's nothing
twisted about wanting to bonk little kids or wag their weenies in front of
old ladies in wheelchairs. I know the difference between what's normal
and what's weird. And I'm not making up excuses for myself when I
admit that what I did was stupid, because it was illegal and I sort of knew
it, but I did it anyhow. That's not an excuse and it's not blaming anyone*

*else. It's just a fact. Everybody does shit that they sort of know is illegal.
Even you, Professor. Right?*

P: *Yes. Right.*

K: *So what do you do that's illegal? Smoke weed? You don't look like you're
into blow.*

P: *To tell you the truth, nowadays I don't do anything that's illegal. Nothing that I'm aware of anyhow.*

K: *"Nowadays." So you have a shady past, Professor.*

P: (chuckles) *You could say that.*

K: *Big-time? I mean shadier than smoking weed or cheating on your taxes.*

P: *Big-time.*

K: *Cool. Can you tell me about it?*

P: *No.*

K: *You ever do time?*

P: *No.*

K: *That's why you can't tell me about it. Your side of the story. You can only
tell your side of the story if you got caught. If the story has an ending.
Right?*

P: *Right.*

K: *And your story's still running.*

P: *In a sense. But yours isn't. You got caught. So tell me your story. If I ever
get caught I'll tell you mine.*

K: *I hope you get caught, Professor. I'd like to hear what a guy like you did
that was big-time illegal and shady, a famous professor and all, respected
pillar of the community, guy in a three-piece suit and necktie doing valuable
research on down-and-out homeless convicted sex offenders like me living
like rats under the Causeway. I'd like to hear that story.*

P: *Let's hear your story for now. Maybe someday you'll hear mine.*

K: *When you get caught for what you did.*

P: *It won't happen.*

K: *That's what you think.*

P: *Tell me about it.*

CHAPTER SEVEN

He rode the bus south from Fort Drum all the way to Calusa without getting out except for coffee and a take-out sandwich at the bus stops and he sat alone the whole way—fifteen hundred miles and four days and three nights—depressed and angry at himself and the U.S. Army regulations against distributing pornography that couldn't make a distinction between distribution for a profit and giving away DVDs to guys in your outfit who you wanted to respect you and be your buddies so that when you got to Iraq or Afghanistan they'd watch your back. Now he has no place to go except to his mother's house, his old bedroom and his tent in the backyard next to Iggy's cage. He has no job to go back to—the new guy who took over the light store after Tony Perez got killed in the robbery acted like he still believed the Kid was somehow involved even though thanks to his mother's lie he had an ironclad alibi. No friends either, male or female, except for Iggy of course, Iggy being one of the reasons—a minor reason—for no friends since most people especially people his age thought it was weird to have a full-grown thirty-pound iguana for a pet or else they were scared of it or disgusted. So no posse just like when he was in high school and the other kids and even the teachers thought he was boring and not very bright and short and skinny with a personality that had no specialty. They never even bothered to bully him in school. He might actually have liked it for the attention if once in a while his fellow students had slammed him against a wall or a bank of lockers or stuck his head in a urinal and flushed or yanked off his backpack and tossed his books and notebooks into a toilet. A loser. That's what he was before he joined the army and that's what he was while he was in the army and now that he had been kicked out of the army he was even more of a loser than before.

His mother seemed to think so too. The only reason she was glad to see him when he arrived back at her door was because she was sick of taking care of Iggy. Within days of his departure for Fort Drum she had given up following his careful instructions for feeding and watering the iguana and cleaning its cage but couldn't quite bring herself to ignore the creature altogether and had started tossing unopened loaves of white bread into the cage and the occasional leftover pizza crust and had started hoping for Iggy's death or escape and disappearance. Several times a week she forgot to close and latch the door of his cage and managed to be both surprised and disappointed when she returned in the evening from work and saw that the cage was open and Iggy was still inside it. It was more or less how she had treated the Kid himself in recent years. Most of his life actually, even when he was a baby. She believed that she was not cut out to be a mother, that's how she put it to her friends and lovers. Which allowed her to give herself extra credit for keeping her son fed and clothed and housed, however inadequately it may have appeared to a social worker, for example, or to someone who in fact *was* cut out to be a mother.

So the Kid moved back in with her. Temporarily, he figured, until he got a job and could afford a place of his own preferably over on the Barriers where you could walk along the beach or sit at one of the outdoor cafés on Rampart and let your eyes caress the shoulders and thighs of girls and young women in their bikinis and wonder about their hidden body piercings—nipple- and clit-rings and so on. But he hadn't been honorably discharged from the army and when he applied for jobs at McDonald's and Starbucks and the other fast-food chains and even the supermarkets and especially Walmart they ran him through the usual databases and came up with a reason not to hire him. It's what they wanted, a reason not to hire him. He was a lousy interviewee and got worse as he went along—sullen, inarticulate, evasive—and with each interview grew more pessimistic and discouraged until he came to believe that he was worse than unemployed, he was unemployable and ought not to be hired. His message to the person sitting across from him was *Don't hire me, I'm unemployable.*

Soon he gave up reading the want ads altogether or visiting once a week the state unemployment office to check the listings there. When they saw the Kid walk through the door the clerks rolled their eyes and sighed audibly and he noticed and slumped down in the chair and waited until finally one of the clerks called him over and gave him a shorter and shorter list of potential employers and sent him out to be interviewed and not hired again. He made them feel like failures and they in turn passed it back until to break the downward spiral he stayed home at his mother's and let night turn into day and day into night and talked to Iggy and watched porn on his computer until he ran out of money and maxed out his debit card.

That's when he started clicking his way onto the sex-talk chat room that he didn't know at first was a sex-talk chat room. He thought it was a regular discussion forum open to all subjects. It's how he met brandi18. He followed his mouse from *craigslist.org* to *Calusa* to *jobs* to *food/hospitality* as if he were looking for a job on the Internet. In minutes he was depressed and discouraged by the curt clean language of the job requirements and knew he was defeated before he even started, so he followed his mouse back out to *Calusa* again and clicked on *services* and from there to *adults* where he declared he was over eighteen years of age and watched a little free porn for a while and when he had jerked off into a tissue he zipped up his fly and clicked out to *Calusa* again and tried checking out discussion forums thinking maybe somebody out there with a female iguana was looking for a stud like Iggy and he could raise a little cash on stud fees.

He knew people did that with dogs and horses, so why not iguanas? Iggy was ready. Once a year since Iggy was three years old and sexually mature as summer came on and there was a slight increase in the length of the day and a rise in humidity and temperature, starting at his head and dewlap and ending at his tail Iggy turned orange. Male iguanas have two penises hidden in a pouch between their hind legs and in breeding season the pouch swells and the iguana grows restless and lustful and will try to mate with anything animate or inanimate shaped even vaguely like a female iguana, biting down where it thinks the neck is supposed to be located and humping its backside with one of its penises until it splats a dollop of semen and relaxes its grip and sleeps for a short while, when it starts all over again with the second penis. Then a short rest period and it's back to the first. And on and on.

Usually the Kid filled an athletic sock with wood chips and tied off the open end and tossed it on the floor of Iggy's cage for him to mate with and a week or ten days later Iggy's color would slowly turn back to its normal green and he'd calm down and resume his old habits and quiet routines, finished for the year with sex. This time the Kid thought he'd try to put the iguana's annual sexual crescendo to some money-making use and save himself a sock in the process.

He typed: *healthy full-grown m iguana available 2 mate w healthy f.* And waited for a response. His handle was iggyzbro.

Almost immediately he received a reply.

brandi18: Huh?

He wasn't going to dignify the question with an answer—obviously brandi18 knew nothing about iguanas—but when no one else after a day and a night responded to his text, iggyzbro wrote: *my iguana rdy 2 breed. do u have a f and want babies? stud fee neg.* He would have written *negotiable* but wasn't sure how to spell it.

brandi18:	*stud fees r for losers. r u a ho?*
iggyzbro:	*no way.*
brandi18:	*way. illegal 2 sell sex on craigslist u no.*
iggyzbro:	*im selling iguana sex.*
brandi18:	*gross!!! u serious???*
iggyzbro:	*do u have a f iguana?*
brandi18:	*that's not what i call it.*
iggyzbro:	*what do u call it?*
brandi18:	*pends on my mood.*
iggyzbro:	*mine's called iggy.*
brandi18:	*cool. how big is iggy?*
iggyzbro:	*huge. what's yrs called?*
brandi18:	*like i said, pends on my mood.*
iggyzbro:	*what mood u in today?*
brandi18:	*kinda curious abt u. lol.*
iggyzbro:	*k. what's yours called when yr curious abt me?*
brandi18:	*kittycat. get it?*
iggyzbro:	*no.*
brandi18:	*gotta go. my mom's calling me. how old r u?*
iggyzbro:	*21*
brandi18:	*yeah, sure.*
iggyzbro:	*how old r u?*
brandi18:	*2 young 4 u and iggy 4 sure.*
iggyzbro:	*pends. iggy likes iguanas younger than him if theyre sexually mature. is yrs sexually mature?*
brandi18:	*what do u mean?*
iggyzbro:	*how old r u?*

By this time the Kid knew they were no longer talking about iguanas and was scrambling to keep up with brandi18. At first she said she was eighteen and when he asked if she was on Facebook and had any pictures of herself posted there and said maybe he'd check her out and be her friend she admitted that she was only kidding, she was really fourteen. But she looked older, she wrote.

The Kid pulled up Facebook and signed on and peeped her, then came back and told her she did look seventeen or even eighteen but was real cute. *yr a hottie,* he added after a pause. He decided not to ask her to friend him and instead continued their conversation on the craigslist forum. It was their own more or less private thread and felt safer to him than Facebook if she really was only fourteen— although he couldn't imagine why a girl would lie about that, say she was younger than she really was. Until they're eighteen or so under-age girls usually say they're older than they really are to keep the guy from logging off and deleting the evidence.

No harm just chatting with her, he decided. If he ran into her at a bus stop or sat next to her in a café he'd feel safe asking her about herself like this and telling her a few things about himself. Especially someone as pretty as brandi18, cute and a hottie: in the picture on Facebook she had long brown hair with blond streaks tied back in a ponytail and cream-colored skin and didn't seem to be wearing any makeup or jewelry except for pearl studs in her ears. Her eyes were large and round and either blue or hazel, he couldn't quite tell from the photograph, and she appeared to be looking slightly up at the camera as if she had taken it herself with her cell phone with her arm extended and the camera held above her head a ways. It gave her a flirty look that he liked—warm and reassuring but also invit-ing. Promising. Tempting. She was wearing a Disney World T-shirt, he noticed.

She told him her real name was Brandi and she used brandi18 online because there were seventeen other Brandis in front of her subscribing to the same Internet provider. She said her mom and dad were divorced and she lived with her mom alone in West Calusa Gardens, a suburb that she said was boring and she hated. *sux,* she wrote. Especially because she could only get to the mall by bus except when her mom drove her and that she said *sux 2*.

He agreed. He told her he had a car, a two-year-old Beemer that he'd almost totaled a few weeks ago so it was in the body shop forcing him to take the bus too. *which sux*, he wrote. *so i no how u feel*. He wished his Beemer was fixed so he could drive her around in it and she wouldn't have to rely on her mom.

that wld b cool, she wrote.

He said he was living with his mom too but only temporarily because he'd just gotten out of the army and was still getting adjusted to civilian life and planned to take night courses at Calusa Community College in the fall in computer programming.

She asked him if he'd been in Afghanistan in the army and he wrote: *ya*.

She thought that was really cool and did he see anybody get killed or anything?

He wrote: *don't want 2 talk abt that*.

She understood. She hoped he hadn't been wounded or anything over there and he said he was lucky because he came home in one piece and some of his buddies didn't.

He asked brandi18 if she had a bf and she said she just broke up with him after three months of going steady. But she was over him now. He was a real loser even though he was older and a senior with his own car.

He asked her why she broke up with him and she said he cheated on her with her best friend and now she hated them both.

plenty of fish in the sea, he typed.

what abt u? she asked.

no gf, he answered. Before he went to Afghanistan there was someone but it wasn't all that serious. *mostly just sexual*, he told her, ready to back off and get light again if she took it the wrong way.

She wrote: *same with my ex-bf and my ex-bgf*.

He told her that it probably wouldn't last then and the bf would soon come back to her on his knees and ask to be her bf again.

She didn't think so. Not unless she agreed to have sex with him.

> iggyzbro: *u dont want that?*
> brandi18:   *am scared 2 do it.*
> iggyzbro: *y?*
> brandi18:   *dont want 2 get preg.*
> iggyzbro: *what abt protection? u no. condoms.*
> brandi18:   *he says only gays use condoms. true?*
> iggyzbro: *no!!! r u a virgin?*
> brandi18:   *my moms coming. got 2 go.*

He asked for her e-mail address and gave her his so they could talk later, he said. In privacy instead of on the craigslist forum.

Then brandi18 logged out and left the Kid staring at the screen reading and rereading the thread from start to finish, trying to determine if he had written anything to her that he couldn't have said to her in person in public and finally deciding that even though he had been more intimate with her than he had ever been with a girl before he had been respectful of her youth and the difference in their ages. He was surprised that he had dared to ask her if she was a virgin though. He'd never asked that of anyone before, male or female, and wondered what he would have said if she had answered yes. What if she'd said no? Where in the conversation would they have gone next? Would she have asked him if he was a virgin? Probably not. He was twenty-one, after all. No one his age was a virgin except maybe a few Jesus freaks and you couldn't be sure about them.

He was sorry he had lied to her about the Beemer and Afghanistan and the rest—although maybe it really was a good idea to take a course in computer programming at the community college in the fall. Maybe it was more than an idea grown from a lie to impress a girl online. Maybe it was a plan. It was the first plan he'd come up with since arriving back at his mother's house from Fort Drum. Talking to brandi18 was good for him and he felt better about himself than he had in a very long time.

The next night shortly after ten the Kid checked his e-mails and there she was again. It was a different format than the craigslist forum—no ads, no columns of subjects and lists of offerings to click onto, just the simple in-box and subject line. It was like she had showered and changed clothes and her hair was still a little wet from the shower. He could almost smell her soap and a touch of cologne when he saw her name *brandi18* under sender and read *hi again* on the subject line.

He was in his bedroom in front of his old Dell laptop, his mother was out with her girlfriends from the shop making the rounds of the bars—younger women than she, in their late twenties, heavy drinkers and dopers who like to do shots of tequila and get high on weed in guys' cars in the parking lots outside. Iggy lay on his back sleeping in his cage under the heat lamp, his belly full and rounded from his supper of a pound of spinach leaves, his twin penises engorged in their pouch, ready for action as soon as he converted the spinach into pellets. The Kid opened brandi18's e-mail and she said *wassup? been thinking abt u since last nite.*

He answered *nuttin up* and hoped he hit the correct jocular tone. Harder to do with e-mail than in a chat room. E-mail was a step or two closer to actual conversation, almost like writing a letter which made it harder to control his tone of voice especially with a girl at the other end, a fourteen-year-old girl he was trying to impress. He wanted her to think he was intelligent and worldly and handsome and knew he was none of those things.

She answered right away: *u mad @ me?*

Okay, wrong tone. Better try sincere and confidential, even though that won't help make him sound worldly. His idea of worldly was sarcasm. He told her he'd had a hard day. Flashbacks to Afghanistan. Beemer's still in the shop. Can't get a decent job because his computer skills aren't up to speed which is why he needs to enroll at Calusa Community College. Money problems. His mother was nagging him to pay rent for his room (that part was true) and the insurance company wouldn't pay for the repairs to his Beemer (not true since the Beemer was a total lie) because his driver's license had expired while he was in Afghanistan. (Only partially true as he never had a driver's license in the first place. All he had for an ID was his old high school photo identification card that he was still using as a bus pass. He looked younger than twenty-one and the bus drivers never checked the birth date on the card when he flashed it getting on. He didn't tell her any of that.)

Sincere and confidential worked despite the falsity of almost everything he told her. She said she was really sad for him. *that sux.* She had problems too, she said. But nothing as bad as his because she was only a kid still and her mom was too cheap to let her have a cell phone of her own and too strict to let her go out alone with guys who had cars even though her mom was almost never home because she traveled a lot for her job and couldn't know what Brandi was doing when she was away anyhow. And her dad only checked in on her when he wanted to fight with her mom about his alimony and support payments. He was a total asshole, she wrote.

so do u like have guys over when your mom's away? he asked. *do u party when she's gone?*

She said not big parties that the nosy neighbors would notice but sometimes friends came over with beer and weed. She asked him if he smoked weed.

ya, when it comes my way, he typed. That sounds worldly, he thought. *btw, u never answered my q yesterday.*

what q?

r u a virgin?

lol, she wrote back.

He asked her why it was funny—funny to ask or funny to answer? *just curious,* he said, *so I can no how 2 talk 2 u better.*

She said he could say anything he wanted. She knew all about sex, she said, even though she'd never really done it with a guy.

what about w a girl?
ew!! no way!!
what about bjs?
not saying.

He said he'd take that as a yes to blow jobs and suddenly had an erection: *gets me excited,* he typed.

She changed the subject then, asking him if he had a cam on his computer or cell phone so she could see what he looked like.

No cam, he told her, and no cable to download pictures from his cell phone to send as a PDF from his computer.

She asked him if he looked like anybody she'd know from TV and how tall he was. She said he must be muscular from being in the army like all those guys in the TV ads that try to get guys to enlist.

He admitted he was short, five eight, he said, adding three inches. But yeah, pretty muscular though not bulging like a body-builder. He wasn't sure if he looked like anybody she knew from TV but people sometimes told him he reminded them of Michael J. Fox who had some kind of disease he was always going on about, Parkinson's or epilepsy or something, although he looked pretty normal to the Kid. It was his mother who had pointed out his resemblance to Michael J. Fox which at the time he had not taken as a compliment except for the fact that the actor was famous and presumably rich. *i don't have any diseases,* he reassured Brandi. *i'm clean and healthy as a teenager.*

lol, she wrote back. *u don't know teenagers.*

used 2 be 1 myself a few years ago.

She asked him his real name and he told her. Why did he use

iggyzbro for his online name? she wondered and he told her his pet iguana was named Iggy.

She was surprised to learn that there really was an iguana after all and wanted the Kid to describe Iggy in detail because she had never seen one before and wondered why anyone would want an iguana for a pet.

So he described Iggy in affectionate detail and when he got to the part about the two penises and that Iggy was going through his brief sexually active cycle and was turning from green to orange he realized he was starting to flirt about sex with brandi18 again as if he himself were turning from green to orange and had two erect penises. He didn't mean to go there. He didn't need reminding that she was only fourteen and he was twenty-one but somehow her questions and comments kept drawing him back to sexual innuendo and inquiry until they both, the Kid and brandi18 too, were getting dangerously explicit—dangerous at least for the Kid. When he read back over their string of e-mails it seemed she was only being playful yet her play kept drawing him forward until finally he typed *id rly like 2 hang with u some nite when your mom's away.*

> *what wld we do?*
> *whatever we want 2 do. just c what happens. i could bring beer and*
>   *a movie.*
> *what kinda movie?*
> *a sexy 1. u ever watch p?*
> *whats p?*
> *u no. porn.*
> *o ya, i watched a couple on pay-per-view when my mom was away.*
>   *she found out frm the bill and was pissed.*
> *turn u on?*
> *ya!*
> *were u alone? or w yr bf?*
> *no!! only alone.*

wld be fun 2 watch p 2gether.
maybe.

The Kid asked her for her street address and she gave it to him which he took as a clear invitation to visit her. He asked when her mom would be away next and she said this coming weekend she was going on a gambling cruise on a ship out of Calusa with the people who worked at her office.

all weekend? he wondered.

ya!

He said he'd come over.

She reminded him that his car was still in the shop. He'd not be able to drive out to West Calusa Gardens unless he could borrow a car. Better wait till his Beemer was fixed.

He said no, he could take a bus. He'd do a search on MapQuest and find the closest bus stop and walk from there. He lived in the north end of the city and there were buses running west to the suburbs and back every half hour till midnight and every hour after that. Even if they hung out till late he could still get home, he said and waited for her answer to come up on his screen.

After a long five minutes he finally heard the *ping* signaling the arrival of a new e-mail and the announcement from the AOL woman, *you've got mail.* It was brandi18. Who else? He never got e-mail, never heard that announcement except for spam. He clicked it open.

sorry. had a phone call from my mom checking up on me. i'm sorta
    grounded.
what 4?
grades. so r u coming fri or sat?
i'll come fri. c what happens and maybe sat. 2 if u like. u might
    invite me 2 stay over.
yr 2 old. and a guy. my moms'll kill me if she finds out.
she wont.

bring the beer. my moms counts her stash when she gets home.

k. i'll bring some surprises 2.

like what?

u'll see. Around 10 ok?

k. bye. gotta log out and delete. my moms is home. sometimes she reads my e-mails when she gets home. she's a bitch. c u fri around 10.

He pushed back from the computer and lighted a cigarette. He was sweating and noticed that his hands were trembling. He was frightened of what he was doing, had done, would do if given the opportunity. But it was too late to back off now. What had begun as an itch had turned into a barely conscious fantasy that had become a plan and now a promise. He wasn't frightened because she was only fourteen—he had almost blocked that out and besides she looked and sounded older on Facebook and in her e-mails. He was scared and nervous because he had never invited himself to visit a girl at her house alone, had never dared to—no girl had let him believe that he wouldn't be laughed at for even asking her for more than the time of day. And here this pretty girl was asking him to bring beer and a skin flick and see what happens.

Okay, he'll see what happens. He'll have to buy some condoms. How many or what kind or size he wasn't sure. He'd never bought condoms before, had never even checked the rack to see if they came in different sizes. He figured he'd need extra-large probably unless they only came in one size and were really flexible.

And he'd have to rent a movie from the adult section of Moviemasters, nothing too hard-core, no gangbang or cum-shots although maybe cum-shots are sexy to girls and not just guys. He wasn't sure what was sexy to girls. Except for vibrating dildo films and the occasional chick-on-chick lesbian films which didn't really get him excited anymore porn seemed pretty much designed for guys. She was white so she'd probably only want to see white people

fucking at least this first time. Maybe down the road she'd be interested in watching a black dude with a donkey-dong getting blown
by a white girl.

She'd probably want to see something with a story attached at
least at the beginning—one of those movies that start out with the
husband going off on a business trip leaving his beautiful wife home
alone and horny and this young stud comes over in his tight cutoff
shorts and no shirt to clean the pool while she's watching from the
window upstairs and getting all wet so she puts on her bikini and
goes down to the pool and lies on a chaise to sunbathe. The pool
guy checks her out and asks for a glass of water and she brings it to
him from the kitchen and when he finishes and sets the glass down
she runs her finger down his bare chest to his crotch. And then the
action starts and you don't need the story anymore till the end where
the husband comes home and suggests jazzing up their tired sex life
by inviting someone to join them and they look out the window at
the pool guy and the next scene has both guys fucking the wife one
from behind and her blowing the other and the two guys come at
the same time: The End.

He'd look for one of those at Moviemasters tomorrow which
was Thursday and watch it alone first to make sure it had enough
of a story to interest a fourteen-year-old girl. It wouldn't matter if
it didn't interest him because he'd already seen it and hundreds of
others just like it. He'd be dealing with reality this time. Not illusion.
He'd be watching and actually touching a real female human being's
body, skin, breasts, legs, ass, vagina, instead of just pictures made from
electronic pixels whose colors and movement and arrangement on
a screen were predetermined and controlled by a script and director
and a half-dozen camera angles. That's what frightened him. That's
why his hands were trembling as he lighted another cigarette. He was
about to bump up against and break through an invisible membrane
between the perfectly controlled world locked inside his head and
the endlessly overflowing unpredictable, dangerous world outside.

CHAPTER EIGHT

EVEN THOUGH HE'S STILL NOT SURE WHAT exactly the Professor is after especially with the treasure map bit the Kid mostly trusts him now. Since the night he took the bus out to West Calusa Gardens to visit brandi18 he hasn't trusted anybody. Period. No one is who he or she seems to be. Not even the other men living under the Causeway. Including the Rabbit who probably made up all those stories about teaching Kid Gavilan how to throw the bolo punch.

That's okay, the Kid's not complaining, it's just the way things are. Everybody has a secret agenda and a secret life. Starting with his mother and moving out from there. Tony Perez had a secret agenda at the light store. Benbow and his goofy sidekick Trinidad Bob. The U.S. Army. It didn't matter who, people near or close to him, individually and in groups were all using him to advance their own hidden interests. Even brandi18. The Kid was nothing to her except an entertaining fool for her to laugh at and feel superior to. She was maybe the worst. The real problem is that the Kid doesn't know what his secret agenda is or if he has one.

But something about the Professor has gradually made him seem trustworthy to the Kid. It begins with his size, his enormous body and the way he dresses it. What you see when you first see him is what you get for the duration, a man so fat and tall and wide that you never get used to it—no matter how many times you see him he never looks normal. The bushy beard and long hair and the three-piece suit only add to his size and make no attempt to hide or disguise it. Most fat guys wear loose Hawaiian-style shirts or guayaberas and floppy trousers and try to make their beach-ball faces look smaller with short hair slicked back and going beardless or maybe keeping a trim little Vandyke beard so when you look at them you focus on their eyes and nose and lips and ignore the wide expanse of skin surrounding them. Nothing about the Professor's appearance is part of a disguise. He doesn't even wear sunglasses. Just squints in the glare looking like one of those Japanese sumo wrestlers.

The way he talks is trustworthy too. At least to the Kid it is. He talks like a professor, using long clearly pronounced words carefully in complete sentences but slowly said with a noticeable southern accent that the Kid guessed right away was from Alabama or Mississippi where the Kid has never heard of there being any professors so maybe he's actually more of a regular person than a professor. He's smart and educated, that's obvious, but he doesn't talk like he feels superior to people who aren't as smart and educated as he is. Most of the people the Kid has met in his life who are smarter and better educated than the Kid either talk down to him from a great height or else try to sound like they aren't really very intelligent and haven't even graduated from high school which only makes the Kid suspicious of their attitude. He's thinking of the social workers and psychologists he met in prison and a couple of teachers he had in high school who tried to get him to join in classroom discussions of current events or the books that were assigned even though the Kid never read newspapers except the headlines or watched the TV news or listened to radio newscasts and had not once read more than the first few pages of any of the books that had been assigned over his entire four years of high school. Most of what he knows about the history of the world and human life he's picked up from scraps of overheard conversation on the street and at the light store where he worked after school and weekends and from remarks exchanged by his fellow students and later the guys in his outfit at Fort Drum and now the men living with him under the Causeway. The Kid is one of those people who have made up the mass of mankind since the species first appeared on the plains of East Africa two or three million years ago. Most of his troubles arise because he's a twenty-first-century American and not some ancient East African or an early Cro-Magnon living with his extended family of hunter-gatherers in a cave in prehistoric Spain or a turnip-planting serf in medieval Russia or one of the early Calusa Indians harvesting oysters in the bay as the first ships from Europe hove into view.

He doesn't think of himself this way, of course—he never heard of Cro-Magnons or Russian serfs and can't tell East Africa from West—or he didn't until the Professor came into his life and started interviewing him, just getting him to tell his story and then showing him ways to improve his life by being better organized and more cooperative with the men living under the Causeway with him.

Now slowly he's starting to realize that he might be not exceptional but at least he's important simply for being who he is, that he's not really like the mass of mankind from the beginning of time whose entire lives and everything they chose to do or not to do is determined by their givens, the conditions and circumstances they were born into and the people they found there to accompany them in life. Until now the only living creatures who seemed to care what he did or thought and were therefore affected by his actions and thoughts were Iggy and Einstein the parrot and Annie the dog as if the Kid were closer to being reptile, bird, or four-legged animal than a human being alive and conscious in time with a beginning, middle, and end to his life, all three parts existing simultaneously in each separate part. His subjective life—his accumulated memories, wishes, fears, and reflections in the last few days—has started to take on an importance to him that it never held before. And consequently he's begun to have a new interest in the subjective lives of the people who are connected to him starting with the Professor but including the men who live alongside him under the Causeway. Even the Shyster whose story up to now he has had no desire to know since he had no story of his own to compare it to.

In the past it never occurred to the Kid to ask questions of the people he associated with. When they volunteered information— bits and pieces of their past and their longings, their dreads and anxieties, opinions and beliefs—he listened more or less politely but did not invite them to continue, to tell more, to clarify and amplify those bits and pieces and he mostly forgot what they told him soon after the telling. Now he finds himself wondering how the Greek got stuck down here under the Causeway, a mechanically clever and entrepreneurial guy who probably ran a successful machine shop or auto garage before he became a convicted sex offender. And P.C.— what's his story? And how come a smart guy like the Shyster with a law degree and married with a big-time successful political career gets obsessed with having sex with little girls without knowing how weird and harmful it is? What's up with that? What crossed his wires and when so that he couldn't recognize evil when he saw it in himself? What's going on inside the Shyster? the Kid wonders for the first time. And Rabbit, an old black dude busted up by the cops for probably the tenth time in his life hobbling around down here in the gloom and the damp surrounded by filth and rats and a colony of outcasts—what did he do to deserve this?

And then there's the Professor. The Kid wonders especially about the Professor. What's his story? They are in his van headed to the gigantic Paws 'n' Claws store for supplies and medicine for Einstein and Annie and the Kid asks him to tell how he came to be a professor. He's never known a real professor before and has no idea how you become one.

Indirection and serendipity. Belatedly. Not by the usual route. For years after I got my Ph.D. I was a paid consultant. For governments, our own and others. And for private interests. Here and abroad. Then I opted for a more settled life, so to speak. Academia.

Cool. What did you like consult about?

Various things. Cultural anthropology, let's call it. Local customs and politics in far-flung places.

The Kid would like to interview the Professor. He'd like to ask him what *serendipity* means. And *cultural anthropology,* what's that? There's a lot the Professor could teach him. And now that he's starting to have a story of his own he'd like to know the Professor's story even though very little of it would be of any use to him. He has no desire to ever become a professor himself and never intends to use the word *serendipity* in a sentence no matter what it means and the only reason he wants to know the meaning of *cultural anthropology* is so that he can better understand the Professor's story.

But the Professor's a hard guy to interview. You ask him a simple direct question and he goes all complicated and indirect on you. The Kid tries asking him his age and the Professor answers with a question and chuckles as if he's amused, *Why do you ask?*

The Kid explains that it's hard to tell how old he is because of the beard and his size—he chooses not to say *fat.*

How old do you think I am? Another question.

The Kid guesses fifty and the Professor says, *Close enough.* Not really an answer.

He tries another tack: *So where are you from? Originally. You got sort of a southern accent, you know.*

Do I?

Yeah. What's up with that? I didn't know professors could have southern accents.

It's sort of a disguise. Most of my students have southern accents. It puts them at ease if I have one too. It's become a habit.

The Kid decides to come from another angle: *What about a wife? You married?*

The Professor just nods. Again, not really an answer but it'll have to do. The Kid pictures the hugest woman he's ever seen, a woman the size of a small car. It's hard to imagine a man this fat being married to a woman not equally fat. But the Kid doesn't know how to ask if his wife is as fat as he is. It's what he wants to know though. Interviewing this guy is like trying to pry open a giant clam with only your fingers.

Kids? And here the Kid is obliged to picture the Professor having sex with his enormous wife, both of them naked and pink and hairy, their arms and bellies and thighs flopping and smacking against one another like slabs of beef and the Kid is sorry he asked—it's the worst porn film he's ever called to mind—and hopes the Professor says No. No kids.

But instead he says, *Your curiosity piques my curiosity. Why the sudden interest in my private life?*

I dunno. I guess on account of you being so interested in my private life. Interviewing me and all.

My interest in your private life, my friend, is strictly professional. I'm a social scientist and right now you are my object of study.

Like I'm a lab rat, you mean? In some kinda experiment?

In a manner of speaking, yes. But you needn't worry. In the social sciences we take excellent care of our lab rats. Their life expectancy is nearly twice as long as in the wild.

The Kid says, *Thanks a lot,* and the Professor chuckles again and pulls the van into the parking lot of the Paws 'n' Claws box store and parks.

CHAPTER NINE

Since childhood, though the Professor has been celebrated for his remarkable memory, he's a man whose life and mind are carefully compartmentalized, methodically divided into boxes that rarely share a single side, and when he's living in one box or remembers having lived there and can therefore recount it to himself or to someone else, his wife, for instance, or colleagues or students or strangers or even the Kid, he has no memory of ever having lived anywhere else. It's one of the reasons, when asked a direct question about his past or present life, he answers vaguely, indirectly, ambiguously, or changes the subject altogether. His life has no single unifying narrative. It has many distinct narratives, each of them internally consistent, with a beginning, middle, and end, but none of them is connected to the other, and for the most part none of them is even aware of the other's existence.

He's not a person with multiple personalities, however. In all his memories and accounts of his memories, no matter how they differ from one another in cast of characters, locale, and resolution and no matter the variety of roles he plays, he always presents the same personality to the world, just as he always presents the same physical body. All his adult life he has looked more or less the same as he looks now. As a child his body was merely a child's version of the body he came to inhabit later. And all his life, man and boy, he has had the same affect, the same manner of speaking, the same set of facial expressions and physical gestures, the same bemused, slightly condescending chuckle. It's why when he was a child he seemed so oddly and captivatingly adultlike.

Nor is he a pathological liar or even in the strict sense a liar at all. Because he's able and is actually compelled when living in one box to forget the existence of the others, his descriptions of his life are truthful. He could have been a great actor. Perhaps great actors possess his same ability to play many different roles, from Caliban to Othello to Lady Macbeth, from Uncle Vanya to Blanche Dubois to Mother Courage, all the while never changing their essential personality, and in the Professor's case never changing his costume either.

It would be easy to credit this unnatural mix of variety, inconsistency, and relentless constancy to his early childhood obesity and his amazing intelligence, to note how at the start of his life they situated him at the extreme outside edge of human interaction, imposing early on in an unusually sensitive and emotionally responsive child a sense of himself as both different from other children, almost freakishly so, and as special. His parents reinforced his sense of specialness, his exceptionalism. Everyone else helped him to feel at the same time strange and ill-formed, both more and less than human.

The Professor knows this much about his formative years. He wouldn't argue that his oversize body and wildly praised and publicized precocity simultaneously alienated him from everyone and at the same time made him feel superior to everyone, even to his parents. Though his parents doted on him and they genuinely loved him, they also exhibited him to the world and basked in his reflected light, as if his unusual intelligence and intellectual and academic achievements embellished their own. They saw themselves as having been inexplicably exiled to a small mining town in Alabama where their natural aristocracy and refined educations were insufficiently honored, where no one, except each other, properly appreciated them, where the Professor's mother was merely the town librarian, a position formerly held by unmarried older ladies not quite qualified to teach school, and where his father was merely the manager of the local absentee-owned coal mines, a kind of plantation foreman whose authority was derived from a higher authority located elsewhere, in a mansion on a hill in Pittsburgh.

Their son, therefore, was their homegrown exotic orchid, and they nurtured and nourished the innate qualities that distinguished him from the garden-variety flowers their neighbors grew. He was a large baby at birth, over eleven pounds, which amazed and delighted the doctor and nurses who helped deliver him, and led his parents to overfeed him from the day they brought him home. His appetite and expectations regarding food soon turned into need, as if he would shrivel and die if he were not overfed, and they now had no choice but to continue providing him with great heaping quantities of food at every meal and before and after meals until by the time he was three years old he spent more of his waking hours eating than doing anything else. By the time he was four, when not asleep he was reading and thus was able to take nourishment full-time. His mind and his body grew apace, and the world, at least the world of Clinton, Alabama, took notice of both and marveled. This pleased the Professor's parents. The child saw this, and though it made him wish to please them still more, just as their overfeeding him had only increased his hunger, so too he came to feel superior to his parents at the same rate and in the same way that he felt superior to other children and their parents. By the same token, he felt different from everyone, including his parents. Alienated, isolated, alone. Utterly alone.

Perhaps that's the one constant that is shared by all those separate compartments he lives in—a profound sense of isolation, of difference and a solitude that is so pervasive and deep that he has never felt lonely. It's the solitude of a narcissist who fills the universe entirely, until there is no room left in it for anyone else. In every life he has led, every identity he has claimed for himself and revealed to others, his profound sense of isolation was then and is now his core.

While the Professor knows most of the facts of the various lives he has led and the public and private, often secret, identities he has held, he has no conscious memory of being inside them. No memory of living those lives from one day to the next, from month to month, in some cases for years, or of being that person in a continuing way. For the Professor it's as if all the separate lives he has led belong to other people. And the life he leads now, it too belongs to someone else. He's privy to the facts of each, but little more. For him, that's enough. The facts. There is no use or point for him to remember what he actually experienced when he was perceived many years ago by his college and graduate school classmates and professors as a radical activist in the civil rights and antiwar movements, a founding member of the Southern Christian Leadership Conference and the Students for a Democratic Society and for a few harrowing months a member of Weatherman. There is for him no reason to try to remember what he felt back then or believed when he first agreed to work for the government agency that wanted to protect the American people from the unintended consequences of the civil rights and antiwar movements. As far as he remembers, he felt nothing. He believed nothing. It was a game, a puzzle, a test of wits and intelligence, and the higher the stakes the more interesting the game, the more challenging the puzzle, and thus the greater proof of his superior wit and intelligence.

He believed he was smarter than the government agents he reported to and smarter than the people he reported on and needed to prove it, to himself if to no one else. For him it was merely a contest between patriotic careerists and dope-smoking ideologues, both equally deluded, equally utopian, equally clannish. And though both believed that he was one of them, he belonged to neither clan.

He stood out too much, could never disappear in a crowd, was odd-looking and grossly overweight, spoke in a peculiar manner, was regarded by both groups as asexual, and was not known to drink alcohol or take drugs and seemed not to be interested in money. He remembers only that he loved the game, the secrecy, and took pleasure from knowing twice as much as either of the groups to which he was thought by the other to belong, even though within each group he was a minor figure. To the political activists in college and later in New Haven, the peculiar fat man was a carrier of signs in demonstrations, a late-night manager of the mimeo machine, a foot soldier in their small army of revolutionaries. To the several government agencies that over time employed him to report on the activities of that army, he was merely one of thousands of informants on college campuses and in ghetto flats and basements, garages, meeting halls, and safe houses all across the country. And later, as he traveled to Asia and Central and South America, ostensibly to extend his knowledge of languages and further his education, he was designated an asset, a reliable asset, but not an essential one, because for the most part the information he provided the agencies was of the type that merely corroborated what they already knew or confirmed what they believed. He was aware of that, of course, and didn't mind at all. His relatively low status in both groups—or was it three or four organizations or five, and was it one government he worked for or two or three?—suited him perfectly.

He was as easily replaceable an asset in their ranks as among the activists and revolutionaries. If he didn't volunteer to print and deliver to every dormitory room at Kenyon a copy of The Port Huron Statement, someone else would. If he weren't available to be a link in the human chain blocking access to the administration building, there were hundreds ready to take his place. If, after he left Yale and on instructions from the FBI, went to San Francisco, he backed out of selling methamphetamine to the biker gangs of Oakland, there were dozens of entry-level undercover agents eager to step forward and do the deed. Those were the years when the government feared a possible coalition of biker gangs, Black Panthers, Weatherman, famous Beat poets, rock musicians, movie actors, and heiresses, so it was glamorous to be selling and delivering drugs to Hells Angels. You might run into Peter Fonda or Allen Ginsberg or Huey Newton. And when he hit the hippie trail to Kathmandu to learn Urdu and reported back to his handlers from there and ducked down into the Andes to learn Quechua and then off to research the descendants of escaped slaves on the Mosquito Coast until he finally came ashore in Calusa and found employment as a writer of policy papers on the Caribbean for a think tank called the Caribbean Basin Institute and had his papers vetted by the CIA—he was always just another easily replaced asset who appeared to be doing one thing while he was in fact doing another. He was a small enough cog in such a huge machine that he could well have been employed at the same time by the KGB while maintaining a safe house for the last of the Weather Underground to come in out of the cold.

He too came in out of the cold, inasmuch as when he quit working at the Caribbean Basin Institute and accepted a position in the sociology department at Calusa University, he created for himself a life that no longer had one, two, or three false identities. Merely a series of false pasts. For the first time since college he was more or less who he seemed to be, even if there was a disconnect between who he seemed to be and who he once had been. Though he had been many things—political radical, civil rights activist, antiwar warrior, drug dealer, independent scholar and student of exotic languages and cultures, hippie seeker of Eastern enlightenment, FBI and CIA informant simultaneously reporting to at least two other independent intelligence-gathering agencies and one or possibly two foreign government agencies as well—all these identities could conceivably have led separately to his becoming the man he now appeared to be, a happily married father of two children living in suburban Calusa, a somewhat eccentric, tenured professor of sociology at the local university, a member of the library board, a deacon in the Congregational Church, a man once portrayed in the newspaper as the smartest man in town, possibly the state.

But only if none of the men he had been once upon a time was aware of the felt, subjective existence of any of the others. They remained separate and distinct identities that knew of the factual existence of the others but did not identify with the others. They could not remember what it was like to actually be the others. And he, the Professor, can only remember what it was like to be himself in the years since he came in from the cold and ceased being an informant and gradually came to be solely who he seemed to be.

He is a man, therefore, without a past. A man with many pasts, who can, if forced, make a report on his life, but cannot tell his life's story. Each of his pasts was designed at the time strictly to deny the existence of the others, just as his present life denies the existence of all his previous lives, giving him the freedom to make them up at will. He can claim to one man that he fought in Vietnam and tell the Kid that he was a draft-dodging opponent of the war and not in either case be lying. If everything is a lie, nothing is. Just as, if everything is true, nothing is.

That's the story the Professor tells himself.

CHAPTER TEN

K: *Yeah, sure I was scared. I thought about not going out there at all, just fuck it, stay home again and bash the bishop in front of my computer pretending I was getting a BJ from brandi18, who was a real person with probably bee stings for tits and scared of me, instead of an actress with inflatable boobs and a cooch-light shining on her bush moaning Fuck me harder fuck my ass et cetera. It wasn't on account of brandi18 said she was only fourteen and a virgin, which I didn't believe anyhow, the virgin part at least, because of her Facebook pictures which she must've snapped with her cell phone in her bedroom wearing what looked like pj's with valentines all over and the top half unbuttoned and the other picture with really short cutoffs and a too-tight Disney World T-shirt.*

P: *The fact that she was fourteen and you were twenty-one wasn't why you were scared?*

K: *Well, she only said she was fourteen. You can be a talking dog online. She could've been a fifty-year-old guy for all I knew. Although I did believe her. I thought she was fourteen, only not as innocent as she was saying. I was thinking I'm the innocent one, I'm the real virgin, all I've ever done is beat my banana and watch porn and tell lies to guys that nobody believes. I never even kissed a girl before. Still haven't.*

P: *Why are you telling me this? It's the truth, isn't it?*

K: *You're the only one who's interested in the truth. Not the cops. Not the judge. Not even the shrink in prison or my parole officer. Whenever I told* them the truth, even the guys in my therapy group in prison, they thought I was lying, so I stopped telling the truth. I dunno, maybe you think I'm lying too.

P: *That you've never kissed a girl and yet you're a convicted sex offender? No, Kid, I believe you. Not that I don't think you broke the law. Obviously you broke the law. There you were, arranging to meet a fourteen-year-old girl at her mother's home, all alone, bringing her beer, a pornographic movie, condoms. Anything else?*

K: *Well, when I bought condoms I saw this tube of stuff, K-Y jelly, which I bought, I figured on account of my dick being pretty big and in case she really was a virgin it might come in handy. I mean, even though I was totally inexperienced at sex I actually know a lot about it from watching so much porn and listening to other guys. You can learn a lot about sex from porn, y'know. And from just listening.*

P: *Really? Like what?*

K: *You learn what gets you off, for instance. And what doesn't get you off. Like I'm not all that into bondage. Or chubbies. No offense. And guys on guys kinda leaves me limp. And you learn what girls like or at least what they say they like. And from listening to what guys talk about when they talk about sex you learn how to talk about sex. With other guys, that is. I'm not sure how to talk about sex with girls. Not in real life anyhow. I can do it online, okay? Or I could. Like with brandi18.*

P: *So you went out there to her mother's house in West Calusa Gardens?*

K: *Yeah. I took the bus and it let me off a couple blocks from the address, so I walked the rest of the way. It was dark but she had the porch light on and I could see the number. Nice neighborhood and all. Two-car attached garages, mowed lawns, pools in back. I had the beer and other stuff in my backpack and was wearing shorts and sneakers and a Bob Marley tee on account of it was pretty hot that night. I stood there awhile on the side-walk and checked out the house, which looked normal with lights on in the kitchen I could see and most of the rest dark except for a room upstairs that I figure is brandi18's room, and thinking about that got me sort of hot and made me forget that I was doing something that could get me in a* lot of trouble. Then I see brandi18 walk past the kitchen window. She has a little ponytail and is wearing a pink tank top, has little tits which turn me on more than jugs do, and is sort of short so the rest of her is below the windowsill and I couldn't see but figured she had on cutoffs, and I'm already getting a woodie just from that glimpse of her in the kitchen. She stops and looks out and sees me standing on the sidewalk out front in the streetlight and kind of waves like she isn't sure it's me, so I wave back and she gestures like come on in. So I go up the front walk to the door which is open except for a screened door and she hollers from the kitchen in this teenage girl's kind of voice, I gotta switch the laundry to the dryer! I'll be right there! There's some cookies and lemonade on the counter so help yourself, she says from someplace beyond the kitchen, a laundry room, I figure.

P: So you walk through the door. You cross the line, so to speak. A line once you're over you can never cross the other way.

K: You got that right, Professor. I walk through the living room and dining room which are pretty fancy with wall-to-wall rugs and designer-type furniture, I notice, even though the only lights on are in the kitchen which is where I settle on a stool beside the counter where there's a plate with Oreo cookies and a glass of lemonade with ice cubes, like she just poured it when she saw me standing outside. I'm thinking this is cool. I feel like frigging Santa Claus. I put my backpack on the floor and eat an Oreo and take a sip from the lemonade when the door to what I figure is the laundry room swings open and this dude in a suit and tie walks into the kitchen, a guy like in his forties with blow-dry hair who looks like a TV Christian telethoner.

P: Uh-oh.

K: Duh. I stand up and he says sit down. So I sit down and try to swallow the Oreo, but it's crumbly and dry so I gulp some lemonade and try to look natural. The guy has a wide face like a frog and this orange dyed hair. He asks my name and I tell him my first name only and say what's his name. Dave, he says. Dave Dillinger. I say are you her father? He says who? Brandi, I say. The girl who lives here. I'm hoping maybe it's

Brandi's mother's boyfriend or a preacher for real that Brandi's mother asked to check on Brandi while she was away. But he doesn't say. Instead he asks me what I'm doing here and I say I came to see a friend. Brandi's your friend? he says. Yeah, sort of. We like met online. He goes, What were you planning on doing with Brandi tonight? I dunno. Watch TV. Hang out. Whatever. Now I'm thinking maybe this guy Dave Dillinger is Brandi's real boyfriend even though he's in his forties and he thinks she's fucking me on the side because he's an old guy and I'm closer to her age group. I don't want to have to fight the guy even though I'm still in good shape and know a few moves from the army, as he's quite a bit bigger than me and looks in good shape too. It's okay, I say. I'll leave. I was just stopping by. He goes, No, sit down. He has a few questions. For the first time I wonder if he's a cop so I ask him. No, he's not a cop, he says. He asks me what I've got in my backpack. I tell him beer. A six-pack of Bud Light. Do you know how old Brandi is? he wants to know. I say I dunno, maybe eighteen or nineteen. I was gonna drink it myself, I add. Eighteen or nineteen? he says. Then I notice he's carrying a file folder and he takes out a bunch of papers and he reads down a couple of sheets. iggyzbro. Is that you? he asks. I say yeah, I guess so. He reads from the papers. iggyzbro: how old r u? brandi18: 18. iggyzbro: r u on facebook? mayb I'll check u out 4 real. brandi18: u can friend me if u want. iggyzbro: K. brandi18: I'm really 14 like it sez on facebook. Sorry.

P: *So he has a transcript of your e-mails? Which he no doubt got from Brandi. Assuming there is a Brandi.*

K: *Yeah. Anyhow, he reads some more. Like where I ask her if she's a virgin and everything. And where I suggest watching porn and tell her I'll bring condoms.*

P: *You wrote that down? And now this man has the printed transcript?*

K: *I didn't know brandi18 was like a real person. I mean, we were just e-mailing. Of course it turns out she wasn't a real person anyhow.*

P: *What do you mean?*

K: *I mean she was like one person online and another person that night in her mother's house when I went out there thinking we were gonna hook* up. It's complicated. Anyhow, I ask the guy if he's her father or is he like her boyfriend, since I'm remembering that brandi18 told me her ex-boyfriend was older but I didn't think this much older. The guy reminds me of the dude on a TV show called To Catch a Predator on MSNBC that I sort of watched a couple of times, and I suddenly think maybe I'm on the show and I'm like this week's contestant. I always thought they had like a script and the sleazoids they trick online into trying to have sex with underage girls were all actors 'cause some of them were really old, and this one guy was even a rabbi and another was an ex-cop and a couple of them had teenage daughters of their own. I thought it was like a situation comedy reality TV series only not funny. I never knew it was reality. So I'm getting ready for a TV cameraman and another guy with a mike on a boom to come out of the laundry room like they do on the show, when the old dude says he's Brandi's father. I go, Whoa! I thought this was Brandi's mother's house and shit, and he says it is and he thanks God that Brandi called him to come over when she learned I was coming here to the house tonight.

P: Wait a minute. Brandi called him? And gave him the printout of your chats and e-mails?

K: Yeah. Which is pretty fucked up, if you ask me. Totally fucked up. Anyhow, the guy asks me, How old are you? I tell him twenty-one, and he asks was I in the army like I said to his daughter Brandi, which is how I'm thinking of her now instead of brandi18, and I go, Yeah but I'm not now. And you were in Afghanistan? he says. And I go, No. I was only like talking that way, the way you do when you're online. He looks really happy to be disgusted. He wants to know what else I've got in my backpack besides the Bud Light and can he have a look? I just shrug why not. Whatever happens happens, I'm thinking. So he goes into my pack and pulls out the condoms and holds the package up. Condoms? he asks. Yeah. Were you planning to use these with a fourteen-year-old girl? he wants to know. Actually, he already knows. He just wants me to confess it. Not really, I say. I wasn't planning on anything. This is true, because I was mostly hoping, not planning. He goes back into my pack and pulls out the

DVD and reads the title out loud, Willow's Day Off, and notes that it's quadruple-x-rated. Not exactly appropriate for a fourteen-year-old girl to be watching with a twenty-one-year-old man, is it? he says. I shrug again and say it was all I had, which is pretty lame, I know, but also happens to be true. He pulls out the tube of K-Y jelly and says what's this? I tell him it's a lubricant. That really gets him off into happy deep disgust. A loo-bricant! he says. He repeats it a couple more times with his voice going lower each time like any minute he's going to come just from saying loo-bricant! Finally his eyes clear again and he asks if I'm married, and I say no, and he wants to know where I live, and I tell him North Calusa. Long ways out here, he says. Did I drive? No, I took the bus. So it took some effort and planning to get out here to meet up with a fourteen-year-old girl, he says. Yeah, it did. Pretty late to come calling on a fourteen-year-old girl, wouldn't you say? It's not a school night, I point out, meaning to joke but he doesn't get it. It's like he's not just her father, he's also a cop or he thinks he's a cop because that's how he's treating me. It's like all of America has turned into a cop whose main job is to protect their fourteen-year-old virgins from creeps like me. He asks me who I live with, and I had to say I live with my mother, which let him ask me what would my mother think if she knew I was arranging to meet a fourteen-year-old girl alone late at night apparently for sex and brought beer and pornography and condoms and a loo-bricant with me.

P: How'd you answer that one?

K: I told the truth. I said my mother'd probably think it was kind of weird. But not weird the way he thought I meant. Weird because my mother hasn't a clue about who I really am, especially when it comes to my sex life, which wasn't really a sex life anyhow until that night. And even that was only happening in my head so I might as well have been online the whole time or watching porn and jacking off, except that now my sex life such as it was had turned out to be illegal. I asked Brandi's father if he was going to arrest me. He said no, he had no power to arrest me. I was free to leave, he said. I stood up and put Willow's Day Off and the condoms and lubricant back in my pack with the beer. Then I looked

*at Brandi's father and said, Listen, Mr. Dillinger, this was a big mistake,
coming out here tonight. I'm really sorry. It was stupid, and I promise
I'll never do it again. I'm really glad that you were here to catch me and
nothing happened. Then I picked up my backpack and headed for the
door.*

P: *And that was it?*

K: *No. I get outside and I'm really feeling like cheese but also relieved to
be away from Brandi and her father. Only I'm not, okay? Because suddenly there's lights all over the yard, and five Calusa cops rush me from
both sides and do like a SWAT team takedown and shove my face into
the pavement front walk and yank my hands behind my back and throw
cuffs on me, all the time screaming, Get down get down get down! Like
I had any choice. This one cop takes out a little book then and reads me
my rights and says I'm under arrest for soliciting sex with a minor. I go,
Yeah yeah yeah, whatever, and they toss me into the back of a cruiser and
take me to the West Calusa Gardens cop station where they interrogate
me and book me and lock me in jail. And that's the end of my big night
with brandi18. I never saw her again. Not even at my trial where her
father testified about everything I told him and the DA read the whole
transcript of my chats and e-mails with brandi18 out loud, leaving out
of course the parts she wrote that got me to write the other parts. Actually
I never saw her at all. Unless you count through the kitchen window
when she was putting out the Oreos and pouring lemonade. But that
wasn't really brandi18 anyhow. Was it? That was Brandi, Mr. Dillinger's
daughter.*

CHAPTER ELEVEN

THE TEENAGE CLERK AT PAWS 'N' CLAWS refuses to sell the Kid and the Professor a tube of selamectin for Annie's scabies infestation. Tall and boney, wearing heavy-rimmed eyeglasses, mud-colored hair in a Prince Valiant cut, he's got skin problems of his own. *You're gonna need a vet's prescription for that,* the clerk declares.

They're standing in front of a wall of medications for dogs and cats. Pet owners stroll up and down the aisles of the huge warehouse outlet with their dogs in tow, cats in cushy carriers, birds, turtles, miscellaneous reptiles, and small ratlike mammals in cages, brought by their owners to the box store like children by their parents to a candy store. The Kid and the Professor have Annie and Einstein beside them, Annie at the end of a piece of clothesline rope, Einstein in his cage. Outside in the parking lot when he saw everyone else doing it, the Kid insisted on bringing them into the store. *It's like they just got outa the can, man. Let them enjoy their newfound freedom. You don't know how they feel, maybe, but I can relate, man.*

Einstein's gone mute and has a nasty habit of plucking out his own breast feathers. The Professor claims that all the parrot needs is a larger cage and regular interaction with humans. *He'll soon open up. African grays are like chimpanzees, highly social creatures that become depressed and self-mutilating when not sufficiently stimulated,* the Professor explains as they return to the van lugging Einstein's new cage, which is nearly as large as the Kid's tent, and bags of dog food and parrot food. The Kid didn't have a clue as to the cause of Annie's crusted sores and bald patches, but back at the Causeway the Professor had diagnosed it immediately by stroking the poor animal behind one ear, invoking an involuntary scratching motion of the hind leg on that side. Then the other ear, and her other hind leg automatically tried to scratch her loose belly.

The Pedal-Pinna reflex, he pronounced.

How'd you know that?

It's the most common disease afflicting dogs in the Third World. For all practical purposes, Annie is a Third World dog.

Still, the Kid is having second thoughts about Einstein and Annie. He's wondering if he should have liberated them from Benbow's in the first place. He says, *I got a dog with skin cancer and a parrot who needs to fucking party. How'm I gonna take care of them when I can't even barely take care of myself?*

The Professor flips open the rear door of the van, and together they lift the cage, the bags of food, the dog, and the parrot in his new cage and place them carefully inside the vehicle. The Professor wipes his brow with a handkerchief and says, *Believe me, you'll take better care of yourself if you have to take care of Annie and Einstein. I've studied the relationship between homeless people and their companion animals. Trust me.*

I can't afford shit like cages and humungous bags of food. And vets and medicine for scabies. It's only 'cause you're shelling out for it that we got it now. But what about two or three weeks from now? You still gonna be covering costs? I don't think so, man.

Two or three weeks from now you'll be able to pay for it yourself. You're not going to let them starve or die for lack of medicine or attention.

So your theory says.

Right. Now get in. We're going to visit the veterinarian.

.   .   .

ALL'S WELL UNDER THE CAUSEWAY. NIGHT IS coming on. Cook fires are burning, tents pitched, shanties up and tightened against the damp breeze off the Bay. A pair of men fish for their supper with bamboo poles; another pair puts the finishing touches on the latrine. Rabbit hobbles over to the Kid's tent and holds on to Annie's rope while the Kid applies salve to the dog's scabs and raw running sores. The two men talk in low voices to the dog, comforting her. Inside his cage on the ground nearby, Einstein watches and listens. The Professor silently stands over the Kid and Rabbit. Suddenly Einstein speaks. The words are the Kid's, but the voice is Trinidad Bob's: *Good dog. Good dog. Good dog. This'll hurt but it'll make you feel better soon. Good dog. Good dog.*

The Kid smiles and looks up at the Professor who smiles back, all teeth and red lips and facial hair. He tells the Kid he'll check in on him tomorrow and turns and leaves. The Kid and Rabbit go back to applying salve to Annie's sores. *Good dog. Good dog. Good dog.*

THE PROFESSOR STANDS BEFORE THE OPEN refrigerator like a conductor at the podium in front of his orchestra ready to begin the evening's opening performance. Gloria enters the kitchen behind him and leans against the door jamb with her arms folded across her chest. Except for the refrigerator light, the room is dark. The Professor likes eating in the near dark. The pale glow from the refrigerator reflects off Gloria's spectacles, a pair of orange disks.

She says in a low, flattened voice that she received two disturbing pieces of information today.

The Professor seems not to have heard her. He reaches with one hand for a jug of sweetened iced tea and with the other for a plastic container of macaroni and cheese and carries them to the table. He returns to the refrigerator for a meat loaf wrapped in aluminum foil and places it on the table. Methodically he carves off half the meat loaf and slides it onto a dinner plate and ladles the macaroni and cheese onto the plate, covers both with plastic wrap and puts the plate into the microwave and sets it for seven minutes' cooking time. Gloria remains silent throughout. The Professor fills a tall glass with iced tea, takes a sip, turns to his wife and says, *Really? "Two disturbing pieces of information"?*

Yes. From a phone call this morning. And from a visitor this afternoon.

The Professor's alarm system has been triggered: his wife sounds not angry or hurt, as usual, but confused. *Really? A phone call and a visitor?*

A phone call from a man claiming to be your father. And a visitor claiming to be a detective in the Calusa police department.

Really?

Yes. He showed me his badge and ID.

And what did you tell the man claiming to be my father?

At first I thought he was some kind of con artist. I told him what you have always told me. That your father and mother were killed years ago in a car crash in Alabama.

But he convinced you otherwise. Thus your disturbance.

Yes.

May I ask you how he convinced you that he was my father?

He didn't want anything from me or you. Money or credit card numbers. And he knew things.

Such as?

About us. Me. And the twins. Their names. And your childhood and college years. Things he didn't need to lie about.

And I do?

I didn't think so. Until the detective came to say that he wanted to speak with you. There were two of them. Your father, the man who said he was your father, he said the same thing on the phone. About the detectives. They asked him questions about you.

Did the men claiming to be detectives say what it was they wished to discuss with me?

No. They wouldn't tell me anything.

What sort of questions did they ask the man claiming to be my father?

He didn't say.

They are both silent for a moment. The microwave timer dings, and the Professor removes the plate of food and carries it to the table and sits down before it. He removes the plastic wrap carefully and picks up a fork and begins to eat rapidly, voluminously, one heaping forkful after another, washed down with great gulps of iced tea, as if he is alone in the room eating in the near dark.

Who are you? She has a stricken look on her face and stands stock-still, as if she dare not move or the room and all it contains will fly apart and suddenly reveal itself to have been only a stage set, replaced by another stage set that is about to be replaced by a third and a fourth and so on. *Really, who are you? Who am I married to? Who is the father of my children?*

I am entirely whom I appear to be. Glory-Glory-Hallelujah.

But your father, your parents . . .

Yes, I said they were dead. And it's as if they are dead. As if they were killed in a car accident years ago. As if I were a Jew and cut off my hair and sat shiva seven days for them. The Professor lowers his head and resumes eating.

I don't understand. He said, your father said, the police were asking him questions about you. And then they were here, a pair of them. Detectives. She lays a business card next to his plate and returns to the doorway. *They left that card and said for you to call them or come to police headquarters downtown.*

Did they say what it was about?

She shakes her head no.

It's probably nothing. One of my students in a spot of trouble. He gets up from the table and refills his plate and pops it into the microwave and waits, watching the timer count down to zero.

But your parents, that's not nothing. They're alive?

No, it's not nothing. And yes, they are alive. I have been profoundly, painfully alienated from them for many years. Painful for them, perhaps. Not so painful for me. Since long before we met, Gloria. Glory. Hallaloo . . .

But why would the police be questioning them about you, if it were only a student in a spot of trouble? Like you said.

I have no idea. The timer rings, and he carries his overloaded plate back to the table and sits down. With his yard-wide back to his wife, the Professor resumes eating.

I have never asked you about your past. Even when you made me tell you everything about mine, all the way back to childhood. Even when you made me tell you about my sexual experiences.

Thank you, Gloria. It's one of the reasons we are still married.

Yes, I know. But now it's different. Because of the children, the twins. I need to know about your past, so that I can protect our children if necessary.

From me?

From your past. If necessary.

Well, it's not necessary.

Are you going to tell me about your mother and father? And why you lied to me about them? My God, if you'd lie about that, what wouldn't you lie about? And if you'd lie to me, who wouldn't you lie to?

He turns in his seat and looks at her in the gloom, still lean-ing against the doorframe, in her pink cotton bathrobe and pale gray nightgown, her arms crossed over her breasts. He imagines what he is to her at this moment: a big fat liar. How ridiculous he must look. How pathetic. The smartest man in Calusa, eh? A genius. One in a million when it comes to IQ, the puzzle-meister, the professor with the photographic memory who seems to have read and remembered everything ever printed in a half-dozen dif-ferent languages. But here, now, at table in his kitchen seated in the dark before his second heap of food, he is just a big fat liar. A liar caught out somehow by his own parents, whom he long ago disowned, prompted by some local police detective's curious visit to his parents in another state two hundred miles north of here. A visit occasioned by what? Gloria is right, it can't be merely because some student got into a spot of trouble and invoked his professor's name as guarantor or alibi or character reference. And it can't be because he himself has broken the law. He's been a model citizen for years.

He knows where and how his parents live now, just as they know where and how he lives and that he is married to a woman and that there are two seven-year-old grandchildren his mother and father have never met and have not seen even in photographs. He knows they have tracked him on the Internet in recent years, ever since he ended up in Calusa. His father even managed to uncover his university e-mail address and for a few years every six months or so has sent him a brief report on their lives and politely asked for a return e-mail, photographs, confirmation of receipt—anything. No explanations for his long silence necessary. No apology requested. Just write back, please. All the old man—for he is old now, in his late eighties—and his wife want is their son's acknowledgment of their existence. *We're happy here at Dove Run, as happy as can be expected,* the old man types into his computer. *Except that we do not hear from you, son. Your mother and I do not understand what we have done to deserve this. Please tell us so that we can say we are sorry and can again be your parents as we once were. Love, Dad.*

The Professor knows from his father's e-mails that his mother is ill, suffering from early-onset Alzheimer's disease, and that his father has become her caretaker. The two of them have sold their house in Clinton and moved into an assisted-living compound outside Tuscaloosa. They have a small apartment and there is an attached full-time nursing unit where the Professor's mother can live when his father can no longer care for her by himself. The Professor, when he read that bit of news six months ago, felt a small ripple of relief wash over him. Soon she will forget she has a son, if she hasn't forgotten already. As her past gets erased so in a sense does his. That's the Professor's ideal lived life—one with no witnesses, or as few as possible.

From the evidence, his father's memory of the Professor's child-hood and youth, up to the point when he left Kenyon College and went off to graduate school at Yale, is intact. And the old man knows as much of his son's life since then as he can learn from the Internet: his publications, articles about him in the Calusa newspaper, mentions of his name in certain sociology blogs, his e-mail address, and his home telephone number; he knows his son's academic rank and place of employment; he knows that he is married to the former Gloria Bennett, who is employed as a librarian, and that there are two children by that marriage, fraternal twins, a boy and a girl.

Of the years between his son's departure for Yale and his arrival thirty years later in Calusa the old man knows nothing. His letters went unanswered and then after a year were returned stamped ADDRESSEE UNKNOWN. Phone numbers in his son's name were not listed anywhere in America. Eventually the Professor's father gave up trying to contact his son, and gradually the Professor's mother began to forget that she had a son and needed to be reminded of his name, and she would brighten then and ask where was he. When will he be here? Then, early in the century, along came the Internet, and the Professor's father was able to renew his search with a more thorough and efficient tool at his disposal than he'd had in the early years. He finally located his son and learned about his present life. Not all of it, of course, but enough to excite his desire to know more and a powerful fantasy of presenting his son and his wife Gloria and their two children to his son's mother before she forgot altogether that he had ever existed.

But now it looks to the old man as if it's too late. In his most recent, unanswered e-mail to his son he wrote: *Your mother's memory of all but her own childhood is pretty nearly gone. She recognizes me, but she confuses me with her father. It's very sad,* he added, hoping to make his son sad enough to want to see his mother again. But he has never seen his son sad, even as a child, so it was probably useless to try arousing in him an emotion that he appeared incapable of feeling. Still, he had to try. But when the Professor read his father's e-mail he felt relieved, not sad. Then he hit *delete.*

He clears his throat. *So now, after all these years, now you decide you need to know my past. We agreed, didn't we, from the beginning that there was much about my life before we met that I could not reveal. Not to you, not to anyone. There were oaths I had taken and pledges I had signed. And you understood and accepted that. It was to protect you. You and the children.*

Yes, I understood. I did. I knew enough about you and your past, the public part anyhow, to accept not knowing more. But your parents? Why would you say your parents were dead, when they weren't? Why would you lie about a thing like that?

That, dear Glory, is one of those things I cannot reveal to you. So that when the police or anyone else comes 'round asking questions of you or of my parents, none of you has to lie in order to protect me. You're free to tell the truth, the whole truth, and nothing but the truth, so help you Jesus. You don't know enough about me to feel obliged to lie. I withhold information so that you don't have to, m'dear.

He has slipped into his genteel southern accent, and she knows what that means: he's told her all of the truth that he's going to. She reminds him that she promised the police detective that she would deliver his message to her husband. *Will you be speaking with the police tomorrow?*

Tomorrow is Sunday. The Sabbath. The Lord's Day. I'll call him early Monday.

All right. Good night, then.

Gloria, I won't be going to church with you and the twins tomorrow.

You won't?

No.

Why not?

I b'lieve I should have me a little private discussion with my daddy.

Your "daddy"? That's a word I never thought I'd hear from you.

Yes. Now that he exists, I can use it.

Can't you speak to him by telephone? It's a day's drive, practically.

I said "private discussion." I suspect his telephone ain't private.

She nods, turns away, disappears into the darkness. The Professor returns to his meal. For the first time he hears the heavy drumming of rain on the roof and the slosh of gutters overflowing. It has been raining steadily, he realizes, for at least the last half hour. If it's more than a late-summer shower, it'll slow his drive north to Alabama. He gobbles the last of the meat loaf and macaroni and cheese and empties his glass of iced tea and places the dishes into the dishwasher. The rain, he notices from the sound, is wind driven. He decides he'd better leave now.

CHAPTER TWELVE

THREE TIMES THE PROFESSOR STOPS ON his journey west and north to Alabama, twice for gas but otherwise for food, truck-stop food—stew and biscuits and pie and ice cream—and fast food—Big Macs and fries and more pies. He does this without deciding to do it, as if his hunger is a constant ongoing need that can never be satisfied. He has no reason to check in on it and ask whether he is actually hungry again. It's always there, like his breath. It is who he is and has been for as long as he can remember, a never-ending appetite.

The only thing that obliges him to push his plate away and pay the cashier and leave is the pressure of time: he's obliged to keep driving. After all these years he has to speak with his father. Before he faces the Calusa police detective, or the man claiming to be a Calusa police detective, he has to learn what the man asked his father and what the old man answered. He has to know if the walls that separate the compartments that contain his past have started to erode and collapse. He cannot allow that to happen, not now, after so many years of constructing and reinforcing those walls, making the chambers they contain impenetrable even to the Professor himself. He's not just trying to preserve and maintain the life he's built for himself in the last decade here in Calusa; he's also trying to hold on to the inner integrity and coherence of each box in the set of boxes that precedes his life in Calusa. The story of his life from Kenyon College on is like a long row of rented storage compartments in a warehouse outside a city that he never wants to visit again. As soon as he's swung shut the door and snapped the lock, he deliberately misplaces the key. A year or two passes, and he departs from Kathmandu or Lima or one of a half-dozen other cities, even a few American cities, small towns, rural communes, and as if renting a new storage unit in the warehouse, he packs up all the details of the year or two of his life just ended and deposits them in the new compartment, clicks the lock shut and moves on, not forgetting to lose the key—tossing it from the window of the taxi on the drive to the airport, dropping it through a sewer grate on his way to catch the train, flipping it into a Dumpster as he approaches the security check at the shipyard.

North of Calusa traffic on the Interstate is light. Rain beats against the flat front of the van. By the time he veers west and passes above the vast Panzacola Swamp on the old Panzacola Highway connecting the Atlantic to the Gulf, the night has worn on, and the only vehicles now are trucks with deliveries crossing from the cities on one coast to the cities on the other and the occasional beat-up pickup driven by a member of one of the remnant Indian tribes still making a life for themselves in the roadside camps and small ramshackle settlements along the northern edge of the swamp.

The lights of Calusa and its suburbs have long since faded and gone dark behind him. Soon out ahead the lights of the cities along the Gulf Coast will begin to tint the western sky. There are no stars. No moon. It's raining hard, slanted against the van by the wind out of the west. But the Professor barely notices. Since leaving the house, he's not once thought of the Kid or of his wife and children, not even of his father or the reason for this sudden journey. He's not thinking of anything or anyone in a focused way. For perhaps the first time in his life the Professor is experiencing panic. The Professor never panics. He admires that fact. But he's panicking now, and knowing it frightens him and makes it worse.

He's sweating slick sheets and loosens his necktie and collar and turns on the air conditioner.

At the Gulf Coast where the Panzacola Swamp merges with the sea, the old Panzacola Highway connects to the north-running Gulf Turnpike. The wind-blown rain slaps the van on its flat left side now, and he has to wrestle with the wheel to keep the vehicle in its lane. There are suburbs and cities clustered alongside the turnpike here, cloverleaves, overpasses, and exits to attend to and an enormous plaza where he refills with gas and eats another meal, pushes his way through the rain back to the parked van and resumes his drive on up the coast of the peninsula.

Windshield wipers flop rapidly back and forth, but the rain is too heavy for them to wipe away, and his view ahead is blurred. Twice he narrowly misses vehicles moving slowly in front of of him, and several times like a drunk man he loses sight of the white line that divides the lanes and has to slow down almost to a stop before he finds it again. His pulse is racing, and it occurs to him to play some music. Yes, for God's sake, play some music. Music will calm him, he thinks, and let him focus and organize his mind, his most powerful tool, his weapon against the world.

For the last few hours, since Gloria revealed that she had spoken with his father and that the police had visited the old man at the home in Alabama and had come to his own door in Calusa asking to speak with him, since that moment the Professor has not been himself. He's been out of his mind, and his mind, he believes, is his true self. He needs to get back inside it, and music will help.

He punches up one of the hundreds of compilations of jazz standards he's burned onto CDs and keeps in a black plastic CD file box inside the armrest next to the driver's seat, and soon his mind comes back to him: Tommy Flanagan's "I Fall in Love Too Easily" and Art Farmer and Bill Evans on "The Touch of Your Lips" and Roy Hargrove's "The Nearness of You." By the time he hears the opening chords of Bud Powell's "My Heart Stood Still" he's found his true self again and is located there: calm, logical, detached. In control. And his body is where he wants it—on its own again.

His panic has passed. The music, as it has always done, helps to separate his mind from his body. For most people it's the reverse. Especially for people who, like the Professor, listen to classic American jazz. Jazz is one of the few subjects he never explains to other people. He's perfectly willing to hold forth on the subject of European classical music from the Baroque to Post-Modern serialism or disco or funk or raga or reggae. But jazz is like a secret drug to him. It alone has the power to alter his brain waves and neurotransmitters such that he feels autonomous, immunized against the contamination of his body, which otherwise is nearly impossible to make go away.

The wind is shifting gradually around to the north and the rain has intensified. It's nearly dawn when he crosses the state line into Alabama, and finally it enters his mind that a hurricane has come in off the Gulf and he has been driving straight through it for the last several hours. He remembers a buzz off the CNN news loop on the TV monitors at the turnpike plaza earlier and glimpsing a headline in the morning paper that he neglected to pick up when he left home yesterday to meet the Kid at the Causeway. Hurricane George they're calling it. A medium-size hurricane, it's expected to pass over the northern half of the state and the southern half of Alabama and Georgia and spin out to the Atlantic where it will weaken and break up. No big deal. But a hurricane nonetheless, high winds and torrential, swirling rain, dangerous to drive through in a slab-sided van or any vehicle lighter than a sixteen-wheeler, especially up the Gulf Coast and into Alabama like this.

Palm trees sway like plumes and palmettos thrash the ground. Now and then his headlights or the lights of oncoming vehicles illuminate overflowing ditches and canals alongside the highway. Thick skeins of water erupt in fantails as the van plows through them.

He's driving much slower now, losing time. He planned on arriving at the home—Dove Run: An Assisted-Living and Life-Care

Facility, it's called—early in the day, spending an hour or at most two with his parents, and then departing for Calusa well before noon. He planned on getting home by early evening, in time to prepare his class for Monday. He briefly considers turning back now, forgoing an in-person interrogation of his father and risking a call from a pay phone at one of the rest-stop restaurants. It would be foolish to call from his cell phone. But it's too great a risk even from a pay phone—the old man's phone is as surely tapped as his own. Besides, the hurricane is on top of him now, and he'll no more escape it by turning south toward home than by plunging on ahead.

He could, of course, pull off the highway and park at a truck stop and wait for the hurricane to pass to the east. That would be the sensible thing to do. It's apparently what the all-night truckers, the only other drivers still moving, are doing now, he observes, as a pair of sixteen-wheel behemoths pulls slowly off the highway into a parking lot illuminated by arc lamps atop tall aluminum poles. The rain drifts in shuddering sheets through the cones of pale light. He should have checked the weather report, he thinks. But no, it wouldn't have made any difference. He'd still have left the house in the night and driven up here for the information he believes he needs in order to protect himself from whomever it was that came calling first on his father and then showed up at his door in Calusa claiming to be a detective in the Calusa Police Department. He knows it's got nothing to do with his present life, or they wouldn't have contacted his father. It's his past that has come calling—but what part of his past? Which chapter? Which episode or linked series of episodes?

Over on his right the dark eastern sky has started bleeding to gray. Near the horizon the boiling clouds are dark green. He can make out flooded citrus groves, crushed gravel side roads, a soaked wind-flattened landscape with wildly scattered palm and palmetto fronds and here and there abandoned cars and pickups, mobile homes with water to their thresholds looking like houseboats set adrift, tricycles and brightly colored plastic yard toys half-drowned. And no people.

Everyone is huddled inside waiting for George to pass over and on to wherever hurricanes go when they're no longer here—onto the TV screen, the radio report, the Internet, someone else's reality and thus no longer real at all.

The wind has ceased to buffet the sides of the Professor's van, and he no longer struggles to hold it to the road, and the rain has let up. He's situated at the eye of the storm, he thinks, the center of a two-hundred-mile atmospheric coil of low pressure twirling its way across the Caribbean and the Gulf like a colossal dervish. Right here at the still center is the place to stay, if only he can manage it—no wind, no rain, no turbulence or uncertainty. The morning sky is a smooth-sided pale green bowl, the pressure so low it feels like a huge vacuum pump has siphoned the air away. The music plays on—Bud Powell's arpeggios and stomps—and the Professor feels calm and lucid and safe: almost invisible. The eye of the hurricane: it's a metaphor for the mental and emotional space where he's lived most of his life. He thinks this and smiles inwardly. Never quite thought of it that way. Nice, the way the world that surrounds one, the very weather of one's existence, provides a language for addressing the world inside.

Delighted, he notices that the eastward direction of the storm has shifted ten degrees to the north, and soon after, as he drives on, fifteen degrees, so that he's able to stay inside the eye, its still center, moving northeast with it into Alabama as if personally escorted by Hurricane George straight to Dove Run: An Assisted-Living Facility and for the first time in over forty years the physical presence of his father and mother.

THEIR HOME IS A TWO-STORY REDBRICK COLlection of small apartments, administrative offices and meeting rooms, recreation rooms, dining areas, and emergency medical facilities, with a wing that functions as a nursing home for the assisted-living residents who need more care than mere assistance provides. It resembles a large Holiday Inn, temporary quarters for travelers who will never return home, except to a funeral home or, for the believing Christians, the home prepared for them by their Lord and Savior.

The Professor knows what he should be feeling as he enters the building. He knows what a man his age meeting his parents for the first time after nearly a lifetime of silent, willed absence ought to be feeling, regardless of the reasons or excuses for his absence. He should be feeling dread, anxiety, fearful curiosity, shame, all mingled with a thickened low-key joy: a muddle of intense, conflicted emotions. And yet he feels none of it. Only a mild irritation, as if while reading a difficult text he's been interrupted by a small household mechanical breakdown that must be attended to before he can continue reading where he was obliged to leave off. For most of his life it's been a strength, to know what other people, normal people, feel in any given situation, without possessing those feelings himself. It began in his childhood as a consciously willed means of protecting himself against ridicule, on the one hand, and on the other as a response to his parents' utter absorption in each other to the exclusion of everyone else, even their precocious, morbidly obese, increasingly eccentric and alienated son.

As a couple, the Professor's parents, Jason and Cynthia, loved the couple itself and the idea of the couple as much as they loved themselves. They felt incomplete when apart and pined for the presence of the other, as if mourning the other. And when they were together they each became the happy center of the other's universe, a solar system with twin suns at the center orbited by a single lonely planet spinning in darkness, except for the light cast by his parents as they danced on the porch to the music of those old 1940s jazz standards, while he sat on the wooden glider and pushed himself back and forth in slow time to the music and watched from an increasingly cold distance.

He knew what they felt for each other, and because it was for them essentially self-love, he could not share in it. Their feelings not only excluded him, they rejected him. He felt attacked by his parents' strange mutual narcissism, causing him from an early age to cultivate his differences from them. Another child of such a pair might have tried to enter their charmed circle by emulating the qualities they seemed to admire in one another—their physical beauty, for both Jason and Cynthia were unusually handsome and healthy individuals; or their pragmatic, mechanical turns of mind, socially useful kinds of intelligence that are much admired in communities like theirs; or their natural ease, the ease of the oblivious, among people wholly unlike them, their friends and neighbors in Clinton, Alabama, their colleagues at work, U. S. Steel in Jason's case, the Clinton Public Library in Cynthia's, and the people they employed, everyone from the housekeeper and yardman to the inmates Jason hired from the state prison system to work for little or no pay digging the coal out of the Alabama hills. Although it was a variant of a folie à deux, his parents' marriage was the kind that people with little or no knowledge of its implications and true nature envied. A pretty couple, a smart couple, a socially useful and reassuringly gregarious couple; and because they were from distinguished northern families and well educated and were probably left-leaning Democrats who made no attempts to impose their political views on anyone else, they were a slightly exotic couple as well. The Professor had none of this moderately attractive couple's qualities. None.

Sheets of plywood cover the large windows of the lobby. The glass doors and remaining smaller windows facing the deserted street have been X'd with tape. The Professor parks his van in the lot adjacent to the sprawling compound and walks slowly up the path to the main entrance. He is sweating and breathing with difficulty, as much from the very low atmospheric pressure as from the humidity and heat.

The receptionist, a stout white-haired lady in a bright red nylon tracksuit, makes him sign the visitors' register. Recognizing his last name, his parents' last name, she smiles with a fake slick and says, *First time you all been here to visit your momma and daddy, am I correct to say?*

He nods yes. She tells him the number of their apartment and gives him a floor plan of the building, which is laid out like a medieval monastery. He feels nothing, or no more than if he were making a delivery for the dry cleaner. The receptionist appears to know this and waves him on dismissively in the direction of the carpeted corridor that leads to the independent-living wing. The walls and carpeting are the color of oatmeal. *You'll find 'em waitin' in unit 119,* she says and picks up the house phone to notify his father that he has a visitor, thinking, A very odd visitor, more like a circus freak than the son of those nice-lookin' folks in 119.

At the door, the Professor raises his open hand, about to make a fist and knock, and he looks at it—it's the hand he had as a child, the same fingernails, knuckles, thin blue veins, the same small purse of flesh between thumb and forefinger—and when he turns it over he recognizes the palm, the same creases, lines, and whorls. For a moment he studies the hand, then puts it out in front of him and fans out the fingers and waggles the hand slowly back and forth, as if from the window of a departing train.

A sudden wave of fear surges over him, and he wants to turn around and flee from the eye of the hurricane back into the storm's full fury. He's panicking again, afraid to go forward, unable to retreat. And no music to calm him, nothing to bleach out his wild emotions and make his mind translucent and hard and rational as a ladder. His eighty-nine-year-old father and his mother with her perforated memory are on the other side of the door waiting for him. They're waiting to present him with himself, as if to introduce him to his fratricidal twin.

T HE PROFESSOR DROPS HIS PALE HAND AND turns away from the door of unit 119 and pumping his heavy arms walks rapidly down the long corridor of numbered doors to the lobby. He strides past the surprised receptionist who calls out, *Your folks are home! They expectin' you, mistah!* Then shakes her head in disgust as, ignoring her, he hurries past.

Don't that beat all? she wonders. First he comes finally to check on his poor momma and his daddy to make sure the hurricane ain't gonna get them, after never once showing his face before this, and then he acts like they ain't worth the trouble. You got to wonder what they done to deserve that from their own flesh and blood, she thinks. But she's seen hundreds, maybe thousands, of grown men and women who don't seem to know they're somebody's flesh and blood, sons and daughters who put their mommas and daddies into Dove Run and say good-bye and are never seen walking through that door again. It's not like it was in the old days when she was a girl and Grandma died in the upstairs back bedroom. Back then parents and grandparents grew old and died before your very eyes, and it was as if a part of you yourself was growing old and dying alongside them. You didn't have these Dove Runs where you could park and hide old people, and back then, if you wanted to forget that you too would someday grow old and die, which is natural to want, you couldn't. She thinks about her own grown son and daughter and their children, and she wonders if she's flesh and blood to them—kin—and decides, sadly, that the answer is no. They're just like the man who blew past her a moment ago, and when the time comes they'll make her live in Dove Run or someplace like it, while they go on living in a world in which no one, no one visible, grows old and dies before their very eyes. She sighs. She's almost sixty years old, and in her lifetime the world has changed, and human beings have changed too.

How can that be? She always believed that human nature was permanent, unchangeable, that human beings were the same always and everywhere, for better or worse, and when conditions changed for the better, as they sometimes did, like for black people and for women, it was because people, including white people and men, were essentially good and their better nature was letting them recognize their kinship with black people and women. Such were the receptionist's thoughts as the Professor in flight from his intended meeting with his parents bustled past her desk, pushed through the door, and rushed across the parking lot to his van.

PART IV

CHAPTER ONE

FOR HOURS THE EYE OF THE HURRICANE HAS enveloped the Professor like a moving bell jar. It has shifted its course just as he has shifted his, and now the storm slides south along the peninsula with him inside it toward the Great Panzacola Swamp, where it veers off to the east, crossing the state again, headed this time for Calusa and the open ocean beyond. The Professor's van is inside an enormous meteorological bubble that protects him from the fury of the storm that rages beyond and behind him. Hurricane watchers and meteorologists and TV weather forecasters say that the hurricane was briefly stalled over land by an enormous offshore high-pressure area, slowing and turning it away from its predicted eastward path toward the Atlantic, gradually spiraling it back over the Gulf for a few hours, where it regained force and refilled with moisture, then resumed its slow assault on the land and the cities at the lower end of the peninsula. But for the Professor, cosseted by the eye of the hurricane, the storm has ended; it's dissipated; gone. The wind has abated, and the rain has ceased to fall. The sky is pale yellow, except at the horizon way out there in front of him over the Atlantic, where it's dark green and sooty gray, and above the Gulf behind him, where great masses of black clouds have piled up.

The only storm the Professor is aware of is the one raging inside his brain. The music blasting from the van's speakers doesn't work anymore to cool his roiled mind. He's sweating and has shucked his jacket and necktie and loosened his collar. He has the music cranked up to top volume, trying to make a wall of it around his secrets, but they keep breaking through the sound and make him feel like he's under attack from them, as if they are hornets and he's accidentally bumped their nest and busted it apart with his unprotected head. He's not in physical pain, but he howls as if he's being stung again and again, and he slaps at his cheeks and neck and the top of his head, slaps at the sides of his enormous, soft arms and his pillowed chest, twists and turns in his seat like a man possessed by a demon.

The Professor knows very little about his deepest self, but as one who has studied the field and the phenomenon, he knows that this is the point in a secretive man's long life of compartmentalization and disguise that one's thoughts turn longingly toward the idea of suicide. This is when the walls fall and the contradictions collide openly with one another. He's read the literature, the journals, the reports, and has paused over them in deep reflection and vague recognition. There was the Polish writer Jerzy Kosinski, who may or may not have been a Holocaust survivor, and many master spies, and another writer, Michael Dorris, who may or may not have been an American Indian, and doubtless thousands upon thousands of unknown others. That's as close as he himself can get to the pure idea of suicide, of self-annihilation—close enough to know that it's a desire felt by others who found themselves in his present situation.

It's a desire not yet felt by him, however. He expects it to arrive soon, if he can't somehow put his lifelong secrets back into the boxes that have held them all these years, held and kept them from knowing of one another's existence. He drives down the Gulf Turnpike inside the eye of the hurricane, howling in pain and slapping at his body, twitching and twisting away from himself, batting at the idea of suicide, as if fighting off an avenging angel sent by an angry god to torment him.

One hundred miles east of the Professor's van, the leading edge of the swirling hurricane has hit the city of Calusa and its sprawl of suburbs and malls, sucking the ocean inland in a widening surge that lifts the waters of the Bay and floods low-lying streets and boulevards. Torrents of rain wash across the highways and turnpikes in foot-high waves. The entire city is in an official hurricane evacuation zone, and most residents of the Great Barrier Isles have already started to migrate inland by car and bus to the county evacuation centers and the suburban homes of friends and family members.

The winds have followed the rain, quickly increasing in velocity, and soon sixty- and seventy-mile-an-hour gusts are bending the stalklike trunks of palms and tossing their fronds like unraveled turbans, ripping off the branches of live oak and cotton trees and flattening palmettos, disassembling carefully planted hedges and shrubs, shredding flower gardens and municipal park plantings, kicking trash cans over and blowing the contents into the streets and roads and into the canals and the Bay. The sky is low, thickened as if bearing a great weight, and though it is midmorning, it's dusk-dark, and long lines of vehicles with their headlights on crawl bumper to bumper off the chain of man-made islands over bridges and causeways onto the mainland, merging there and flowing slowly on widening roads toward the slightly higher ground miles from shore, headed in the direction the Professor is coming from, still driving his van inside the eye of the storm somewhere out there just north of the Great Panzacola Swamp, still howling and slapping at his arms and chest like a gigantic, bearded baby lost in a tantrum.

CHAPTER TWO

THE CITIZENS OF CALUSA ARE ACCUS-
tomed to hurricanes at this time of year, and most of the
residents who have actual residences have followed the
detailed instructions distributed by the Federal Emergency Manage-
ment Agency. The day before the arrival of the storm they will have
secured their homes as best they could by clearing their terraces
and patios of outdoor furniture and toys, and those who have them
will have double-tied their boats to pilings or put them in dry-dock
storage, brought their satellite dishes inside, rolled their bicycles and
garbage carts into their garages. They will have charged their cell
phones and portable TVs and installed fresh batteries in their portable radios, gone to the nearest ATM machine and withdrawn as
much cash as permitted by their bank, filled the car with gas, shut-
tered, taped, and in some cases boarded over windows with five-
eighth's-inch plywood, especially the windows with the nice view
of the sea or the Bay. They will have put together a family disaster
kit, its contents recommended on FEMA's "Are You Ready" website (http://www.fema.gov/areyouready/hurricanes.shtm): bottled
water, nonperishable packaged and canned food, manually operated
can opener, change of clothing, rain gear, and sturdy shoes, bedding,
first aid kit and all prescription medications, extra pair of glasses,
battery-powered radio, flashlight, extra batteries, extra set of car keys,

phone list of family physicians, special items for infants, elderly, or disabled family members, pet supplies, and should their neighborhood be secured by authorities after the storm due to damage, a current utility bill to prove residency. They will have an evacuation plan, especially those who live on the Barriers or adjacent to the Bay. Many of those who have pets will have packed a pet disaster kit with a two-week supply of food, bowls, water, portable carriers, collar, tag and leash, cat litter and litter box for the kitties, paper towels, plastic Baggies, and hand sanitizer for the doggies. They will bring their birds' caged homes with them when they evacuate their own homes, carry their hamsters in closed boxes with air holes cut in the top, their pet snakes, turtles, and lizards, their ferrets and pet tarantulas. They will have had sufficient time, thanks to the official hurricane warning system, to be ready for the storm, and when the storm finally smashes into the city, they will simply slip under it and wait until it passes over and drifts out to sea.

The men who reside beneath the Claybourne Causeway, however, have neither been warned of the approaching hurricane nor would they be able to prepare for it if they were. Yes, they knew it was on its way, some hearing about it on the radio, a few others reading about it in newspapers pulled from Dumpsters and trash cans, or noticed the citywide preparations and the gardeners and yardmen employed at the hotels and condominium buildings cutting down low-hanging coconuts that the rising wind might otherwise toss through the air like cannonballs. Most of them know the storm is arriving soon, maybe today, possibly in five or ten minutes, but when you have not the means to follow the emergency instructions put out to the citizenry via radio, TV, newspapers, and Internet by city, county, state, and federal agencies, when you are in fact not a member of the citizenry, you tend to discount the warnings to the point where you simply are not aware of any emergency. For you, since you can't do anything to protect yourself from it, there is no emergency. And so the men who live beneath the Causeway go about their usual domestic business as if a hurricane were not about to descend on them.

First the rain, then the surge. The pounding rain the Kid can handle. He's got Einstein and Annie dry inside his tent with him. He's got his own emergency kit—a half-gallon bottle of Sprite, a big bag of Cheez-Its and a jar of peanut butter to dip them in, his favorite between-meal meal. He's got his stove and three cans of Spam and six hard-boiled eggs, a week's worth of parrot and dog food, and a plastic bucket set outside under a drip off the Causeway to catch drinking and wash water. He's chain-locked his bike to a steel stanchion. He's got candles, a headlamp with fresh batteries, and the wind-up radio and telescope that the Professor gave him. It's not exactly FEMA's kit, but it'll get him through the worst of what he's expecting: a couple of boring days of heavy, wind-driven rain.

The rain hammers on his tent. He's lit a candle and has pulled out the Shyster's Bible again and is reading in the book of Numbers. This section of the Bible makes no sense to him because there's no story. But he likes reading it anyhow. Mostly it's rules and regulations being laid down by God and His main human Moses upon the ancient Israelites after they got away from the Egyptians. It's a kind of moral menu for religious fanatics, the Kid thinks. He planned to return the Shyster's Bible and the packet of papers in the briefcase he grabbed the other night during the police raid but has decided that he'll read them first, both the Bible and the papers, before trading them back for something useful. Like money. The Shyster has the most money of anyone in the encampment and has been hiring the others to build his shack and buy his groceries and wash his clothes and his dishes and pots and pans. He's even got Otis the Rabbit doing his cooking.

The Kid has started reading the fifth chapter of Numbers and it gives him a sudden chill, makes him sit up in his sleeping bag and keep reading: *And the Lord spake unto Moses, saying, Command the children of Israel, that they put out of the camp every leper, and every one that hath an issue, and whosoever is defiled by the dead: Both male and female shall ye put out, without the camp shall ye put them; that they defile not their camps, in the midst whereof I dwell. . . .*

Not cool, the Kid thinks. Even lepers deserve a break and shouldn't be abandoned and put under a bridge someplace outside the city like garbage just because they're sick. That's what hospitals are for. And who doesn't have issues anyhow? Everybody's got issues with something. You don't have to be a convicted sex offender to have issues. He's not sure what it means to be defiled by the dead but it can't be as bad as defiling the dead which he thinks means sex with dead people, a thing he's heard about but has almost as hard a time imagining as sex with little children like the Shyster and most of the other guys under the Causeway are guilty of doing. Even they wouldn't have sex with dead people but if they did instead of putting them outside the city you'd want to get them to try and talk about it and figure out why it interested them so much. Which probably goes back to their early childhoods and not having any confidence because of stuff that happened to them back then so that the only people they could picture having sex with was people who couldn't reject them. Like dead people. Or little kids. The trick would be getting them to have enough confidence not to be sexually attracted to dead people. Or little kids.

Maybe the Professor's theory about sex offenders is right, he thinks. Put them in charge of something. Something they can't fail at. So they'll get enough confidence not to worry about being rejected if they decide to hit on a living adult woman instead of a little kid or a dead person.

The Kid has charged his windup radio and with the volume up as high as it will go is listening on earbuds to WBIG which plays mostly rap with very few advertisements and no news. Rap suits him fine as background music because he can't understand most of the words and doesn't especially want to since all the music with words that he's ever heard hasn't got anything to do with his real life unless of course it's used as background music for pornography or for a pole dancer in a strip club for instance. Songs that are just songs are sung by and to people whose lives aren't anything like his and all they do is remind him of that fact. It's the steady pulsing beat of rap and the rhymes—the pure sound of the words and not their meaning—that he likes. It's the same for him with any music, even when it's just a soft-rock or pseudosamba sound track for a porn film. When the words happen to come in standard white people's English which is the only language he understands except for a little Spanish he almost always tunes them out and hears only the rhythm and the instrumentation and the rise and fall of the human vocal sounds and uses them to help him concentrate on what he's looking at which in this case instead of pornography or a stripper is a page of the Shyster's Bible.

So he hears neither the rising wind that batters the sides of his tent nor the angry shouts and frightened cries of his fellow residents. The water off the Bay has risen over the sloping ledge at the edge of the concrete island and is now flooding the low-lying flats where many of the men have built their shanties and pitched their tents. Several of the shanties have already been demolished by the surging waves and washed into the Bay. The nearly completed latrine has been tipped over by the wind and floats like a narrow coffin-shaped raft toward one of the support pillars where it is smashed back into scrap lumber. The Greek has pulled his generator up under the overpass to the highest level place he can find there and parked it in the dark cavelike area where until now none of the residents has elected to settle because there's barely room to stand and it smells of rotted food and human feces and urine. It's where only the rats have made their nests. No people.

Otis the Rabbit and Paco have abandoned their flooded tents and moved their possessions including Paco's Harley up the steep grassy slope toward the highway and have stopped there in the wind-driven rain to take what appears to be a last look back at the disappearing encampment. Their island home is being absorbed by the Bay. The Shyster and most of the others stand in the doorways of their camps, shacks, and tents helpless and confused, unsure of whether to wait out the storm or flee. If they stay and try to protect their possessions from the rising water and the winds which have now reached Category 3 hurricane force, will they be blown into the Bay and drowned? But if they give it up and flee their island, where will they go? For the men who live beneath the Causeway there is no private or public shelter from the storm anywhere in the city or the adjoining suburbs.

The Rabbit says to Paco, *Where the fuck's the Kid? You seen the Kid?*

Paco can't hear him over the roar of the wind. He cups his ear and leans in close and the Rabbit asks it again.

Must still be in his tent! Paco hollers back. *With his dog and the bird!*

We better get him outa there! Water's almost up to his tent! Wind's gonna fucking blow it away any minute anyhow! the Rabbit shouts. He starts to hobble on his crutch back down the slope and stumbles and nearly falls.

Paco grabs the old man by the arm and steps in front of him and tells him to stay here by the Harley, he'll get the Kid. He likes being a hero. He's wearing a black muscle shirt and gym shorts and high-tops, his usual workout clothes. His tanned shoulders and biceps flex and glisten in the rain as he descends to the encampment, makes his way along the embankment and crosses under the Causeway toward the Kid's flapping tent.

The waters off the Bay have risen to within a yard of the tent and the wind pummels its thin nylon skin and yanks on the taut cords the Kid so carefully tied to cinder blocks and stanchions when he pitched it. The Kid thinks of himself as ex-military and therefore an expert by-the-book camper who as head of the Executive Committee tries to set military standards for the rest of the men even though in spite of his and the Professor's exhortations and warnings most of them seem not to care about keeping their quarters foursquare, neat and clean. The Kid doesn't understand why everyone isn't as orderly and fastidious as he is especially when it's the only way to keep the police and the sanitation department from coming back and breaking up their camp again like it's a filthy rats' nest and sending them scampering away to darker dirtier more dangerous hideouts. Or if they can't escape, if they don't scamper into greater darkness and invisibility, putting them in cages, tossing away the key. Next time they'll lock them up permanently, even the Shyster unless the men beneath the Causeway demonstrate that they're basically good neighbors and citizens of Calusa who aren't violating any municipal regulations or laws.

A few of them have tried to follow the Kid's example—Otis the Rabbit and Paco and P.C. and Plato the Greek have pitched their tents correctly or built themselves foursquare huts out of plywood scraps and polyethylene with the Shyster paying them to build his to the same high standard and were instrumental in constructing the latrine and organizing trash and garbage collection and disposal—but the rest have set up their households like drunks and druggies who all they think about is getting or staying high so they pay minimum attention to how and where they actually live. Which shouldn't surprise anyone since many of the residents down here in fact are drunks and druggies in spite of having settled beneath the Causeway solely because they're convicted sex offenders who have served their time for their crime and have nowhere else in the city to live.

In most cases it's the only reason they're homeless. It's the one thing they have in common. A bond that unites them against everyone else, even other homeless people. Just yesterday a bushy-haired bearded guy in a long topcoat who wasn't a convicted sex offender wandered down under the Causeway from a park or abandoned building elsewhere in the city and tried to settle among them but they stood together shoulder to shoulder and cast the guy out. The Kid as spokesman for the group explained to the guy that standard-issue homeless people have easy access to dozens of public and church-run shelters that are not available to convicted sex offenders because sometimes there are children being sheltered, *So fuck off, dude, or I'll turn Paco and our other security guys loose and let them kick the shit out of you.*

Paco unzips and flings back the tent flap and the Kid takes out his earbuds and says, *Wow, I was just thinking about you, man!*

Paco says, *You got to abandon ship, Kid! We gettin' flooded out! This a fuckin' hurricane!*

The Kid takes a look outside and his eyes widen. *Holy shit! It's fucking Noah and the flood!*

Working frantically he and Paco shove his belongings into his duffel and backpack. He puts Annie on her leash, picks up Einstein's cage and Paco tucks the expedition-size backpack under one meaty arm and wraps the duffel with the other as if rescuing a pair of children from a fire. He says to the Kid, *You take care of the animals, I'll get the rest.*

Einstein squawks and says, *Women and children first! Women and children first!*

Where'd he learn to say that shit?

Not from me, man. He says stuff all the time that he never heard from me. You can have real conversations with him.

Yeah, right. Follow me, Paco says and the Kid obeys, holding Einstein's cage and leading Annie by her leash. Leaning into the wind they make their way up the steep switchbacked path to the roadway where the Rabbit waits beside Paco's Harley and a pile of black garbage bags stuffed with most of his and Paco's clothing, bedding, and cooking gear. The Kid huffs and puffs his way behind Paco up to the Rabbit where he turns and looks back down at the drowning settlement and the men in flight, most of them scrambling to salvage their possessions by moving to higher ground and stashing as much of it as they can in the dark underside of the roadway, a few others following Paco's, the Rabbit's, and the Kid's example by abandoning the settlement altogether and lugging what few possessions they can carry uphill toward them.

Suddenly the Kid says, *Jesus, I forgot my bike! I gotta try and get my bike. And my tent too.*

The Rabbit puts a hand on the Kid's arm and stays him. *Too late, Kid. They're gone. You're lucky you got yourself and them fuckin' animals out.*

The Rabbit's right. The Kid's tent and bike are half underwater. The wind- and tide-driven surge off the Bay is rising faster now and is coming in waves with a heavy three-foot chop. The Kid hollers over the wind, *Maybe we should try to wait it out under the Causeway where it ain't flooded yet! Up high underneath, like those guys're doing, the Greek and Shyster and them!*

Paco hollers back, *Forgetaboutit, man! Them guys're gonna get trapped under there and drowneded!*

That's fucking harsh, Paco.

That's reality. Those guys're too stupid to abandon a sinking ship. Even your fucking parrot knows reality.

Paco sets a pair of garbage bags onto the back of his seat and straps his bundled goods onto the Harley with bungee cords, leaving barely enough room for him to ride. He slings one leg over the Harley and starts the engine.

Where you goin', man?

Inland! If the wind don't blow me over!

What about us?

Paco flashes a white-toothed grin at the Kid and Rabbit. *It's every man for himself. Better start walking!*

The rain falls on the pavement faster than it runs off and the highway looks more like a shallow rippling river than a six-lane roadway. It's entirely empty of vehicles; from the Barriers to the mainland not a car or truck of any kind, a ghost of a road from nowhere to nowhere. Except for the men who live under the Causeway everyone who wants to be evacuated from the Barriers has been evacuated and there's no one on the mainland foolish enough to be driving in the opposite direction. Paco guns the engine and cuts a wide arc across all six deserted lanes and rides his Harley up and over the long arch of the Causeway and in seconds has disappeared in the distance.

Bracing himself with his crutch the Rabbit leans against the wind. He looks exhausted from the effort as if he's about to fall over. Both he and the Kid are soaked through and are shivering from the cold rain. The Kid says, *What're we gonna do, man?*

You heard him. Start walking.

What about you? With your busted leg and all? The Rabbit doesn't look like he can walk across a room, let alone get himself over the high arching Causeway and hobble down the highway for more than a mile to the mainland. Especially in this wind which the Kid estimates at fifty to sixty miles an hour with gusts in the eighties. And once on the mainland where would they go? They could find some sort of temporary protection against the hurricane maybe—a bridge they could hide under or a mall where they wouldn't get busted for loitering—and could wait it out. But what then? Whatever they had going for them under the Causeway a day ago is pretty much smashed now and if Paco's right and a bunch of the men living there end up drowning the city will put a high fence around it. And who would want to live down there after that anyhow? Who could sleep there with all those ghosts haunting the place?

Shouldn't we do something about those guys up under the bridge?

Like what?

I dunno. Tell 'em they're gonna get drowned.

Rabbit speaks very slowly and with effort as if struggling to get his breath. *They won't listen to you, Kid. Besides, maybe they won't drown.* Then after a few seconds, *Yeah, you're right. I'll tell 'em. They'll listen to me. You gotta take care of yourself, Kid,* he says.

The old man swings around on his crutch and starts moving down the soaked muddy pathway. The Kid shouts against the howling wind for him to wait, then to be careful, for chrissakes, it's slippery, when the old man's crutch slides out from under him and he

collapses onto the ground and keeps falling. As if he planned on falling and even desired it he offers no resistance to it. His body crum-
ples and seems to come apart, legs going one way, arms another, head
lolling loosely on his skinny neck, as if he's a marionette made of
wet papier-mâché. He rolls some twenty feet off the zigzagged path
to a ridge where the long slope from the highway to the settlement
below turns into a sixty-degree drop. The old man drags himself to
the ridge and goes over. It's almost a precipice and he falls faster and
faster tumbling down the incline all the way to the bottom where
there's now three feet or more of rapidly rising water and he ends up
lying there facedown half in the water and half out.

The Kid quickly ties Annie's leash to the guardrail and scrambles
down the long hill after him, pushing past P.C. and Ginger making
their way up with their loads on their backs like hobos hoping to
hop a freight. By the time he reaches the bottom the tidal surge off
the Bay has already risen another foot and the Rabbit is floating
away. The Kid wades into the water and reaches for Rabbit's pants
leg but before he can grab it a wave hits him in the chest, driving
him back. The wave catches the old man and shoves him farther
out. Otis the Rabbit floats away from the Causeway and the sunken
settlement toward the open Bay. He does not resist. He's gone.

Struggling against the undertow the Kid backs slowly free of the
waist-high water and turns and looks up under the bridge. The rest
of the men are huddled up there in the shadows watching him like
gargoyles. Above him on the right Ginger and P.C. have crossed the
guardrail onto the empty highway and are trudging west heading
inland.

The bastards. They watched the old man fall and not a one of
them made an effort to come to his aid. Not a one of them moved
from his perch. But the Kid knows that the Rabbit had finally given
up on living like an abandoned animal and didn't want anyone to
save him. He fell down that hill like a man jumping off a bridge. And
who could blame him? Maybe they should all give up the struggle—

just let go and fall down whatever hill you were trying to climb until you end at the bottom and the sea rolls in and takes you away like it took away Iggy and now the Rabbit. What's the point of trying to solve your problems and get ahead in life if the only problems you can solve are the little meaningless housekeeping ones and you're never going to get ahead in life anyhow because you're a convicted sex offender and are condemned to be one for the rest of your life even if you never commit another sex offense. Your name and face are always going to show up on that registry and scare the shit out of people who will make you live outside the camp as if told to do it by Moses under orders from God.

He casts his gaze over the flooded encampment and notices that the surge seems to have receded a foot or two. The wind has diminished to a steady breeze and has shifted from the east around to the west and the rain has let up slightly. The men squatting up under the bridge have ventured out a ways to where they can stand in a low crouch and they're talking to one another excitedly as if surprised at not having drowned, as if they think that soon everything will return to the way it was yesterday—as if the way it was yesterday was worth living for.

But the Kid knows it'll never be like it was before the flood and the hurricane. Once you've seen your life and where you live for what they are they never look the way they did before. Illusions die hard especially when like the Kid you've only got a few to hold on to and when they're dead and gone you can never get them back. He knows now what the Rabbit knew when he let himself fall: this life is the only one available and it's not worth the effort. Fuck the Professor and his theories.

The rain has stopped and the sky is turning from dark gray to a buttery shade of yellow. The water is receding rapidly as if the Bay is being emptied out through Kydd's Cut back into the ocean. His tent is gone, swept away by the flood. Like Rabbit. All the tents and huts have been demolished and dumped into the Bay. Chained to the stanchion his bike lies buried beneath a huge pile of dripping debris, garbage, old boards and plywood, and tangled sheets of polyethylene. He can barely make out its twisted and bent wheels and frame. Everything is beyond repair or simply gone.

He can't think of what to do now or where to go. Maybe he should just stand where he is and wait for something to happen and react to whatever it is. As if he were an object, a thing instead of a human being. Because that's what he feels like now.

Then he remembers that his water-logged duffel and backpack and few remaining possessions are up by the highway. What the hell, he can be a thing up there as easily as down here under the Causeway. Head down he starts trudging up the path and halfway to the top he lifts his head and sees Annie soaked and shivering tied to the guardrail and on the pavement next to her is Einstein miserable in his cage with his head tucked under a wing, his long tail-feathers a soaked mat on the floor of the cage.

The Kid never should have taken responsibility for Annie and Einstein. What was he thinking? It's all the Professor's fault, he thinks. He never would have taken them with him when he left Benbow's if the Professor hadn't given him the illusion that he was capable of taking care of them. That illusion is gone now too. Those two helpless creatures are way worse off with him than they were at Benbow's.

Then to his amazement just as the Kid reaches the top and steps over the guardrail he sees the Professor's van coming down the highway from the west. Every time he thinks about someone that person suddenly appears in reality. He should start thinking about people he actually wants to see except that he can't think of anyone he really wants to see. Nobody he knows in person anyhow. He wouldn't mind seeing Willow the French Canadian porn star. He wouldn't mind seeing Captain Kydd the pirate so he could ask him about the buried treasure.

The van crunches to a stop beside the Kid. The Professor gets out of his vehicle and hurries up to the Kid. He's in shirtsleeves with huge sweat circles under his arms and a gray wet blotch across his heaving chest. His face is red and he's breathing rapidly as if he's climbed several flights of stairs.

Put the animals and the rest of your gear in the van!

The Kid answers, *You can take the animals if you want. But I'm stayin' put. I don't need you.*

The Professor slides open the side door and lifts Annie into the back and sets Einstein's cage beside her. *Yes you do. The storm's only half over. You can't stay here.* He reaches for the Kid's backpack but the Kid yanks it back from him.

Fuck you, fat man! Like I said, I'm stayin' put.

Look at you! You're soaked through. He glances down the hillside at what was once the settlement beneath the Causeway. *Your camp is wrecked. You can't stay here.*

Fuck you.

The Professor picks up the Kid's duffel and places it on the back-seat. *Come with me. I'll take you to my house. You can come back here and rebuild tomorrow or the next day, after the hurricane's passed out to sea.*

The Professor takes hold of the backpack again. This time the Kid doesn't resist. He's remembered that he's an object, a thing, not a human being with a will and a goal, and that he's only capable of reacting, not acting. The Professor's the human being here, not the Kid. So he opens the passenger door of the van and gets in.

CHAPTER THREE

To the Kid as they drive across the city and along deserted suburban streets the Professor seems agitated and uncharacteristically urgent. Usually he's calm, slow-moving, and talks in long complete sentences that keep your attention but today he rattles on about how until now he's been protected and that's all going to change so he's going to have to protect himself. The Kid's not sure what he's talking about and thinks at first that it's the hurricane that's got the Professor in a lather so he asks him if he means protected from the hurricane.

No, no, of course not, the Professor's not afraid of the storm, he's been in far worse storms than this, he insists. He's been in typhoons at sea in an open boat.

No shit, the Kid says, not knowing what a typhoon is exactly but admitting to himself that it does sound worse than a hurricane. Especially at sea in an open boat.

And besides, the Professor adds, *wherever I go, the eye of the storm goes. The I of the eye.* He laughs loudly at this, a joke the Kid definitely does not get. *As you may have noticed,* the big man says and laughs again.

Yeah, whatever.

Dodging fallen tree branches and uprooted foliage to the end of a looping tree-lined residential street, the Professor turns the van onto a driveway and pulls up before a double bay garage attached to a sprawling ranch house. He raises the overhead door with an electronic remote and drives the vehicle into the garage and parks it.

Lugging Einstein's cage and leading Annie by her rope leash, the Kid follows the Professor into the house. The Professor, still in shirtsleeves and sweating, drags the Kid's expedition backpack and duffel across the carpeted floor and drops them by the entrance to the living room. It's a large comfortable tastefully furnished home, a professor's and a librarian's home with floor-to-ceiling bookshelves, paintings and framed photographs on the walls, Oriental carpets, an elaborate stereo system and racks of CDs, a large flat-screened TV, and a long shelf of DVDs next to it. The Kid can't remember ever being inside a house like this before. He wasn't aware that comfy good-looking rooms like this even existed except in magazine ads and on TV. It's more like a set for actors to use for an upscale porn film than a real home for real people, he thinks. Then he flashes on the night he got caught by Dave Dillinger and the girl he thought was brandi18. Except for the books and pictures this house is a lot like that one.

You don't have like any hidden cameras or anything here, do you?

Of course not! What made you ask that?

Just wondering. Is this where you live?

Yes, it is.

You live here alone or with a wife?

With a wife and our two children.

They around?

Yes, yes, of course. They wouldn't go anywhere in this storm.

Maybe I oughta leave. If there's kids in the house.

No! You have to stay! Wait out the storm, and I'll cover for you.

Too late now anyhow.

They pass through the dining room into the kitchen, a large open space with stainless steel restaurant-size appliances and copper-colored tile countertops and floor to match. The Professor heads straight for the refrigerator and then abruptly stops. A sheet of white paper with a long typed paragraph on it has been taped to the door.

The Professor peels the paper off the refrigerator door, reads it quickly, and passes it to the Kid. He opens the refrigerator door and caresses its brightly lit interior with his gaze. *At least she left us plenty of food,* the Professor says and starts carrying bowls and plastic containers to the table. He sets out two plates and forks, sits down at the table and opens several of the plastic containers.

Soaked and chilled to the bone the Kid stands by the refrigerator reading:

I have taken the twins and gone to my mother's in Port Vitalie. It may be temporary, it may be permanent. I don't know. I need time to think this through without you present. I need to decide how seriously to take all your secrets and lies. I realize that I'll never know the truth about you and that you will probably always keep secrets and will continue to lie to me. I have to decide if in spite of that I can go on living with you. Right now I don't think I can. Please don't call or e-mail me. Please don't try to speak with me at the library when I'm working or at my mother's. I need to listen to my own voice and the kids' voices, not yours. If you want to speak to the kids, call my mother's number, not mine, and ask for them. If they want to speak to you, I will let them call you. Please don't try to contact them when they're at school as my mother will be driving them in and picking them up afterward, and as you know, her view of you has always been negative and will likely be even more so now. When I have made up my mind about what to do with this marriage, I will let you know. —Gloria

The Kid lays the sheet of paper next to the Professor's loaded plate. *So I guess no kids. But, dude, that's cold.*

The Professor glances at the letter and goes back to eating.

Between mouth-filling bites of cold macaroni salad he says, *Yes . . . but appropriate . . . and in some sense . . . useful.*

Useful? To who?

To her. To our children. And to me.

I don't get it, man.

You will, you will. He stops eating and looks at the Kid. *You're really wet. Go down the hallway on the far side of the dining room. There's a guest bedroom and bath at the far end. Take a shower and get dried off, and then we'll feed you and look after this poor dog and parrot. I think like you they'll be fine once they've gotten dry and are fed.*

The Kid points out that his duffel and backpack are soaked through and he doesn't have any dry clothes. The Professor says there's a laundry located next to the guest room, he can run his clothes through the dryer while he's showering, and he better do it now while they still have electric power. If the storm knocks out the power, they'll have to get by with candlelight. The Professor estimates the hurricane will last the rest of the day and abate during the night. *We're lucky it's only a Category Three. Now that we're safely sheltered here the eye of the storm can move on. By tomorrow everything will be back to normal. Damage should be minimal, except out at the Barriers.*

Yeah. And under the Causeway. That's totally trashed, man. I'm never going back there.

We'll discuss that later. Meanwhile, go on and dry your clothes and shower and come back to the kitchen for something to eat. I'll still be here.

Yeah, I can see that. At the door the Kid stops and turns back. *How come you're so jumpy and nervous, man? I mean, your wife just took your kids and left you. Shouldn't you be all sad and fucked-up? Or at least all pissed off?*

You'll understand soon enough. Go on, go on. We've got work to do.

Whaddaya mean, work?

We need to film another interview.

No fucking way, man! No more interviews. I'm done with that.

This time you're going to interview me, Kid.

That's stupid. Why would I want to interview you?

I need you to interview me. For me, for my wife and children. Don't worry about it, just do as I say.

The Kid shrugs and heads off down the hallway dragging his duffel and backpack behind him. Annie has collapsed in a puddle on the kitchen floor. From his cage next to her Einstein says, *Do as I say! Do as I say!*

CHAPTER FOUR

P: *You sit there, Kid, off camera. I'll sit here on the sofa in front of it.*

K: *Whaddaya want me to ask? I mean, I never done this before, interviewed somebody.*

P: *No, but you've been interviewed. You start by asking a question that you want answered, and then I decide if and how I'm willing to answer it. Then you ask a follow-up question that's generated by my previous answer. Simple. Especially for the one asking the questions.*

K: *Okay. How about what's the fucking reason for making this interview in the first place?*

P: *Excellent first question! The simple answer is that in the coming weeks or possibly months my body will be found, and it will look like a suicide. This interview will provide evidence that it was not a suicide.*

K: *No way, man! Why would you commit suicide? I mean, you're kind of jolly. You don't seem the type to kill yourself.*

P: *I'm not.*

K: *So how come your body's going to be found? A heart attack maybe, I can sure see you having a heart attack. On account of being so overweight. But how come it'll look like a suicide?*

P: *That's two questions. Which one do you want answered?*

K: *Okay. How come it'll look like a suicide?*

P: *There will be a scandal, a public exposé. I know who I am, a man with a publicly certified, locally celebrated, genius IQ, a respected university pro-*

*fessor with a wife and family, a deacon of the church, et cetera, and what I
look like, morbidly obese, bearded, eccentric, et cetera. A popular parody of
an intellectual. Given that profile, the scandal will be of an embarrassing,
probably criminal, sexual nature. That's how they do these things. I know
the script. I practically wrote it myself. First a complaint is made to the
local police by someone claiming to have been raped by the targeted party
or sexually molested by him in the distant past when the accuser was a
child. The police quietly begin an investigation. Then the targeted party
mysteriously disappears. The accusation of rape or sexual molestation is
surreptitiously leaked to the news media. Weeks pass, sometimes months.
Eventually the body of the targeted party is "discovered" under circumstances and in a condition that indicates suicide. By now the accuser has
disappeared. The investigation ends. Case closed.*

K: *You're just making this shit up, right?*

P: *No, I'm not making it up. I wish I were, believe me.*

K: *Okay, now I got a hundred questions! If you're not just shittin' me.*

P: (chuckles) *Pick one, and we'll go from there. I'll answer them all eventually.*

K: *You are one really weird dude, Professor. So okay, who's the "targeted
party" you're talking about?*

P: *In this case, me.*

K: *Okay. That's what I thought. Who's doing the targeting?*

P: *I'm not sure yet. It could be one of at least three of my previous employers.
Let's call them government agencies.*

K: *What government? You mean the government of the United States of
America?*

P: *Yes. And the government of at least one foreign nation and possibly a
second. Or all three in collusion.*

K: *So like, are we talking FBI and CIA and shit?*

P: *Not really. There are agencies that aren't as well known as the FBI and
CIA whose purposes and activities aren't as closely monitored by Congress and the public. Agencies that are off the books, so to speak. Black-
box agencies. But we needn't go into that here. I don't want to put you*

in any danger, and I certainly don't want to endanger my family any more than I already have. My sole use for this interview is to provide some small comfort to them after my body is found. So I'll spare you, and therefore them, some of the details.

K: *Are you not really a professor then?*

P: *Oh, yes! I am who I say I am! A professor, husband, father, deacon, library trustee, et cetera. All that and more.*

K: *But you're saying besides being a professor and all you're also like "targeted" by these super-secret agencies.*

P: *That's correct.*

K: *So why the fuck would they do that, target you? Why would they set it up so they can like kill you and make it look like you committed suicide because of some sex scandal?*

P: *(sighs) It's a long story, Kid. I was recruited very early. While still in college, in fact. I was recruited because of my intellectual and linguistic gifts, no doubt, but also because my psychological and social profiles fit certain known and tested templates. I arrived early and stayed late, let us say, and consequently over the years I saw and heard and participated in much that if they became publicly known could cause great harm to powerful political and economic interests. Especially now that both political and economic interests are so intricately connected. Simply put, even though I was never anywhere near the top of the pyramid, I saw and heard and participated in too much. Those on top operate strictly on a need-to-know basis. It's the people nearest the bottom, people like me, who know too much. More than they need to know.*

K: *Yeah, but so what? Lots of people know too much. They don't get killed for it, so long as they don't talk about it to anyone. Even me, I know shit for instance about the guys who live under the Causeway that I'd never tell about, stuff they told me or I saw them do that could get them sent back to prison, and nobody wants to kill me. They just trust me not to tell anyone what I know. Were you like planning on telling what you know about these secret agencies and so on, going on TV or writing it in a book or something? And somehow these guys found out about it?*

P: *No, nothing like that. But it's assumed among my previous employers that people who lived as I did for years, for decades, can only be trusted as long as they are not who they say they are. It's when they become who they say they are that they can no longer be trusted.*

K: *I'm confused. Trusted to what?*

P: *Not to reveal what they saw and heard and did in the past.*

K: *So now that you are what you say you are, a professor and such, married and all, you can't be trusted anymore to lie about who you were in the past? Like you might start by telling your wife and then a priest or a shrink or the guys in your therapy group if you had one, and pretty soon some newspaper writer would hear about it or a book writer, and then the whole world would end up knowing what you know. And that would fuck up a lot of important people like in politics and so on?*

P: *Correct.*

K: *So that's why they want to get rid of you?*

P: *Yes.*

K: *This sounds like a fucking movie. Are you sure you're not making this shit up?*

P: *I'm not making any of it up. Unfortunately.*

K: *Were you like a spy, then?*

P: *Informant first. Then mole. Then spy. Counterspy. Double agent. That's the usual progression for someone with my particular abilities and temperament.*

K: *How do you know they want to do you? The suicide thing.*

P: *Like I said, I know the script. The Calusa police have started an investigation. Two plainclothes officers came to my home asking to speak with me. They have already gone to the trouble to question my parents, which means the scandal will no doubt be set in my distant past. It will be a crime that I am accused of having committed when I was a young man, when my parents and I were still more or less in touch, before I decided to distance myself from them. It will therefore have to be an act for which there is no statute of limitations.*

K: *What's that mean?*

P: *Misdemeanors and most felonies have to be prosecuted within a limited amount of time following the commitment of the crime. Crimes that society regards as particularly repulsive, however, have no statute of limitations. First-degree murder, for instance. Also, in most states, rape, distribution and possession of child pornography, and sexual abuse of children, especially in cases when the victim doesn't remember the event until years later. My best guess is that someone has recently uncovered long-repressed memories of having been sexually abused by me when she or he was a child and has taken those resurrected memories to the Calusa Police Department.*

K: *But you didn't, right? Abuse anybody. You're not a fucking chomo, right?*

P: *Correct.*

K: *Dude, that's some serious shit! You could end up living under the Causeway yourself!*

P: *It'll never come to that. I'll never be indicted or even arrested. I'll never be tried or convicted. I'll simply disappear. Then my accuser, whoever she or he is, will allow her- or himself to be interviewed by some local investigative journalist, or else one of the police officers will leak the nature of the accusation and investigation to the press. Sometime after that my body will be found, and the official cause of death will be ruled a suicide. Naturally, they can arrange it so my body is never found. But then my disappearance would remain an open case and would invite a long-term ongoing investigation. Who knows what would turn up? No, they want my wife, my children, my colleagues and students, the entire city of Calusa and especially the press and other news media to believe that I killed myself because I was about to be exposed as a child molester or rapist. It'll make a titillating, convincing story. "So-called genius professor of sociology, an eccentric, bearded, fat man doing research on homeless convicted sex offenders, is a sex offender himself."*

K: *How come you're telling me all this in front of a camera, instead of telling your wife in person, say? Or the cops. Or why not go on TV and tell Larry King or some news guy? Or here's an idea, why don't you put it up on YouTube?*

P: *First of all, if I tell Gloria what is about to happen, she will want me to save myself in a way that will basically destroy her and my children's lives. She'll want us to flee to some undeveloped country and assume new identities, for instance. Which wouldn't work anyhow. It would only shatter their lives and postpone the inevitable. All it would do is buy me a little extra time until they found us. Ten or fifteen years ago it might have worked. But the world is digitalized now and interconnected, so it's impossible for a high-profile American man with a wife and two small children to flee the country and change his and his family's identity. The first time one of us went online we'd be located. And if I go to the police, as you suggest, they will merely assume I'm lying in order to protect myself against my accuser. That would make my accuser go away, which is good, and the suicide script would be scrapped. Also good. But they'll know I've been alerted to their intentions, so a different way to make me disappear will be contrived. Which is not good. In that script there's usually an accident or a fire that takes out the whole family or several other people associated with the target, fellow workers or innocent bystanders. If I'm killed alone it will appear that my story is true. An "accident" that takes others with me is messy, perhaps, but not incriminating. The same thing will happen if I go public with it by posting this interview on You-Tube, for instance, or tell my story to a journalist.*

K: *Okay. So why don't you just cut out by yourself? Leave your family here. Go to Jamaica or someplace, change your name. Shave your beard and get a haircut. If you lost a lot of weight nobody'd recognize you, man. Even your wife when she came and visited you there once in a while. If you really are an ex-spy and all, you oughta know how to disappear. Even in the digital world.*

P: *If I fled alone, it would put Gloria and the children in great danger, especially if they knew where I was. To get to me these people would go after my family. My parents would be in danger too. It's the reason I broke off all contact with my parents in the first place. It was to protect them. I suppose it was also to let me more freely become who and what I wanted to be, regardless of who and what I said I was. That was a long time ago.*

It's only in recent years that I began to think I could become the same as who and what I said I was. (long pause) I forgot that I was still being watched. And that I was expendable. And because of the life I built here in Calusa, I had become a danger to them.

K: *Are you sure you're not like paranoid or something, Professor?*

P: *(chuckles) I wish I were!*

K: *Here's a question. Maybe my last, unless you still have stuff you want to add. Why tell me all this? Why don't you just talk to the camera by your- self and then download it onto your computer and burn it onto a DVD and drop it into the mail to the wife? If that's what you're planning to do anyhow. Besides, if you're not nutso paranoid and what you're telling me is true, then I'm in trouble too, just for sitting here listening to this shit. If they're watching you, they're watching me now. What're you thinking, I'm expendable too? Are you sure this place doesn't have hidden cameras and microphones?*

P: *Don't worry, I do an electronic sweep of the house every few days. As for your last question, why tell you all this? There's a very simple answer. I trust you, Kid. I do. For decades I've trusted no one but myself. But I trust you. After I burn a DVD of this interview and erase the original from my computer, I trust you to keep the DVD in your possession until my body is found. It'll be in the papers and on TV, so you'll know about it. I trust you then to deliver the DVD to Gloria and no one else and never to say a word about it to anyone for the rest of your life. I don't trust anyone other than you to do that. No one. I don't even trust the postal service. Besides, I can't mail the DVD myself if I'm dead. It has to be hand delivered. By you. I trust you to do that. I've studied your character closely these last few days. Also, you are probably the only human being I know personally who is not being watched.*

K: *C'mon, I got a GPS beeper on my ankle. I'm being watched closer than you. I don't know, man. If you're telling me the truth about all this and you're not just fucked-up in the head or playing some kind of weird col- lege professor's game with me to prove how much smarter than me you are, like with that treasure map game, then I'll end up with some very*

*dangerous information on my hands that these guys would like to elimi-
nate. Which would make them want to eliminate me. That DVD is like
Captain Kydd's treasure, man. If anybody thought I figured out where X
marks the spot, they'd torture me for it and then kill me.*

P: *Don't worry, Kid. That map's a fake.*

K: *Yeah, well, I thought it was, anyhow. Why'd you try to make me think it
was real? That wasn't cool, y' know.*

P: *I apologize, Kid. I was testing you. I knew you were honest, but I wasn't
sure if you were imaginative.*

K: *So I passed the test?*

P: *With flying colors.*

K: *First test I ever passed. Is this what happens when you pass a test?
Okay, forget it. Here's something else I just thought of. What if this whole
super-secret spy agencies story is just a cover story? What if you're not an
ex-spy, which can't be proved anyhow one way or the other, so it doesn't
matter, and you're really just some old ex-chomo, and you're about to get
busted for something you actually did to a kid or maybe several kids way
back before you were a professor and married with kids of your own and
so forth, and you know it's gonna hit the papers and TV? What if you're
planning to kill yourself first, so you don't have to go through all that and
do time and end up living under the Causeway with an electronic anklet
like the other sex offenders, and you've got me making this interview
with you so it'll look like it was really homicide, not suicide, at least to
your wife and your kids, and you weren't really guilty of sexually abusing
kids? What about that, Professor? The camera's still on, isn't it?*

P: *Yes, it's running. Hm-m-m. Maybe you're more imaginative than I
thought. Well, yes, Kid, you're right, you may never know for sure if I'm
telling you the truth. But will it make any difference to you? Will you
refuse to keep the DVD in your possession and deliver it to Gloria when
my body is found and my death is declared a suicide?*

K: *Depends.*

P: *On what?*

K: *On what's in it for me.*

P: *Ah! You mean money, I assume. I hope not Captain Kydd's treasure. I'm not a rich man, you know. And when my death is ruled a suicide, my wife won't be able to collect on my life insurance policy.*

K: *Maybe that's what you want this interview for! So your wife can use it to show that you didn't kill yourself, you were knocked off by some super-spies from Russia or someplace. So she can collect on your insurance.*

P: *They'd never go for it. She'd have to take the insurance company to court, and if indeed I am telling the truth, that would put her and the children in grave danger. You don't want that on your hands, do you? Just tell me what you want in payment for delivering the DVD to Gloria after my body is found and for never revealing the DVD or its contents to anyone else.*

K: *I don't wanna talk about it in front of the camera.*

P: *Understandable. Pretty much everything I wanted Gloria to hear has been said already. Except that I truly love her and the children. I need to say that. And I am not guilty of the heinous acts that I will soon be accused of.*

K: *Are you ashamed, though? Like you asked me when you were interview-ing me about brandi18.*

P: *Ashamed? Of what?*

K: *You know, of spying and shit. Being an informant and a mole and a double agent. All that.*

P: *No, I'm not ashamed. And I don't feel guilty for all those years of deceit and betrayal, secrecy and lies. That was the nature of the world then and now, and those are the rules of the game that runs the world. And once you know that, you either play the game or it plays you. I only regret that I stopped playing the game. Now it's playing me. Except for this one last move. . . .*

K: *Maybe we should shut off the camera and discuss my fee.*

P: *Fair enough.*

CHAPTER FIVE

THE UNBLINKING EYE OF THE HURRICANE swerves east of Calusa and crosses over the Barriers and out to sea. Then the second half of the storm pounces. The wind speed jacks up to eighty and ninety miles an hour and gusts start to reach a hundred and above. Torrential rain floods the streets of the Professor's neighborhood and surrounding yards. At the edge of the neighborhood a tall live oak tree is uprooted and falls against a utility pole, blowing out the transformer and shutting down the electricity for a dozen blocks, including the Professor's.

The Professor breaks out a bundle of candles and several hurricane lamps and lights up the living room. He hands a candle to the Kid, picks up a hurricane lamp for himself, and tells the Kid to follow him. *And bring your bags,* he adds. He waddles back to his study at the far end of the house, his flickering lamp casting a wedge of lemony light against the walls and ceiling as he goes. The reenergized wind slaps relentlessly at the sides of the darkened house.

The study is a small, book-lined room with an enormous blue leather recliner chair and a wide desk cluttered with books and papers. Next to the desk is a black, old-fashioned floor safe. The Professor places his lamp on top of the safe and grunting from the effort gets down on his hands and knees in front of it. He puts his eye close to the dial, spins the numbers several times each way, clockwise, then counterclockwise, and swings open the heavy door. The Kid steps forward and lowers his candle so he can see what's inside. Filling the interior of the safe are stacks of neatly bundled cash.

He says to himself, *Excellent! Finally, Captain Kydd's treasure!*

The Professor turns and looks up at the Kid. *How much is this going to cost me?*

The Kid is silent for a minute. He thinks: If we're supposed to be negotiating my fee, he probably shouldn't have let me see this. But it does make the hard-to-believe ex-spy story a little more believable. He takes a stab at how much cash is in the safe and says, *Ten K.*

No, that's way too much. Try twenty-five hundred dollars. That'll buy a lot of dog food and birdseed.

The Kid remembers that everything the Professor does has a game plan. This money was probably intended for him from the beginning. All of it. Pretending to negotiate is just another of the Professor's little mind games. The Kid says, *If you're gonna get turned into a suicide you're not gonna be needing any extra cash. So how about you put all the money that's in the safe into my duffel and we'll call it a deal. I'll count it later.*

I'll give you five thousand dollars for your services. I need to hold back as much as possible for my family's use. After I'm gone.

Come on, man, your wife don't even know this money's here. If what you told me in the interview is true, you stashed it strictly for this occasion way back. Like you say, you wrote the script. I bet your wife don't know the combination and you don't plan on telling it to her or writing it down for her, neither. If the cops or one of your secret agent ex-buddies decides to crack open this safe after you disappear or after they find your body, you'd want it to be empty. A whole lotta cash left here would make your suicide look real. An empty safe will help back your story in the interview.

The Professor makes his usual fat man's professorial chuckle, *Heh-heh-heh. Okay, Kid, you win this one.*

Yeah, except sometimes with you it seems like whatever I think and say is what you planned for me to think and say. Maybe all you really wanted was getting me to believe your spy story.

Nonsense. I'm barely in control of what I think and say myself, never mind controlling your words and thoughts too.

You're supposed to be a fucking double agent or maybe a triple agent times two. You guys plan everything out in advance. Or maybe you're just playing a made-up role. So who knows what you're in control of? Not me, that's for sure. I'll do what you want me to, though. With the DVD, I mean. A deal is a deal. It don't actually matter to me what's true about you and what isn't. It ain't like this is in a novel or a movie where the whole point is figuring out what's true.

Despite what he says, the Kid is a little scared of the Professor. Especially now. The more the fat man reveals what he claims to be the truth about himself the less the Kid knows who or what the fat man is. Other than weird. If he's telling the truth he's the weirdest dude the Kid has ever known and if he's lying he's still the weirdest dude the Kid has ever known. *Just gimme the fucking money and the DVD of the interview and I'm outa here. I don't know where I'm going but wherever it is, it has to be in Calusa County, so I'll be checking the news for when they find your body.*

The Professor points out that he can't download the interview onto his computer and burn the DVD until the electricity comes back on. The Kid will have to stay a while. Besides, with debris flying through the air and fallen tree limbs and rising waters, it's dangerous out there for someone on foot. He reminds the Kid, who needs no reminding, about Annie and Einstein and suggests that the Kid use the guest room for the night.

The Kid says no way. He's willing to stay put until the storm blows over—but not inside the house. He and Annie and Einstein will sleep in the Professor's van in the garage.

The Professor says all right and proceeds to empty the contents of the safe into the Kid's duffel while the Kid peers down from above. He counts ten bundles of hundred-dollar bills and is pretty sure now that his first guess of ten thousand dollars was correct. Very cool ending to a treasure hunt, he thinks, even though he wasn't exactly hunting. All he was looking for tonight was shelter for himself and Annie and Einstein.

The Kid grabs his duffel and follows the Professor into the kitchen where the Professor sets out a new meal for himself at the table. Before he sits down to eat, he makes a ham and cheese sandwich for the Kid to take with him to the garage and gives the Kid a flashlight and an extra candle. The Kid stands by the door for a minute and watches the fat man go back to the refrigerator and load a second plate with pie and ice cream and he decides to keep the doors of the van locked when he's sleeping. Even though most of what he's heard and seen tonight is probably a lie or a trick or part of a game whose rules he'll never really *get,* he knows too much about the Professor now to turn his back on him. The guy never says or does anything without a hidden agenda. For all the Kid knows it could be sexual and the Professor could have a thing about the Kid's thing. He wonders how a guy that fat can even have sex anyhow. Unless his dick is humungous—longer for instance than the Kid's—he'd have a hard time getting his hands on it under all those rolls of fat.

Maybe he's into giving BJs, the Kid thinks. Not for him. No BJs for the Kid these days or maybe ever. Especially not from the Professor. Not in return for the ten K. Not for any amount of money. Since getting busted that night by Brandi's dad and the cops he hasn't jerked off even once. He actually doesn't like looking at his dick anymore or touching it and he sure doesn't want anyone else looking at it or touching it. He doesn't mind if Annie or Einstein happen to see his dick when he's naked from a shower or changing clothes like earlier in the Professor's guest room and bath. They're only a sick old dog and a trash-talking bird. But no humans, male or female, are going to see it. Or touch it.

CHAPTER SIX

THE AREA OF A CIRCLE IS PI TIMES THE square of its radius. Which means: if you're required to reside 2,500 feet away from anyplace where children regularly gather—a school or a playground, for instance, or a video arcade—you have to live outside a closed circle of 9.25 million square feet. Since every school, playground, or video arcade lies at the center of such a circle and nearly all of the circles partially overlap and often extend well beyond the others, when you step clear of one 9.25-million-square-foot forbidden zone, you immediately step into part of another.

Thus, if you're a sex offender tried and convicted in Calusa County and are required by the terms of your parole to stay in Calusa County, as is almost always the case, there are only three places where you can legally reside: under the Causeway that connects the mainland with the Barrier Isles; in Terminal G out at the International Airport; or in the eastern end of the Great Panzacola Swamp.

The Kid knows he can't go back to the Causeway again. Whatever they had going for themselves down there before the hurricane, it's totally smashed now. The Rabbit is dead. And Iggy is dead. Their ghosts will haunt the place forever. The Shyster, Paco, the Greek, P.C., Froot Loop, Ginger, all the residents are scattered across the city like cockroaches and in any case will be looking out only for themselves now. It's like Paco said when he rode off into the rain. The Kid's got to do the same. Look out only for himself. Forget communal living, collaboration, cooperation. Forget community completely. Except for Annie and Einstein, you're on your own now, Kid.

He can't set up camp in the parking garage at Terminal G or sleep on one of the benches in the waiting area inside. The airport's a favorite cul-de-sac for homeless crazies, drug addicts, and alcoholics to panhandle harried travelers who are usually flush with cash and more or less confined to the terminal waiting for their delayed flights to arrive or depart. People like that are easily hit for a buck or two just to make the panhandler go away, since they're stuck at the airport and can't go away themselves. The homeless crazies, addicts, and alcoholics end up nodding out or falling asleep on a modernist stainless steel bench inside the terminal stinking up the place or else they look for an unlocked car in the garage or failing that break into a locked car where they can hole up till the owner comes back from his trip. Which is why there are so many cops patrolling the area. The Kid would be busted in an hour for vagrancy and sent back to prison for violating parole.

That leaves the Great Panzacola Swamp. The vast grassy marshland is a fourteen-thousand-square-mile national park that sprawls across the entire southwest quarter of the state, extending all the way east into Calusa County to where it was partially drained a generation ago by a concrete grid of thirty-foot-deep canals creating the cane fields, citrus groves, and truck farms that bump up against the expanding suburbs and tract-house developments of Greater Calusa. West of the suburbs, fields, farms, and groves, there is a sizable chunk of the swampy waters, lakes, slow shallow streams, mangrove islands, low hummocks, and grasslands—some five hundred thousand acres of the Panzacola National Park—that remains within the borders of Calusa County. The Kid can legally reside there.

Though less than thirty miles from so-called civilization, the swamp is home to alligators, small deer, the last of the American cougars, and hundreds of species of birds. Out where the freshwater streams and the shallow run-off from the lakes farther north mingle with the saline waters of Calusa Bay and the Gulf there are diminishing numbers of crocodile colonies and manatee pods. Also in recent years many Calusans have released into what looks to them like the wild exotic pets grown too large for their cages or too dangerous for domestic life with humans. The swamp has become the home away from home of twenty-foot-long Burmese pythons and other large Asian, African, and South American snakes, huge snapping turtles captured as babies in Georgia and Alabama ponds, pet wolves, feral cats, parrots and cockatoos, and in a few cases monkeys, macaques, gibbons, and at least two pet chimpanzees grown from cute little humanoids into powerful destructive adults that a year ago had to be shot by park rangers for attacking a group of their *Homo sapiens* cousins visiting the park from abroad.

At the ranger station located near the entrance to the park you can buy a ticket for a thirty-minute tour-boat ride through a small part of the swamp and out into Calusa Bay to watch the sunset. Or if you prefer to penetrate to the heart of the swamp on your own you can rent a canoe by the hour for the day. If you want to stay longer than a day but are not eager to sleep in a tent at one of the flea- and mosquito-infested campsites you can rent one of the half-dozen small underpowered flat-bottomed houseboats, stock it with water, food, iced beer or wine, fishing gear, and plenty of sunscreen and bug spray and with a topographical map of the entire multimillion-acre park in one hand and the tiller in the other you can disappear into the depths of the swamp for days or weeks or even longer if you can afford the rent.

Though he's never been to the Great Panzacola Swamp in person and doesn't know much about anything that he hasn't experienced in person the Kid knows all this. He learned about the swamp and the houseboats from the Rabbit one night back when he first pitched his pup tent under the Causeway. Still unused to the noise of the traffic overhead, the filth, stench, and crowdedness of the place and the sometimes erratic scary behavior of the other residents, he was grousing to the Rabbit who was the only one living down there who had befriended him and didn't seem to want anything from him in return. The Kid whined that there's got to be a better place than this rat hole where they could legally reside.

The Rabbit told him there wasn't. But if they had enough dough they could rent a houseboat and live in the Great Panzacola Swamp and still be in Calusa County. *Nobody hassles you out there, Kid. They got a store at the ranger station where you can buy what you need. You can even rent a post office box there for your Social Security check or if you're on welfare. Once a week or so you come in off the swamp, pick up your mail and restock your supplies, fill up the gas tanks and head back out the same day. 'Course, it's probably pretty boring after a while. And there's all kindsa dangerous snakes and animals out there. And it's buggy. I mean, Kid, it's a fucking swamp! They probably got malaria out there. But nobody can bust you as long as you can pay your rent for the boat and obey the park rules.*

The Kid asked him what the rules were and the Rabbit said he wasn't sure but figured you couldn't toss any trash overboard or pick the flowers or use firearms or make campfires except in designated spots. That sort of thing. He said he heard there were still a few Indians living deep in the swamp way west and north of the Calusa County line, descendants of the Seminoles and escaped slaves who fought the white Americans to a standstill back in the nineteenth century getting by on hunting and fishing for food, living in hidden huts and tents on the mangrove islets and now and then guiding fishing parties out of the lodges located near the highways and in the small towns on the far edges of the park. He thought they signed a peace treaty years ago that gave them some special park privileges. He heard there were a few fugitives hiding out in the swamp too. *Outlaws, Kid. Sort of like us. Only without electronic GPS anklets, so nobody knows where they are. If you cut the fucking thing off your leg, nobody'd know where you were, either. The cops'd never think of looking for you in the swamp. They'd just think you booked for Nevada or somewhere in the West. They'd put out an APB to have you picked up and wait for you to turn up busted for vagrancy in Salt Lake City or someplace.*

The Kid was interested in the idea. *That sounds awesome, man! I hate this fucking bracelet.*

It's an anklet, Kid. And if you cut it off you'd be an outlaw too, the Rabbit pointed out. *A fugitive. You'd have to live in the swamp the rest of your fucking life. For me, no big deal maybe, but for you, different. If you ever wanted to come back to civilization for a visit or to get laid you'd get busted the first day just on suspicion of being alive, and they'd nail you for cutting off your tracker and you'd be back in the can. 'Course, as long as you kept your tracker on and the battery charged, which you could probably do at the ranger station, and didn't go beyond the county line, they couldn't legally stop you from living on a boat in the swamp.*

The Kid asked him if he was up for it. Why not? They could rent one of those houseboats and live in the swamp together. It had to be an improvement over living in a tent under the Causeway.

The Rabbit laughed and agreed, sure, it would be a decided improvement. *But forget about it, Kid. Those houseboats go for like fifty bucks a day. Maybe more. Who's got that kinda bread? Not me. And not you either.*

But that was then. This is now. The Rabbit may be gone to the bottom of the Bay with Iggy, but thanks to the Professor's upcoming suicide, the Kid's got plenty of bread now.

CHAPTER SEVEN

F LATTENED AGAINST THE SIDE WINDOW OF the van, the Professor's fat bearded face peers inside at the Kid stretched out asleep on the backseat. Annie and Einstein stare at the Professor from the rear cargo space. *All hands on deck!* Einstein screeches. *All hands on deck! All hands on deck!* Annie offers a weak whimpering bark—her first attempt to protect the Kid since he kidnapped her from Benbow's. She's gradually getting her strength and health back and evidently with it a small amount of confidence.

Slowly the Kid props himself up on his elbows and checks out the Professor face-to-face. The man looks sad and worried to the Kid, different from last night when he was spinning his tale and the Kid fears that he's going to ask for the money back. Too fucking bad, the Kid thinks. He's not getting it back no matter how sad and worried he looks. A deal's a deal. He checks the van doors—still locked. The keys dangle from the ignition.

The Professor tries the door and when it won't open he holds a DVD in a plastic case up to the driver's window and offers a wan smile. The Kid scrambles into the driver's seat and without starting the engine turns the ignition on and lowers the window an inch. He asks what time is it. The Professor says eight in the morning. *This is yours now,* he says and pushes the DVD through the slot to the Kid.

The hurricane's passed out to sea. It's safe for you to leave now. He offers to drive the Kid back to the Causeway.

The Kid grabs the DVD and reaches around behind him and quickly shoves it inside his duffel next to the money. *Forget that, man.*

You can't stay here, Kid. There's a day care center on the next block and an elementary school three blocks over. Now that the storm's over they'll be checking your anklet's location again.

I don't need to be reminded. You want to take me someplace, Haystack, drive me and my stuff and Annie and Einstein out to the Panzacola Swamp ranger station. Otherwise call me a cab.

The Professor raises his bushy eyebrows in surprise. *Why there?*

The Kid briefly lays out his intentions and reasoning, and the Professor purses his lips and nods in agreement—he doesn't think the Kid will last long out there on a houseboat but he agrees to drop him and his possessions and his two friends at the ranger station. *Now will you unlock the van doors?*

The Kid flicks the lock off and climbs into the back where he positions himself in the middle of the wide seat and waits for his driver to heave his huge bulk up and behind the wheel. The garage door rises and bright white daylight floods inside.

Cock-a-doodle-doo! Einstein cries. *Cock-a-doodle-doo-o-o!*

The Kid smiles and reaches around behind him and pats Annie on the head and gives a friendly wink to the parrot. This is better than he's felt in at least two years. Maybe longer. He's almost happy. If someone asked him if he was happy he'd say yes and he'd only be lying a little.

BEYOND THE SUBURBS MOST OF THE OTHER vehicles on the road this morning are pickup trucks and green and white city and county trucks carrying work crews out to begin repairing the downed lines and road signs and corporate vehicles headed to clean up the ravaged fields and the migrant workers' overturned trailers and shacks. The sky is clear and sapphire blue. West of the city limits a few miles past the last of the industrial parks, gated communities, and suburban housing developments they pass along the concrete drainage canals that run like arteries from the swamp down to the Bay, irrigating the hundreds of square miles of sugarcane and citrus groves. The waters of the overflowing ditches and canals glisten brightly in the sunlight. It's like a gigantic gleaming green game board out there despite the devastation caused to the crops and groves by the wind and the flooding of the canals and irrigation ditches. The blown-down bright green stalks of cane all lie on the ground in the same east-west direction and wide swaths of citrus trees are broken off at the same knee-high height.

The Professor has grown more animated as they drive and as is his wont is explaining to the Kid much of what the Kid is not the slightest interested in: the history of the canals and the draining of a huge chunk of the swamp for corporate agriculture, the political and economic battles waged for decades between the environmentalists who wanted to keep the swamp intact and the businessmen and politicians who wanted to carve it up piece by piece for industrialized farming and the real estate developers who had and still have designs on the fresh loamy soil for tract housing, gated communities, industrial parks, theme parks, stadia, and malls. The environmentalists lost their end of the battle years ago and have had to content themselves with guarding the remaining two million acres protected by the national park, but the fight between the agricultural interests and the real estate and banking interests continues. Meanwhile, the Professor goes on, these concrete canals have come to function not just as conveyors of water to drain and irrigate the land but also to serve a valuable service for the Calusa underworld. *That's the aspect of industrialization that particularly interests me,* he says. *Professionally. How the underclasses and the underworld end up making good use of social environments designed and built for altogether different purposes. Like your Causeway. Or the way you're now planning to make use of the Panzacola.*

The Kid perks up at this and asks how the underworld makes use of the canals. The Professor pulls the van over onto the shoulder near a thick hand-cranked lock on the farther bank where a smaller side canal feeds water into a thousand-acre cane field. *If you want to get rid of a body or a gun or other incriminating evidence or a stolen car stripped of its resalable parts, you drive out here at night and drop it into a main canal like this. Look down. You can't see a thing. It's twenty to thirty feet deep. The water's darkened by the tannin off the mangroves that grow around the lakes miles north of here, where most of the canal waters originate.*

The Kid asks why the canals don't eventually fill up with all those bodies and guns and stolen cars and shit and turn into like garbage dumps and clog up the canals and the Professor explains that once every few months the Calusa police and county sheriff's departments send crews and divers out to drag and search the canals and when possible identify the bodies and whatever else they fish out of the dark waters and try to attach them to unsolved crimes. *Usually in vain, of course. Bodies of missing persons can often be identified, and the serial numbers of guns are sometimes still there, and there's usually a way to trace a stolen car back to where and from whom it was stolen. But there's almost no way after it's been in the canal for a month or two to determine who put the body there or who used the gun or stole the car.*

That is very cool, the Kid says. I mean the way criminals and gangsters and what you're calling the "underclasses" like me get to reuse things like canals and causeways and swamps for their own purposes. Sort of like recycling. So is that what you teach at the university?

It's not of general enough interest to justify an entire course. It's merely one of the things I like to investigate and think about. In the future it's all that will be left to us, Kid. Recycling. You're readier for the future than most people. Before long we'll all be recycling buildings, roadways, industrial machinery, everything we've built for the last two hundred years or so, recycling them for purposes other than what they were originally designed and built for. And it won't just be the underclasses and criminals doing it. We'll all be living that way.

So I'm sort of like a pioneer, right?

That's right, Kid. You're the future. Now, remember this spot, Kid.

Why?

No special reason. It's just a spot where we had an interesting discussion about the future. Maybe our last.

Yeah, okay. Drive on, Haystack. The Kid's got an appointment with destiny in the Great Panzacola Swamp.

So the Kid's speaking of himself in the third person now? Money talks, I guess.

Yeah, it does. Unless you're a parrot.

The Professor, chuckling, drives on.

CHAPTER EIGHT

THE COUNTY ROAD INTO THE GREAT PAN-
zacola Swamp ends at a crushed limestone parking lot the
size of a football field. Adjacent to the parking lot a grove
of tall slash pines draped with scarfs of Spanish moss slopes down to
the shallow end of a long, narrow estuary where the swamp empties
into the southern end of Calusa Bay. It's the first of dozens of small,
meandering, island-clotted estuaries where freshwater slowly slides
off the swamp and mingles with the salty depths of the Bay and the
Gulf. All the way west to the Gulf and north to the lakes, except for
the turnpike that slices off the top of the park with a single straight
stroke, there are no more paved or unpaved roads. Nothing but endless miles of floodwater sluiced off the lakes in concrete canals and
poured into the swamp where it spreads out in a thin slowly drifting
plane of water that passes through tangled thickets of mangrove and
saturates wide knee-high saw grass veldts. It's a primitive ancient
landscape, Paleozoic. From time to time the shimmering watery
plane gets split by low tree-covered hummocks into mazes of dark
shifty streams and sloughs, making thousands of impenetrable islets
where water moccasins lurk and alligators wait patiently in the mud
for their next meal. Here and there along the outer edges of the
park ripples of dry sandy ground and a long broken chain of oyster-
shell mounds, ten-thousand-year-old midden heaps left by the first

human residents of the swamp, are laced with narrow footpaths and board catwalks, nature trails for day-trippers winding in circuitous routes to dark green observation towers that stick up from the flat expanse of the vast swamplike sentries.

In the shady grove by the parking lot most of the Spanish moss has been ripped from the branches of the slash pines by yesterday's wind and several of the larger, older trees have been uprooted and thrown to the ground. Palmettos and torn palm fronds lie scattered around the lot and under the trees, yellowing in the morning sun like abandoned brooms. The Professor's van, a red national park service pickup truck, and a dark green minibus with the county seal on the side door are the only vehicles in sight. On the seaside of the estuary where the swamp flows into the Bay a quarried limestone breaker and a wide bunkerlike concrete dock with a half-dozen empty slips and a boat-launch ramp appear to have survived the storm intact and undamaged. Opposite the slips and the dock four young black men in baggy dark green trousers and pale green T-shirts lug aluminum rental canoes from a rusted corrugated iron shed and place them gently down on the grassy bank of a slurred black-water stream that flows out of the dense jungle beyond. A portly middle-aged white man in a dark green short-sleeved shirt and trousers with a rifle cradled in the crook of his arm stands nearby smoking a cigarette. He watches the Kid and the Professor as they pass, flicks his cigarette butt into the water, and turns back to his prisoners.

A forty-foot open tour boat with a canvas canopy extending its length has been let back into the water and tied to stanchions. A teenage white boy near the bow of the boat wearing the same inmate's uniform as the young black men pointedly grunts from the effort of lifting an overturned ticket booth back into a standing position ready for business. At the edge of the dock a peeling gasoline pump and beside it another for diesel wait for takers. A tipped hand-painted sign, PAY INSIDE! CASH ONLY! points toward a low flat-roofed cinder block building where a lizard-skinned man in a baseball cap, sleeveless undershirt and cutoffs and a tanned white-haired woman in denim overalls and tie-dyed T-shirt pry sheets of plywood off the plate glass store windows. Signs on the glass advertise groceries, fishing gear, beer, bait, and sundries, an ATM, and a United States post office, Panzacola branch.

Behind the store and adjacent to the parking lot is the ranger station, a low stucco Bahama-style building with a covered porch on three sides and open floor-to-ceiling wood-latticed windows. There's a small office for the rangers in back and in the front an information center with a pamphlet stand and public restrooms, a beverage-dispensing machine and not much else. There are no visitors to the park this morning. Only the Professor, the Kid, Annie on a rope leash, and Einstein in his cage.

A heavyset red-faced ranger in his late thirties with a pale blond buzz cut and rumpled uniform, his short-sleeved shirt already wet with sweat, sits at his desk in the office and talks into the radio to fellow rangers located deep in the swamp checking on storm damage to the lookout towers and catwalks. The ranger glances up and notices the Professor and the Kid. *Park's closed today, folks. On account of the hurricane. No visitors. Not till tomorrow at least.*

I was gonna rent a houseboat.

The ranger says he'll need a permit. He speaks in short crisp sentences. No permits issued till tomorrow. Still have to clear some trails out there.

Without meaning to the Kid imitates the ranger's way of speaking. He says he's ex-military. Back from Afghanistan. Needs to clear his head.

The ranger crinkles his brow and thinks a minute. Ex-military, eh? He asks the Kid if he knows how to handle a canoe.

The Kid lies and says sure. He's never been in a canoe in his life but figures it can't be all that hard to stick a paddle in the water and push. Or maybe you pull.

The ranger says that the guy who runs the rentals is short of workers today. All he's got is a small crew from the county jail that the guard won't let him send into the swamp. *Willing to work a few hours for no pay?*

Maybe. Why?

Go talk to Cat Turnbull. Guy who runs the store. Help him get his houseboats in from the swamp this morning, maybe he'll rent you one today. If he does, I'll give you a permit to go into the park. In spite of its being officially closed till tomorrow. Seeing as how you already came all the way out here. You both going in? He tosses a skeptical glance at the Professor as if trying and failing to imagine the man paddling a canoe. Hard to imagine him even sitting in one.

No. Just me.

How long you want it for?

Not sure yet. Have to see how it goes. A few days anyhow. Maybe more.

Okay. Costs fifty-something bucks a day. Plus tax. Cat'll want a deposit. You got a credit card?

No. I got cash though.

The Professor grunts.

Okay, go see Cat. Tell him what I said about volunteering. Take it from there.

The Kid snaps him a military salute, turns on his heels and marches out to the parking lot. The Professor, leading Annie and holding Einstein's cage, trails along behind.

At the store, where Cat Turnbull and his wife are still removing plywood sheets from the windows, the Kid makes his deal for the houseboat. The leather-skinned old man is surprised and pleased to hear the Kid's offer to help bring the boats in from the swamp where they rode out the storm. And he's very glad to have what looks like a cash-paying rental in hand, especially at this time of year, four months before the start of tourist season. From March to December the only business that comes through the door of his store is brought by fishermen from Calusa who drive in with their own fishing gear and boats with the gas tanks already topped off and park in the lot and launch their boats straight into the Bay; and bird-watchers who want only to walk the marshes on the footpaths and catwalks and bring their own binoculars and sandwiches, cold drinks, and coolers with them. From June to early October, hurricane season which is where we are now, even the local fishermen and bird-watchers stay away. This kid is the first cash customer he's seen in nearly two weeks. And now he's offering to paddle into the swamp where they parked the houseboats and bring them in. Good deal.

How long you gonna need the houseboat for?

Not sure. I'm thinking maybe five days, maybe more. I'm sort of recovering from the war. Afghanistan. I'm just out of the military. Need to get my head together. Post trauma whatever.

Semper fi, sonny. Retired Marine. What branch?

Army. First Mountain Division out of Fort Drum, New York.

Well, damn! Welcome back, soldier. America thanks you for all your sacrifices. And we're real glad you're back home alive in one piece. The old Panzacola's a good place for a man to get his head together. Especially after what you been through. Nothing out there but gators and slithery snakes and pretty birds. And they won't bother you none. You can do a little fishing. Catch your own supper. No fucking rag-heads blowing themselves up and cutting off people's heads on TV. It's real peaceful.

That's good.

I'll give you a military discount. You gonna need supplies? Food, water, gas, and so on?

Yeah. Five days' worth anyhow. And some dog food and birdseed if you got it.

We'll fix you up good, son. He tells the Kid to leave his bags and animals here at the store and take one of the canoes that the colored guys are bringing out. *There's three houseboats tied to the mangroves about a hundred yards upriver. You won't get lost. The river's blazed. You'll have to make three trips. Just tie the canoe to the boat when you bring it in and paddle it back for the next one. Shouldn't take you more'n an hour a trip. You know how to drive a houseboat, sonny?*

Sure.

There ain't much to it anyhow. Pontoon boats, little pissy twenty-five-horse outboards, no wheel or tiller to worry about. They only draw about ten inches. Moron could drive it. Lots of 'em have. Water's pretty deep out there now on account of the storm and you might run into some drowned trees coming in, so don't try no water-skiing, sonny. Heh-heh.

Cat's wife has been looking the Kid up and down in a kindly, warm open-faced way as if she recognizes the young man from someplace pleasant and can't remember where it was. The Kid catches her gaze and feels the warmth of it and grows uncomfortable. It's a familiar enough gaze to him, one that he usually gets from women. Especially older women. They seem automatically to trust him. He doesn't trigger their usual alarms against strange young males nor does he in any way invite their erotic attention or desire, subliminal or otherwise. He doesn't even make them feel maternal. It's as if he's outside all sexual potential, is without an erotic marker of any kind, has no sexual past or future. Somehow in his presence middle-aged and older women seem released from all their usual forms of sexual anxiety and feel instead a physical warmth toward him, unrestrained and unedited. It's almost as if he's a very old woman himself.

But whenever the Kid perceives this warmth flowing in his direction—which due to his deflective nature isn't all that often—he grows itchy and uncomfortable. A little fearful. It makes his stomach churn, and his breathing speeds up and goes shallow. He's afraid that if he doesn't turn away from that onrush of female warmth he might literally start to cry.

So he ignores Cat's wife, refuses even to look at her. Instead he walks a few yards away from the couple and turns his attention to the Professor.

Well, Haystack, I guess this is good-bye.

Yes. I doubt we'll meet again. I'll leave your backpack and duffel up at the ranger station.

Okay. Thanks. Well, it's been . . . interesting knowing you. The Kid doesn't understand why he suddenly feels so sorry and sad for the Professor. He can't remember when he last felt both sorry and sad for someone—even the Rabbit whom he felt sorry for when the cops busted his leg and sad about when he drowned but never both at the same time. Most people seem to him not quite real, as if they're on a reality TV show and are only pretending to be themselves like the guy who's supposed to be the park ranger and the old guy who calls himself Cat Turnbull and his wife who the Kid doesn't want to look at. It's like they're on a reality show called *Swamp People*. They're not actors like you see in soaps and movies or even porn because they're playing themselves instead of people invented by a writer to say words written in a script and do what a director tells them to do, smiling or crying or taking off their clothes and screwing each other or just talking to each other on their cell phones. The ranger and the old guy named Cat and his wife and pretty much everyone else the Kid meets aren't actors, he knows that—they're just not real in the same way that he himself is.

But the Professor is different. He's starting to feel real to the Kid the same way the Kid feels to himself and he's puzzled by the feeling. He's never much liked the Professor or enjoyed his company the way he enjoyed Rabbit's for instance or even Paco's because of his goofy concentration on something as useless as pumping iron that turned him into a cartoon character. On the other hand he didn't particularly dislike the Professor either, not the way he disliked the Shyster and certain other deviants under the Causeway or O. J. Simpson for instance whom he never actually knew personally but definitely did not want to know personally anyhow, not just because he was a stone-cold wife killer but because he was an arrogant asshole. On the likability scale until this moment the Professor has fallen somewhere between the Rabbit and O. J. Simpson. Which for the Kid is about where most people fall. Even his mother. That's how he prefers it. It's how he's always preferred it.

You know all that shit you told me in the interview? About how you're gonna get whacked and everything from becoming "expendable and therefore dangerous"? Only it's supposed to look like it's a suicide?

Yes.

That's not true, is it? You just made it up so your wife will feel better if you kill yourself.

Kid, it's all true. You don't believe me?

Why do you want to kill yourself, Professor? If your wife and kids come back, except for being so fat you got a lot to live for. Even if they don't come back and she wants a divorce, you still got a lot to live for. Nice house, big prestigious job at a college, all those books and pictures and nice stuff you live with. You can travel wherever you want, live wherever you want, get credit cards and bank loans, take friends out to fancy restaurants for dinners. If you lost some of that weight you could even probably get a fairly good-looking girlfriend if you wanted one. Christ, look at me, I'm the one who should be talking about suicide, not you. I can't even vote in this state. Why do you want to kill yourself?

I don't. And I won't. Someone else will do the job. Only he'll be masquerading as me. As it were.

That means he won't really be you? People will just think he's you?

Correct. Except for you and Gloria.

It doesn't add up, Professor. You must be really bored with life. Like you're too frigging smart for reality and other people so you make up this complicated spy story about how you're not really gonna kill yourself, some secret government agent's gonna do it, and then you go and kill yourself anyhow but you get to feel superior about it. 'Course, that doesn't make much sense either. Once you're dead you don't get to feel superior to anybody. You don't feel anything. Unless you're a Christian who believes in God and heaven and all. But you're a professor, so you don't believe in any of that, do you?

No.

Me neither. Maybe you're too tricky for your own good, Professor. You ever think of that?

I'm touched by your concern, Kid. Seriously.

Yeah, well, I guess the truth is I'm gonna miss talking with you. I kind of wish what's gonna happen wouldn't . . . you know, happen. Maybe it won't. I actually hope it doesn't. No shit. But if it doesn't, do I get to keep the money anyhow? You know, in case you don't end up dead. Otherwise I'll be back to squatting under the old Causeway with the rats again.

The Professor smiles and says, *The money's yours, Kid. No matter what happens.* He extends his hand and the Kid shakes it firmly. *Listen to the news on that radio I gave you, Kid. And check the newspapers whenever you can.*

The Kid nods, and the Professor hands him Annie's leash. He turns away and the Kid watches him waddle slowly up the long slope toward the parking lot and his van. He watches him the whole way. That's the last time the Kid will see the man: a huge hairy figure sweating inside the ten yards of brown cloth it takes to cover him with a suit, a man submerged in a body as large as a manatee's, graceless, slow moving, arms and thighs rubbing themselves raw, spine and knee and ankle joints stressed nearly to the breaking point by the weight they must support, enlarged heart thumping rapidly from the effort of shoving blood and oxygen through all that flesh, overheated lungs gasping from the work of getting that enormous bulk up the incline to the parking lot, liver, kidneys, glands, digestive tract, all his organs overworked for half a century to the point of exhaustion and collapse—a man with two bodies, one dancing inside his brain, a hologram made of electrons and neurons going off like a field of fireflies on a midsummer night, the other a moist quarter-ton packet of solid flesh wrapped in pale human skin.

CHAPTER NINE

I F   Y O U ' V E   N E V E R   P A D D L E D   A   C A N O E   B E F O R E
it can at first be surprisingly difficult—you have constantly to
correct the tendency of the bow of the canoe to swing in the
direction opposite your paddle. At first you may try correcting the
tendency by alternately dipping your paddle into the water on one
side of the canoe, then switching to the other, but all this does is
drive the bow from right to left and back again, and you waste a
great deal of energy and time making corrections instead of moving
straight ahead on your desired course. Eventually to keep the canoe
from wagging its bow from side to side you learn to lean forward
from your seat in the stern, dip, pull, and curl the paddle away from
the canoe in what's called the J-stroke. A beginning canoeist who is
physically intuitive can figure all this out on his own fairly quickly,
and if there is no strong current to fight or the water is still, in a
matter of minutes he will be on course, slipping smoothly upriver
through overhanging foliage, past mangroves and dense palmettos,
the only sound the soft plash of each stroke of the paddle as it breaks
the surface of the dark water. Overhead, bands of sunlight streak the
bright greenery of swamp willows, gumbo-limbo trees, and strangler
figs, drift downward past epiphytes and flowering red mangroves and
end up lying across the water in flattened stripes.

The canoe rounds a long slow S-bend in the narrow stream startling a snowy egret into awkward flight. A pair of small chartreuse parrots stares down at the slender craft from high in the branches of a cottonwood tree. As the canoe comes out of the S-bend the streambed straightens for twenty or thirty yards and the canoeist sees the first houseboat tied to the trunks of three stout cypress trees. The houseboat is nearly as wide as the stream, a raftlike platform carried on tubular aluminum pontoons with a small box of a cabin set in the center, a short deck aft and another at the squared bow. As he approaches the houseboat he makes out two more beyond it, also tied to cypress trees. He brings the canoe alongside the first, steps aboard, and ties the canoe to the stern. Five minutes later he has the outboard motor started and has untied the moorings and is ready to bring the houseboat back downstream to the settlement at the estuary, where he will by then be feeling utterly competent at this, and with a certain pride he will bring the rectangular boat out to the end of the pier and pull it into a slip, shut down the motor, and tie the boat to a pair of stanchions there.

He will do this twice again—paddle his canoe upstream to the houseboat, bring the houseboat down to the dock and tie it there. The convicts cleaning up the campground and the area surrounding the store will stop in their work and watch him come and go, and on his final trip downstream to the settlement as he passes the convicts he will impulsively smile and wave to them. Look at me, guys! They will look at him, but with expressions approaching disgust and irritation, and the guard will toss him a hard angry look and with a push of the flat of his hand will tell him to keep moving, unless you want to end up alongside these poor souls yourself.

THE THINGS HE CARRIES FROM TURNBULL'S Store and stashes aboard the houseboat named *Dolores Driscoll*:

waterproof charts of the channels, sloughs, and streams of the Great Panzacola Swamp

topographical map of the Great Panzacola National Park
compass
fishing license
filet knife
fishing rod and reel with hooks and lures
plastic container of earthworms
mosquito netting
mosquito repellent
water purification tablets
5 one-gallon jugs of drinking water
first aid kit
sunscreen
10 cans Alpo dog food
2 pounds mixed nuts
1 pound sunflower seeds
rice
3 loaves Sunbeam bread
peanut butter
Rice Krispies
powdered milk
instant coffee
sugar
tub of coleslaw
3 large bags Cheez-Its
Tang
6 cans Dinty Moore beef stew
1 dozen eggs
1 dozen oranges
1 case Budweiser Light
6 flashlight batteries
6 candles
20 pounds of ice
10-gallon plastic cooler

white gas for Coleman lantern
1 rented one-man dome tent
1 carton Newport 100 mentholated cigarettes

When he's paid Cat Turnbull for everything on his list he asks the old man if he can charge his cell phone battery from a wall plug he noticed when he used the restroom at the rear of the store, and Cat says yes indeed, adding that it's probably a good idea to have a cell phone out there in case he needs to be rescued by the rangers. *People wake up lost in the swamp all the time 'cause they forget how they got to where they anchored the night before. Some of 'em are just drunk, of course, or on drugs, but some of 'em are purely stupid. Good idea to mark on the topo each night exactly where you anchor. You ain't stupid, sonny, I can see that, but you might decide to drink that whole case of Budweiser the same night or smoke too much pot sitting out there all alone in the swamp listening to the tree frogs.*

I don't touch no drugs, the Kid says. *No, sir. And I never drink more'n three cans a day. I keep count of everything. Same as with cigarettes. I'm down to eleven a day, and next week it'll be ten. Ten weeks from now it'll be one. And then none. Quit.*

That's the military in you, sonny. Better than being a goddam Boy Scout Christian. Can't trust those types. It's always the damned Boy Scout Christians who get drunk or stoned 'cause they think they're on vacation from the wife and nobody's watching so they can do whatever the hell they can't or won't do the rest of the year, and either they get lost or they fuck up the boat somehow and don't want to pay for it afterward.

I ain't no Boy Scout Christian. Though I've known a few, the Kid says, remembering the Shyster and his Bible in particular.

He heads for the back of the store and locks himself into the restroom with a copy of the *Calusa Times-Union* and plugs the charge-cord for his anklet into the wall socket. He sits down next to it on the closed toilet seat with his ankle extended and reads the newspaper for a half hour until the battery is topped off with enough juice to report his whereabouts for the next seventy-two hours. He switches over to his cell phone charger's cord, sets the phone on the back of the toilet and returns to the store and commences loading his large pile of purchases, his duffel and backpack, Annie and Einstein onto the *Dolores Driscoll*.

The boat is the first that he brought in from the swamp. A floating house trailer, it has an eight-by-ten-foot cabin minimally furnished with a fold-down table and two stools, a pair of collapsible cots, a propane-powered stove and refrigerator and a row of low cabinets with cookware, plastic dishes, and eating utensils stored inside. He has his radio and flashlight, his own sleeping bag, the Shyster's Bible and packet of purloined papers for reading material, clothes, the telescope given him by the Professor in case he wants to look at distant birds or stars at night, and the rented tent in case he decides to spend a night camping at one of the island campsites over near the Gulf.

The *Dolores Driscoll* is named after Cat's girlfriend and business partner, the same white-haired lady the Kid caught looking at him with such affectionate regard a while earlier. She watches him now from behind the deli counter as he comes and goes between the store and the boat. Then he disappears from her sightline for a while, gone to the ranger station for a park permit, she figures. She'd like to talk with him, find out where he's from, who his people are, how old he is and so on, but instead when he returns to the store to pay Cat she hangs back in silence. She can see that he's extremely shy and averts his eyes from her, and though he speaks forthrightly if a little stiff in an odd loud way when he's talking with Cat, whenever he appears to know she's in earshot he mumbles and looks down at the floor. He's a strange boy with his derelict yellow dog and caged parrot and what looks like all his worldly effects paying for the boat and supplies with hundred-dollar bills like a sudden millionaire. He doesn't ever smile, even with Cat who has a humorous way of putting things and is the friendliest man she's ever known.

Cat told her that the kid's just back from Afghanistan, which explains a lot about his manner and affect and probably all the cash, but it doesn't explain the dog and the parrot or the fact that he seems so alone in the world now that his fat bearded friend has driven off. They were a mismatched couple, the short skinny young man with the buzz-cut hair in T-shirt and worn jeans and sneakers who looks barely old enough to shave and the enormous hairy middle-aged man wearing a dark three-piece suit like a TV professor or that fat TV detective, Whatzizname, Nero Wolfe. The two seemed intimately connected but formal; attached to one another but determinedly independent: they acted like a father and son who love one another, who are stuck with one another for life, but have no idea of who the other is.

The young man reminds her some of the little schoolboys she knew back when she was driving a country school bus up by the Canadian border years ago, before her invalid husband died and she moved as far south as she could go and still be in America to get away from the memories of all that and try to start her life over in her late fifties, which, thanks to finding Cat Turnbull, she has pretty much succeeded at. She remembers how every year or two a scrawny pale boy several years short for his age and looking almost malnourished would show up on the first day of school at the school bus stop outside a falling-down shingled wreck of a house or one of the rented dented double-wide house trailers on the outskirts of town, a new boy in town who couldn't make eye contact with anyone, not even with the other children. They were born to lose, those little boys, no other words for it, and the other children recognized it instantly and turned on them the way a flock of hens will single out the weakest member of the flock and start pecking at its head and eyes until it bleeds and tear out its feathers one by one until they've made it so ugly and deformed that lying panting on its side in the dust it looks more like a grotesque version of a newborn chick than an adult hen. You couldn't protect those persecuted boys from the other children, any more than you could protect the poor pecked-to-death hen from its flock, because those boys mistrusted adults, no doubt with good reason, even more than they mistrusted other children, as if the protective adult were merely a larger stronger version of the worst of the other children. If you tried to help them they turned surly and pulled away in sullenness from your extended hand and stumbled back into the eagerly waiting flock.

From her post behind the deli counter she looks out the screened door and along the dock to the slip where the young man is untying the houseboat that Cat so sweetly named after her when she first moved into the trailer with him. Cat stands off a ways watching him with more than usual interest though it's probably mostly because like Cat he's ex-military and Cat never got over his time as a Marine in Vietnam and to him anyone who once wore a uniform is a brother or nowadays a sister. The way he does for everyone who sets off in a rental Cat salutes the young man who from the afterdeck of the boat salutes him back. He squats down and starts the motor and slowly steers the craft away from the dock out into the open water of the estuary. He brings it back around and heads it into the quickly narrowing Appalachee River. Seconds later the *Dolores Driscoll* has disappeared up the river and into the jungle.

Cat walks into the store with a worried frown on his face. *I prob'ly shouldn'a done that.*

Done what?

Rented him a boat. Took his money.

For God's sake, why not? A cash customer at this time of year? Five days' rental. All those supplies.

He ain't straight, that kid. Paying with cash, all hundreds, even for the deposit. And using a state-issue ID instead of a military one. Not even a driver's license. You see what he was wearing on his ankle?

On his ankle?

Noticed it when he sat down and started the motor. His pants leg come up a ways and he had one of them electronic whatchamacallits on, like they make people wear who're under house arrest.

You think he's some kind of criminal? He did seem a little odd to me. Actually just unusual, not odd. Kind of sweet, I thought. And shy and sad, like he's trying to get over a busted romance or something. The one I didn't trust is that big fat guy who brought him in. Maybe that thing on his ankle is just a kid thing. You know, some new kind of cell phone or electronic game machine or one of those gizmos they use for playing their music like the joggers wear on their arms.

Maybe. Still, I think I oughta look him up on the computer. The Internet. Assuming his ID ain't a fake. See if the cops're looking for him or something.

Cat, my dear, underneath that good nature of yours lies a suspicious nature. He's just one of those born-to-lose kids who probably lives most of the time in his head because he hasn't got any friends, except that big fat guy.

You could use a little more suspiciousness yourself.

As my dear departed late husband Abbott used to say, I have a sanguine personality.

Cat grins and pats Dolores on her rump and nuzzles her with his leathery face. *Yeah, yeah, yeah, that dear departed late husband of yours. Him and his unforgettable words of wisdom. "Short-term profits make long-term losses." "The biggest difference between people is their quality of attention." "Everyone must sometimes serve."*

She nuzzles him back. *Sweet of you to remember.*

You never let me forget. Still, despite your sanguine nature, whatever the hell that is, I'm gonna go over to the trailer and crank up the computer and see what I can find out about the kid.

You think the computer's going to tell you about a total stranger?

'Course! Everybody's on the Internet now. Even you, sweetheart.

CHAPTER TEN

THE KID IS IN AS BLISSFUL A STATE AS HE
has ever experienced and he knows it and truly appreciates
it. He's not thinking about his past for once and he's not
thinking about his future either. It's late afternoon and he's miles
upriver not far from where the Appalachee flows out of Turner
Slough on its winding way to Calusa Bay. From the map the slough
appears to be a quarter-mile wide and two miles long, a narrow shallow collecting basin for a veiny network of streams draining the farther reaches of the swamp and the watery saw grass prairies beyond.
The slough is where he intends to anchor and spend the night.

Annie lies half asleep on the foredeck in shifting splotches of
afternoon sunlight falling through the breaks in the overhanging
foliage and Einstein released from his cage has taken a watchful position on the flat roof of the cabin. It's the first time the Kid has let
Einstein out of his cage—a true experiment because he conducted
it without preferring one result over another: all he wanted was
knowledge of whether the parrot despite his broken wings could fly
up into the cypress trees and into the jungle where he could join a
flock of other parrots most of whom are descended from escapees
from urban and suburban cages themselves and live a normal free
life up there among his own kind which would have seemed natural
to the Kid. Or would he hang around the boat with him and Annie

like a regular member of the crew where he didn't have to hunt for food in a strange land or need protection from predators? Which also would have seemed natural to the Kid. But when the parrot stepped from his cage and did a little dance on the deck and showed no inclination to fly any farther than up onto the roof of the cabin the Kid was relieved and smiled and said, *Looks like you got first watch, man.* He decides it's time to teach Einstein some new words and expressions. Like *Land ho!* and *Fifteen men on a dead man's chest* and *Yo-ho-ho and a bottle of rum.* Time to teach the parrot how to be a proper shipmate. Annie, the Kid figures, due to her age and condition, is more of a ship's mascot. Retired.

So far on his trip upriver he's seen dozens of wading birds—egrets and ibises, great and blue herons, anhingas and even a huge brown stork, although he doesn't know what they're called, they're just beautiful strange birds to him that stand or walk slowly in the water looking to snag a fish or a frog near the banks and in among the mangrove tunnels that branch off the Appalachee. When the houseboat approaches they flutter clumsily to the upper branches of nearby cypress trees or take a position among the clusters of bright green fan blades that top off the tall Panzacola palms where they stare down at the Kid and his crew with what looks like irritation and when the boat has passed return to the water to resume their interrupted hunt for food. He's seen dark brown mahogany trees hugged almost to death by strangler figs and peeling red gumbo-limbo trees looking like sunburnt tourists. He's seen six-foot-long alligators and their babies that look like mechanical toy alligators and striped mud turtles the size of bicycle helmets all snoozing together side by side in the muck. He watched a water moccasin as thick and long as his arm slip from a boney black mangrove root into the water and swim slowly alongside the boat for a few moments as if hoping for a handout before veering back toward shore and he decided right then that he'll be bathing aboard the boat with water taken from the slough with a bucket and not do any swimming which he almost never does anyhow because he doesn't know how to swim and for once is glad. He saw an otter dive off a log into the stream and at first thought it was a giant rat but quickly realized it was an animal that lives off the land and the slow-flowing waters of the Panzacola instead of eating human waste beneath the Causeway and took comfort in the thought and was once again very glad to be exactly where he was. He's seen soft white orchids dangling from the trees among long strands of Spanish moss and orchids with strings of blossoms like small yellow butterflies and three-foot air plants with blushing red blooms pushing through long green wraps and thickets of gigantic ferns some of them growing on dead logs, ferns so large and ancient-looking that as a private joke he keeps an eye out for dinosaurs. From time to time he's cut the speed of the boat almost back to zero and peered down into the water and spotted crayfish and whole schools of bluegills and sunfish and once saw what he thought was a largemouth bass and decided then and there that when he anchors at Turner Slough later he'll make like the egrets and herons he's been disturbing and for his first supper aboard the old *Dolores Driscoll* he'll serve fresh-caught fish.

At half past four in the afternoon the houseboat reaches the headwaters of the Appalachee and slips through the grassy marsh into the glistening still waters of the slough. There is no overhanging foliage here, no deep dark mangrove tunnels off the stream to peer into. The sky is enormous, the light bright enough to make him wish he'd bought a pair of sunglasses back at Cat Turnbull's store.

Now that he's had some time to reflect on it he's sorry that he lied to Cat about being just back from Afghanistan because he likes the man and respects him for having served in the Marine Corps in Vietnam. Whenever the Kid lies about himself or hides the facts that he's a convicted sex offender who got kicked out of the army before completing basic training for distributing porn he feels like even more of a creep than he actually is. As if he's something worse. A child molester like Shyster. And when he pretends that he served in Afghanistan like he did in person with Cat and online with brandi18 he feels as if he's worse than a Shyster or a chomo. He feels like he's a cold-blooded wife killer who got away with it, an O. J. Simpson. Secrets and lies, they eat your insides until all you have left is a hard thin skin that covers you like the shell of one of those eggs you poke a little hole in and draw out its eggy contents before you dye it for Easter.

He's glad that Cat's wife didn't try to talk to him and instead just hung back and watched him with her smiling eyes because it's harder to hide who you really are from a trusting woman like her than from a skeptical man like Cat Turnbull and he might have ended up telling her the truth about himself. Cat's the kind of man who like most men expects you to lie to him but she's the kind of woman who expects you to tell her the truth so before you know it you're telling it to her. When you lie to a woman like that you feel twice as bad as when you lie to a man who expects you to lie anyhow. Most men take it for granted that people have secrets and tell lies. Most women, especially older ones, don't. The Kid figures that's because men have lots of secrets and tell lies on a regular basis like the Professor for instance and just about every other man the Kid has ever known. It's just something in their masculine nature. Whereas most older women are pretty much who they seem to be and usually tell the truth at least when they're not trying to get laid. Even the Kid's own mother. With her what you see is what you get for better or worse. She's 100 percent truth in advertising. Although maybe it would have been better for him growing up if she had kept a few things from him and had lied now and then about herself and about what she did in her spare time and after work in the bars of Calusa and later or when she went off with her girlfriends on cruises. Too much information, he thinks. TMI. He knows all that wasn't his mother's fault and he doesn't blame her for the way his life ended up but knowing your mother's secrets and always being told the truth by her can hurt you. Especially when you're a child.

But these are thoughts he doesn't want or need right now. It's peaceful here. He's anchored the houseboat about twenty feet off the eastern shore of the slough and he wants to concentrate on catching his supper which he just saw break the water in the weedy shadows cast by a stand of slash pines at the edge of the slough: a silvery swirl and slosh and then expanding rings of concentric ripples. It's within easy casting distance from the boat even for the Kid who has never used a casting rod before. He's seen it done of course by Rabbit and other denizens under the Causeway fishing in the Bay and can imitate them: a little flick of the wrist, an overhand toss of a squirming worm impaled on the hook, follow-through with the arm extended and the worm and red-striped white plastic bobber plops into the water and you watch the bobber go still until it's suddenly pulled under and you jerk back on the rod and start reeling in what turns out to be a bluegill the shape and size of the Kid's open palm.

Excellent first catch! Life as it was meant to be lived in the Bible when God gave human beings the Garden of Eden and told them to be fruitful and multiply. He cuts the fish open and guts and beheads it and realizes that without its head and tail it'll barely provide two or at most three small bites so he's going to need to catch five or six more bluegills if he wants to feed himself and his crew properly tonight. Which does not displease him. He's happy to have to continue catching fish here in the Garden of Eden with Babylon completely out of sight and mind.

Except for the whir of the reel and the plop of the worm and bobber hitting the water at the end of his cast the only sounds are tree frogs creaking like rusty hinges and a chirping choir of crickets. The sun has slipped closer to the treetops on the western shore of the slough. Mosquitoes have begun to cloud around his face and arms but he has plenty of repellent which he spreads over his skin and he has a mosquito net to hang over his cot later. He catches two more bluegills in quick succession. Then two more. Almost enough. He cracks open a can of beer chilled in ice and takes a thrilling first gulp—the first swallow of a cold beer is always the best. It's what you remember when you want another swallow and another beer and though they're never as thrilling as the first the memory lingers on anyhow so you can't complain. Reeling in his sixth bluegill in twenty minutes the Kid can't complain about anything right now. If this isn't heaven, which he doesn't believe exists anyhow, it certainly is paradise.

PART V

CHAPTER ONE

I T'S A NEW WORLD THE KID IS LIVING IN. Literally as well as figuratively. In geological time the entire state, and especially its waterlogged southwestern corner, have only recently been delivered from the ocean. Toward the end of the Pleistocene period barely twenty thousand years ago the planet entered a last great ice age, and glaciers expanded south and north from the Poles. As the air cooled, evaporation of seawater into the atmosphere slowed, and for millennia sea levels dropped six and ten feet a century, until at last, in the shallow waters of the Caribbean off the blunt southern edge of North America, waves from the Gulf of Mexico and waves from the Atlantic begin to crash against one another and then to part and fall upon newly risen banks of coral and sand, and the long narrow subtropical peninsula gradually surfaces dripping and puddled from beneath the blue-green Caribbean.

Seeds from Cuba, Jamaica, Puerto Rico, and Santo Domingo float northward on the warm currents and winds and float south from the North American continent in the new streams and rivers and take root in the freshly emerged land, and soon there are grasses and tropical and subtropical trees and flowering shrubs and all manner of flora spreading over the land. And large schools of fish and mammals from the seas, porpoises, manatees, and seals, swim into the saline estuaries and up into the streams and marshes where they meet freshwater fish and mammals swimming down from the northern highlands into the rivers, lakes, marshes, and estuaries of the peninsula. Sun-blotting flocks of birds break their long winter migrations to the South American and Caribbean tropics and make landfall here and stay and build nests in the new trees and in among the mangroves and marshes and take up year-round residence and are fruitful and multiply. Solitary panthers and packs of red wolves in pursuit of smaller fangless prey, antelopes, squirrels, and rabbits, lope down from the wintry hills of the Alleghenies into the high-grass veldts expanding between islands of subtropical deciduous, pine, and palm trees and begin to thrive here. The large grass-eaters, bison, deer, and elk that have been roaming in hungry herds across the freezing upland plains, drift south, munching their way toward the abundant green year-round leaves and tall grasses. Behind them come lumbering onto the peninsula the very large animals slowest to roam, the megafauna—gigantic bears, mammoths, and mastodons, horse-size sloths and enormous land turtles. Until finally, following the megafauna, killing off the huge slow-footed animals with reckless abandon, come the humans—the spear-carrying, fire-making, highly intelligent and organized descendants of Asiatic hunters and gatherers migrating south and east onto the newly risen peninsula where there is a seemingly endless harvest available winter and summer from sea and land alike, where the temperature rarely drops below freezing or rises above what is pleasantly tolerable, a climate perfectly suited to their nearly naked, tattooed and painted, furless bodies.

The Kid knows nothing of this five-millennia-long sequence. He only knows what has happened to him in his personal twenty-two-year-long narrative. And of that he's aware of mostly unconnected bits and thus has no comprehensive sense of his lifetime's arc. But while he sleeps in paradise beneath the stars and the moon aboard his houseboat deep in the Great Panzacola Swamp with his old yellow dog sprawled on the deck beside him and his companion parrot in a cloth-covered cage next to the dog, he dreams the pictures and sounds of the slow making of his paradise.

A dream can compress eons into minutes, and that way the Kid lives through thousands of years of silence broken only by the sound of the waves lapping the shore and the clatter of palms in the warm winds off the sea, centuries of birdsong and the mating calls of frogs, the hoot of owls in the night, the splash of a gar snagging a mullet and an alligator's scrambling rush from shore into the water in pursuit of the gar, a sudden thrash in the saw grass as a panther brings down an unwary deer: everything heard and seen in his dream signifying merely the constant presence of the wind, the sea, and the slow-flowing waters over the land, the search by all the creatures living on the land and in the waters for mates for procreation and the necessary death of one creature strictly to feed another: the natural world in its evolutionary passage through time.

Centuries pass quickly into millennia, and while the Kid sleeps aboard his boat, continental and global weather patterns shift again. Rainfall, especially in summer and autumn in the north and central parts of the peninsula, is heavy now, creating large shallow inland lakes that seasonally flood and spill over their southern banks onto the drought-dried flatlands beyond, the floodwaters flowing slowly in sheets and wide meandering streams toward the Caribbean and the Gulf where gradually in the lower southwestern corner of the peninsula a vast wetland grows, the beginnings of the Great Panzacola Swamp. Old temperate flora and fauna from the late Pleistocene and the Ice Age get gradually displaced by tropical and subtropical wetland plants, insects, reptiles, birds, and mammals. Large stands of cypress trees appear along the coasts, and mangroves proliferate and spread from the estuaries into the inland waterways, clogging the streams and regularly rerouting them. Tidal ridges laid down at the birth of the peninsula by the action of ancient waves and midden heaps built by the first humans become low-lying tree islands and densely forested hammocks surrounded by sloughs and threaded by slow-flowing rivers and streams.

It's on these tree-covered ridges and hammocks and the wet grasslands beyond that the new natives, the domesticated descendants of those early hunters, settle. Calling themselves the Calusas and the Tequestas, they begin to fire and decorate clay pots and manufacture elaborately carved shell and bone ornaments; they develop societies divided into classes of ruling priests, administrators, and workers and build communal longhouses and places of worship with cypress, slash pine, and thatch.

This is the moment when the serpent enters Paradise. At least in the Kid's dream that's how it happens. From the underbrush near the mouth of the Appalachee a half-dozen Calusa men step forward to greet the bearded pale-faced strangers and admire up close their shiny helmets and breastplate armor, their brightly colored pantaloons and their, to the Indians, colossal triple-decker canoe. It should be a simple matter to exchange food and other locally processed and manufactured goods with these humans for some of their steel and woven possessions. For decades they have been hearing about white-skinned people from a faraway land, heard tales of their several gods and their marvelous inventions and weaponry from fellow tribesmen and -women who have traveled overland along the canals and rivers to the peninsula's eastern coast where the white people are rumored to have made a permanent settlement at the mouth of a river flowing to the sea from the mountains of the north. The Europeans who have settled over there are said to be for the most part peaceful and mainly interested in trade with the natives and fighting off other Europeans at sea.

It's hard for the six Calusa men to know which of the two types of Europeans has come ashore here—the traders or the slavers. These fellows seem friendly enough however and are not carrying manacles or chains. In fact they have rowed from their great canoe to the mouth of the river and have spread out on the grassy shore large bundles of beautiful cloth and steel axes and knives apparently for trade.

The six native men emerge from the palmetto bushes and holding their bows down and their arrows stashed walk gingerly but with a basic trust in their shared humanity toward the Europeans—who draw their steel weapons and quickly surround them and clamp manacles on their ankles and wrists and chain them together.

The Kid wakes from his dream that has turned into a nightmare. He is swiftly relieved for he realizes that all along he has been asleep and dreaming. Everything's going to be okay. But then, seconds later, years have passed. Centuries. The last of the twenty thousand Calusas and Tequestas, fewer than three hundred of them now, mostly children and old women and men who have not been enslaved or killed by the Europeans, in a final raid are rounded up by Spanish soldiers and shipped to Cuba.

There are now no human inhabitants of the swamp and the marshlands surrounding it, no one living on the tree islands and hammocks and in the saw grass plains north and east of the wetlands. From the thousand estuarine islands along the coast to the large central lakes inland the entire region has returned to its paradisal state. The mounds and midden heaps and the cultivated gardens and cornfields are covered over with trees and palmettos, and the longhouses and thatched huts of the villages have fallen to the ground and rotted and disappeared into the soil. The banks of the canals and irrigation ditches have been washed away by flood and hurricane and invaded by mangroves, coco plum, and strangler pine. The man-made grid of canals and ditches has been integrated into the swamp's vast constantly shifting natural system of waterways, marshes, and sloughs.

Once again the only sounds and sights in the Kid's dream are those of a semitropical world in which there are no humans. He believes that he is lying half-awake aboard his houseboat on a mattress beneath a cheesecloth mosquito net with his dog and parrot asleep beside him. He thinks he is awake. He is still trembling but is relieved to have escaped from the Spanish slave catchers and the British soldiers and now from agents sent down from Georgia and the Carolina plantations to sail along the coast hunting escaped African slaves.

For nearly a century the Kid is the only human being residing in the Great Panzacola Swamp—until he learns that there are many people besides him scattered throughout the wilderness. He's been joined by people driven south from their ancient Appalachian homeland by the American army, Creek and Miccosukee Indians. He smells the smoke from their fires, hears them chopping trees on the hammocks to build huts, sees them pass along the streams in their canoes, fishing in the sloughs, gathering oysters from the bays. They hunt with rifles and weave beautiful multicolored fabric for their clothing. They call themselves Seminoles and this entire corner of the peninsula has become their homeland, their Seminole nation.

Gradually in the last few moments the Kid has begun to realize once again that he has not wakened. He only thought he woke: he is still asleep and dreaming. He feels an unease, a serious discomfort with that information. He fears that if he cannot wake from his sleep and break off this dream, something really bad will happen to him. He is afraid that whatever will happen to the Seminoles at the hands of the white people in the century and a half yet to come will also happen to him. It's as if his personal history has been locked down in a cell alongside their tribal history, as if their fate and the fate of the Panzacola wilderness are now his as well.

He tries to concentrate and will himself awake. He grunts and groans, trying to make animal noises that he can hear in his sleep and that ought to wake him. But he stays asleep. He says to himself, *It's only a dream, a fucking dream. If I can wake up, everything will be okay, and I'll be in Paradise again. Really bad things won't happen to me. I won't be a loser with no place to live and no friends or family to turn to for comfort and help and company, I won't be a pathetic convicted sex offender on more or less permanent parole with a tracker clamped to my ankle, I won't be an ex-whackoff addict and an ex-porn freak kicked out of the army and without a job, paying my way with probably dirty money taken from a superfat weirdo professor of sex-offensiveness studies who for reasons unknown is paying me to help make people think he's on a secret spy agency's hit list. If I can just wake myself up, I won't be a total limp dick in every way possible. If I can only wake myself up and stop myself from dreaming, I won't be me anymore!*

CHAPTER TWO

LARMED BY THE KID'S GROANS IT'S
Annie's single frightened bark and a squawk from Einstein
that wake him from his multilayered dream. And while it
would be truly a paradise for the Kid if when he awoke he was not
himself anymore he is in fact still the same person he was yesterday
when he took his rented houseboat up the Appalachee and anchored
it at Turner Slough. The sole consequence of his dream is that he
knows today that he's not living in Paradise like he thought he was
last night but in a fallen world and if he had a computer he'd probably be watching porn and jacking off right now.

But he remembers that he has to feed his companion animals and
though his lascivious desires dwindle they don't quite go away. He
learned from the group therapist in prison that there's a difference
between a desire to get high and a craving for it and that the same is
true for any addiction, even for an addiction to porn and jacking off.
The main difference—according to the therapist who was explaining all this to the inmates in the group which except for the Kid
was made up of drug addicts and alcoholics—is that a desire doesn't
go away until it's satisfied but if you think about something else like
feeding your companion animal, a craving unlike a desire will disappear. She told them addicts have cravings, not desires. And although
the Kid mostly believed her at the time lately he's begun to wonder

why the cravings keep coming back if they're not desires. Maybe the psychologists distinguish between the two even though they know there's really no difference between them so you'll use a few mental tricks and be able to go for a long time without satisfying either and they figure you'll lose the desire eventually along with the craving and it won't matter that there's no difference between them.

Until today it was working pretty well for the Kid—since the night he got busted by Brandi and her father he's had no desires to watch porn or whack off and no cravings either that he couldn't make dissipate by thinking deliberately of something else. But finding himself in the middle of the Panzacola wilderness alone on a houseboat with Annie and Einstein and feeling first like he was in Paradise and then having to fight his way out of a densely tangled dream of slaves and dead Indians and alligators and other wild animals and reptiles have left him feeling the old cravings for porn again and desire for what has passed for sex since he was ten or eleven years old.

Glumly he anchors away and steers the *Dolores Driscoll* out into the slough on a northwest heading in the direction of the Turner River which flows into the slough from what appears on the map to be a chain of small lakes linked by streams wide and deep enough to accommodate a houseboat. By noon he's already bored with this adventure. It sounded exciting back when he and the Rabbit were discussing it under the Causeway and when he told the Professor of his plan and later when he rented the boat and bought all his supplies from Cat Turnbull. But now it just feels weird and lonely to him in spite of having Annie and Einstein aboard. It's just water and mangroves and the occasional stand of trees and some jungle flowers and birds he doesn't know the names of. It's thickets of mosquitoes and heavy wet heat. Sometimes it's open water and sometimes it's dark tunnels winding under overhanging mangroves on streams that curl through the jungle to another stretch of open water. There are plenty of alligators to look at as he passes along the muddy shores of islands and now and then water moccasins and turtles and twice he sees a large silver long-nosed fish with a mouth full of saw-teeth that reminds him of his dream. But the landscape and waterways and the animals, birds, and reptiles and the abundance of tropical and semi-tropical vegetation and the blood-sucking mosquitoes don't distract him from his cravings or desires much because even though he's only been doing it for one night and two days, being on a houseboat in the Great Panzacola Swamp is basically boring to him.

Maybe what the psychologists and the shrink in prison were try-ing to get the addicts to overcome was boredom instead of desires and cravings and in reality the main cause for addiction is being bored and his desire for porn and his cravings for a good chub-a-dub are only ways to make his life seem interesting to himself.

By late afternoon he's made his way up the Turner River into the second of the chain of three Mullet Lakes, the one called Little Mullet. He decides to put in there for the night and instead of fish-ing for his supper he'll heat up a can of Dinty Moore beef stew. He's already sick of fish even though since he shipped out on the house-boat he's only eaten it once. Fishing in Little Mullet is boring. Eating fish caught in Little Mullet is boring. He's thinking that maybe after supper he'll flop a while in his cot and try running a porn flick in his head and go for a blanket bop and afterward smoke his ninth and tenth cigarettes of the day.

Then he remembers that he should give Annie a land-walk so she can do her daily business, an idea that partially distracts him for a while. He draws the boat up to an island campsite close enough to step ashore without getting his sneakers wet with the dog in his arms and Einstein perched on his shoulder like a pirate's parrot and stands at water's edge watching Annie circle the open sandy space where people who are obviously not scared of alligators or snakes pitch their tents and sniff at the blackened fire pit until she finally squats near a clump of palmettos and does her business. The Kid uses a stick and buries the turd in the sand.

When he gets back aboard the houseboat with Annie and Einstein he realizes that for about five minutes he didn't once think about watching porn or jerking off, confirming his theory about boredom being the main cause of addiction because during those five minutes he was wholly and solely interested in watching his dog take a shit and for part of it pretending he was a pirate with a parrot on his shoulder looking for a good place to bury his ill-gotten gains although all he had to bury was a fresh dog turd, and that was all he thought about until he got back to the boat.

While he cooks and then eats his supper of canned beef stew and drinks two warm beers he wonders what the Professor would think of his theory. One good thing about being with the Professor is that the Kid was never bored. He was sometimes pissed, once in a while suspicious, occasionally admiring, and most of the time confused. Which causes him to remember the crank-powered portable radio that the Professor gave him when he first visited him at Benbow's and he realizes that he can kick back and be distracted by listening to the radio as long as he's not too far from so-called civilization to get any reception and if he is then he can always wave off his cravings by doing a little reading in the Shyster's Bible instead or maybe he'll check out the Shyster's briefcase full of papers that's still in his duffel and which he only glanced at quickly the night the cops raided the Causeway and busted Rabbit's leg and killed Iggy.

Okay, so his situation isn't perfect here and he's spending a lot of time and energy just fighting off boredom and addiction and still going through porn and masturbation withdrawal but he's glad all that's behind him now—living under the Causeway and getting fired from his job at the hotel and camping at Benbow's and the deaths of Iggy and Rabbit bound together forever beneath the dark waters of Calusa Bay and the hurricane that wrecked the Professor's planned community for homeless sex offenders. Maybe he was never bored back then like he is now and therefore wasn't tempted by mental porn flicks and a real-life woodie waiting for his wet hand but he was definitely in a lot of continuous ever-complicating mental pain.

He digs through his duffel and comes up with the little red plastic radio with the crank. He turns the crank for five minutes or so until he's generated enough juice for the power indicator to register green. Switching the radio on he runs the dial up and down without locating a station anywhere except for one signal that's reasonably free of static and turns out to be the National Public Radio affiliate broadcasting from the town of Belvedere where there's an air force base and not much else about forty-five miles north of Little Mullet Lake. NPR—the Kid hates that network and all its affiliates that you can't get away from no matter where in America you go and has never been able to stand listening to it for more than twenty or thirty seconds before flipping the dial on to something else, anything else, even soft rock like James Taylor and Joni Mitchell or college baseball, anything other than National Public Radio with the puzzle-master Will Shortz setting little language-and-number mousetraps designed to make you feel stupid and that weird deep-throated guy who sings folk songs his grandparents liked and tells definitely not-funny stories about pie-eating Lutherans from Minnesota and some breathless woman interviewing writers and politicians you never heard of and of course constant news, national and local news and weather told by people trying to sound like they're English.

But it's the only signal he can get way out here in the Panzacola so he leans back on his cot with the one pillow propped behind his head and smokes his ninth cigarette and listens to news about the stock market and the Federal Reserve Board that makes no sense to him since he has no idea of what they sell at a stock market or what's reserved at a reserve board. As the newscasters drone on and on from national to regional to local news the Kid starts to nod and his eyes close. His cigarette drops from his hand onto his belly and burns through his T-shirt and abruptly wakes him. He slaps at the hole in his shirt and rubs the still-burning cigarette out in the empty Dinty Moore can and says aloud, *Dude, whoa! Fucking bad idea, smoking in bed!*

The Kid checks his belly and decides that he needn't break out the first aid kit. Besides the T-shirt with the burn hole looks cool to him, as if he took a bullet and somehow survived, when he realizes that the NPR local newscaster is talking about the mysterious disappearance of a well-known Calusa University professor of sociology once described as a genius and the smartest man in Calusa County.

CHAPTER THREE

THE KID WANTS TO WEIGH ANCHOR AND start back right now but it's already dark and he knows he'll get lost even with a nearly full moon and clear sky so he waits all night half awake—not dreaming this time, no way he's going back there—and restless until the sun finally comes up and he can see the markers and follow his map back through the swamp the way he came. It's downstream all the way and only takes him half the day to get from Little Mullet back to Turner's Slough and down the Appalachee to the Bay where as soon as he ties up the *Dolores Driscoll* he hurries down the pier, enters Cat Turnbull's store and without even a hello as if he's just stepped out for a minute instead of most of three days he asks Cat for a copy of today's *Calusa Times-Union*.

In a flat expressionless voice Cat says, *Over there on the rack by the door,* and turns his attention back to a man standing at the counter in front of him, a heavyset fellow in his mid- to late sixties. He has short white hair and a close-cropped white beard and sunburnt face. He wears a Boston Red Sox cap pulled low over aviator sunglasses, a white short-sleeved guayabera shirt, cargo shorts, and running shoes with no socks. Now that the Kid notices him he thinks the guy looks like the famous writer Ernest Hemingway whose books the Kid has never read of course but he's seen his picture in magazines and on TV even though he's pretty sure the writer's been dead for a long time. He must be really famous though if the Kid's heard of him.

The Kid quickly opens the newspaper and leafs through it, taking special care to scan the Metropolitan section carefully. Nothing. He refolds the paper and lays it down on the counter and says to Cat, *You hear anything about that professor who disappeared?*

Cat shakes his head no—he's been to the National Sex Offender Registry online and doesn't really want to talk to the Kid if he can avoid it—but the man who looks like the famous writer says, *I saw a bit about it on TV in my hotel over in Calusa last night. It was on the late-night local news.*

They show a picture of him or anything? The guy who disappeared?

Yeah. Big fat bearded guy. Sort of a mug shot, actually. I didn't catch his name though.

Dolores has come out of the back room and has been listening. Unlike Cat she's actually glad to see the Kid and relieved that he's apparently no worse for wear for having been in the swamp for most of three days and two nights. He's more resourceful than he seems. It's none of her business, but she does want to ask the Kid about his appearance on the sex offender registry and find out what he did to get himself on that list, because to her he doesn't seem in the least dangerous or creepy and not especially weird, either—at least not in the way she'd expect a sex offender to look and act. A little eccentric maybe, and there's a lot about him that's not easily explained without having a good long personal conversation with him, which is what she's interested in initiating somehow. She asks the Kid, *Do you think it might be your friend? The man who drove you out here?*

It's possible. I heard about it last night on the radio and didn't hear all of it. They might have said his name but I didn't listen to the whole story until it was almost over. And there wasn't anything about it when I checked this morning. I could only get NPR out there.

Dolores says, *We don't even get that here. No cable TV either. And all we've got for Internet is dial-up. Slow as molasses. Makes you not even want to use it. I keep telling Cat we need a satellite dish, but he isn't much interested in TV or the Internet. He likes things slow. Don't you, honey? Cat's a real nineteenth-century man. A swamp fox.*

Cat casts a hard look at the Kid. *I don't watch TV maybe, but I do use the Internet from time to time. To look stuff up. Research.* He turns to the other man and asks him if he ever uses the Internet for research in his line of work.

Dolores says to the Kid, *He's a travel writer. He's writing an article about the Panzacola for a big fancy magazine in New York. He promised we're gonna be in it.*

That explains the Hemingway look, the Kid thinks.

She asks the Writer to remind her what the magazine is called.

Outsider. It's not really that fancy. The Writer has a crooked smile and speaks partially from the left side of his mouth as if he may have suffered a minor stroke long ago and did not fully recover his speech. He turns to Cat and says that he does indeed use the Internet for research. It was how he learned about Cat and Dolores's store and their houseboat and canoe rental service.

Cat notes that you can also learn about individual people on the Internet. He tells the Writer, as if it were news to him, that if you know an individual's name all you have to do is type it in and everything about the individual that's posted on the Internet will pop up on the screen immediately.

Not immediately, honey. Not if you're stuck using dial-up. Now let's change the subject, shall we? Do you think we could learn from the Internet if the professor who disappeared is this young man's friend? I really hope not. I mean I hope we don't learn that it was his friend.

Cat ignores her. He says to the Writer, *Say I happened to know a young fellow's name because he rented a boat from me and showed an ID to do it. Paid cash in hundred-dollar bills. Claimed to be U.S. Army just back from Afghanistan. Said he was home on dwell-time. Say for the hell of it I typed his name into the computer. You know, just to check, since he's got my five-thousand-dollar houseboat out there in the swamp. You might do that yourself in your line of work, right?*

Let it go, Cat. He's worried about his friend who's disappeared, Dolores says.

The Writer shrugs and says yes, he might do that. To check a source's background.

What if your source turned out to be a convicted sex offender? Listed in the national registry of sex offenders? And he wasn't in Afghanistan with the U.S. Army like he said.

Could be meaningless. Or it could be a negative. Could even be a plus. Depends on what I'm using him as a source for.

Cat wonders what the Writer means, especially what he means by saying it could be a *plus*. How could secrets and lying be a plus?

Say I'm writing about the swamp, not sex offenders, and my source simply withholds the fact that he happens to be on the national registry. A meaningless omission, right? Or he mentions in passing that he saw combat in Afghanistan. A meaningless lie. No one has to tell you everything about himself, and no one has to tell you the truth about himself. But let's say I'm interviewing a guy here for a piece about sex offenders and he lies and says he's not a convicted sex offender. That would be a negative. Same thing if I'm writing about the war in Afghanistan and later it turns out my source lied about having served there. Definitely a negative.

Cat says, *Okay, but how's keeping secrets and lying a plus? A positive.*

Well, let's say I'm writing an article about sex offenders and for some reason neglect to ask the guy if he's one himself and he doesn't volunteer the information, and later it turns out he is one. That would be a plus. Because his secrecy would become part of the piece, maybe the key to it. Same thing with the war. Say I'm writing about why so many American men falsely claim to have seen combat, and I never bother to ask my military source if he's one of those liars himself, but then discover on the Internet that actually he never served in the military. That's a plus, too. He'd be my Exhibit A.

Dolores asks the Writer what he'd do then.

I'd go back and interview them both again. And one of my main ques-

tions would be to ask the first guy why he withheld the fact that he was a sex offender. I'd ask the second why he lied about having seen combat.

And what if it was the meaningless case? Dolores wants to know. She has caught the Writer's drift. *The case where you weren't writing about the subject in the first place. What would you do with the new information that you took off the Internet?*

Nothing, I guess. Like I said, no one has to tell you everything about himself. And no one's obliged to tell you the truth about himself either. We all have our little secrets, no? And we all tell little lies, sometimes for innocent reasons. To make friends, for instance, or to avoid embarrassment. Or just to keep things simple. Sometimes the truth is too complicated to pass along in a short conversation or interview. And sometimes it's just irrelevant.

Dolores says, *There you go, Cat. Irrelevant. Meaningless. Got that? You've kept a few secrets yourself, you know. We both have. And told a few lies over the years, even to each other. And I'm here to tell you that it's not always useful to know all of someone's secrets or every truth behind every lie. You know that as well as I do.*

The Writer agrees. *Couldn't have said it better myself.*

Cat feigns a large sigh of capitulation and smiles at his woman. She's a better person than he is, and he loves her for that. He believes that a person's weaknesses are also his strengths: Cat's weaknesses are skepticism and suspiciousness; Dolores's are trust and open-mindedness; and if her weaknesses are morally superior to his, and Cat believes they are, then so are her strengths. Ergo, she's a better person than he is. He's a lucky man and he knows it. And when he forgets it she's there to remind him. He says to Dolores, *You're right. Compared to you I'm a total pain-in-the-ass estupido.*

Throughout the conversation the Kid has remained silent. At first he was freshly ashamed for not having told the man that he was a convicted sex offender and felt once again like a chomo like the Shyster and then when he saw that Cat also knew that he had lied about having been in combat in Afghanistan he felt like he was O. J. Simpson again. But listening to Dolores and the Writer lay out what

kinds of secrets and lies were meaningful and what kinds were meaningless he began to feel a little better about himself and when even
Cat came around to essentially forgiving the Kid for his secrets and
lies he was able to see himself briefly through Cat's eyes—although
not through Dolores's which were a little too wet with sympathy for
him and not through the Writer's either who for all he knew might
now be thinking about writing an article for a fancy magazine about
sex offenders or about American males who lie about having fought
in a war instead of writing an article about the Great Panzacola
Swamp and will next be wanting to interview the Kid on one or
both of those subjects.

The Kid has been interviewed enough for a lifetime thanks to
the Professor and shrinks in prison and judges and public defender
lawyers and cops and parole officers going all the way back to Brandi's father and before that at his army discharge hearing. Except for
Iggy the best thing about his life before he joined the army is that
back then no one ever wanted to interview him which meant that
he never had to lie and didn't have to keep any secrets. He was no
more or less than what he seemed to be—a fatherless white kid who
graduated high school without ever passing a single test or turning
in a single paper, a kid who could barely read and write or do math
beyond the simplest level of arithmetic, who was hooked for years
and maybe still was hooked on porn and jacking off and never had a
girlfriend or a best friend and belonged to no one's posse—but that
was okay to the Kid back then. He might not be the kind of kid he
wanted to be but at least back then he didn't have anything to hide.

The Writer asks the Kid if the missing person, the fat bearded
professor, might really be a friend of his, and the Kid says, *Yeah. I'm
sure of it, in fact. He's not exactly a friend, though. More of an acquaintance.*

You got any idea of where he is?

Yeah. Sort of.

The Writer is intrigued. So are Dolores and Cat. All three turn
their full attention on the Kid and wait for him to say more. He stays

silent for a long minute until finally the Writer asks if the missing professor has been having marital problems. The Kid shrugs as if he doesn't really know. *Maybe,* he says. Although he knows of course that the Professor's wife Gloria has recently taken their two children and gone to live with her mother.

Financial problems?

The Kid shrugs again.

But you do have an idea of where he might be found. Correct?

It's only a guess. It's probably not him anyhow. I'd hafta see a picture. Most professors are fat and wear a beard anyway, aren't they?

Dolores suggests they go over to the trailer and check out today's *Calusa Times-Union* on the Internet. They print the paper a day early but the Internet's up to the minute. There'll likely be a photograph of the missing professor to accompany the article. *And if it is your friend, and you have an idea of where he might be, then naturally you'll want to help find him.*

The Writer thinks that's a great idea, and Cat says, *Yeah, sure, why not?* He's still a little embarrassed for having used the computer to check on the Kid. Maybe he'll feel better if he apologizes to the Kid. Which is a little tricky for Cat to pull off, since he'll be apologizing to someone who's a convicted sex offender and has committed a sin that's cardinal to a Marine vet by falsely claiming to have served his country in wartime. He tries anyhow, for Dolores's sake and says to the Kid, *No hard feelings, I hope. About me not believing you and all. And looking you up on the computer and such. I probably shouldn't have done that. I mean, it isn't like we was gonna hire you for a babysitter or something.*

My late husband Abbott, Dolores chimes in, *used to say that a person's private life ought to be kept private. That's why it's called private life. 'Course, that was before the Internet and all.*

Thank you, Dolores, for your late husband's words of wisdom. Anyhow, sonny, I guess I just got a suspicious nature. Must come from dealing with tourists all the time out here.

That's okay, man. I'm actually kinda relieved. When people know the truth about me there's not so much for me to keep track of.

Ha! You're starting to sound like Dolores's late husband.

The Writer is impatient to check out today's online edition of the Calusa newspaper. He says so, and Dolores leads the group from the store along the pier and up the grassy slope to the double-wide trailer where she and Cat make their home.

THAT'S HIM ALL RIGHT!

How come it's a whachacallit, a mug shot? Like he's been arrested for something. What's the article say? Is he a fugitive from justice?

Says he's a "person of interest" in an ongoing investigation but has not been arrested. Doesn't say what kind of investigation, though.

So how come they took his mug shot?

Maybe it's off his ID. Or from some previous arrest. Does it say anything about that?

No. Just says he was last seen leaving his home in his car Sunday morning in the company of an unidentified teenage boy and when he didn't show up for his Monday classes university officials called his home. His wife and two children were visiting her mother and have no idea of his whereabouts. I'm summarizing here.

So he hasn't been gone very long. Maybe he had a family emergency.

He has two children? And a wife? Wouldn't have figured that.

Why not?

Well, I guess on account of he's so fat.

Gimme a break, Cat. That's a prejudice. Plenty of fat people get married and have kids.

Mentions he's well known in the city for his civic work and in academic circles. A popular teacher. That sort of stuff.

Maybe he just wants to be alone. Or is on a bender. Is he a drinker?

The wife's gone ahead and filed a missing person report. She obviously doesn't think he just wants to be alone.

I don't think he's a drinker. But I don't really know him that way. Like for drinking.

What's with the teenage boy? Is that a reference to you, sonny?

Probably. Only I ain't teenage.

You look like it, sweetie. Especially to a stranger and from a distance.

So maybe you were the last person to see him alive.

Assuming he's no longer alive. He might be living it up in Rio, for all we know.

Actually, Cat and I were the last people to see him alive too.

Where was he headed, sonny? After he left you off here?

Didn't say.

But you think you know where he might be? Like you said earlier?

Yeah. Actually, no. I don't.

C'mon. We all heard you.

Okay, he maybe was doing some research. For his work as a professor. He's interested in those old Army Corps of Engineers canals back toward Calusa. He was telling me all about how they get used by criminals and such for hiding the evidence of their crimes.

Any particular canal?

Yeah.

You know how to find it?

Yeah.

Maybe we oughta take a ride over there for a look-see. What do you think? I'm driving back to Calusa later today. My work here's about done, only got to interview one of the rangers for my piece, and this disappeared-professor story is a lot more interesting.

I don't think he'd want you writing about it in some big New York magazine.

It's not that interesting. I'm just curious is all. I'll even bring you back here afterward if you want. I can interview a ranger later.

You should do it, hon. Go with him. Or at least tell the police about the canal. Especially since the last person he was seen with is you. Clear your name, so to speak. We'll watch your pets and your stuff.

Clear his fat friend's name is more like it.

There you go! Exactly, clear the professor's name. Who knows, out there in the sun investigating a canal, the guy might've had a heart attack or something. He looks like a heart attack waiting to happen anyhow. I'll drive you there and we'll check around for him. If we see his car, we call the police. If not, not. And since they're probably also looking for you, you being the last person seen with him, I'll do the calling. You can stay out of it completely if you want.

Dude, I'm not that hard to find. See? Check this out. Speaking of which, I got to charge this thing before I turn into a pumpkin. It's a good thing I came outa the swamp when I did. I didn't know there wasn't any electricity in the houseboat or at the so-called campsites.

Wow. I've never seen one of those before. They make you wear that?

Yeah.

For how long?

Like ten years.

You poor thing! That's horrible! Look, Cat, it's like he's a prisoner or a slave in shackles.

No comment, Dolores. No damned comment. He's paying his debt to society, that's all. Same as those guys the corrections department sends over. We don't know what he done. Frankly, I don't want to know. And I don't want to hear what your late husband Abbott would say.

He'd be horrified.

So what about it, friend? Shall we take a little ride in my rental? It's a Lincoln Town Car. Great air. How far is the canal? About an hour?

Hour and a half, maybe.

Is that a yes?

I dunno. I gotta charge my shackle.

I rented a GPS when I picked up the car. Maybe the outlet jack's the same size as your thingie there and you can charge it while we drive. Let me take a look. Yeah, it's the same. No problema.

Okay. But if we see his van, you be the one to call the cops. I don't want nothin' to do with finding his body.

How do you know he's dead?

I don't. It's just . . . like you said, he's a heart attack waiting to happen.

Well, if he is dead we can prove you had nothing to do with it. He was certainly alive when he left here, and we can testify that you've been in the Panzacola the whole time since.

You still have three days' rental on that houseboat, sonny. You gonna want a refund on that?

No. I'll be back. Maybe I'll just not take it into the swamp again. It's kinda primitive out there. Maybe I'll just keep it tied up here at the dock this time.

Suit yourself.

First I gotta get something from my backpack.

Terrific. Meet you at the parking lot up by the ranger station.

CHAPTER FOUR

C ANE FIELDS STRETCH FROM THE CANAL nearly to the horizon where a rough line of citrus trees divides the green earth from the cloudless blue sky. Half-a-dozen police cars—Calusa County Sheriff's Department, local police, state troopers—and a white Sheriff's Department tow truck and at least three vans from local TV stations are lined up on the shoulder between the two-lane road and the canal. Uniformed and plainclothes officers in twos and threes mill around the edge of the canal talking and smoking. Occasionally one of them breaks off and peers down into the dark still waters of the canal as if he dropped a coin in for luck. Wearing oxygen tanks and weight belts, a pair of divers in dripping black wet suits lean against a fire engine red EMT rescue truck.

Highway traffic is backed up for a quarter of a mile in both directions. Waving impatiently, a single state trooper tries to keep the rubbernecked drivers moving their vehicles in a single lane past the site, and as the Writer's Town Car approaches the trooper, the Kid slumps in his seat and turns away. The Writer does the opposite: he stops the car, lowers his window, and hands the trooper his business card. He says he's covering the story for his magazine and asks where the officer would like him to park.

The trooper glances at the card and shakes his head with irritation. *Boy, you guys're all over this one, aren't you? Park down there beyond the TV guys and stay the hell there till we get this done.*

You find the body yet?

It's still down there. We got to get his van out first. Get moving now. You're holding up traffic.

How'd you know to look here, officer?

Sir, I said to keep moving! There'll be a press briefing later. Save your questions for that.

The Writer takes back his card and salutes the trooper and drives on, parking the car a short ways past the TV vans and several non-descript civilian sedans on the shoulder of the highway. Reporters and cameramen and sound technicians drink coffee and smoke and wait. The Writer swings open his door and tells the Kid he's going to try to speak with one of the divers. *Always talk to the guys you won't see later at the press conference. You coming?* he asks the Kid.

No way, man.

Why not? You could identify the body for them. Assuming it's your friend they bring up.

They probably got his wife here for that. Besides, I barely knew the guy. Plus I'm a convicted felon, remember? They'll be all over me like white on rice. I don't need no added scrutiny. The Kid likes saying that, "white on rice." It's an expression the Rabbit used to slip his way now and then and for some reason for the last few moments the Rabbit has been flashing across the Kid's thoughts. He's been replaying the instant out there on the Causeway in the hurricane-force wind and rain when the Rabbit stopped trying to stand on crutches and just gave it all up, when he ceased to fight gravity and pain and let his tired broken old body tumble down the hill into the rising floodwaters. For the first time the Kid thinks he knows how the Rabbit must have felt in the last months of his life when his only counter to the loneliness and shame of banishment and harassment official and otherwise was his sometimes sly wit and his guarded friendship with the Kid. Then the city officials sent the cops to bust up the camp and scatter the residents like cockroaches and when that didn't work and they all sneaked back because they had no other place to live and under the guidance of the Professor rebuilt their camp, the hurricane came along and did what the cops couldn't. By then the Rabbit's life despite having almost no options had gotten too complicated to bear or even to understand. So he let gravity take over. Which is what the Kid feels like doing now.

Why? You don't have anything to hide, do you?

Dude, I got a lot to hide. Everyone does.

The Kid imagines being frisked by a cop and the cop coming up with the DVD of the Professor's final interview which will implicate him in the Professor's death even if after watching it they actually buy the super-spy story which is highly unlikely. Either way, to nail down the Kid's exact relation to the death of the famous college professor they'll go out to Turnbull's Store to check out his alibi with Cat and Dolores. They'll have a warrant to rummage through his duffel and backpack where they'll discover over nine thousand dollars in one-hundred-dollar bills which the Kid will have a very hard time explaining to anyone. It's money beyond money. It's like winning the lottery only not. He has a hard time explaining it even to himself. All it's done for him so far is complicate his life. He almost wishes he'd refused to let the Professor pay him for his services so he could simply drop the DVD into the canal and let the Professor's wife think whatever she wants.

The Writer has disappeared. All the reporters and cameramen have seen what the Kid sees now and have scrambled down the line of vehicles where they're bellying up to the yellow crime scene tape watching and already filming the tow truck that's been backed up to the edge of the canal. The operator locks the brake and steps down from the cab and walks toward the rear of the truck. He's a professional and moves slowly and methodically so everyone can know it. He takes his position at a panel fixed to the bed of the truck and checks the gauges and levers that control the tension of the steel towing cable.

Cautiously the Kid makes his way to the tape and stands among the reporters and TV cameramen. The police officers and EMT technicians crowd forward and peer into the canal. The black steel cable curls loosely over the concrete edge of the canal and drops into the water and disappears. The operator shifts his hands from one lever to another, the engine digs in and the winch at the rear of the flatbed truck slowly starts spooling the cable, gradually straightening and tightening it until it's taut as a steel bar that when reaching the turning drum seems magically to soften into coiled black rope. Then the dark waters of the canal rise into a green bubble that bursts apart, and the front bumper and chrome grill of the Professor's Chrysler van appear, dented and dangling, headlights smashed. The waters part and the vehicle keeps coming like a whale emerging from the depths of the ocean, until it's half in and half out of the water, held tight to the truck by the cable as if harpooned. The operator locks his levers and walks forward to the cab and climbs up into the driver's seat. Very carefully he puts the truck in gear and edges it ahead a few inches at a time, bringing the van slowly up and out of the canal onto the embankment where it ends shuddering on all four wheels, sheets of water slithering off its roof and sides and pouring out from under the doors and hood. A police officer steps to the rear of the van and swings open the wide door and a wave of water spills onto the ground. Another officer pulls on the driver's side door. It suddenly opens and another, smaller wave breaks onto the ground. Slumped forward in the driver's seat, his forehead resting on the steering wheel, as if he fell asleep while parked, there he is: the man known to the Kid as the Professor.

CHAPTER FIVE

ON THE DRIVE BACK TO APPALACHEE BOTH the Writer and the Kid for most of the first half hour are stuck deep in separate and distinct thoughts and stay silent until finally the Writer tells the Kid he doesn't get it. Why would the cops immediately say to the press that the Professor's death is an apparent suicide, no foul play, et cetera, when they don't even have a coroner's report yet and can't produce a suicide note?

The Kid shrugs and notes that they only called it an "apparent" suicide. And maybe there is a suicide note except it's at the Professor's house. Or he sent it to his wife in the mail. Or maybe the police know something about the Professor's past that could cause him to commit suicide but to protect other people's privacy they can't reveal it to the public. Also it is possible they're only saying it was a suicide just in case he actually was murdered and they want whoever did it to think he got away with it until they gather enough evidence to make an arrest. *Cops do that sometimes,* the Kid adds. *I've seen it on TV.*

Sounds like you buy the official version, though. But then you knew the guy personally.

Sort of.

The car has left the main road and turns onto the narrow lane leading into the Panzacola National Park. They pass clusters of green-uniformed work crews, chain gangs made up of young black convicts still clearing away debris and fallen trees, the aftermath of Hurricane George. The Writer glances over at the manacles and chains linking the men and asks the Kid about the fact that the Professor's hands were chained to the steering wheel and his foot to the gas pedal. *Before they could remove his body from the van they had to use bolt cutters to cut his hands free of the steering wheel and his foot from the accelerator, remember? That's a far-fetched and fanciful way for a hugely obese man to kill himself. Especially one who's supposed to be a genius. There have to be a hundred better ways for a man that smart and that fat to make his death look like a simple accident.*

The Kid says he must have wanted to make sure he couldn't change his mind at the last second. Besides, they weren't really chains, he points out. They were combination bicycle locks made from steel cables and the cops didn't know the combinations to unlock them. Which is why they used the bolt cutters. It's the same type of eight-millimeter cable the Kid used for locking his own bike back when he had one and is probably where the Professor got the idea. That could be why he opened the driver's side window too—so the van would fill with water immediately and he wouldn't have enough air inside to give him time to escape. *It must be wicked hard to kill yourself while you still have time to change your mind,* the Kid says.

The Writer agrees. But something about the way the man did the deed suggests that it wasn't a garden-variety suicide. If he wanted to make some kind of point or issue a statement to the survivors or to the general public—a not uncommon desire among people who kill themselves—there are ways to do it without making it so strange and ugly.

Unless that was the point. Unless that was the statement. The Writer reminds the Kid of the damage done to the Professor's face by the crabs and who knows what other underwater creatures that got into the van through the open driver's side window and ate at his eyes and ears. There are eels in those canals, and alligators.

True, it was very ugly. And strange. The Kid doesn't want to remember how the Professor looked when the EMT guys finally succeeded in getting him out of the van.

Hemingway blowing off his head with a shotgun in the kitchen while his wife is asleep upstairs. There's a statement for you.

Yeah? What was he stating?

He spent his life killing animals with guns. Big dangerous animals like lions and water buffalo and rhinos. He wasn't about to kill himself in bed with a bottle of vodka and a jar of sleeping pills or by taking a flying leap off the Golden Gate. Not a big dangerous animal like Ernest Hemingway.

Who was he stating it to? That he was a big dangerous animal.

History, naturally. Literary history.

That seems dumb to the Kid but he doesn't say it. He can't imagine wanting to make a statement about who you really are to history. Especially "literary history"—whatever that is. Unless you're a Hitler or a George W. Bush talking to history is a waste of time. You'd have to believe that people hundreds of years from now would give a shit about knowing who you really were. Still, the Writer is showing him something he never thought of before: that when you decide to kill yourself you also get to choose the method and therefore how you kill yourself in a sense can reveal who you really are. You don't get to find that out for yourself of course because you're dead by then but it is like a form of self-expression, your true last words after you've already said what were supposedly your last words. For the Kid this casts a slightly different light on many things: the Professor's telling his super-spy assassination story and recording it onto a DVD; making the Kid agree to be the story's delivery boy; then there's the one hundred Benjamins nicely wrapped and waiting in the safe, the van in the canal, the bicycle locks—all the details that lead up to the Professor's death and come shortly after it. With only one carefully planned detail yet to play out: the Kid's actual delivery of the video-taped interview with the Professor to the Professor's widow.

But what kind of man would think up and then arrange all that? If he did kill himself—and the Kid is now pretty sure that he did—

then what does the way he went about it say to those who are still alive, to his wife and children, to the Kid himself, to the Professor's students and fellow professors, to everyone who ever knew the man? Even to history like the big dangerous animal Ernest Hemingway?

It says the Professor was somebody with lots of secrets, the Kid reasons. With maybe a whole secret life. And that he was somebody who wanted people to believe that he was smarter than everyone else. Also a man who got off from observing people from a safe distance. A man who didn't want to be known for what he was but at the same time did want to be known for what he was. A man who loved hiding the truth but also loved revealing it.

The Kid asks the Writer if at the press briefing he found out how the cops knew to search for the Professor's body at that particular spot in that particular canal. There are hundreds of miles of canals in Calusa County that they could have searched just as easily and logically as this one only they would have come up empty-handed. It might've taken a year before they happened onto the right spot at the right canal. *Somebody must've dropped a dime on where the van went in,* he says.

Couldn't have been the wife. The police told us she and their two kids were living with her mother temporarily and she hadn't seen or spoken to him for days. That leaves only one person who could have done it.

Who?

You.

Very funny.

Well, when we left Appalachee you seemed to know precisely where they'd find him.

C'mon, I just remembered he was kind of interested in that one canal. Besides, I was way deep in the swamp since before he went off the radar. I couldn't've called the cops.

Cell phones, Kid.

For a minute or two the Kid wonders if maybe he did call the cops from way deep in the swamp. He remembers being surprised by the NPR news coming as it did from what seemed like another planet than the one the Kid was on with Annie and Einstein in his houseboat out there in the sloughs among the mangroves like the crew of the starship *Enterprise*. And he remembers being frightened at first because he wasn't sure how he was connected to the Professor's disappearance but knew that somehow he was connected and it could turn out to be dangerous to him. He was backsliding right then, bored and generating head-porn and jerk-off fantasies which has always had a dulling effect on his awareness of what else was going on at the time and not much memory of it afterward so that often the next day if he was no longer bored he would remember his thoughts and actions of the previous day as if he had only dreamed them. Did he call the cops and tell them where they were likely to find the missing professor? Or did he only dream it? Or wish it?

He could have made the call. You just dial 911 and say, *Look for the missing college professor at the Route Eighty-three Canal at Lock one-oh-seven.* Then hang up. And the Writer's not wrong, the Kid did have his cell phone with him out there and if he was in NPR range he was possibly in cell phone range too. He pulls his clamshell from his pants pocket and checks the recent-calls list. His next-to-last call, he notes with relief, was placed the morning after the cops busted up the encampment under the Causeway and before he got fired from his busboy job at the Mirador when for a few moments that morning he thought of renting an apartment for him and Iggy to live in and called a few Realtors before he was interrupted by the two Babes on Blades. His last call was to his parole officer from Benbow's.

I never dropped no dime on the Professor, man. Not unless they got pay phones out there in the middle of the Panzacola. Which they don't, believe me. But you already know that since you're writing about it for your magazine and all.

I didn't know that. Never thought of it, actually. No pay phones in the Panzacola? Nice detail. Mind if I use it?

Be my guest.

Wonder if you're out of cell phone range there. Did you happen to check your reception out there?

Not that I remember. How come you hafta ask about stuff like this? Don't you hafta be like some kinda expert on the Great Panzacola Swamp in order to write about it for a big fancy New York magazine?

Not really.

You ever actually been inside the swamp? Like in a canoe or a houseboat? Or even take a walk on one of those hiking trails they got for bird-watchers?

Not really.

But you're okay with writing about it anyhow?

Sure. Jesus Christ, what's that!

The Writer hits the brakes and brings the car to a sudden stop ten feet short of a gigantic mocha-colored serpent as long as the one-lane road is wide crossing the road slowly from left to right as if sleep-crawling over the hot pavement, sucking the heat through its scales into its cold blood as it undulates its way from greenery over concrete to more greenery and seems to be trying to make it last but is obliged nonetheless to keep moving in order not to get cooked by the sun-baked pavement or hit by a car or truck before succeeding in making it all the way across and into the safety of the jungle. Its head is as large as a Doberman's and its swirling muscular body is as thick as the Kid's body so that if its mouth could open wide enough it could swallow the Kid whole. This snake is evil. Its eyes are open but cold and not afraid or angry or curious and they're nothing like Iggy's, the only other eyes the Kid can think of comparing them to, eyes that always seemed friendly toward the Kid at least if not toward other people.

Though he's never seen a snake like this before—never seen a snake that's so big and scary it blocks everything else out of his field of vision—he knows that it's a full-grown Burmese python, one of those three- or four-foot-long pet snakes somebody got tired of feeding live mice to and dropped off one night in the Panzacola where it grew to maximal size and gradually moved its diet up the food chain to the top, so forget about mice and rats, now it's eating deer and feral cats and dogs and the occasional pig that wanders off the farm into the swamp and if it got hungry enough it could grab and crush and devour without dismembering a human being.

Despite the air-conditioning inside the car the Kid is sweating. His thumping heart rushes blood to his face making his ears ping like high-pitched alarms. His palms are wet and for a few seconds he's afraid he'll pee his pants. If he starts talking he'll block out enough of his fear with his own voice and be able to control his body better so he says to the Writer, *It's a fucking giant python, man! Don't get outa the car or do anything to piss it off 'cause even though they're not poisonous like water moccasins they can move really fast on the ground and they can break every fucking bone in your body and eat you, man. They're pure evil and they know no fear. In fact you better put the fucking car in reverse and back it the fuck up in case it decides to attack the car.*

The Writer laughs. He pulls out his iPhone and reaches for the door handle. *I want to get a picture of it.*

Dude! Are you fucking nuts?

The Writer ignores him and gets out of the Town Car and steps to the front fender a few feet away from the middle of the slow-motion body of the snake. He props his elbows on the hood and holds up his iPhone and snaps off half-a-dozen pictures of the serpent as it slithers past the car and slides into the gully at the far side of the road and disappears into the high grass and palmettos.

Grinning in triumph the Writer returns to the car and gets in and clicks through his iPhone photos. *Wow! Amazing! My editor's going to love this. Perfect ending to the story, a twenty-foot Burmese python living in America's Great Panzacola National Park. And I've got photographic proof.*

Crossing his arms over his chest the Kid slumps down in his seat. *You're just lucky he wasn't hungry right now. That snake is evil, man. Pure evil.*

Where do you think you are, Kid, the goddam Garden of Eden? Snakes aren't evil any more than they're good. They're just following their nature. Which as long as we don't screw them up by putting them in cages and zoos is snake-nature. Good and evil, Kid, that's strictly for us humans. It's only human nature that's divided into good and evil.

No way, man. Everything in the universe especially human nature is good and evil mixed. But that fucking snake is pure evil, man. Which is why God put him in the Garden of Eden. Don't you read the Bible?

The Writer smiles, drops the car into gear and drives. A few miles farther on as they approach the Appalachee ranger station the Writer says to the Kid, *I'm going to assume there's no cell phone service out there in the swamp. For my article. But also with respect to the question of whether you called the cops and told them where to look for the Professor's body.*

Thanks. A lot.

But if you didn't do it, who did?

Whoever put him there, I guess. Or else the Professor himself called it in.

Right. But judging from the condition of his body, the Professor must have been in the canal since he first disappeared, which was right after he dropped you off out here. Hard to phone in your location when you've been underwater for four days and half-devoured by crabs and eels. So it must've been whoever put him there.

I guess.

But why would the person or persons who chained him to his van and drove it into the canal want the body discovered?

Beats the shit outa me. Anyhow, they were bicycle locks, not chains.

And why would the police decide so quickly that it was suicide?

Like I said, beats the shit outa me. Is this what writers do all the time, sit around asking themselves questions that can't be answered?

Yeah. And when they can't answer them they write about them.

Why?

To give somebody else a chance to answer them.

Does it work?

Sometimes.

The Kid lightly taps the DVD in his cargo pants pocket. He

brought it with him from Appalachee because he thought he might see the Professor's widow at the canal and if so he planned to give it to her then and there without comment and just walk away whistling. But she wasn't there. Now he's almost glad she wasn't because he's thinking of telling the Writer about his interview with the Professor, get the Writer's take on the Professor's story and maybe even let him watch the DVD even though he promised he'd not give or show it to anyone but the Professor's wife Gloria.

Then he changes his mind. He can't let the Writer play the DVD on his computer. That would rip up his deal with the Professor and it would be like he stole the ten K from him instead of being paid legitimately for a job yet to be completed.

Maybe he could get away with telling him about it though. Don't tell him everything. Long-story-short kind of thing. See if he thinks it's one of those unanswerable questions the Writer likes so much.

WHEN THE KID AND THE WRITER ARRIVE at Turnbull's Store Cat and especially Dolores are eager to hear all about the recovery of the disappeared professor's body from the canal which the Writer gladly reports in detail, even including his speculation as to how the police knew to search for it at that exact spot. The Writer is the excitable talkative type and seems to want to upgrade Cat's and Dolores's level of excitement as if to compensate for their generally low-key personalities. The Kid tries fading from the scene inside the store and hangs back by the door at the edge of earshot with Einstein and Annie. Something about hearing the Writer's version of events makes him uncomfortable: in his telling the story gets simplified and crude even though everything the Writer says either is factual or if the facts aren't known is rational.

The Writer checks his watch and announces that he's off to interview the ranger for his magazine article before the man leaves the park. As he passes the Kid at the door he asks him if he plans to spend the night in the houseboat and the Kid says why the hell not, he's got no place else to stay and he's already paid for it, so yeah.

Will you be taking the boat into the swamp tonight?

Not after seeing that fucking snake, man. I'm gonna keep it tied tight to the dock. I got a dog and a parrot to protect.

The Writer laughs at that. *How about I drop by later for a visit? Check out what it's like to cruise the Panzacola in a rented houseboat.*

Whyn't you just rent one and take it for a ride yourself? Maybe you'll run into one of those giant snakes and snag some more pictures.

No time. And not necessary, Kid, since you've already done the boating for me. Anyhow I've got to get back to Calusa tonight. Early flight to New York tomorrow, he says and hurries off to interview the ranger.

The Kid shrugs and reaches down and scratches Annie's boney forehead. The dog lies down and closes her eyes with pleasure and flops her tail twice against the tile floor. From his cage Einstein watches the Kid and Annie with what looks like empathy for both. The Kid is surprised by how relieved and glad he is to see Annie and Einstein after being away from them for only a few hours and they seem relieved and glad to see him too. He thinks all three of them must be scared of being abandoned and their shared fear is drawing them closer together. Of course they don't know about his past habits and longings and his many failed attempts to be a normal person but then they're animals—or rather an animal and a bird—and are therefore innocent and if the Writer is right they are beyond good and evil and cannot judge him. And will not abandon him. And he will not abandon them.

Dolores has walked up behind the Kid and touches him on the shoulder startling him. *I spoke with Cat, hon, and he says it's okay for you to stay on the boat and keep it tied up in the slip, if that's what you want and can afford to keep renting it. It's off-season anyhow. Not much call for houseboats this time of year.*

Cat watches from the far end of the counter, his expression halfway between a scowl and a look of defeat.

In a voice that's practically a whisper the Kid says to Dolores, *You don't mind having a convicted sex offender in the neighborhood? It's gonna be on the Internet watch list, y'know. Where I'm living.*

Whatever you did, hon, I don't believe you're a danger to me or Cat. Are you?

I'm not a danger to anyone. What I did was I guess just stupid and con-fused. And I'm not as stupid and confused now as I used to be.

That's what I figured. C'mon, I'll help you take your pets and your bags to the boat, Dolores says and she lifts his duffel and Einstein's cage and walks from the store. Einstein hollers, *Man overboard! Man overboard!* and Dolores laughs and tells him to shut the hell up and he obeys. The parrot seems to like Dolores.

The Kid takes Annie's leash in hand and grabs his backpack. As he leaves he stops and turns to Cat for a second. *Thanks for letting me stay on awhile, Cat.*

Thank Dolores. She's the one with the soft heart.

Hey, I'm really sorry I lied to you, man. About the army and all that. It was very disrespectful.

Beats me, though, why everybody wants to say they been in combat when they weren't anywhere near it. It's like wanting to say you worked in a meat processing plant when you never got closer to meat than eating a Big Mac. Consider yourself lucky, Kid, that you didn't get sent over there. And don't be ashamed to admit it next time somebody asks. You got enough stuff you should be lying about. You don't hafta lie about your military service too.

Yeah. Thanks for the advice.

So what got you kicked out of the army anyhow? "Don't ask don't tell"? You're not a gay guy, are you?

No. I got caught distributing porn films to my outfit in basic.

Jesus! G'wan, getthefuckoutahere. Next time lie about that too. Say you're a gay guy or something.

The Kid can't tell if Cat is serious or not. But he's right, the next time someone asks him about his military service he'll admit it right up front, he'll say he got shit-canned by the U.S. Army before completing basic training. If they ask him why he was discharged he'll say it was because of "don't ask don't tell" and they found out he's gay. It's what he should have told brandi18. It would have saved him a world of trouble.

·   ·   ·

IT'S NEARLY NIGHTFALL WHEN THE WRITER strolls aboard the *Dolores Driscoll*. He finds the Kid in the gloom of the cabin seated cross-legged on his cot among a batch of loose sheets of paper, some of the pages on his lap, others fallen to the deck, several held in his hands. With small surprise the Writer notes a Bible lying among the papers on the cot. The Kid's normally suntanned face is chalk white and his hands are shaking. The Writer pulls up a folding chair, sits down, and asks the Kid what he's reading.

Some weird shit, man.

The Bible yours? I didn't take you for a Christian particularly.

I'm not particularly. The Bible's not what's weird. It belonged to a guy I knew. I ended up with it and started reading in it by accident, you might say. Same as these papers. They're like printed-out e-mails that I guess the guy was saving for a case. Or in case of a case. Something like that. He's a lawyer. Or used to be a lawyer.

The Writer can see that the Kid is upset by what he's been reading, upset and perhaps frightened. *Do you mind if I take a look?*

Be my guest, the Kid says and he gathers the sheets of paper, takes a moment to put them carefully in sequence, and hands the packet to the Writer.

As the Writer reads his eyebrows lift and he purses his lips as if to whistle. Then he does whistle. *Who is this guy, Big Daddy?*

I'm pretty sure he's the guy I know, the lawyer, since they were in his stuff. I sort of got them without his knowledge, I guess, and forgot to give them back. His name is Shyster. Actually his real name is Lawrence Somerset. Used to be some kind of big-time state politician named Larry Somerset who was on TV a lot until he got caught for being into kiddie porn and arranging over the Internet to set up a love nest for a couple of little girls supposedly being pimped by their mother. Only it was a sting and there wasn't any mother or any little girls either. You maybe read about him in the papers or heard it on the news. It was a big deal for a while when he first got caught. Mainly because he was this big state legislator with a wife and grown kids and all, and when he opened the motel room door for what he thought was a couple of little girls but instead turned out to be the cops, he was naked or almost naked with a dildo in his hand and a kiddie porn DVD playing on the TV. Asshole probably had a hard-on too. And I thought I was stupid.

Good lord! How on earth do you know a man like that? the Writer asks and the Kid briefly describes life beneath the Causeway, its unintended necessity and nature. He adds that he doesn't know where the Shyster has been living since the hurricane and points out that he never liked the guy anyhow and especially doesn't like him now after reading these e-mails which the Shyster must've been saving in case he needed to keep the other guy from blowing his whistle on even worse things than kiddie-dipping. The Kid calls the other guy *"the recipient."*

The one who calls himself Doctor Hoo?

Yeah.

Let me take a wild guess. Is that our *professor?*

'Fraid so. Read the rest.

The Writer asks if there's a reading lamp and the Kid places a kerosene lantern on the table next to his chair and lights it. A splash of orange covers the wall behind him and shadows dart around the cabin like bats. The Writer resumes reading. The two of them remain silent. When he reaches the end of the stack of e-mails, the Writer exhales loudly, passes the e-mails back to the Kid and simply says, *Jesus Christ.*

Yeah.

Did you know your professor friend and this guy Shyster or whatever he's called were coconspiring pen pals?

No. But they didn't either. Check the dates on their e-mails. They're all from a couple years ago, back before the Shyster got busted and did time. They're from when he could still legally use a computer for e-mailing and cruising the Internet for kids. I didn't know the Professor back then. Or Shyster either. And since it sounds like Big Daddy and Doctor Hoo never actually met in person in real life, despite being heavy into swapping kiddie porn websites and exchanging kiddies-for-hire contact info, when they did meet in real life under the Causeway a few weeks ago it was a kind of coincidence and they didn't know who they were meeting so they didn't recognize each other.

Why on earth would this Shyster want to keep these e-mails? They're disgusting.

Maybe he thought he could make a deal with the cops. Like if he turned in his pen pal they'd let him get rid of his anklet and get off parole and maybe get his old law license back. I dunno. Everybody makes deals if they can.

The Writer goes back to the e-mails and quickly scans three or four in particular, wincing as he reads. He asks the Kid what makes him think this Doctor Hoo is in fact his professor friend.

The Kid hesitates before answering, as if afraid of the answer. Finally he says, *I just know it's him. I mean, I believe it's him. Because of all that stuff in there about little buried treasures, which you can tell are in reality little kids for sex, and secret maps, which are Internet kiddie-porn sites, and the mentions of Captain Kydd, who is himself. It's like a code. It's not really about pirates. It's about sex with little kids and how to find them on the Internet. And it's like all a big joke to those two. Anyhow, the Professor sort of talked like that. Nobody else talked that way. Nobody I ever met anyway. Especially that stuff about Captain Kydd. He used the same words when he was telling me about him and the map and so on. Only I thought at first he was talking about a real secret treasure map and an actual pirate's treasure and that there was a real island where it was buried. I even got into trying to find the treasure using this old map that he gave me that was supposedly Captain Kydd's secret map. I thought maybe it was buried under the Causeway, which was originally an island before they paved it with concrete and built the Causeway over it. That's how dumb I was. I even thought because his name is spelled the same as mine maybe he was related to me.*

The Writer scratches his bristly beard and continues to peruse the e-mails, as if looking for something to argue against the Kid's conclusions. He doesn't want to find himself trapped in dark self-designed delusions: he's all too familiar with his affection for bad news and conspiracies. It's had a negative effect on his career. After a moment he asks the Kid if he thinks the person who told the police where to find the Professor's body was Big Daddy. The Shyster.

The Kid says no, the Shyster wouldn't have known where to send the cops unless the Professor tipped him off in advance where he was going to drown himself. Which he wouldn't have been able to do via e-mail since the Shyster can't go online anymore due to being a convicted sex offender. Plus the Kid is pretty sure that when the Professor met the Shyster in person down under the Causeway he had no way of knowing he was actually meeting Big Daddy. Any more than the Shyster knew he was meeting Doctor Hoo. No, it had to be somebody else who called the cops.

Who?

Yeah, Hoo. Could've been Doctor Hoo himself, assuming he was definitely gonna kill himself then and there. So maybe he made a last-minute 911 call or mailed a tape to the cops or a letter scheduled to arrive a few days after he did the deed.

The Kid goes silent for a moment. The Writer asks if he has anything to drink and the Kid says sure and gets up and digs two cans of beer out of the cooler, apologizing for their not being very cold. He forgot to buy more ice from Cat earlier. The Kid sits on the edge of his cot again and goes back to stroking Annie's forehead. Without looking up he says, *Or else it was somebody else. Somebody not Big Daddy or Doctor Hoo. Somebody who bike-locked him to his van and then drove the van into the canal. Somebody who wanted the Professor's body discovered and ID'd and declared a suicide.*

The Writer looks him over carefully. *You know something I don't know?*

Sort of. I shouldn't be telling you all this. You're probably gonna write about it.

The Writer shakes his head. *No way I'll write about it.*

Yeah? Why not?

Who'd want to read it? Kiddie porn and child molesters, pedophiles and suicidal college professors? Jesus! Besides, I'm just a freelance travel writer, not some kind of investigative journalist or a novelist trying to depress people. I have to make a living. The stuff I write is designed strictly to make people want to spend money on hotels and airlines that advertise in my employers' magazines. Believe me, this is not a story likely to be welcomed by the Calusa County Chamber of Commerce or the local tourist board. They'd probably pay me not *to write it.*

Throughout this conversation, throughout the entire afternoon, the Kid has felt himself warming to the Writer, feeling less and less suspicious of his motives and intentions, enjoying the man's company, not because the Writer is amusing or especially friendly like Dolores or even interesting in a challenging way like Cat but because the Writer's jumpy ongoing attention makes him feel less alone in the world. Even before the Professor disappeared, from the moment that he turned over the DVD of their interview and paid him to deliver it to his wife Gloria the Kid has felt unaccountably lonely. Up to this point the Kid has rarely felt loneliness—he had been merely one of those people who later, after it comes out that he's an assassin or a terrorist, is described in puzzlement by people who knew him as a "loner," a quiet solitary boring person who seemed to have no family or friends going all the way back to childhood, someone who was incapable of committing the act that made him however briefly the center of the known universe. And with the Professor's DVD in hand and ten thousand dollars in his duffel the Kid has unexpectedly gone from being a mere loner to someone desperately lonely, as if for the first time in his life he's potentially the center of the known universe only nobody knows it yet.

It's because the Kid possesses information that no one else has. And he's starting to believe that if he shares it with the Writer it will give him the feeling of actually being at the center of the universe which will in turn end his loneliness, at least until everyone else has the same information. Maybe then he'll have to come up with something else that only he possesses and find someone else like the Writer to share it with. But for now he decides to tell the Writer about the DVD in which the Professor aka Doctor Hoo predicts his own assassination by secret government agents who will stage his death as a suicide caused by the threat of imminent public exposure of a shocking sexual scandal.

He begins with the dark and stormy night of Hurricane George after the Professor picked him and Annie and Einstein up at the flooded encampment under the Causeway and brought them to his house. He adds in passing that the Professor's wife had just left him and had gone to her mother's with their two kids. He doesn't mention her note taped to the refrigerator door.

So you were alone with him. Did he try anything? Anything . . . sexual, I mean.

The Kid laughs at that and says that the Professor's only interest in him was for testing out some dumb theory he had about making homeless convicted sex offenders into sexually normal people. It had something to do with organizing them into little committees and voting on how to run the camp under the Causeway and various aspects of personal hygiene and the Kid and the other men living there had more or less gone along with it for a while until the hurricane hit.

It takes the Kid fewer than five minutes to summarize the content of his interview with the Professor, partly because he neglects to include in his account anything about the ten thousand dollars. Though from the beginning it must have been a part of the Professor's plan, taking the money is more about the Kid than the Professor and it still slightly embarrasses him. He merely says that he was charged with the responsibility of getting the DVD of the interview into the hands of the Professor's estranged wife so that she will believe that he did not kill himself and the sexual scandal was bullshit.

To the Kid's surprise the Writer who he thought was the skeptical type, being a writer and all, easily believes his brief description of what the Professor said in the interview. He buys into the Professor's account of why he will be murdered and who will do the murdering. He believes that it will be made to look like a suicide and that information about the Professor's involvement in a sexual scandal probably involving pedophilia, child pornography, and child prostitution, though false, is about to be made public. The Writer believes all this because he believes in conspiracies and that in fact there are hundreds, perhaps thousands, of secret government operatives with supernatural competence, double and triple agents, spies and moles working outside the law. And apparently for many years the Professor was one of these operatives—he was a certified genius after all—and must have been about to go off the reservation as they say in the movies and perhaps write a tell-all book or turn a stash of secret documents over to a blogger or testify to a congressional committee and reveal all the heinous deeds committed for decades by agencies that we don't even know exist. The Professor had become a threat to national security and was therefore dispensable.

The Writer says, *So it wasn't a suicide after all! Wow! That explains a lot.*

Like what?

Like how the cops knew where to look for his body. The quick official designation of his death as a suicide. The way he was chained to the steering wheel and accelerator. Et cetera.

Suddenly, having revealed to the Writer the Professor's account of his approaching death and seeing how easily the Writer accepts it as the truth, the Kid no longer believes it himself. There's a big difference between knowing something is true and believing it's true and the Kid doesn't want to be a believer. *They were bike locks,* he points out again. *Not chains. Bike locks are cool. Chains are definitely uncool.*

The Writer cocks an eyebrow and stares at the Kid. *You think he was trying to tell us something?*

Maybe. Yeah. That the suicide is a phony. Maybe he was trying to tell us he didn't really kill himself, someone else did it. So his wife and anybody with a suspicious nature wouldn't buy the Big Daddy and Doctor Hoo kiddie-porn and suicide story, which he figured was gonna come out and is why the Shyster was saving those e-mails. The Professor must've known it was coming. Like he says on the DVD. But when you think about it, it's like he went to too much trouble to make his so-called suicide look phony.

What do you mean, too much trouble?

If these super-spies and all are so good at killing people who they don't trust anymore, they oughta be able to fake a suicide without clamping the guy to his car with bike locks and driving it into a canal, right? I mean, he's such a fat guy they could've made him run on a treadmill or up and down a beach dune until he had a heart attack and died and they could just leave him there. They coulda pushed him off a bridge if they wanted to fake his suicide. Drop him off a boat in the Gulf. There's a hundred different ways to make it look like a suicide without also making it look like a murder. If that's what you want. The only one who wanted it to look like a murder was the Professor. But he also wanted to make it look like a suicide. He needed it both ways, or nobody'd believe his story. The murdered ex-spy cancels out the child-molester professor. And vice versa. They both disappear. Like that snake slithering into the swamp.

And we end up not knowing which one he really was.

Maybe he was both, the Kid says. *Maybe neither. He was supposedly a genius, remember. And he liked playing games with people.*

What're you going to do with that DVD?

Take it to the wife. Like I said I would.

Tomorrow?

Yeah, I guess so.

I'll drive you there. I'll cancel my flight back and take you to the Professor's wife.

You're not gonna write about this, are you?

God, no!

Where you gonna stay the night?

I'll rent myself a houseboat so I can write about sleeping in a houseboat deep in the Great Panzacola Swamp instead.

Research.

Yep.

CHAPTER SEVEN

WHEN THE PROFESSOR'S WIFE ANSWERS the Kid's light knock on the door she opens it only a crack at first, as if expecting someone she doesn't want to speak to: another reporter or a nosy neighbor faking concern and offering condolences and a casserole; or a police officer with more of her husband's "effects" as they call his clothing and the contents of his pockets and car. Her skin is chalky white and dry and she has large dark circles under her green eyes. She doesn't appear to have been crying, but she looks haggard and exhausted as if she hasn't slept for days. Her shoulders are slumped and her hands, even though both are clamped to the edge of the door, tremble visibly.

She pushes the door open a few more inches and peers out at the Kid and the big bearded white-haired man in the Hawaiian shirt and baggy shorts standing behind him and asks them what they want. Something about the small young man with the military buzz cut is familiar to her. Did he do some yard work for them? He looks like the kind of young unskilled white man who does yard work for people in neighborhoods like this. Or maybe he's selling magazine subscriptions and the older man behind him is his supervisor who's training him.

The Kid asks if she's the wife. He can't remember her actual name—the only time he saw it was on her typed good-bye note that she taped to the refrigerator and the Professor barely mentioned her by name, just referred to her as *my wife*. To the Kid therefore she's the Wife so that's what he calls her.

She says yes and asks them again what they want, a little less confrontational now than the first time. She opens the door farther. She's starting to remember that she met the young man briefly at the library once, but is unsure of the circumstances or when—recently no doubt. Possibly she interviewed him for an afterschool job but did not hire him. But if she met him at the library and it was about a job she never gave him, why would he seek her out at home?

Oddly—at least it strikes her as odd—she likes his looks, especially compared to the looks of everyone else she's had to talk to lately: she likes the angle of his cocked head and the way he stands at an opposing angle with all his weight on one foot like a watchful bird. He seems slightly bored and a little annoyed with having to stand here at the door. He doesn't appear to want anything from her. She likes that too. Everyone else has wanted something from her—information about her husband mainly, his disappearance and death—and has tried to conceal that fact with false expressions of sympathy and insincere offers of comfort and help: neighbors, friends and colleagues from the library and from her husband's university, the several reporters who called on her, the police. Even her mother. *If there's anything I can do . . . , Don't be afraid to call on us . . . , I know how hard this must be for you, ma'am, but. . . .*

She knows what people thought of her husband when he was alive—he was not a popular or particularly admired man to anyone except his wife and his children—and she knows what they think of him now that he's committed suicide and abandoned that loving wife and those well-behaved pretty children, the only people who knew him and did not think he was odd and ugly and arrogant. But he is or rather *was* a very intelligent man, people always note that. A genius.

But nobody likes a genius. Especially one who is obese and

eccentric. And she knows—because of the way he killed himself and because he was a fat weird opinionated genius—that everyone thinks the Professor had secrets, dark secrets, probably secrets of a sexual nature. People who are neither fat nor geniuses always think fat people who are geniuses have strange secret sex lives. And because she was married to him and bore him two children, people probably believe that she too has, or rather had, a strange secret sex life. She senses the presence of that belief especially now in friends and colleagues as much as in strangers. Even in her mother. It's one of the reasons she was hesitant about leaving the children with her mother while she dealt with the aftermath of her husband's disappearance and death. But her mother had said, *Please, dear, please let me help by taking care of the children for a few days. You have enough to handle, Lord knows, and with me they'll be more protected from the . . . from the facts of the situation.*

As if the facts were somehow sexual. And peculiar. But they weren't. Were they?

The Wife's mind is primed by her darting dark thoughts, so when the Kid says, *I have something your husband wanted me to give you,* and holds out a clear plastic case with what looks like a CD inside she remembers suddenly and clearly her one and only meeting with the Kid. He's the same skinny young man who walked stiff with anxiety into the library on Regis Road one afternoon and asked her to help him look up his neighborhood, his own house in fact, on the National Sex Offender Registry. His is the face that came up on the computer screen, the convicted sex offender who said he was sorry and she told him not to be sorry. Although she had no idea what she meant by that. Ever since, she's wondered what she was thinking then and has wished he had not fled and instead had stayed and told her what he was sorry for. Whatever it was, she was sure, from the horrified expression on his real face when he saw its digitalized version on the computer screen and from the rigid quick-stepping way he steered his body from the library like a mortified comedian in an early silent movie, that he could not have done something that he should be sorry for. She has believed ever since that she was not wrong to tell him that.

At the same instant the Kid recognizes her too. She's the fizzy red-haired research lady at the library he was dumb enough to ask for help the afternoon he wanted to see for himself what anybody in the world with a computer and an Internet connection could see. He remembers the afternoon with embarrassment and shame. It's how he remembers most of his life up till then only sharper because that was the afternoon before the night the cops tore up what passed for his home and killed Iggy. It was the afternoon before the next morning when he was humiliated by the bikini babes on Rollerblades and then got fired from his job at the Mirador on account of his joke about the guy at O. J. Simpson's table who wanted half a pear. His first and only visit to the library was when everything started going from bad to worse, from simple to complicated, obvious to confusing. It was the day before the night the Professor first came knocking at the door of his tent. And now it's suddenly all come full circle and feels almost like he's back at the library again looking at his mug shot on the computer screen with the nice research lady except that it's much worse this time because not only does she know some of his secrets he knows some of hers.

The Wife's tired eyes get very large and her mouth opens to speak but nothing gets said. She nods and takes the plastic case from the Kid's extended hand in silence. For a moment the Wife and the Kid stare at each other as if waiting for an answer to a question that neither of them wishes to ask.

Finally it's the Writer who speaks. *The young man knew your late husband, ma'am. We're very sorry to intrude at such a time, but your husband instructed my friend here to deliver the DVD to you personally. They filmed an interview together. Your husband, in the event of his untimely death, wanted you to have it. We thought it was important enough to risk intruding on you like this. I hope you don't mind.*

Without answering him, the Wife as if brushing away cobwebs passes one hand over her face and gestures with the other for them to come inside.

She asks the Kid if she should watch the DVD now since he knows what's on it. *Can it wait until I'm a little over the . . . the shock of it all? I don't need any more bad news.*

The three of them stand awkwardly together in the middle of the living room. The blinds and curtains are drawn, filling the room with thickened shadow and gloom, as if no one has ventured into it in months. The Kid says, *I dunno, I think maybe you oughta check it out now. Before you do get any more bad news.*

She says, *Oh!* He's told her more than she wanted to hear.

I mean, I think the Professor wanted you to look at it right away. Like, as soon as they found his body and said it was a suicide.

Well, it was suicide!

The Writer clears his throat and asks, *Was there a note or a letter to that effect, ma'am?*

No. But he was despondent. There were things you couldn't know. He and I . . . we were recently estranged. I'm afraid to watch it, the DVD. He may say things about me or the children that I don't want to hear.

The Kid says, *No way. He only says nice stuff about you and the kids.*

The Wife looks pleadingly into the Kid's eyes: *Will you watch it with me? I'm scared to watch it alone. I don't know who else to ask. You were there, weren't you?*

Yeah. I was sort of like the cameraman.

She asks the Writer if he knows what's on the DVD, and he says yes, although he hasn't watched it himself. The Kid summarized it for him.

She says, *All right, then if you don't mind, we'll watch it together. Come with me, there's a computer in my husband's office,* she says and leads the Kid and the Writer down the hallway to the Professor's office.

The Wife sits down at the desk and opens the computer and turns it on. As the Kid and the Writer take positions behind her, the Kid glances over at the big black safe and feels a twinge of guilt. He wonders if he should have told the Wife about the money and decides no, it would only complicate things even further. Maybe someday.

When the computer screen has opened and the screen has filled with icons, the Wife slips the DVD into the slot. A few seconds later the Professor's bearded plate-shaped face appears on the screen.

You sit there, Kid, off camera. I'll sit here on the sofa in front of it.

Whaddaya want me to ask? I mean, I never done this before, interviewed somebody.

The Kid interrupts his digital self: *I guess I was more than a camera-man. Sorry.*

The Professor continues: *No, but you've been interviewed. You start by asking a question that you want answered, and then I decide if and how I'm willing to answer it. Then you ask a follow-up question that's generated by my previous answer. Simple. Especially for the one asking the questions.*

Okay. How about what's the fucking reason for making this interview in the first place?

Excellent first question! The simple answer is that in the coming weeks or possibly months my body will be found, and it will look like a suicide. This interview will provide evidence that it was not a suicide. . . .

For nearly twenty minutes the Kid, the Writer, and the Wife watch the DVD on the Professor's desktop computer. Finally the interview comes to an end:

Pretty much everything I wanted Gloria to hear has been said already. Except that I truly love her and the children, and I am not guilty of the hei-nous acts that I will soon be accused of.

Are you ashamed, though? Like you asked me when you were interview-ing me about brandi18.

Ashamed? Of what?

You know, of spying and shit. Being an informant and a mole and a double agent. All that.

No, I'm not ashamed. And I don't feel guilty for all those years of deceit and betrayal, secrecy and lies. That was the nature of the world then and now, and those are the rules of the game that runs the world. And once you know that, you either play the game or it plays you. I only regret that I stopped playing the game. Now it's playing me. Except for this one last move. . . .

Maybe we should shut off the camera and discuss my fee.

Fair enough.

The screen blanks out. The Kid backs away from the Wife, who sits stunned in front of the computer. The Writer hunches over beside her, still staring at the screen as if wanting more. The Kid moves slowly toward the door thinking: I never should've said that shit about my fee because now they're going to ask me how much he paid me and the Wife's going to ask for the money back and I'll have to give her what's left of it if she does on account of she'll need it for her kids and it isn't like I actually earned the money by working for it but then I'll be broke again and homeless with no job and I won't be able to feed Annie and Einstein or even myself except by Dumpster diving so now I'm totally fucked again!

But they don't ask him about his fee. They don't ask him about anything. For the Wife and the Writer, the Kid's interview with the Professor has provided nothing but answers. Instead of asking questions, they make statements.

Her pale face soaked with tears, the Wife turns and looks up at the Kid, who's never seen a woman cry before: *Thank you,* she says. Then to the Writer: *Thank you both. I know the truth now. I finally know who my husband really was. Finally! And I know what to expect. And when it comes, no matter how awful it is I'll know how to deal with it and how to protect my children from it. I'll be able to tell them that whatever people say about their father it isn't true! And someday when they're old enough to understand such things I'll play this for them. So thank you! For their sake as much as mine.*

The Writer places a hand on her shoulder. *Some people would consider your husband a hero. I'm one of them.*

The Kid stops at the door not so much surprised as appalled and stares at the two. They believe the Professor's stupid story! Both of them! The Writer has leaned down and embraced the Wife. She sobs onto his shoulder wetting the sleeve of his yellow and red Hawaiian shirt.

The Kid slips out the door and waits in the Town Car.

CHAPTER EIGHT

O N THE DRIVE BACK TO APPALACHEE THE
Kid slumps in the passenger's seat in sulky silence with his
arms folded across his chest and his feet propped against
the dashboard while the Writer natters on—at least from the Kid's
perspective—about the Professor's courage in accepting the fatal
consequences of his past associations and the man's loving-kindness
toward his wife and children by making sure they knew the truth.
Arming them against the coming scandal, he says.

The Kid tamps back an impulse to ask the Writer if he's forgotten about the sick e-mail correspondence between Big Daddy and
Doctor Hoo. Buried treasures and secret maps. Captain Kydds and
Peter Pans. Disgusting! The Writer believes what he wants to be
true, not what he knows to be true. Who does he think told the
cops where to find the Professor's body anyway? Who else had a
motive? No one. It had to be the Professor himself. It was the only
way he could be sure his cover story would get delivered to his
wife, the only way he could defend himself from beyond the grave
and also go out feeling smarter than everyone else. He probably
holed up in a cheesy by-the-hour motel at a minimall somewhere
west of the city for a few nights until his disappearance got on TV,
then drove out to the canal and made an anonymous phone call to
the cops with the motor of his van already running, lowered the

window, and tossed the phone into the water, snapped the bike locks onto his wrists and feet, somehow shifted the van into drive and floored it. It would have given the crabs and eels only an hour or so to do all that damage to the Professor's face but maybe that's enough when they're hungry. Complicated—maybe too complicated—but just complicated enough if you were married to the man like the Wife was or are slightly paranoid and believe in conspiracies like the Writer does to make suicide not quite believable which is exactly what the Professor needed to make his story believable to his wife and no doubt someday to his kids and evidently to the Writer as well.

But not to the Kid.

The Kid's not buying it. Though he'd like to. It would help him sort out how to deal with the money. His fee. If the Professor's story is a big fat lie and he was a big fat chomo into kiddie porn and worse then the money the Kid received for filming the story and delivering it to Gloria makes him an accomplice in the Professor's big fat lie and life. Which makes the money dirty and he ought to hand it over to Gloria and her kids the same as if the Professor stole it from them. But if the Professor's story is actually true then the money's clean—it's payment for the Kid's services which involved a certain degree of risk for him and maybe still does if those secret agents assuming they exist ever find out about it—and he's entitled to keep what's left of the ten K and spend it any way he wants.

It's in the Kid's interest then, his financial interest, to believe the Professor's story is true. It's the only way he can afford to rent the houseboat and live out there with Annie and Einstein in Appalachee at the edge of Paradise among normal people like Dolores and Cat and the ranger. Otherwise he'll have to give the money to the Wife and he'll be penniless and without a job or a home and will have to go back down under the Causeway and live with the ghosts and whoever else among the convicted sex offenders of Calusa County shows up there. And he won't be able to take proper care of Annie and Einstein or even feed himself except by stealing garbage from behind restaurants and supermarkets after they close.

He says to the Writer, *You really believe the Professor's story, right?*
Definitely!

But how do you know it's true? Instead of just believing it's true.

You mean, do I have proof? Like scientific proof? No, of course not. Hardly anything about human behavior can be known that way. Even our own behavior. We just have to choose what to believe and act accordingly, Kid.

Yeah, well, I need to know if his story is true or not. Because as far as believing goes, I can come down on either side. And if I come down on one side my "human behavior" will be different than if I come down on the other and vice versa. No matter which side I come down on, I'll worry it's the wrong side and my human behavior will be wrong too. This ain't a novel or a movie, y' know, where that shit don't matter as long as you know by the end what really happened.

The Writer laughs and shakes his head. *You're shoveling some heavy shit there, Kid. But I wouldn't worry about it if I were you. Whether he killed himself or someone else known or unknown did it for him, the Professor is dead and gone. You delivered his DVD to his widow and presumably you collected your fee, which I understand from Cat amounted to a rather large supply of hundred-dollar bills, right?*

Yeah. Right.

So whether you believe the Professor's story or not, your life will go on pretty much the same tomorrow as yesterday. You can live out there on your houseboat like Huckleberry Finn on his raft until your money runs out and then probably work for Cat and Dolores at the store until something better comes along. Sounds pretty nice to me, little buddy. I don't see how your "human behavior" will be affected one way or the other by your not having scientific proof that the Professor's story is true. You gotta believe, Kid! You just gotta believe.

Not, the Kid says. *'Course, that's easy for you to say, you're a writer. For people like me it's not so easy to believe things. Every time I believed someone or something I totally fucked up my life. So you can let that one go, man.*

Sorry, sorry, sorry, Kid.

A FULL MOON ABOVE THE BAY SPLASHES WIDE
stripes of cool glimmering light across the dark waters of the Appalachee estuary. There is a weak offshore breeze, and low waves lap
the sides of the pier. The boats rise and fall slowly as if the sea
were breathing. The Writer has rented the boat next to the Kid's
for one night only. He plans to structure his travel magazine article
around a weeklong exploration by houseboat through the practically unmapped constantly shifting mazelike interior waterways of
the Great Panzacola Swamp. He figures a single night spent aboard
one of Cat's boats at the pier ought to provide him with enough
details to make his account believable. *Sort of like* African Queen.
Only without the leeches, he tells the Kid.

The Kid points out that he'll be making the whole thing up and
asks if that's the way it is in the magazine article world, if what you
read and what you think is true is actually mostly made up.

The Writer explains that in a sense everything we read is mostly
made up.

Even the news?

Even the news.

Even on the Internet?

Especially on the Internet.

What about pictures and videos? Pictures don't lie, man.

Everything lies.

If everything's a lie, then nothing's true.

*You got it, Kid. Sort of. It means you can never really know the truth of
anything.*

Where'd you learn this? In college?

Yeah. Brown.

What the fuck's a Brown?

Where I went to college.

They're sitting in deck chairs at the stern of their respective
houseboats, side by side and only a few feet apart. Einstein is perched

atop the Kid's cabin like a lookout and as if to amuse himself every now and then mumbles, *Land ho,* and Annie sleeps curled like a comma at the Kid's feet. When the Kid returned earlier from Calusa both creatures seemed happy and relieved and the Kid's chest and throat filled with thick emotion and he felt himself almost start to cry but quickly got hold of himself and knocked his feelings back and was okay again.

But then when he went into the store for ice and more beer Dolores too and even Cat seemed oddly happy and relieved to see him—odd to the Kid since they know he's a convicted sex offender but don't yet know the exact nature of his crime when it could be anything from child abuse and rape to exposing his dick in public—a thing he wouldn't be caught dead doing—and everything in between, the kinds of things that he would do and a few that he actually did and that lots of more or less sexually normal people would do too if given the chance. And again his emotions almost welled over.

What's going on? he wondered. Am I losing it or are they?

Dolores actually hugged him and Cat didn't charge for the ice. They knew only that he and the Writer had driven into the city so the Kid could deliver a message to the widow from his friend the dead Professor since he was probably the last one to see the Professor while he was still alive—that was all he told them and what he instructed the Writer to say—and they were impressed by his kindness and loyalty to his strange friend. They were closing up the store, planning to barbecue ribs for supper and Dolores asked the Kid if he'd like to join them but he just shook his head no and grabbed the beer and ice and backed out the door, turned and headed quickly for his boat. Their trust and seeming affection for him was scaring him. It was a lot like Annie's and Einstein's trust and affection but Annie and Einstein are innocent animals and to make animals and even reptiles respect and like you all you've got to do is first do no harm and second make sure they have enough to eat and a safe place out of the rain. It isn't all that clear on the other hand if you're a human yourself what makes humans trust and respect you.

The Kid cracks open his second can of beer and says to the Writer, *If everything's a lie and nothing's true like you said, then it doesn't matter if the Professor's story is bullshit, right? Is that what you're saying?*

What you believe matters, however. It's all anyone has to act on. And since what you do is who you are, your actions define you. If you don't believe anything is true simply because you can't logically prove what's true, you won't do anything. You won't be anything. You'll end up spending your life in a rocking chair looking out at the horizon waiting for an answer that never comes. You might as well be dead. It's an old philosophical problem.

Then I got an old philosophical problem, the Kid says.

Tell.

It's sort of about the money, he begins. *My fee.* Leaving out the numbers the Kid admits that he received a very large amount of money from the Professor for delivering the DVD to his widow, money he has no trouble keeping on account of the risk he was taking. But that's only if the Professor's story is true. If it is he can in good conscience keep the money and stay on the houseboat for a long time, maybe cut a deal with Cat to rent it for a year or more and live like a regular Huckleberry. But if the Professor's story isn't true and he drowned himself in the canal because the Shyster or somebody else gave evidence to the cops that the Professor was actually this guy Doctor Hoo and was into kiddie porn and sexually abusing little kids then the Kid has let himself be drawn into a chomo conspiracy of lies. If that is the case he should give the money back—what's left of it which is almost all of it. Besides with her husband officially a suicide and no insurance and two kids the Wife could probably use the money.

Well, you can take that out of the equation, Kid. Gloria doesn't need the money. Your late friend was a very successful player on the commodities exchange for years and apparently he got into gold early.

How do you know that?

I asked and she told. You don't have to worry about Gloria, Kid.

I guess that's good.

You're trying to think logically about this, but you're being way too sloppy. Not that it would help if you were rigorous. Anyhow, let me show you the limits of logic. First, forget good and bad. Forget all about 'em. And forget the money, even. The Writer tells the Kid to remove everything from the equation except considerations of pure logic.

What equation?

Either the Professor's story, X, is true, or it isn't, Y.

The fuck you talking about?

They can't both be true, right? X and Y? So one of them has to be false.

Yeah. I guess so.

So that means either X or Y is the case for P.

What the fuck's P?

The Professor.

Right. The Professor is P.

Okay. Your problem, if you rely on logic, is that you can't assert the proposition such that X is the case for P, and you can't assert the proposition such that Y is the case for P. All you can assert is that either X or Y is the case for P.

Dude, that's where we started. That's the fucking problem.

It's only a problem if you rely on logic. That's my point. What you've got to do, Kid, is forget logic, admit its limitations, suspend your disbelief, and believe! It's the only way you'll be free to act. Otherwise you're stuck, frozen in disbelief. As good as dead.

For a long while the Kid remains silent. He tries to replay in his mind what the Writer has just told him but he can't untangle enough of the sentences to remember and understand what the man said—except for the last part, that he's frozen in disbelief and is as good as dead. He thinks it's true. It is the case that he is as good as dead.

He listens to the waves lap against the sides of the houseboats. He looks up and notices a few raggedy clouds, their edges soldered silver with moonlight, sliding in from the west. The breeze off the water has kept the mosquitoes back in the swamp all evening which he's glad of. He forms a sentence and says it aloud: *It's actually pretty nice here.* He reaches down and scratches Annie's forehead.

Finally he asks the Writer if he'll be driving back to Calusa in the morning.

Yeah. I'm about done. I thought I might stick around the city a few days. Type up my notes. Knock out a draft of my article. Get to know Gloria a little better.

Gloria?

The Wife. Yeah, we kind of hit it off back there. She and I. While you were waiting in the car we talked about a lot of things. Gloria's pretty special.

Right. The Wife. So maybe you wouldn't mind giving me and my stuff a lift?

Where to?

The Causeway.

Why the hell would you want to go back there?

It's where I live.

CHAPTER NINE

THE KID RISES EARLY TO FEED HIS ANIMAL friends before he feeds himself and walks Annie along the grassy bank of the Appalachee so she can do her business. While Annie squats and pees he glances back at the pier: no sign of the Writer stirring in the boat next door. He returns to his own boat where he builds himself a quick double-decker peanut butter sandwich for breakfast, packs his belongings, and makes the cabin shipshape.

Before Cat and Dolores arrive at the store the Kid walks the length of the pier to the end. It's a bright cloudless morning and off to his left metallic plates of sunlight glitter on the Bay. He sits down on the concrete pier beside a rough plywood belt-high table used mainly for cutting bait and cleaning fish. Folding his right leg under him he extends the other, exposing the electronic monitor clamped to his ankle. In the Bay a short ways off the pier a pair of dour pelicans perched atop two channel-marking pylons watches him carefully as if puzzled by the way he's seated himself on the pier. Usually people stand behind the table and gut and chop the bodies of fish and toss the gooey insides and bits of flesh into the water for the pelicans and gulls to fight over. It's not clear what this one is up to.

He unravels a stringy black charger cable and jacks one end into a socket on the anklet and plugs the other into an electrical outlet bolted to the table's two-by-four wood frame. The metal shackle presses against the bare skin of his leg, and the Kid feels the juice flow not from the battery into his body but from his body out to the battery as if instead of being filled with electrical power he were being drained of it. It happens every time he gets the battery charged: he imagines his way from his body out to what he rationally knows is the source of the current but visualizes it instead as the ultimate receptacle for the current—as if he and millions like him were spinning the turbines at the farthest end of the line and not vice versa. He sits on the pier and stares at the dime-size battery linking his skin to the charger cord.

It takes half an hour to fully charge his monitor battery and during that half hour the Kid feels intimately connected to the millions of other convicted sex offenders young and old and in-between, rapists and child abusers and men who exposed their genitals on a bus, public masturbators, voyeurs and escalator gropers, compulsive seducers of teenage boys, coaches who couldn't keep their hands off their athletes, men who talked dirty in Internet chat rooms to people they thought were teenage girls and then arranged to meet them for sex, fathers and uncles who drunkenly reached out for their teenage daughters as they passed by the sofa, porn addicts and fantasists lost in the misty zone between reality and imagery, no longer able to tell the difference—all of whom at this moment have plugged their electronic shackles into outlets and are sitting in the bedrooms, living rooms, and basements of houses and apartments and mobile homes, in garages, homeless shelters, public parks, in airports and train stations, in waiting rooms, offices, and the back rooms of fast-food restaurants and under causeways and overpasses—as if they were all trembling leaves on the branches large and small of a vast electrical tree that casts its shadow across the entire country.

AN HOUR LATER THE KID DROPS HIS DUFFEL and backpack beside the Writer's Town Car. Leading Annie on her rope leash, lugging Einstein in his cage, he steps inside the store.

Dolores is sweeping the floor behind the deli counter and Cat is in the back room breaking down cardboard boxes. Smiling warmly at the sight of him Dolores puts aside her broom and comes around to the front of the counter and asks what's he got planned for today, another voyage into the heart of darkness?

She's never read the book but has caught onto the phrase and knows it's supposed to refer to the African jungle and be scary. She thinks the Panzacola must resemble Africa and is dangerous in spite of being so close to civilization, which is one of the things that attracted her to Appalachee when she first arrived from upstate New York—that and Cat Turnbull who resembled an old-time expat running a store at the mouth of the river for the natives who come in and trade their crafts and pelts for goods manufactured in Europe and the cities of America. Except that the natives are mostly tourists and fishermen. But she lived all her life in the mountains of the North far inland and has romanticized the South and the sea and the slow-moving meandering dark rivers that empty into it and the people who live there and even the people who visit there.

The Kid says, *Actually, I gotta move on.*

Listen, it's okay by us if you keep the houseboat a while. We won't get much call for houseboat rentals for another month anyhow. Cat'll want you to pay for it, of course. But he'll give you a discount.

Naw. I got to get back to where I belong.

Where's that?

It's where they put all us convicted sex offenders. Out here I'm the only one. And it's kind of uncomfortable.

I don't understand.

That's okay. You don't have to.

You don't look very happy about it. But I guess you know what's best for you.

Listen, can I ask a favor of you? You and Cat?

Certainly.

It's about Annie and Einstein, he explains. He tells Dolores that where he's going will be rough on them. There's grass here for Annie to walk on and fresh air and normal people coming and going and lots of interesting birds including other parrots for Einstein to relate to. Maybe she and Cat could use a watchdog with a good bark even though she's old and a little decrepit and a friendly tame talking parrot to amuse the tourists even though he's kind of eccentric. He'll leave enough money to pay for their food for a month and if it works out, once a month he'll send whatever it costs for their upkeep.

I don't know. They seem awfully attached to you. Why would you give them up?

I can't provide them with the kind of home they deserve.

Look at you, hon, she says and pats his hand. *You're tearing up. Someone should give you the kind of home you deserve.*

They have, he says. He retrieves his hand and turns away from her. He stares manfully out the window and sees the Writer strolling down the pier toward the store. *I gotta go now,* he says. *Here comes my ride.*

Dolores nods and reaches out and takes Annie's leash from his hand and lifts Einstein's cage and places it on the counter. The Kid digs into his pocket and pulls out a single hundred-dollar bill and passes it to her. Then he turns and quickly walks away.

THE WRITER'S TOWN CAR APPROACHES THE Causeway from Calusa heading toward the Barrier Isles. It crosses over the concrete arch to the far side where the Writer pulls the wide vehicle onto the gravel shoulder and parks it next to the guardrail. Cars and trucks and motorcycles roar past in both directions. He cranes his neck and peers down the steep slope into the shadows beneath the six-lane bridge. He can't see much down there—flotsam and jetsam, a jumbled mix of building materials, trash, cardboard boxes, torn sheets of polyethylene. A tidal dump.

The Writer says to the Kid, *You're not going down there, are you?*

Without answering, the Kid steps from the car and retrieves his backpack and duffel from the backseat. He walks up to the passenger's side window and the Writer lowers it. The Kid leans in and says, *Thanks for the ride, man. For all the rides, I mean. Thanks for everything.*

Not a problem, Kid. But I'm a little worried about you going down there. You know, to live. It looks . . . dangerous.

It's not. Not for me anyhow. Listen, the Kid says, *I gotta ask you not to write about this. About any of it. You know what I'm saying? Like for a magazine or something. Or for the Internet. Definitely not for the Internet. Blogs and shit. Or on Facebook.*

Why not?

I dunno. It's just sort of private. My life, I mean. And the Professor's and even the fucking Shyster's. In spite of the fact that we're on the Internet and anybody who wants to can look us up and think they know all about us, it's still our life. It's all we got. Know what I mean?

Don't worry, Kid, it's not my kind of material. Besides, as long as you and I and Gloria know what really happened out there at the canal, it doesn't matter if no one else knows.

Yeah, but we don't. We don't know what really happened out there.

We know what we believe, Kid. That's all anyone gets in this life.

Yeah. Sure. The Kid gives the Writer a small wave and hefts his backpack onto his shoulders. He lifts his duffel off the ground and steps with care over the guardrail as if about to trespass. Slowly he makes his way down the steep slope and disappears from the Writer's sight into the heavy wet shadows beneath the Causeway.

For a few moments the Writer sits in the car trying to imagine the life the Kid will lead down there. Then he gives up trying—not his kind of material—puts the Town Car in gear, makes a quick U-turn and enters the flow of traffic heading toward Calusa and drives away.

FROM THE HEAPS OF TRASH PILED BY THE water's edge the Kid like a shipwrecked sailor scavenges a batch of two-by-fours and a sopped sheet of paint-stained polyethylene. In bright sunlight a dozen or so feet above the high-tide line he props the two-by-fours into an upside-down conical frame, ties the poles together at the top with a piece of found wire, and covers the frame with the plastic sheeting. Two hours later he's built himself an eight-foot-tall rainproof teepee with a wide view of the Bay and the sky-scrapers of downtown Calusa. Sweet.

He stashes his belongings inside his teepee, then stands outside it for a moment in the late-afternoon breeze and admires his work. Things could be worse than they are, he notes. A ragged ridge of pink-edged clouds has moved in from the east. The sunset should be awesome. He scans the concrete islet to see if there's anything else worth salvaging—a plastic cooler or some cooking utensils, maybe a bucket to use for a toilet. Finding nothing useful he glances into the darker recesses of the Causeway for the first time and realizes that he's being watched. Probably has been watched from the beginning. He's not as alone on his island as he thought.

It's Paco. Senor On-Your-Own. Still the bodybuilder, still wearing his muscle shirt and nylon gym shorts, his Harley on its kickstand parked off to one side, his old weight bench on the other, some kind of junk wood and wallboard shanty behind him. Wherever Paco fled when the hurricane hit it must have been deemed illegal once the storm passed out to sea. The dude had nowhere else to go.

By way of greeting him Paco slowly lifts and folds his ham-size arms across his chest and nods his heavy head twice. The Kid nods back. Having adjusted his sight to the darkness back there he can make out now a few more shadowy figures lurking amid what appears to be the beginnings of a resettlement, one that's modeled on the old settlement but a lesser more dilapidated version—a col-lection of hovels that he initially thought was just trash and tide- and storm-tossed wreckage heaped up against the inner supports of the Causeway. It's the squalid remnants of the old colony. And the rem-nants of the colonists.

Coming forward from the gloom is P.C. wearing a crooked smile of recognition although he's not exactly welcoming the Kid with open arms and beyond P.C. stands the Greek holding a large adjustable wrench in his hand and behind him are a half-dozen other impassive men—among them red-haired Ginger, the goofball Froot Loop and finally in his navy blue lawyer's suit and stained white shirt and loosened tie there stands the Shyster. They all regard the Kid with an expression mingling welcome with suspicion that to the Kid signifies a reluctant acceptance of his presence among them. It's as if thanks to the chaos of the hurricane the men living under the Causeway pulled off a mass jailbreak, but then one by one each man was hunted down in most cases probably by no one other than himself, captured by himself and returned by himself to his cell. They gaze almost mournfully out of the shadows at him, as if his return is the final proof of their collective defeat. As if their last hope after the storm was that he alone of the original settlers, the last of the lost colonists and the first, the youngest and the scrappiest, had somehow permanently escaped. And now by coming back to the Causeway he's let them down. Of all the settlers the Kid was the one thought most likely to survive above the Causeway among normal people. And if the Kid is back it's certain that those who haven't yet returned will soon be caught and brought back too—by the police or their parole officers or caseworkers. Or if not caught and returned by the authorities, they like the Kid will catch and bring themselves back here on their own. There's no escape from under the Causeway.

No one steps forward to greet him; no one says anything.

Wussup, Paco, the Kid finally says.

You pitch your tent too far out in the light, man. They can see you from the highway.

P.C. says, *New rules, Kid. We can't stay here unless no one can see us. So you better take down your tent and move it and your shit all the way inside like the rest of us.*

The Kid squints and looks past the group into the jumbled damp darkness that surrounds them. *No way, man. You guys're like fucking bats scared of the light living inside a wall. I ain't moving in there.*

The Shyster says, *We don't have much of a choice, Kid. And they don't either.*

"*They*"? *Who're* "*they*"?

The police. The authorities. The upholders of the law. And those who make the law, the frightened citizens of Calusa.

Yeah, well, fuck them. And besides, scumbag, I don't want you living next to me. I don't even want you talking to me, man. Suddenly the Kid's heart is pounding and he's breathing rapidly and hard. He spits on the ground to calm himself, looks straight at the Shyster, focuses his mind and in a voice barely above a whisper he says, *Big Daddy.*

The Shyster raises his eyebrows as if surprised by hurt feelings. Or in mockery of surprise. Or both. *You're judging me? Really, Kid? You think you're better than I am? Sorry to break it to you, but no matter what we're guilty of, we're all down here for the same reason. That includes you.*

The Kid turns away and starts back to his teepee. At the entrance flap he stops, spins on his heels and calls back to the Shyster, *I seen your e-mails, man! I know what you did! You and Doctor Hoo!*

Ah! So you have my briefcase. I wondered where it ended up. Better you, I suppose, than the police.

You want it back? You can have it. The e-mails make me want to puke, man. They're so dirty they make everything they touch dirty. I thought I'd seen dirt before but nothing comes close to the e-mails between you and Doctor Hoo. Nothing. Too bad you didn't fucking drown yourself like he did.

Drown? Again the Shyster raises his eyebrows as if in mock surprise. It's his default facial expression. *Poor old Doctor Hoo is certainly dead, which turned out to be a problem for me. But he didn't drown.*

Yeah? How'd the fucker die, then?

Oh, he shot himself in the head. Right after I was arrested, unfortunately. Nearly two years ago. Before my trial. You might as well burn those papers, Kid. I don't know why I kept them. They're of no use to anyone now, not even to me. They were part of my defense, which obviously didn't work, and ended up in the trial transcript. I would like the briefcase back, however. And my Bible.

What're you telling me? The Kid has made his way back to the Shyster and stands close enough to him now to see the man's nearly black pupils—they're opaque. Nothing visible on the other side. Like the eyes of a snake. *What d'you mean, they were part of your defense?*

The jury didn't buy my claim that by posing online as Big Daddy I was merely trying to entrap a child molester who happened to be a well-respected Calusa pediatrician known in certain Internet circles as Doctor Hoo. It's the old legal strategy of trying to confuse the jury or at least one member of the jury by providing too much information. One holdout and you've got a hung jury. Surprised me that the judge admitted the e-mails as evidence, since by then the good doctor was dead and no longer available to testify on his own behalf. Or on mine, as it were. Wasted effort.

Was it true?

Was what true?

That you were trying to entrap this doctor. This fat perv who was all into kiddie porn and sex with little girls. Or was it boys?

In his case, boys. And he was hardly fat. He was one of those Ironmen. A competitive triathlete. Zero body fat. But puh-lease, I was merely trying to avoid going to jail. The same as everyone living down here. It's the same for everyone everywhere, Kid. It's what people do. We tell stories that proclaim our innocence. All of us. We tell them to ourselves and to anyone who'll listen. Even your old friend the late lamented Rabbit with his boxing stories did it. No doubt your professor friend too. Even you. And it's not just us pervs. Everyone has a story that proclaims his innocence. It's human nature. I'm a lawyer, Kid. I've heard them all.

The Kid lowers his face and looks down at his feet. He turns slowly away from the lawyer and returns slump-shouldered to his teepee. Brushing the plastic door flap aside he steps in and sits down on the cement floor facing out. The view of the Bay and downtown Calusa isn't as appealing as it was a few minutes ago. Nothing is.

He's almost back where he started. If the Professor wasn't Doctor Hoo then the Shyster couldn't have been the one who told the cops where to look for the Professor's body. The Kid realizes that he's disappointed: on some deep level he *wanted* the Professor to have been Doctor Hoo. Even if repellent and disgusting it would have made him finally known to the Kid. There isn't much about people that he lets disgust him because there's always a chance people aren't what they seem to be or say they are. But if he knew the Professor really was a chomo then he would at least be free to be disgusted.

But if it wasn't the Shyster who phoned in the location of the Professor's body, it must have been whoever put him there. The Professor's story proclaiming his innocence, his story about the spies and counterspies, could still be true, right?

Unless it isn't. Unless the Professor himself was the one who told the cops where they could find his body and then drowned himself in a slightly suspicious way so Gloria and other people like the Writer would believe his story and think he was assassinated because he knew too much. It's a plausible story after all. Even the Kid believes it happens sometimes, that secret agents murder other secret agents who they think can't be trusted anymore. Even in America. So it could be true.

He doesn't know which story to believe—the one in the Professor's filmed interview or the report from the Calusa County coroner's office. His mind is bouncing off competing versions of reality as if he's living inside a video game and it's making him feel dizzy and nauseated. He wonders if the Writer's harsh theory about knowledge—that you can't ever know the truth about anything—is true after all. Maybe it is. Maybe it isn't. But the Kid can't even know that: he's stuck between believing the Writer's theory and not believing it.

He does know however that if nothing is true then nothing is real. Logic tells him that. And if nothing is real then nothing matters. Which means you're free to believe whatever you want—unless you've got an innocent soul like Iggy had and Annie and Einstein. Unless you're an animal, that is. Except for the Snake which is neither a human being nor an animal. Because once you're born a human being and the Snake talks you into doing something that you have to lie about you're no longer innocent. That's when you start making up stories that proclaim your innocence like Adam and Eve did after they ate the forbidden fruit and like the Shyster says is what everyone does. It must happen very early in life when you're still new at being human, the Kid reasons and he wonders when it happened to him, when he got talked into doing something that he had to lie about and as a result no longer had an innocent soul.

Maybe the Internet is the Snake and pornography is the forbidden fruit because watching porn on the Internet is the first thing the Kid remembers lying about. He was only ten years old that summer and he remembers getting his first real hard-ons from listening to his mother screwing her then boyfriend in her bedroom. The Kid can't remember which of three boyfriends she was making it with that summer, Dougie or Sal or the retired U.S. Airways pilot. They kind of blend together in his memory. The only thing that helped him ignore her orgasmic shouts and the thumping of the headboard against the wall was sitting in his room in front of the computer screen of her old Dell desktop, clicking onto free porn sites. Later he memorized her credit card number and whenever his mother and her boyfriend of the moment were screwing he got into watching pay-per-view hard core and then a year or so later he was watching it when she was out with her women friends cruising the bars or after he got home from school and she was at work and he was alone. It relaxed him. When he sat down and booted up the computer and mouse-clicked his way straight to the porn sites he favored he could feel and almost hear a corresponding series of clicks in his brain. A warm spot would emerge at the back of his skull and spread up over the top of his head until he felt like he was wearing a heated cap.

He didn't lie about it to his mother—except about using her

credit card which she discovered on her own anyhow when he finally maxed it out prompting her to read the whole statement for once instead of just checking the minimum monthly payment due. But she knew he was deep into porn—maybe not how deep—and although she shook her head and clucked her tongue whenever she caught him at it she didn't seem to care. She treated his growing addiction to pornography like it was little worse than a waste of time better spent doing his homework or helping out with housework. So it wasn't his mother he lied to or anyone else either since no one else knew or ever asked him about it. He lied to himself.

And it wasn't watching porn that he lied about or even his constant jerking off. He lied about the way they made him feel, both the porn and jerking off. He told himself it was normal, everyone did it—especially guys. Well, maybe only guys. And it was no big deal anyhow. In fact it was boring, he told himself. Even the quintuple-X hard-core multiple black-on-white fisting double anals. Porn was boring; beating his meat was boring. The same-old same-old. He just did it because it felt better and less boring than not doing it, he told himself, like chewing gum or wearing sneakers instead of shoes. That's what he told himself.

But he knew better. He did it because he couldn't stop himself. He couldn't stop himself because watching pornography and masturbating were the only times he felt real. The rest of the time he felt as if he were his own ghost—not quite dead but not alive either. A dust bunny shaped like a person. So for years whenever he was alone with a computer he watched pornography and masturbated. Until the night he let himself get lured by brandi18 into a house in the suburbs and got busted by her and her father.

He doesn't know why but everything changed that night. Suddenly for the first time in his life he was visible to himself. The police who took him down in Brandi's yard when they interrogated him at the station later opened a laptop on the table in front of him and put in a disc and showed him a video of him and Brandi's father in the kitchen that Brandi's father had taped with a hidden camera and the second he saw himself on the screen he felt like all his atoms were instantly reconfigured. It was as if he had never seen himself in a mirror before. It was like being touched by an angel. He had an actual body and it was not just his body, something he merely possessed, it was *him*! And who was he? He was the digitalized body of an about-to-be convicted sexual offender, a grown young man with a six-pack of beer, a porn movie, condoms, and a tube of lubricant trying to hook up in the suburbs with a fourteen-year-old Internet girl—and because now it was on a computer screen for everyone in the world to see, it was reality.

From that moment on he no longer felt even the slightest desire to watch pornography or jerk off because now he was a convicted sex offender, which provided him with the same feelings he used to get from sitting in front of his computer screen with his hand wrapped around his cock watching one or two or more naked men with huge erect penises pushing their penises into the orifices of one or two or more naked young women. Three holes and two hands per woman. He no longer had to lie to himself. He no longer had to endure mind-numbing boredom in order to feel partially alive. He had been made human—as wholly human as he could then imagine anyhow. And those women—those three holes and two hands each—for the first time the women on the screen were almost human too and not just two-dimensional pictures. They were as real as he was!

There's a difference between shame and guilt. And the Kid has begun to realize that he's not ashamed of having spent most of his life so far watching pornography and using it to give himself orgasms: he's not a bad person, he knows that much, and being a bad person is what makes you feel shame. No, he's guilty instead because that's what you are if you do a bad thing. And if the women being abused on camera by facial cum shots, gangbangs, and double anals and so forth as if they were just images designed to make his dick hard enough to whack off with were in fact as almost-real as he, then paying money to watch them being abused and degraded was a bad thing. It was like paying money to watch someone beat a dog.

Ever since the night he got arrested and then was convicted and sent to jail and the months he's spent as a convicted sex offender he's thought and acted like a man who was ashamed, a bad man who deserved to be cast out of the city. For reasons he will never fully understand—although he knows its origins go back to his child-hood way before Iggy came into his life—he got sluiced into being a nearly full-time consumer of Internet pornography and because he didn't realize it was a bad thing that he was doing and should therefore feel guilty for doing it which would have made him stop doing it, he felt ashamed instead: a bad person doing his typically bad things instead of a good person doing one bad thing. Or maybe two.

Remembering the night he was arrested for soliciting sex from a minor via the Internet and how as a result he went from feeling like a dust bunny to a flattened image of a man seen on a computer screen, the Kid wonders for the first time if there is a way for him to give that two-dimensional image on the screen a third dimension and become wholly alive.

Maybe if he just acts like he has a third dimension whether he's seen by others or not—whether he's seen by practically everyone in the world on YouTube and is monitored by his parole officer on a computer screen with beeps from the GPS on his ankle or instead is invisible to the world, living underground in darkness beneath the Causeway and well out of sight from passersby on the highway—if he acts like a three-dimensional man then maybe, just maybe he'll turn into one. Isn't that how everyone does it? By acting?

But he's not sure how to behave as if he were already a man with three dimensions. It has to be done mentally from the inside out, he knows that much: it can't be just an act put on for the cameras and the Internet as if life were a gigantic reality TV show that you can download onto your computer or your phone. That would only make things worse. No, it has to start way inside you down in the black hole of antimatter that sits at the exact center of who you are. Diddle that spot even a little and the rest will follow and out of nothingness will come heat, light, and a strong wind blowing across the universe, and they will combine and bring into existence fire, earth, and water, and out of fire, earth, and water will emerge flesh, bone, and blood wrapped in his skin.

So the Kid decides to believe the Professor's story. All of it. That's the first move. The rest will follow.

He decides to invest some of the Professor's money in a new generator for the Greek and go into the battery-charging business with him. That's the second move. If he's stingy with it he can maybe make the Professor's money last a year or possibly more, at least long enough for him to luck onto a job as a busboy again at one of the hotels out along the Barriers. The way he lives he could get by just on panhandling plus his cut of the Greek's battery-charging fees but a real job will help establish him as a man in the world beyond the Causeway.

Third: he decides to give back the Shyster's briefcase and not to judge him or feel superior to him. He may even apologize for woofing him the way he did.

Fourth: unfinished business; miscellaneous loose ends. In a week or two he'll hitch out to the Panzacola and visit Dolores and Cat and see how Annie and Einstein are holding up at the edge of the jungle. He won't bring them back to the Causeway with him though. This is no place for a dog on her last legs and a restless talkative parrot. He'll buy a bicycle. Maybe he'll start pumping iron with Paco.

He needs to move fast if he wants to stay synchronized and ready because the pace of change is picking up. He can feel it spreading out from inside his body in the general direction of his skin.

He'll check in on his mother but will only stay long enough to let her know he's alive in case she's worried about him. He may visit Gloria and her kids and encourage them to continue believing the

Professor's account of how he died, although he figures the Writer will be taking care of that. By now he's probably getting ready to move in with them.

The Kid stands and drags his duffel and backpack—all his worldly possessions—outside the teepee. The other men gaze at him in silence from under the Causeway, a Greek chorus standing in the shadows offstage watching their disillusioned hero accept his fate. He's not as sad and beaten down as he looks however. Heroes never are. Otherwise they'd be victims and the Kid is not a victim. He rips down the plastic sheeting and unties the frame and lets the structure collapse of its own weight. Grabbing his pack and duffel he lugs his possessions toward the damp darkness beneath the Causeway.

He will make his home here among the other men. He is after all like them: a convicted sex offender. Guilty. Guilty. Guilty. He has nine years to wait in darkness out of sight deep beneath the city before he is no longer on parole. No longer guilty. Nine years before he can remove the electronic shackle from his ankle and can emerge from under the Causeway and mingle freely again with people he believes to be mostly normal people with mostly normal sex lives; nine years before he can live among others in a building above-ground that's less than 2,500 feet from a school or playground and circulate inside the city walls without fear of being rearrested, buy a one-way ticket on a bus bound for a distant city and live there if he wants to and not be breaking the law; nine years before he can stroll into a public library and legally use the public computer to go online and check out the job listings and apartments for rent on craigslist.org—a website that may not even exist by then—and while he's online and nobody's nearby he'll be tempted to linger over a little free Internet porn as long as he keeps his fly zipped and no one reports him to the librarian. He decides to stop quitting cigarettes. He wonders what pornography will look like nine years from now. He wonders if it will get him hard again. He'll be thirty-one years old by then.

ACKNOWLEDGMENTS

Special thanks to my assistant, Nancy Wilson, and to Liz Moore for their help with research. Thanks also, as always, to my agent, Ellen Levine, for her ongoing support, and to my irreplaceable friend and editor, Dan Halpern.